***This is** not going[...]*

*This is going to be hard. [...]
done before. And you're going to do anything it takes.*

Because I knew I would. I'd do anything to get Anyan
back. And that fact scared me a little.

"We can't begin to thank you enough," I said, my hand
resting on the book on my knee, when two robed monks
rushing into the hotel suite interrupted us. They were
speaking frenetically in their language, and I had no idea
what they were saying. But I knew it was bad when the old
man paled visibly. Turning to me, he spoke urgently.

"There are dragons. On the roof."

Praise for the Jane True Series

"Jane is sure to endear herself to new readers with her
charm, sass, and vulnerability, while longtime fans will
be thrilled by her magical and emotional growth."
—*Publishers Weekly*

"Peeler is like the Janet Evanovich of paranormal
fantasy..."
—**Paul Goat Allen, bn.com**

"Witty and fun, with a dash of dark suspense."
—**Scifichick.com**

"Peeler pulls out all the stops in this heart-stopping tale
with a cliffhanger ending that will leave you gasping!"
—*RT Book Reviews*

By Nicole Peeler

JANE TRUE NOVELS

Tempest Rising
Tracking the Tempest
Tempest's Legacy
Eye of the Tempest
Tempest's Fury
Tempest Reborn

Tempest Reborn

Nicole Peeler

www.orbitbooks.net

Copyright © 2013 by Nicole Peeler
Excerpt from *Blood Rights* copyright © 2011 by Kristen Painter

Orbit
Hachette Book Group
237 Park Avenue
New York, NY 10017
Visit our Web site at www.orbitbooks.net

Orbit is an imprint of Hachette Book Group. The Orbit name and logo are trademarks of Little, Brown Book Group Limited.

Printed in the United States of America

First edition: May 2013

10 9 8 7 6 5 4 3 2 1

This book is dedicated to Rebecca Strauss,
the invaluable other half of Team Us.

The story so far...

At the end of *Eye of the Tempest*, Jane found herself the champion of her supernatural brethren, cast to battle an ancient evil. Forces working for her nemesis, Morrigan, wanted to awaken the Red and the White, beings that took the shape of dragons and who thrived on chaos and destruction.

In *Tempest Fury*, Jane traveled with Anyan and the Original, Blondie, to Great Britain in order to keep Morrigan from her goal. There, Jane learned more about her supernatural heritage and the structures that kept it both secret and secure. Morrigan, however, threatened both. Her behavior became increasingly erratic, including very public attacks that risked the secrecy of their species.

For Morrigan was keeping her own secrets. She'd merged with the Red, whose corporeal form was mostly destroyed by the former champion, Blondie. But the dragon had found a way to resurrect herself by merging with another. Morrigan/the Red could shapeshift between Alfar and dragon, or a hybrid of both.

Having a way to resurrect themselves, the Red's goal was now to awaken her consort, the White. Jarl, Morrigan's lover who murdered his own brother, King Orin, was the Red/Morrigan's chosen vessel for the White.

Jarl, however, was less keen on merging with a dragon than Morrigan, and had to be kept under armed guard while Jane, Anyan, and Blondie were themselves busy trying to keep the bones of the White out of Morrigan's hands. Morrigan needed those ancient relics to resurrect the White, and so Jane's mission appeared simple: Keep Morrigan away from the bones.

Nothing was ever simple in the Great Island, however, the supernatural name for Great Britain, as both the Alfar who ruled and the rebels who wanted their own power both sought to use Jane against the other. Anyan and Blondie managed to keep her mostly safe, but besides those two, there was really no one she could trust.

A lesson she learned the hard way after a trap was laid for the Red, using the White's bones as bait. Everything was going according to plan until the Rebel leader's brother turned against them, releasing Morrigan's minion, Graeme, whom they were keeping prisoner. He also brought Jarl to Morrigan, so that she could complete the ritual and resurrect the White.

Before Morrigan/the Red could complete the ancient rite, however, Blondie—already grievously wounded herself—killed Jarl. Thinking themselves triumphant, Jane turned to the Red . . .

Who, in dragon form, lashed out her tail, sending Anyan crashing onto the pile of bones. A few chanted words later, and the Red's magic hit like a nuclear strike. Struggling to her feet minutes later, Jane was relieved to see Anyan still breathed.

Her relief was short lived, however, for when her lover sat up and blinked...

His eyes were the green, slit eyes of a dragon. Jane's great love shifted into a dragon and flew away with the Red. And then she discovered her greatest ally, Blondie, was dead.

Leaving Jane all alone.

Tempest Reborn

CHAPTER ONE

The agony was excruciating, a white heat at the center of my consciousness. Like that pinprick in space that pulls everything into its ever-widening gyre, the black hole inside me expanded.

Only moments had passed since Anyan, in the shape of the White, had flown away with his consort, the Red. The bones that had once held the White's spirit lay scattered in front of me. The ivory shapes blurred as unshed tears glazed my vision.

Behind me, Magog, the raven, raised her voice in mournful ululation, keening for the woman she knew as Cyntaf, and I knew as Blondie. My friend and my mentor lay a corpse in Magog's arms.

Meanwhile, my grief beat its own cadence, an infernal drumming reminding me, at all times, of my losses.

Blondie dead. Anyan as good as. Blondie dead. Anyan as good as . . .

For I knew better than to hope. I'd hoped once before,

looking down into my first love Jason's staring blue eyes, that reality could be malleable. But reality was always exactly that—real, no matter what we told ourselves or how many delusions we tried to build. Like sandcastles, they always crumbled.

[My child,] came the voice in my head.

Creature, I sobbed, feeling its love wrap around me. It, too, was unimaginably stricken by Blondie's death. It felt she was a daughter, and one of the only remnants of a time long ago, before time began, when the world had been a different place.

Many of Blondie's memories were its memories, and they died with her.

We mourned then, crooning into each other's minds.

[Join with me,] it pleaded, and I instantly understood. We would live together in my mind, until we could function again. We would support each other, and we could heal.

I will never heal, I told the creature, that pit of hopelessness I knew so well yawning in front of me.

In my own mind, I took a step toward that pit.

But the creature was there, appearing as a single great eye. It flooded my consciousness as it went everywhere, wrapping around me, cocooning me...

Awake, I slept.

The pyre had long since burned out, but we could still imagine the heat on our face. Behind was more heat—Gog, Magog, and Hiral were pressed behind me, literally guarding our flanks, our back.

Combined together, an amalgamation of creature and Jane, we hadn't moved in a day.

Instead we let the cool, wet English air blow the ashes of our friends and enemies against our cheeks, into our long, black hair, and we refused to think. We lived in our memories—a steely gray gaze, the flash of a tattooed bicep, the touch of a strong hand, a wave of power so unique it could only be our child...

The part of us that was the creature touched the part of me that was Jane again, a mental stroke as if to assure the other we were there.

Because alone we might break.

Our friend, daughter, ally was dead, and our lover was gone. Blondie had fallen at the claws of the Red, while Anyan had become the White.

We'd watched Blondie burn, thrown on the same pyre as the allies of the Red. Lyman, the rebel leader's brother, and Jarl, the Alfar we had thought our greatest enemy, had burned with her.

It wasn't logical to build an extra pyre when one would suffice.

Together they'd all turned to ash as Jane and the creature leaned on each other, together, here in this body where we could take shelter.

"Jane?" came the squeaky voice of the gwyllion, Hiral. "Are you about ready to leave?"

We ignored him.

"She hasn't moved in twenty-four hours," the raven, Magog, told her lover, the coblynau Gog. "Nor eaten. Nor peed. Nor slept."

"Is she blinking?"

"Rarely," replied Hiral.

We ignored them all.

"What do you think is happening?" Gog asked, his

voice concerned. For even though he and Magog had
originally been set to spy on Jane, the creature knew
they'd come to like the girl.

"No idea. What should we do?" Magog said.

"We've got to keep her from the Alfar," the gwyllion
said, referring to the official supernatural leaders of the
Great Island, or what the humans called Britain.

"We can't do so forever," the raven responded in her
singsong Welsh voice. "She is the champion, after all."

The part that was Jane stirred nervously, but the creature responded with a warm rush of power. Nothing
would keep us from our grief.

"They're going to want her to, er, champion," said
Gog.

Hiral snorted. "I don't think she could manage
'champion.' "

Magog's retort was sharp. "Don't mock. She's lost
everything."

"She has people, doesn't she? Do we contact them?"
Gog was, as always, kind and practical.

"The Alfar will have our hides if we let the champion
get away," Magog said, a tone of warning in her voice.

The gwyllion spat. "They won't have my hide. You get
me names, I'll get them word."

Gog and Magog looked at each other, whether in
agreement or in fear was anybody's guess.

"But if she goes, what will we do to fight the Red and
the White?" Gog's question was fair.

"Don't be stupid, coblynau. Can she fight as she is now?
She's like your girlfriend with clipped wings—useless."

Gog put a protective arm around Magog, as if to ward
off Hiral's cruel jape.

In the meantime, we went inward. We were tired of the others' words, tired of their concern. We were in mourning...

More memories came flooding in, at our beckoning. The first time the girl who would break our world used her magic. When we realized the dog was a man. The first time...

There were sounds around us. A car arriving. It had come once before.

"Is the halfling recovered?" came a new voice. A cold voice.

Alfar, we recognized.

Our friends remained silent.

"Well?" asked the voice again.

"No," said Magog. "She's not moved a muscle since you first saw her. Nor said a word."

A lean, handsome face appeared before us. Griffin's dark hair brushed his cheek and we thought of the feel of wiry curls under our palm, and a pink Mohawk that defied gravity.

"Jane. Jane! Are you in there?"

We settled further in, so far that even the sharp sting of a slap across our face didn't faze us.

"Don't hit her, you git," Hiral said with a snarl. He liked us, too, although he was loath to admit he liked anyone. In fact, he was bleeding inside at the loss of Blondie. She had been one of the only living creatures to abide the little gwyllion, and he found it hard to imagine a future without her friendship.

The part of them that was Jane marveled at the creature's omniscient viewpoint, even as she shrank away from Hiral's pain. She had enough of her own...

But the creature was there, helping her lapse back into memory...

When they came to again, they were lying in a room. A goblin was flashing a light in their eyes, like a human doctor would. Finally, he sat back, shaking his head.

"There's nothing physically wrong with her. She's in a traumatic fugue state—totally disassociated. You are aware of her medical history?" The goblin spoke with a lovely accent Jane couldn't recognize, but even as she questioned it, the creature supplied the answer—Irish, Dublin, upper class.

"No, we're not aware of her medical history." It was Griffin again. His voice might be smooth to a human ear, but underneath his calm tone lurked annoyance.

"Well, she's gone doolally before, and under similar circumstances."

"Dolally?" Griffin's voice was dry. "Is that the technical term?"

The goblin winced, as if remembering to whom he was talking.

"Sorry, sir. I meant she's had a psychotic break once before, and been committed."

"Great. She's been like this for a week. Our champion is a lunatic as well as a halfling."

There was a time that comment would have amused both the creature and Jane greatly, but now they felt nothing.

The goblin, however, was not amused.

"She's no lunatic, sir. She's traumatized. She suffered an initial experience of loss as a young woman, in which a loved one died. Now this experience mirrors that one, only with two loved ones, one of whom died and one of whom became, excuse me, a great bloody dragon. Her mind needs time to process, to heal itself."

When Griffin finally spoke, his always-cold tones had dropped into arctic temperatures.

"Remember your place, goblin. Healer or no, you can be replaced."

The goblin's Adam's apple bobbed as he gulped in air.

"And this 'trauma victim,' as you call her, is our champion. She is the only one who can kill the monsters that will, at any moment, recommence ravaging our lands. We need her on her feet and ready to fight. Is that understood?"

"Yes, sir." The goblin's voice was quiet.

We stopped listening at that point, in favor of our memories spinning before us like dangling sweets.

Anyan was calling for us, and we were trying to answer. His voice was weak, as if shouted through layers and layers of thick cotton, but we ached to respond.

That's when the mage balls started hitting our shields.

We opened our eyes, unimpressed to find Griffin lobbing missiles at us in a bid to get our attention. Behind him, a spitting, struggling Hiral was held by two goblin guards. Magog and Gog stood to one side, looking uncomfortable.

"There you are," the Alfar said, his voice irritated.

We blinked at him, our only response.

"You do not seem to understand the enormity of this situation," the Alfar said. "You are the champion, and you have been playing this game of yours for two weeks now. We can no longer indulge your little strop."

Our ire rose at his words.

"The Red and the White have been spotted," Griffin continued, his gaze locked on ours. "Our reprieve is nearly over. They will attack soon, be sure of that. And we need our champion."

We did not respond.

Griffin took a step closer, his face now inches from ours. "Look, halfling. Your bedmate is dead. He is the White now, and therefore our enemy. He must be destroyed, and unfortunately, we have to rely on you to help us. But if we attack now, we have a chance."

Jane's fear grew inside us, but we soothed her. Griffin continued.

"The Red and the White are still weak, still recovering. We can send in our best forces—immobilize them for you. All you need do is strike the killing blow. Even a halfling can do that, no?"

We thought over what the Alfar said. We conversed.

What if he's right? asked Jane. *What if Anyan's gone?*

[Do you believe that?] asked the creature.

No. No I don't. But what are our options?

[We don't know our options yet, child. We haven't had time to think.]

No. We haven't. But you do think there are options?

Jane's voice was so sad, so scared, that we suddenly understood one simple fact.

We realized there must be another option, for to kill Anyan was unthinkable.

[Yes,] the creature said. [There are options. There are always options.]

For the first time since Blondie fell and Anyan was flung onto the White's bones, we felt something other than despair. The tiniest glimmer of hope built within us, and we nurtured it as we would a flame. Jane grasped on to that hope, and she made a decision.

She was grateful for the creature's intervention, but now she had work to do.

I need to be me again, Jane said.

[Are you sure?] the creature asked.

Yes, I think so. I appreciate what you did for me, though.

[Nonsense,] the creature said. [You helped me as much, or more, than I helped you.]

And then it withdrew, its ancient power that had cocooned me and kept me together through these last, turbulent days withdrawing. It didn't leave entirely, and I knew that it wouldn't until this whole affair was over.

But I was Jane again. And I wasn't doolally, at least not entirely, or not yet. I could feel an edge there, however. A hard edge, a desperate edge—one that scared me. I knew I could run over that edge without even seeing it in the darkness.

But right now I had to find us some options.

When I raised my eyes to Griffin's, he knew something had changed.

"Hi, Griffin," I said, knowing that both the creature and I would be okay. I could still feel it, inside me, and I knew it wouldn't leave me and that it would continue to comfort me, and that I'd reciprocate. But I had to be me again, for both our sakes.

I was the champion, after all.

"We've noted your concerns. The problem is that you haven't given us any time. And we're tired of your methods."

I went ahead and continued using the royal "we," since I knew that in this matter, the creature and I were partners.

"The fact is that we've spent too much time letting other people work for us, or tell us what to do, or guide us. Now it's time for us to guide ourselves. We're taking control of this little operation. And we're doing it our way."

Then I looked over to where Gog, Magog, and Hiral had all taken a step forward.

"You wanna come with?" I asked, feeling the creature warm at the thought. My friends, for they had become my friends, nodded.

The creature took us home.

CHAPTER TWO

Jane?" shouted my dad's hoarse voice, right before his arms wrapped around me.

For a split second, at seeing my father, my grief nearly overwhelmed me. A ragged sound came from my throat and I felt tears burning down my cheeks.

I also realized it was the first time I'd actually cried over what happened. So I let myself.

My dad led me upstairs, to Anyan's loft bedroom, as I sobbed. He sat me on Anyan's bed and held me till I cried myself out. Then he held out a clean handkerchief he'd dug out of his pocket. I used it to wipe my face up, noticing that I could smell Anyan all around us. That nearly made me cry again, but I choked it down.

"Is it true?" he asked finally.

I nodded.

"Blondie's dead," I said. "And Anyan's been turned into a monster."

"What are you going to do?"

"I don't know, Dad. I really don't. Blondie and Anyan were always the ones who led. They had all the answers."

"Well, it's obvious, isn't it?" my dad said. I looked up at him. His now healthy, pink complexion still looked a bit foreign to me, but the rest of him was so achingly familiar and safe after all the chaos of the past months. A few days unshaven, his craggy features were handsome, and his salt-and-pepper hair thick.

"What's obvious?" I asked, my voice small. Like everyone, he probably thought I had to kill Anyan. Maybe I did have to kill Anyan.

"You've got to get him back, Jane. You've got to find a way to fix this and get Anyan back."

I looked at him, tears welling in my eyes. It was what I'd been longing to hear since I first saw Anyan's beautiful gray eyes gone green, but somewhere deep down I thought I was crazy for hoping.

"I do?"

"Of course. And I know you can. We have to figure it out. We'll all help, of course."

I smiled then, having never thought I'd smile again. It was refreshing to be wrong.

"You'll all help. And we'll figure it out," I repeated, more for myself than for him. The words felt fragile in my mouth, but once they were uttered, they grew in strength.

"Yes," came Iris's voice from the stairway. "We'll all help. And we will figure it out."

I twisted my upper body to see all of my friends, old and new, peering around Iris. Lord knows how long they'd been waiting there.

Overcome with emotion, all I could do was hold out my arms. And then they were there.

Grizzie crowded in, smothering both my dad and me in her ample, enhanced bosoms. My dad looked alarmed, but I was used to it. Tracy was behind her wife, her arms wrapped around us as much as she could, considering her huge, pregnant belly. Iris and Caleb did their part and took the other side. Nell and Trill were in front and back, the gnome levitating herself to sling an arm around our necks. Only Gog, Magog, and Hiral stood back, looking a bit flustered at all the emotion. They were British, after all.

When we'd hugged and cried and everyone had said something about his or her own feelings of loss, we still stayed as we were, hugging each other tight.

Finally, my dad spoke.

"So, are we ready to figure this out?" he asked.

"Hell yeah," Grizzie said, her husky voice growling.

"We're getting Anyan back," Iris told me. I noticed her voice was nearly honeydew again, and I could only grasp her hand tightly in response.

"We need snacks," Tracy said, making her way downstairs, undoubtedly to rustle up some grub.

"I like these people," said Hiral, following Tracy to the kitchen.

"I like them, too," I said to no one in particular as we made our way downstairs. For we had some planning to do.

Operation Get Anyan Back was in full effect.

"So what exactly happened?" Grizzie asked as we all settled around Anyan's large, open-planned living room. Iris made tea while Tracy put the finishing touches on the snacks she was preparing.

My stomach rumbled like a monsoon was about to hit, and I realized I was starving. Keeping one eye on Tracy's progress, I turned Grizzie's question around on her.

"I want to know the same thing," I said. "How much do you know, and how do you know it?"

Grizzie gave me a finger waggle. "You should be in trouble, miss, but your dad explained everything. Keeping secrets from us…"

I hung my head. It had always bothered me that I couldn't tell Grizzie and Tracy about my supernatural life, but it had been as much for their sake as the sake of the secret. The more they knew, the more vulnerable they were, and I wasn't about to risk their getting kidnapped and tortured just because I couldn't keep my gob shut.

Speaking of gobs, my stomach sounded again, rolling over and over in its emptiness. Everyone gave me a queer look as I clamped a hand to my belly.

"Sorry. I don't think I've eaten in a few days. Er, weeks."

My dad shook his head; as if that was the craziest thing he'd heard in the past week. Not me fighting a dragon, as I had in Paris, but me not eating.

"So how did it all come out?" I prompted, still wanting answers.

"You fought a dragon on television," Tracy said drily as she placed a platter of sandwich halves in front of us. I picked up what I thought was turkey and cheddar, biting into it gratefully.

"There was that," I said around my mouthful of food. It came out, "Der wad dat."

"And then your ex showed up, with Caleb and Iris, and they whisked us out to the cabin we thought belonged to our famous local artist, Juan Besonegro, but actually belongs to another of your kind named Anyan, who is apparently something called a 'barghest.'" Grizzie was really glaring at me now. It was one thing to keep my secret identity from her, another thing entirely to keep secret any single scrap of information regarding my love life.

Griz had priorities.

"Sowwy," I mumbled through another huge bite of sandwich.

Tracy set down a platter of sliced-up fruit and a bowl of potato chips, both of which I helped myself to like a toddler confronted with a limited supply of Cheerios.

Tracy took a seat next to Grizzie, and finished what her partner had started. "Your dad explained everything. And he told us that he had only just found out, which made us feel a bit better. I think Ryu would have wiped all of our minds again, but Iris and Caleb talked him out of it, since everyone and their mother had already seen the dragon footage with you in it."

I swallowed the bite I'd been chewing, then looked at both Grizzie and Tracy.

"I hated lying to you, I really did. But it was such a big secret, and it would have sounded so crazy." Grizzie looked ready to protest, and I knew she'd tell me that I could tell her anything.

"But more important," I said before she could interrupt, "I didn't want you involved, because everything about this new world is so dangerous. If the psychos we're dealing with thought you knew something important, the gods only know what they would have done to get it out of you. I didn't want to risk your safety just because I wanted my friends."

That seemed to pacify both women, and Tracy was staring at her distended, very pregnant belly. She and Grizzie were having twins, and that probably put a different spin on things for the two women.

"But I did want my friends," I added, my voice small. "I wanted them very much, and I've hated not being able to ask for their help, or their advice."

"And now you can," Grizzie said, her eyes glazing suspiciously as she placed a hand on Tracy's stomach.

Tears burned again in my own eyes as Nell's voice came from her rocking chair, which she'd set up, as usual, near Anyan's big fireplace.

"Now tell us what happened, child."

And so I did. I told them all about our trip to the UK, and how everything had started out so straightforward. I felt something akin to shame as I talked about how easy I thought it would be. All we'd had to do was keep the Red from recovering the relics, the bones, from which she could cobble together her consort, the White. But between our constantly being a step behind and the political machinations of the Great Island, what the humans called Britain, what should have been easy never was.

And then I told them about that last, horrible day in the seaside town of Whitby, when we'd been betrayed by one of our own. The rebel leader's own beloved brother, Lyman, had not only freed Graeme, the rapist-incubus, to warn Morrigan of our plans, but had delivered her chosen vessel, my arch-enemy Jarl, to become the White.

Even in those first, chaotic moments after Lyman's betrayal, things seemed to be going our way. Blondie killed Jarl, and I thought it was over.

Which was very stupid.

I'll never forget telling my friends, in a dark, grief-stricken voice, about the Red's tail lashing out to strike Anyan's shields, or how he flew through the air to land on the bones, or how she chanted something and it was like a nuke went off in our midst.

When I told them how I'd struggled up from where I'd fallen, my older friends—my father, Grizzie and Tracy, Iris and Caleb, Nell and Trill—all cried for me. My new friends, Magog, Gog, and Hiral, who either had been at the site or had helped mop up the carnage, sat quietly with inward-looking eyes.

I'd sat up to find Anyan sprawled out, and I'd thought he was dead. I told them of my relief when he sat up. But then he'd turned vivid green eyes on me, and I'd felt my world torn from under my feet.

Then he shapeshifted into a dragon and flew away, and I'd discovered that our greatest ally, Blondie, the Original, was dead. She'd bled out from a cut made by the Red, whose claws made wounds that couldn't be healed.

When I'd finished talking, everyone sat in silence. My dad had long since put his arm around me, and I was grateful for its weight.

"Well, shit," Trill said. That seemed to sum the situation up for everyone.

"We need to start at the beginning," Nell said, her sage little grandmother's face looking into the fireplace as she thought. "First of all, we need to list our assets. What do we still have?"

"We have all of us, here," Iris said. "And we all have special knowledge and stuff. Plus Jane's the champion."

"And we have the creature," I said. "It's with me all the time now."

"With you?" Caleb asked, his craggy face startled. "Like...living inside of you?"

I nearly said yes, till I realized everyone was looking at me with horrified expressions, and I put what I'd just said together with what we'd been talking about.

"Ohmygod, no, the creature isn't like the Red or the White. He's not like *in me* in me."

"Then what is it?" my dad asked, obviously affecting calm.

"It's like..." I tried to put into words what the creature and I were, but it had changed so much so quickly that I realized I wasn't sure myself. "Before Whitby, it was like the creature was just somewhere else but we could reach out to each other if we wanted. If I needed it, I'd call, or it would pop in to say 'hi.'

"Now, after Whitby, it's like we...have a Bat Phone to each other," I said, finally hitting on the metaphor I wanted.

"It's not in me all the time, and it isn't *me*, as the Red is Morrigan. It's like we have a permanent line of communication, an exclusive line, but we're still totally separate. And sometimes we're in more communication than others. Sometimes it's like we haven't bothered to pick up the Bat Phone at all for a while, and it's like it's not even there. But then if I need it, voilà! Bat Phone."

Everyone still looked confused, but less alarmed, which was good. I gave it one more go.

"So don't worry about me going all Morrigan, and taken over by the creature. It needs me to have my own agency," I said, startled by that realization. I think the creature had fed that fact to me. "It needs me to be Jane and it wants me to be Jane. I think we did become sort of like the Red and Morrigan in Whitby, but as soon as I was okay, it backed away. But I can pick up that Bat Phone whenever I need it."

"Good," Nell said, nodding brusquely to end that conversation. "That explains everything." Caleb and Iris looked less convinced, but I hoped I'd made some sense. The creature was a part of me, yes, but it wasn't *me*. And we weren't always in direct communication by any means. It was busy doing its own creaturely thing, plus it wanted me to be independent.

The gnome, meanwhile, kept talking, moving swiftly on. "So, we have manpower, brainpower, and, er, creaturepower. Now, what's our goal?"

"Get Anyan back," Iris said immediately.

"Kill the White and the Red," Caleb said.

"But for good this time," my dad added.

Tears really did well up in my eyes when I didn't have to answer that one.

"Great. We have clear goals," Nell said, nodding excitedly. "So, where do we start?"

Crickets chirped.

We all looked from one to the other. Facing ancient evils was bad enough, but facing an ancient evil that, for all intents and purposes, was holding your boyfriend's body hostage while using him as a barghest shield was really bad.

Iris leaned forward, her pretty mouth in a moue of concentration.

"I think," she said, "that we've got to figure out what, exactly, the Red and the White are."

I cocked my head at her, unsure what she meant.

"Like, are they things we can touch, hold, et cetera. Or are they more like . . . souls, or spirits?"

My mind did a little explosion as I realized what she was saying.

"That's brilliant, Iris," I said breathlessly. "They've always had their own bodies to re-create, through their bones. We never thought they were anything but pyhysical. But after what happened with Morrigan and Anyan, they're clearly not. So what are they, if they're not bodies?"

"It's totally like *Supernatural*," Grizzie said, and my dad started nodding like crazy.

I'd seen the show, but my supernatural brethren clearly hadn't. My dad explained what they needed to hear. "In the show, ghosts will be tied to their bones," he said.

"Or in something super personal, like a doll," Grizzie added.

"Creepy dolls," said my dad, then he and Grizzie both shuddered exaggeratedly. They'd obviously been watching a lot of TV together.

"The ghost idea is interesting. Maybe that means the Red and the White can be exorcised?" Caleb mused.

"That's a great place to start," I said, just as my back pocket buzzed. When I took my phone out, it had gone blank, the battery dead.

Almost immediately, Caleb's phone started buzzing from the table in front of him. He snapped it open.

"Yes, boss?... Yes, she's here... Okay, I'll put her on." Caleb held out his phone toward me.

"It's Ryu. He wants to talk to you."

I blinked at the phone in surprise. What could Ryu want?

With hesitant fingers I took the phone from Caleb and raised it to my ear.

"Yes?"

"Jane?"

"Yes, it's me."

"Good. I heard what happened."

I waited, having no idea what my former lover was going to say. When he spoke again, his voice was deep and serious.

"I want to help."

CHAPTER THREE

Ryu, of course, looked fabulous. He was wearing a beautifully tailored button-up in a bright, jewel-like blue that made his gold-flecked hazel eyes glow. Not a hair was out of place, and his strong jaw had an artful smattering of stubble.

He was sitting across from me at the Pig Sty, the place where we'd had our first date. I'd wanted to meet Ryu in public, but alone, rather than back at Anyan's with everyone listening. We had a lot to talk about, and I needed to understand his motivations.

I also needed to make sure he wasn't working for someone else—namely, the Alfar—and was only interested in getting the champion back onside to kill Anyan.

"You look great, Jane," he said, his eyes on mine.

I snorted indelicately. The fact was I looked a mess. My long black hair was completely out of control, my bangs hanging in my eyes. Said eyes were rimmed with almost purple bags of exhaustion, making my black gaze look like it came out of a pit. I also resembled someone who'd just come out of a coma, which in some ways I had. The creature's intervention had meant I hadn't gone completely bat-caca, but it had also meant I hadn't slept or eaten for a few weeks.

"I look like shit, Ryu," I told him, cutting to the chase. "I think my makeup is still somewhere in England, along with my underwear. We had to send a gwyllion over to my house to rescue me some clean clothes. I did shower, though. Just for you."

"Is your house still being watched?"

I nodded. After I'd shown myself to the media as a representative of some "helpful forces" that would take care of the problem at hand—the problem at hand being a rampaging, motherfucking dragon—human authorities were naturally very interested in me.

"Oh, yeah. Thanks for getting my dad and Griz and Tracy out, by the way."

"No problem, it was the least I could do."

Our order came.

"Tuna melt, ma'am," Amy said, winking at me as she set down my plate. I was heavily glamoured so as not to be recognized as Jane True, but our nahual waitress—a shapeshifter and an old friend of mine—could see through it.

"Rare steak," she said, setting down Ryu's food and walking away. I knew we'd see her back at Anyan's that night.

Maybe I can have her bring another tuna melt, I thought as the smell of hot buttered bread, melted cheese, and a whiff of tuna fish rose to my nostrils, causing my mouth to water.

"So, how are things back at the ranch?" I asked,

meaning the Alfar compound. After Morrigan had stabbed her husband, Orin, and run off with Jarl, Ryu and his nemesis, Nyx, had become coleaders of our territory.

Ryu took a moment to gather his thoughts while I paid close attention to his every reaction. I had to try to figure out where he was politically in all of this mess.

"They're great, actually. Nyx, believe it or not, has turned out to be a wonderful leader. I guess she just needed some actual responsibility to propel her into maturity."

I chewed a fry thoughtfully before swallowing. "Really? I find that hard to believe."

"I know. I did, too. But it's true."

"And you? How are you doing with all that power?"

Ryu took a moment to answer. He pushed his food around on his plate, and he wiped his mouth with his napkin. He took a drink. Eventually, he looked up.

"That's why I'm here, Jane. I want to apologize."

"For what?" I said cautiously. I had no idea where this conversation was going.

There was another awkward pause as Ryu struggled to find the best way to say whatever he had to say.

"Because I haven't thought about you at all," he said finally, looking chagrined.

"Okay?" I said questioningly, having no idea what he meant by that.

"What I mean is that I really did think I loved you, Jane. I really did. I really meant what I said back in Boston."

"But?"

"But," he said, "ever since I took over this position, I've been . . . I've been . . ."

"You've been happy," I said with a small smile.

"Yes." He looked relieved. "I've been happy."

"I'm glad, Ryu," I said. "But you know I would have hated it."

He smiled. "Yes, you would have. And that's what I realized. There was the Jane I wanted you to be, and the Jane you really are. The Jane you are would have hated my new life. And it wasn't fair of me to want to remake you."

Part of me was stunned at Ryu's admission, but part of me wasn't. He'd always been willing to admit when he was wrong. It's one of the reasons I'd liked him so much.

He was a good almost-vampire, if not the almost-vampire for me.

In my response I tried to acknowledge all I was feeling, but with a joke.

"I hope you liked the real Jane a little, too?"

He took my hand from across the table, but it wasn't a seductive gesture. He was being as open and honest as I'd ever seen him, which says a lot about our former relationship.

And about whatever our new relationship, our friendship, was developing into.

"I did, Jane. I liked you so much. And I still do."

"I like you, too, Ryu," I said, squeezing his hand affectionately. Then I withdrew, and asked the real question.

"So why, exactly, do you want to help? And what do you mean by help?"

Ryu burst out with his weird barking laugh, cutting a big piece of steak. I took a bite of my tuna melt, still ravenous. I'd eaten scads of Tracy's sandwiches, but then gone for a quick swim in the Sow before showering to meet Ryu, who was already in the area. I figured I'd earned another meal, at least.

Swallowing his mouthful, Ryu answered. "I mean help, as in help. So whatever you want me to do, or whatever you need. I know everything that happened, of course, and I'm assuming you want to get Anyan back?"

Relief flooded through me at his words, and the easy way he said them.

"Yes. And that's okay with you?"

Ryu cut off another piece of steak but spoke before taking his bite. "Of course. I figured that's what you'd want. And I think that's the right course."

I felt my eyebrow drifting up of its own accord. "You do? You're not thinking like the Alfar, that I should kill Anyan?"

Ryu held up a hand, gesturing for me to wait until he could speak without his mouth full.

"The way I see it," he said when he'd swallowed, "is that the Alfar have been doing their thing with the Red and the White for long enough now. And look where it's gotten us. Nowhere. They're still around, still wreaking havoc; only now the stakes are higher. We can't brush their shenanigans under the rug any longer, not with human technology. Our world is in chaos after Notre Dame, and it's just going to get worse. They need to be stopped, for good this time."

"But not by killing Anyan?" I asked skeptically.

"Obviously not," Ryu said, giving me a level look. "Think about it, Jane. The Red and the White have been killed about a million times. Has it worked?"

I couldn't help it then. I looked down at my own plate and voiced my worst fear. "But they're in real bodies now," I said, my voice small. "Maybe that means they can really be killed."

Instead of agreeing with that idea, Ryu openly scoffed.

"That makes no sense. If anything, now we know how little a body, even their own bodies, means to the Red and the White."

Looking up to meet Ryu's eyes, I felt another rush of excitement. "Iris said the same thing. I mean, she didn't, but sort of. I mean, she brought up the idea that we had to figure out what the Red and the White are. Like, are they bodies, or souls, or spirits, or whatever."

"They have to be the latter," Ryu said. "It's the only explanation. It's why they could communicate, even when they were supposedly dead and cut up, with the people they manipulated. It's why they could enter Morrigan and Anyan. We never thought of it that way because they would always come back to their own bones, their own bodies. But they're not things, they're...woo-woo things." Ryu wiggled his fingers in the air when he said "woo-woo," like a person imitating a ghost.

"So if we kill Anyan or Morrigan..." I started.

"All we do is release the spirits again, to find another host," finished Ryu.

To my embarrassment, tears rose in my eyes. I was definitely making up for my not crying immediately after everything happened, by crying at everything today.

Ryu's hand again found mine over the table.

"We will get him back, Jane," he said.

"Why do you care?" I asked, snuffling. I couldn't help it. He was being so good to me, and after everything that had happened between us, I didn't understand why.

"For a few reasons," he said, withdrawing his hand and leveling a serious look at me, so that I knew he wasn't just being friendly. Ryu was also strategizing, and for once I was glad to be on the receiving end of his ceaseless Machiavellian manipulations. "First of all, I've become a leader, too, just like Nyx. I've learned a lot about myself these last few months. I realized how selfish I'd been with a lot of things, including with you. So no matter how I felt about you and Anyan at one time, I have to put aside those feelings for the good of our people. *All* of our people. If the Red and the White aren't stopped, everything we know will come to an end. All life may come to an end. I can't let my own pettiness stand between me and that reality."

Wow, I thought. He really had grown up. I don't think I could think that clear-headedly, if I were he.

"Not to mention, how can I live without Anyan?" Ryu asked, giving me a broad wink. "He's the Moriarty to my Sherlock, the Road Runner to my Wyle E. Coyote, the Tom to my Jerry."

"But you're both good guys." He acknowledged my compliment with a smile and a small nod in my direction.

"Finally, I owe you, Jane."

"What? You don't owe me, that's ridiculous."

"No, I think I do. I did love you, you know. But I loved you in the wrong way. And I know I hurt you because of that."

For the umpteenth time, I blinked back tears. This time, however, they were the good kind.

"Ryu, you're a better person than me," I said, meaning it.

"Nonsense. Although that does mean a lot to me."

We ate the rest of our meal in companionable silence, and then we even ordered pie.

"So how long are you free from your duties?" I asked

Ryu as we ate our desserts—cherry pie for him, pecan for me.

"As long as you need me. Nyx really is capable of running things without me, especially now. Everyone's basically paralyzed, waiting for the next appearance from the Red and the White. Makes ruling easy. Oh, and Daoud will be here tomorrow. Camille is now running things in Boston, although she sends her regards."

"The old gang," I said with a smile.

"Yes, the old gang."

And right then, I knew we had a shot. Because I did have a gang. I had a massive, incredibly smart, incredibly loyal, and incredibly loving team of people whom I could count on.

People who just might make getting Anyan back possible.

So I briefed Ryu on what we had, in terms of our own strengths, and what we knew, which was very little. I also promised to show him the labrys later. I hadn't taken it out since I'd gotten back, partially because I knew I'd think of Blondie when I did.

Grief for her death was something I couldn't deal with at that point, so I'd just bottled it up and stashed it somewhere deep inside. It probably wasn't too healthy, long term, to do stuff like that, but it got me through the short term.

When I was done talking, Ryu looked speculative as he put money down for the check. I had to let him pay, as I had no cash. I actually had no wallet, passport, purse, anything, since it was all still back in London with my backpack.

I made a mental note to ask the creature about that,

forgetting the creature was actually in my mind. So as soon as I had the thought, I felt a feeling of confirmation run through me, and I knew I'd probably return home to a backpack full of dirty clothes.

"Well," Ryu said as we made our way toward the Sty's double doors. "We don't have a lot to go on, but maybe that's a good thing. The fact is, everything we know about how to take care of these monsters hasn't worked. So we have to think up something entirely new."

I nodded as we pushed our way into the warm spring evening.

"That's the next step. Find somewhere to start—"

My sentence was never finished as an explosion rocked Ryu and me off our feet. Protected by our instinctive shields, we bounced harmlessly off the ground. But when we clambered to our feet, mage balls at the ready, we saw that the glass fronts of all the surrounding stores were blown out. Cowering humans, most of whom I knew even if they couldn't recognize me through my glamour, peered up in fright from the Sty, and fury kindled within me.

When the next blast hit, we were ready, and I easily contained it within my shields. I also got a lock on our targets, lurking in an alleyway kitty-corner from where Ryu and I stood.

Beautiful blue eyes met mine from a waxen face, and I strode purposefully forward.

It was about time I dealt with Graeme, once and for all.

CHAPTER FOUR

Morrigan had definitely sent her big guns, as well as a few little ones.

Besides the rapist-incubus, Graeme, who wielded a fair bit of mojo, there were two goblins launching themselves across the street at us. They were the little guns, and Ryu and I flicked them aside with a negligible release of magic.

While we dealt with them, however, Graeme sent another massive blast of magic from a set of charms he held. They were like the magical version of grenades—supercharged, probably by Morrigan herself—to be utilized later by whoever carried them.

Since I was a woman, and better at multitasking, even as I dispatched my goblin I circled the charm's blast with a heavy blanket of damp air. As I did so, I pulled more moisture out of the drenched Maine atmosphere, until the blast was cocooned in water.

[Do as Nell taught you,] came the creature's voice in

my head. Even as he told me what to do, he showed me, and I smiled.

Some of my first lessons from the gnome had been about recycling power. So, when I did things like create a mage light, instead of letting it fizzle out when I was done with it, she taught me to reabsorb the power.

And this charm was really just a massive, fuck-off powerful mage light.

I went deep in my power, grounding myself as I opened my channels to shunt off all that crazy force. Feeling the foreign power whoosh through me, I immediately boomeranged it back at where I knew Graeme was hiding between the fire station and the post office. It came out like a blast of light, clipping the corner of our fire station and blasting away a third goblin that had launched itself from the shadows.

I moved to the right, still streaming that power, until Graeme's alley no longer hid him. He took off running, screaming something incomprehensible, but I felt an answering pull of air power above me.

Harpies, I thought grimly, knowing that Kaya and Kaori must be near. Ryu shouted, pointing upward. Dark shapes darted above us and then a single, magically charged feather came drifting down—but this one had the punch of a missile from a B-52 bomber.

It landed at our feet, and I shielded it even as we separated, throwing ourselves away as we amped up our own individual protections. It exploded in a riot of magic, blowing out the front of the fire station. Our dazed local firefighters—volunteers mostly—poked their heads around a corner, and I begged the creature for help. Like marionettes with their strings cut, the firefighters slumped to the ground, put to sleep by the creature's power.

And that's when I got pissed. It was one thing to attack me, but it was another thing entirely to attack the town of Rockabill. Morrigan was hitting way too close to home.

Graeme was holed up in the front piece of the restaurant a few doors down from the post office. He must have thought it was a good place to hide, but he was wrong.

Because that building—owned by Stuart Grey's nasty parents—was the one building I didn't mind destroying.

"Take the harpies!" I shouted at Ryu. "I'll take Graeme!"

Ryu gave me a startled look, since he'd not seen the evolution of Jane True into someone who took people on, rather than just taking things from buffets.

He looked even more shocked when I pulled the labrys from wherever it hid, waiting to be called.

I swept it through the air a few times, calling to its power even as I remembered my lessons with Anyan with a pang. It responded eagerly, lighting up with a savage gleam. I grinned, admittedly rather maniacally, at Graeme, and started to walk forward.

Graeme shouted gibberish again, lobbing a few mage balls at me, and out stepped ... something.

I'd never seen anything like it. It was squat, about three feet tall and as wide across. It appeared to be made of ... mud? Brown and lumpy, it sort of resembled a toad. Or the nasty brother that gets turned into an actual pile of shit in *Weird Science*.

Its grotesquely wide body shuffled forward on stupidly tiny, SpongeBob legs. It might have been humorous, except that with every step it took earth power boomed forward. The ground shook like we were having a quake, and I stumbled.

"It's a golem!" Ryu shouted.

I cast him a Look, letting him know I had no idea what he was talking about, even as I pulled more water out of the air, pushing against the golem thing.

Ryu lobbed a few mage balls into the air, and we heard a satisfying squawk, before explaining.

"They're basically walking charms, charged with the element of the person who made them. But that person has to be enormously strong."

The blood drained from my face as I realized the implications of Ryu's words.

The thing was using earth power. Anyan's main element was earth. Anyan may have charged this thing.

And sent it to kill me.

Forcing down a lump in my throat, I told myself that this was inevitable. Anyan wasn't Anyan anymore. And although I had to believe he was somewhere inside of that damned dragon, that didn't mean he was in control.

Which meant the White did this. Not Anyan.

And I was the champion, not just Jane anymore.

So this time, when the earth golem took another waddling step forward, looking a bit like a New Zealand rugby player performing the haka, I was ready.

I pushed forward with the labrys's power, meeting the golem's own expenditure of energy halfway. I then arced it up, so it dissipated in the air rather than causing another tremor.

I moved forward, too, until I was close enough to see that it had a creepy version of a face. Mud eyes stared blindly forward, above a crude mud nose and mouth. Its small arms flailed as it called forth more power.

"How do I kill this thing?" I shouted at Ryu, who was now peppering the sky with a barrage of mage balls. We heard another noise from the heavens, this time a cry, and something fell onto the roof of the post office.

One harpy down, one to go, I thought.

Ryu dashed over to where I stood, trying to keep the golem from taking another of those earthquake-inducing steps. He started to pour his own power into mine, but I felt him withdraw it as he gave me a shocked look.

"Most of it's the creature's," I said, knowing he'd realized just how much force I now wielded. "Power's not the issue; how do we stop it?"

A mage ball hit our shield from above, and Ryu started peppering the sky above us to keep the remaining harpy away.

"Golems haven't been created for centuries, so I don't know how it can be killed. But if it's earth, I'd assume use a contradictory element?"

I nodded, narrowing my eyes at the golem. Graeme was behind it, his lips still moving.

He must be controlling it, I realized.

"If we don't know how to destroy it, we should just try to stop it," I told Ryu, a plan forming in my head. "Then we have to take out Graeme."

"Getting it to stop would be a good thing, yes," Ryu said as he scanned the skies, sending up a few more missiles.

"I meant stop-stop, like freezing it…" I stopped talking. Freezing it. Yes, freezing would work.

The golem was mud, after all…

Once I had the idea, all I had to do was execute it.
Unfortunately, what I wanted to do took way more focus
and power than I'd thought it would. So the moment I
went in—seeking out all of those fat, lovely water mole-
cules holding the dirt together and making it mud—I lost
control of the golem. It took another haka-step forward,
and both Ryu and I stumbled, then dove out of the way as
a light pole snapped and fell from right above us, threatening to crush us. I lost my grip on the golem's water, and
it took another step, even as a dark shape hurtled down
from the sky at Ryu.

Graeme shouted exultantly, no doubt some command
for the golem, and I decided I'd had enough.

Clambering to my feet, using the labrys as a crutch, I
sent one arc of power that knocked the harpy out of the air
seconds before her taloned feet found Ryu's throat.

With another wave of power, I clumsily, if effectively,
pushed Graeme over, shields and all. And then I went for
the golem.

Instead of pulling the water out of it, I focused on its
chemical structure. It took only a few tweaks, and a fair
bit of the creature's mojo, and suddenly, it froze.

And I mean froze—its water turned to ice; it couldn't
move. Like a great frozen turd, it squatted smack in the center of Rockabill's Main Street. It'd take a while for it to thaw.

Ryu was up and engaged in a firefight with the downed
harpy. Caught on her two feet, rather than in the air, she
was severely handicapped and I knew that fight would be
short.

Which left Graeme up to me.

The incubus had gotten to his feet, looking dazed,
when I struck.

My first blast peeled away his outermost defensive shields with a surge of power so raw, so undiluted, that even I was surprised by it. But as if some other Jane— some Rambo Jane—were in control, I struck again instantly.

Another raw flood of power kept Graeme from re-forming his shields, even as I started chipping away at his stronger inner shields. They were no match for my fury.

For being angry with someone was one thing. But being angry with someone because they'd been part of a process that took everything from you . . . that was another thing entirely. I'd never wanted to destroy something as badly as I wanted to destroy Graeme, in that instant. He'd been such a nemesis for me, but it wasn't just because of all our past encounters that I wanted to squash him like an insect. It was because he'd helped take away my Anyan, and helped replace my lover with someone who sent mud-people to kill me.

He'd also helped kill my friend.

At the thought of Blondie, I suddenly saw her, lying on the funeral pyre before it was lit. It was like a rage bomb went off inside me, and if I thought I was strong before, I was now ruthless in my strip-mining of every available ounce of power around me.

The blasts that I'd been keeping aimed at Graeme had never ceased, but now they were coming twice as fast, and with twice as much fury.

[Careful, young one,] the creature warned. But despite the emotional storm raging inside me, I knew what I was doing.

I acknowledged the creature's thought with an unvoiced

response of my own, even as I broke through Graeme's inner shields. That left only his personal defenses—the thin skin of mojo we all wore around ourselves as a last resort.

I had them down in seconds.

By that point I was nearly on top of him, having strode forward with each carefully timed blast. So when I peeled away that last layer of shield, pushing him to his knees as I did so, I was able to get right up in Graeme's grill.

It was time to send a message.

I took a page from Anyan himself as I sent my power out like a hand, taking a viselike grip on Graeme's throat. His eyes widened as I squeezed, ever so slowly.

When he was blue and wheezing, I spoke.

"You're going to take home a message for me, you shit," I said, letting up just enough on Graeme's throat that he didn't die and could take a breath. Then I squeezed again.

"You're going to tell Morrigan that I'm coming for her. And that she made a mistake taking Anyan. Before we were ready to play the way she'd always played, but now all bets are off. We're going to find a way to kill her, and for good.

"She's going to die, and she's not coming back from this one."

I let go of Graeme's throat so promptly he fell forward; choking with harsh strangled sounds that were like the sweet tinkling of bells to my ear.

"Now get the hell out of here. And if you ever step foot in Rockabill again, I'm killing you."

With those words I sent a massive arc of power at the frozen golem. It exploded in a magnificent shower of icy mud that rained over Graeme like a riot of chocolate sprinkles.

He looked up at me, then, and although his eyes were still full of the same hate they always were, I saw something new.

I saw fear.

I saw respect.

I saw the Jane I'd become—the avenging Fury who meant it when she said she'd kill someone.

A dark shadow swooped down on Graeme from above, and then he was aloft, carried by the now recovered harpy.

I signaled for Ryu to release the other one, who launched herself in the air with the aerial version of a limp.

She buzzed out of sight, lumbering in the night sky like a pollen-drunk honeybee, following the larger shape of her Graeme-laden sister.

Turning back to Ryu, I found him watching me with a dark, inscrutable gaze. Graeme wasn't the only one who got schooled that day.

It seemed that everyone was learning just what Jane was made of, including Jane herself.

CHAPTER FIVE

Is that the creature?" Iris whispered at me, pointing surreptitiously at the giant eyeball staring at us from the rock wall.

"Yes. Well, its eye at least."

"And the, um, appendages?" she said, giving a furtive flutter of her hand toward the piles of tentacles lying around the cave.

"Yes, they belong to the creature, too."

The creature had apparated all of us down to its underground lair. Graeme had undoubtedly taken my message back to Morrigan, but we knew there was a good chance the harpies were still skulking about, trying to spy on us.

And since harpies, with their control over the air, could do all sorts of things to make listening from a distance easy, the creature had suggested we meet underground, on its turf.

The cave hadn't changed much—it was still dank,

drippy, and muddy. I was relieved, however, that Phaedra's body was nowhere to be seen. The creature had speared the little Alfar like a kebab; only tentacles make much bigger holes than skewers.

It hadn't been a pleasant sight, watching her die, and her corpse would be even less pleasant after time to rot.

With us for this meeting were Iris, Caleb, Ryu, Daoud (in from Boston), Nell, and Trill. At my insistence, we'd also brought my father, Grizzie, and Tracy. Ryu was not convinced that they'd be of any use, but I wanted them there for a few reasons. I wanted their support, if I were honest, but I also knew that, sometimes, those farthest from a problem could often see it the clearest.

We had left Gog, Magog, and Hiral back at the ranch. It's not that I didn't want to trust them, but I also knew that they had divided loyalties, no matter how much they liked and supported me. They'd always have their affiliations to the rebels of the Great Island, and after Lyman's betrayal I wasn't able to trust his brother, Jack, the rebel leader. For even though I knew Jack was devastated by his brother's betrayal and subsequent death, we now knew Jack didn't have the control over his people that he thought he did. If his brother could go that rotten without him realizing, lord only knows what else was lurking in his crew. So while I trusted Gog and Magog to have my back, I didn't trust them not to tell Jack what we were up to.

Hiral was another matter. The little gwyllion had grown on me, and I'd have been willing for him to come. But he'd asked to stay back, to my surprise. It took me a few minutes to realize that he was actually intending to keep an eye on Gog and Magog, but I was grateful when that realization hit.

"Should we get down to business?" Ryu asked, casting a fastidious gaze around his surroundings. The baobhan sith wasn't really a mud person.

[Yes. Let us commence,] rolled the creature's sonorous voice through my mind. I could tell from everyone's startled reactions that he was speaking to all of us, and I suppressed a smile.

Despite what all the fantasy books might lead you to believe, psychic phenomena were actually unheard of in the world of magic. We could manipulate energy, but thought was something entirely different. I'd been more than relieved to learn that fact, as I'd always been rather frightened of the idea of psychic phenomena. Maybe it was so much time spent in the loony bin, but I had a certain respect for the idea that our minds were our own, no matter how fucked up they were. So psychic stuff had always struck me as frighteningly external—like a lobotomy, or really strong drugs like lithium.

Things coming in from outside and wiping out my mind scared me after my stay in the hospital.

Which brought me back to Anyan. We had to save him. I couldn't imagine being trapped in my own mind, and yet I hoped that's what he was. Because if he was just gone, if the White had managed to eradicate Anyan...

I couldn't even consider that outcome.

I also realized that everyone was staring at me expectantly, waiting for me to begin. That was a huge change from our normal modus operandi, in which I was mostly listening to the other supes talk. It struck me that the tagger-along had become the leader.

So I'd better lead.

"I'd like to start by thanking all of you for coming. I know that sounds lame, but I mean it. I now feel like we can actually do this."

Everyone nodded, acknowledging my thanks but also, I think, affirming my words. My father, standing next to me, squeezed my shoulder in support.

"I've been scared this whole time that our only option was to go after Anyan and destroy him, to get to the White. But Ryu had some really good reasons why working to save Anyan is actually a smart course. Ryu?" I said, turning to my ex.

Ryu stepped forward, squaring his shoulders.

"Jane told me that Iris already touched on the ideas that I had, but I'll share them with you anyway. In my thinking, the Red and the White aren't physical, which is why killing them never worked."

Iris nodded manically, her eyes wide with excitement.

"They're not bodies!" she hooted triumphantly.

"They're not bodies," Ryu repeated. "We've always been so focused on their physical selves—their bones— that we never stopped and asked how they could keep resurrecting themselves. But it's because they're souls, or spirits, or something else. As long as they could animate their own bodies, they chose to do so. But when that was no longer an option…"

"They went incorporeal," Caleb said, his gaze turned inward as he thought through what Ryu was saying.

I cast a glance at my dad, Grizzie, and Tracy. Tracy and my dad looked a bit lost, if I were honest, but Grizzie just looked…blank.

Every once in a while, Grizzie's Grizelda mask dropped,

and we would catch a glimpse of the outrageously clever woman who lurked beneath. That woman loved being Grizelda, but she was something both of and apart from her persona. She'd also lived as many different personas, all with very different interests. So I was used to looking over and seeing Grizelda look like somebody other than Grizelda. But I'd never seen this. She looked...empty.

Creature? I asked. *Is someone spying on us?*

I felt a tingle in my head, an acknowledgment of my question telling me the creature had understood and would investigate.

I kept an eye on Grizzie as Ryu continued. "If it is true that they are able to exist noncorporeally, that explains why we can't kill Anyan. All that would do would be just that: We'd kill Anyan, leaving the White still in existence and now free."

"It would just find another host?" Daoud asked, obviously uncomfortable with this line of thought.

"I'm sure. I think that a negative result of the Original using the labrys on the Red and the White was to help sever their last link with their bodies. Meaning that now the process of finding a new host might be even more straightforward than it was before, as they apparently don't even have to worry about their bones or anything. They're spiritual free agents, so to speak." Ryu looked around, his words weighing heavy in the air. I saw Iris shiver, and Caleb put a muscular bare arm around her. Grizzie didn't react at all, but she also hadn't done anything weird. Nor had I heard back from the creature. Maybe she was just tired?

"So if we can't kill the body..." Daoud said, bringing my attention back to the problem at hand.

"We have to kill the spirit," Ryu finished.

[Which means separating the soul from the body,] came the creature's voice, rich and bright in our minds.

"Can that be done?" I asked, my voice breathless.

My supernatural friends all looked at each other expectantly.

Crickets.

"Well, I've never heard of anything like that," Caleb began. He spoke lightly, as if he should have been relaying more positive information.

"Souls," Iris mused, looking up at the ceiling.

Daoud looked down at his pants as if he were wondering what he could pull out of them to help. As a djinn, he could create anything he understood at the chemical level—and then pull it out of his pants. I'll never understand the physics of that trick, but it made for some alarming hostess gifts.

"Is there anything in your history?" I prompted. "Or your legends, that we could apply?"

Caleb shook his head. "I can't think of anything. In terms of the Red and the White themselves, we've only ever attacked physically. And I can't think of any other tales of souls, or spirits. We don't even believe in ghosts, as humans do..."

My dad and Tracy glanced at each other when Caleb said the word "ghosts." But they didn't speak up, although they probably thought all of this talk was crazy. I turned to our big gun.

Creature?

[I'm listening, Jane. You want to ask your tall friend. The human.]

I looked at Grizzie. She still looked curiously blank,

and she was rocking back and forth. Tracy had noticed, and was watching her partner with worried eyes.

"Grizzie," I said, "you all right over there?"

Grizzie was obviously not all right, for Grizzie began to glow. It was just a faint, soft luminescence, but it was definitely not normal.

Instantly, we supes snapped into action. First Caleb was there, dragging Tracy to safety. Iris pulled my dad back, to join Tracy, and Daoud joined his shield with Caleb's to keep the two nonmagicals safe behind their defenses.

Meanwhile, Ryu, Nell, and I fanned out in front of Grizzie. Ryu and Nell had mage balls ready, but I refused to pull a weapon on my friend. Yet.

"Grizzie," I said. "What's going on? Can you hear me?"

"She can hear you, child, and she is safe. Do not fear."

The voice that spoke from Grizzie's mouth wasn't hers. Instead of the usual husky, dark tones I was used to, this voice was resonant. It carried power, and although it wasn't that loud, it felt as if it were booming.

"And who are you exactly?" I asked.

Grizzie's form laughed, a rich chuckle that sent shivers up my spine.

"I am all, my child. I am everything."

We all stared. "That's not very helpful," I said, frantically calling the creature's Bat Phone.

[Hush,] was all I got in reply. [And listen.]

"What have you done with my wife?" Tracy yelled, struggling where Caleb held her in a tight grip.

"I have done nothing to this vessel," Grizzie intoned, casting those eerily blank eyes on Tracy. "Your children will have its mother, have no fear. Both of its mothers.

"I needed a mouthpiece, and this one was perfect. So open, so free, and so fluid in her identity."

Were we about to have a lecture on Judith Butler? "Look, can you hurry it up?" I said, losing patience. "Who are you and what do you want?"

The creature tsked in my brain, but I didn't care. But neither was I ready for the response when it came.

"I represent the universe," the voice said, the glow encompassing Grizzie pulsing faintly.

"The whaaa?" I asked, completely nonplussed.

"You humans are so small," it marveled, causing me to stand at my full (not at all impressive) height. "Do you have *any* idea what surrounds you?"

"Apparently not," Ryu said, doing his "humble supplicant" voice. He was good at these kinds of games, while I wasn't.

"You are part of something greater. You must know this after everything you've seen."

I made a face. This was getting far too religious for me.

"What do you mean, something greater?" Ryu said so I didn't have to. The Friend Formerly Known as Grizzie ignored him.

"Forces must be balanced. There may not be good or evil as you know it, but there is power. And power must be aligned, or all will fall."

I made a face. "What power?"

Grizzie's blank eyes stared directly into mine, and my whole consciousness swam. "Power, child. Power. The power that propels the world!"

That last bit ended in a boom, and Grizzie's glowing form shone even brighter.

"Okay," I said. "And?"

"You must restore the balance."

What the fuck is going on? This is like being lectured by the Sphinx, I said to the creature. It sent a warm wash of thought through my brain, as if to comfort me, but I wouldn't accept it. *Tell me what's happening,* I demanded.

[I am exactly what I say,] came a voice in my head. But it wasn't the creature's, it was the same voice pouring out of Grizzie. My heart beat faster in my chest, but I tried not to panic.

But what is that? I asked silently.

[I told you: I am the universe!] With that, it took control of my vision.

I saw the birth of the worlds, the coming together of powers that exploded, rocketing outward. I saw the creation of first light and then matter—gases becoming solid, solids glomming together, the creation of suns and planets and galaxies.

That power radiated throughout this process, dancing in and through all of creation, as the universe bucked and spun...

Until here and there throughout the galaxies, in pockets where conditions were just right (and those pockets were very few, and far between), life flared.

With life came renewed interest from the powers, which promulgated around these bright beacons of existence. Some life, however, plodded along...never changing, never challenging, never learning. But others were not so staid. Across the universe rose beings that could manipulate the powers that had created them. They were the power, were of the power, and could *use* the power.

The universe shuddered with delight, sensing kinship

and opportunity. Sometimes these new forms of life took too much, however, or tried to throw out the rules of the game. Then balance needed to be restored.

The Red and the White upset the balance, I put together, hints and images and echoes of thought. *But how do we stop them?*

This time, the universe changed tack. Instead of seeing the macrocosmos, I was made party to the microcosmos. I saw it all: how the universe interfered to right the balance. Creatures like the one underneath Rockabill, given power or knowledge at crucial moments in their fight against the Red and the White. Then, as those creatures faded, new creatures were made into weapons. I saw dozens, hundreds, including a stranger with a great destiny saved from a childhood illness. The blond girl who'd been tricked into dividing her kind into factions made into a champion. An ax forged at the critical time with powers beyond the comprehension of even the being that had helped create it. A boy drowned on a beach while a girl hovered over him, keening to the skies…

What does Jason dying have to do with anything? And I already know I'm the champion, I pleaded. Where were the answers?

I saw then the not so lucky. The other beings—elemental beings, preschism Originals like Blondie, Alfar, other strong supes—who could have led, who should have led, struck down before their prime. Suspicious accidents, outright murders…the Red and the White were creatures made of the same power that sought to destroy them, and they could sense the universe's interference…

So truth needed to be hidden. Power needed to be contained as knowledge, and hidden away. And what better place to hide dangerous knowledge than in the ones who could only bear witness to the powers that bore them, never tapping into them themselves.

Humans.

A spate of glassy-eyed, gibbering faces ran by me: artists, hermits, saints, writers, soothsayers, prophets—all men and women made mad by the powers seeking to use their hands, their voices, their minds.

Using these humans, small secrets were buried here and there, as if the universe were a squirrel hiding away nuts.

Then another human was chosen, inspired to collect all these scraps of knowledge. Another inspired to transcribe them. Another to translate. Another to archive. Another to say the right words at the right time...

All humans, made into tools of the universe.

With that, I was given back control over my own body. My eyes sprang open, to find myself recumbent in Ryu's arms, his voice saying my name and his eyes peering into mine. I turned my head to see Grizzie similarly propped up by Daoud, Tracy kneeling next to her while Caleb hovered over both protectively. To my relief, Grizzie sat up, looking as groggy as I did.

"We're looking for a human," I said then, my voice scratchy. "The universe gave us a human."

I think I fainted then, for just a second. That happens when one has the powers of creation rattling around in one's mind. When I came to, I heard more speech in my head. It sounded like it was coming through cotton wool, but I recognized it.

[I've been seeking through relevant minds,] the creature said, its thought colored somehow with its findings. It was excited. [There is a voice calling us. He seems to be expecting me. How curious…I can only take two of you, if you are ready now?]

The choice was obvious, and it flashed through my mind in a second.

And then, like that, Ryu and I found ourselves in another room. I was still lying in his arms, but when I tried to sit up, everything spun.

"Easy, Jane," Ryu said.

"What the hell just happened?"

"I was going to ask you."

I gave him a squinty look, trying to fix my vision, which was swimming alarmingly. "Either somebody slipped me some shrooms or I was talking to the universe."

"The universe?"

"Yeah. The universe."

"The universe," Ryu repeated, looking as skeptical as I'd ever seen him. "You have been under a lot of stress…"

"Don't be so doubtful. The universe is closer than we know," came a chirping, friendly voice from somewhere behind us. I tried to crane my head around, but could see nothing. Ryu helped me clamber to my feet, and we got a good look at our surroundings.

Instead of a cave, this room appeared to be a very sumptuous, modern hotel. Chrome and glass were every-where, and a modern cityscape lurked outside the huge wall of windows. I also located our speaker, sitting a dis-tance away.

Amid all this modernity, he cut a figure not modern at all. Small and bald, with a round, friendly face sporting even rounder glasses, sat a Buddhist monk in full regalia. He sat in a very large chair.

He had tea prepared, waiting on a low table in front of him, and he was definitely expecting us. He certainly wasn't surprised by the sight of two strangers appearing by magic in front of him.

"Welcome," he said in perfect English. "I believe you have a problem with dragons?"

CHAPTER SIX

In this instance, who I am is of no importance," the man said, never losing that wide, welcoming smile. I made a small sound, for although I was pretty sure I knew the identity of the bespectacled figure, I couldn't help wanting clarification.

The man laughed, a lovely, bell-like sound. "So curious!" he said, his eyes twinkling from his smile-creased features. "But while I, as an individual, can acknowledge that there is far more to our world than one answer will ever account for, as a spiritual leader I must toe certain lines. So I'd like to keep our conversation off the record, as it were."

While the monk talked, Ryu wandered toward the wall of windows on one side of the hotel room.

"Hong Kong?" he said. I joined him at the window to see a riotous city, full of signage in all different languages, but mostly in Chinese and English.

"Yes. I'm sorry it couldn't be more convenient," the man said.

It was my turn to smile at him. "Oh, believe me, it was no trouble getting here."

"Now, let us get to the problem of your dragons." The man gestured toward the chairs opposite him.

Ryu and I took our places as the man poured tea. I took one of the shortbread cookies lying on a silver platter, because snacks keep a body going.

"I have been expecting you," the man began, which was not at all what we expected to hear.

"You have?" I said, unable to stop myself from interrupting.

The man gave me another wide smile, but this one held a note of ruefulness.

"Of course," he said. "For what is happening in your part of the world affects everyone. I love Westerners and the West, but you do have a tendency to act as though things only happen to you and your own people."

I blushed, although the chastising was very gentle.

"The truth is that what you call the Red and the White are a global problem. Yes, their physical appearances have, by accident of geography, been bound to your Great Island, but their reach is far wider."

"Really?" said Ryu, leaning forward.

"Of course. They are a manifestation of great power, and as such they inevitably act on the balance of things."

"I'm sorry, I don't understand," I said.

The man took a sip of his own tea, taking the cup and saucer with him as he leaned back to place them on his robed knee.

"As elements, as avatars of the forces that created not only our physical world, but our emotional and spiritual world as well, the Red and the White have far more power than we can really understand. Their thoughts infect the thoughts of those creatures around them that share their nature."

"Beings of fire and air?" I asked, referring to the supernaturals that could wield those forces.

For the first time since we'd met him, the man frowned, but in concentration.

"That is an obvious response, yes, but not necessarily true. There will be creatures of your world that can wield air and fire, yes, but whose *natures* are not of air and fire."

It was my turn to frown. "Huh?" I said intelligently.

"What I mean is that what we are isn't always what we should be. You know creatures, I'm sure, who are big and powerful, yet their souls are gentle. In the same example, I'm sure you've met delicate beings who have the souls of tyrants."

I thought of Gog, who could flatten a door by poking at it with a finger, but who was as gentle as they came. Then I thought of Phaedra, the tiny doer-of-evil, and Morrigan, whose delicate beauty contained a monster.

"Don't judge a book by its cover," I said, turning to clichés to help me understand what the man was saying.

"Essentially, yes," the man said. "The Red and the White were created by forces that permeate all of us, in different measures. We all have many conflicting characteristics. In a single person, goodness sits next to rage, which dines with generosity and pettiness, before going to meet greed that lives next door to empathy. We are all conflicted creatures, but not all in equal measures or in equal ways."

"Are you saying that the Red and the White represent characteristics that we somehow pick up from them?" Ryu said. He didn't appear too invested in the idea.

The man took another sip of his tea, radiating calm as he spoke again. "Yes and no. The fact is that people are a combination of many things, environment being just as importance as genetics. But I do think that the Red and the White spring from something essential. What you think of as your elements are, I believe, similar to our understanding of DNA. They're the building blocks of our world; your people are just able to interact with and to wield them in ways that my people can't. But we all come from the same source, do we not?"

I nodded vigorously. Back when I'd fought Phaedra in the creature's lair, the night I became the champion, the creature had beamed a vision out to me and any of the surrounding minds close enough. Well, it wasn't a vision really. It was the creature's memories, and in those memories was revealed the fact that supernaturals were not a separate species. They were humans who'd evolved to manipulate the elements that were all around them. Supernaturals such as Ryu, born and raised to think of themselves as very much separate from and superior to humans, had been unhappy to discover we were all originally humans. Indeed, since then many had dismissed the vision as impossible. But I knew it was the truth and was thrilled, for it meant I hadn't really changed. I was still essentially the human I had always believed myself to be.

"Yes, we have seen a vision in which that scenario was true," Ryu said, all shifty eyed.

The monk's Cheshire cat smile managed to look even more mysterious at Ryu's obvious discomfort. "Well, if we all come from the same sources—these building blocks of genetics that you supernaturals understand as elements—it means we have all of the same things inside us, but mixed up in different proportions. Hence the fact none of us are the exact same person, except biological twins, of course. And even they can be so very different from each other."

"So what you're saying is that we all have a bit of the Red and the White in us, but some have more and some have less." I was starting to get it. He was really talking about genetics. The Red and the White were formed of the elements that made our earth, quite literally. They'd been spawned of fire and air, and those things existed in all of us, because we were created of the same forces that made them. Humans and supernaturals were just a later version of the life that sprang out of the elemental forces colliding. Life 2.0, so to speak.

"Exactly," said the monk. "We all have a bit of what created the Red and the White. And for those that have more... when the Red and the White appear in our world, it affects those whose natures are more akin to Fire and Air."

"I haven't been paying attention," I admitted. "We've been so busy with everything involving the Red and the White. Have there been things happening?"

"Oh, yes. Crime on the rise everywhere. Domestic violence ending in murder, in households that were always happy. Brothers slaying brothers; mothers slaying their children. And those are only the individuals. There have been mass lootings and rapes, gangs fighting. Armies mobilizing..."

"Holy shit," I breathed, forgetting there was a real holy person already in the room.

"Exactly. But this is not the first time in history. The amalgamation of fire and air, is, after all, an odd combination, existing in a very small minority of the population. But throughout history, there have been times of such utter madness, when whole civilizations have followed single leaders to their doom, that I cannot help but look for an outside influence."

"Hitler?" I said. I'd asked this before, and been shot down, but I really wanted to blame Hitler for something other than human evil.

"Perhaps," the man said, but with a shake of his head that warned me he wasn't finished. "But that doesn't erase the individual's culpability. Someone like Hitler may have allowed himself to be seduced by his worst nature, but he could have resisted. And even if his madness were partially a product of the Red and the White's interference, not all who followed him could have been susceptible to their powers. The vast majority would have followed of their own volition, because they believed in his insane vision and were swayed by the crowd."

"This is all very fascinating," Ryu said. "But what can we do with this information?"

"Yes," I said. "My friend, Anyan, he was basically bodynapped by the White. And we have to get him back."

The small man watched me, but stayed silent. I wasn't sure if he was thinking, or waiting, or what. I began to worry he didn't actually have any answers.

Ryu spoke then, interrupting the quiet. "We also have to end this cycle. The Red and the White need to be destroyed for good."

The man took a sip of his tea, his gaze turned inward in thought.

"I do have some good news," the man said. "I think it's definitely possible to get your friend back."

I sat bolt upright. "You do?"

"Possible, yes. Probable...that will depend on you. The process will be neither pleasant nor easy."

"But if there's a process, we can handle a process," I babbled excitedly. The thought of there being a process was heavenly.

The man chuckled at my excitement before continuing. "The answers you seek are actually in your own tradition, those of the West. They lie in your alchemy."

"Alchemy?" I said, startled. "Isn't that about turning stuff into gold?"

"Yes, and no. For everything in alchemy is a metaphor for something else. So while there was definitely a search for gold, that search was also a metaphor for other things, such as eternal life and the transcendence of the soul."

"Oh," I said, feeling stupid.

"We have our own Eastern alchemical traditions, certainly. And we also have our own Shamanic traditions, which deal with the soul and its relationship to the body. But ultimately, our goals in these spheres were different from the goals in the West."

Ryu nodded sagely, and I tried to imitate him. Then I gave up.

"How do you know all this?" I asked.

For just a split second, the monk glowed, that same gentle, golden luminescence that had bathed Grizzie.

"Oh, my child. There is so much more to our reality. And the universe, despite our intrusions, is self-ordering. It wants balance, and it looks forward." The monk's voice was no longer entirely his own. I shivered.

He continued in that voice that was his, but with something extra. "Think of our conversation of essences. The universe knows that the Red and the White should not exist."

"They were born of violence," I said. "They were not born of choice."

The Red and the White were spawned from Fire's rape of Air. Fire had always been a very nasty piece of work, as had all of its offspring. One such offspring was responsible for killing all of the creature's siblings, just because it could. To be born of Fire and created in an act of such violence made the Red and the White what they were today: pure evil.

The man nodded, his glow pulsing as if in agreement. "They were cursed by their mother with nothingness. No heart, no empathy, no softness. Their father filled that empty place with his greed, his desire, and a lust for pleasure. From both parents, however, they received tremendous power—too much power. They represent, in all ways, a lack of balance. And so the universe understands, and seeks to redress their influence."

"So what does that mean for us?" Ryu said, getting to the point.

The monk's glow increased, and his voice was no longer in any way his own. "It means that visionaries amongst humans have written about things they, themselves, could not understand, but they knew were important."

"Like prophecies?" I said.

"Nothing so mundane. They didn't know what they were writing, or why, and were quite convinced they were writing something else entirely. But their wisdom was guided by something bigger than them, something that knew it would be needed someday."

The man stood. His body moved upward, and upward . . .

until he was hovering a few inches off the floor. Then he levitated, trailing that golden glow, over to a small table where sat a single book. It looked old, while still having a modern bookbinding. It must have been from around the turn of the last century.

He floated back to our tea service, handing me the book. To my surprise, it was a copy of a text in Greek, older than I had imagined. The words on the page were beautiful, if completely illegible to me, since I didn't know the Greek alphabet besides the alpha and omega signs.

Then the monk sat down, and his glow faded. He blinked at us owlishly before finding his voice. It was his own again. The universe had gone back to wherever the universe dwells. All around us, I suppose.

"I've given you my Theophrastus," the man said, rather unhelpfully, as I stared at the unfamiliar lettering on the spine. I looked at him beseechingly for more help.

"Your Greek philosophers loved alchemy, and this book contains a certain poem by Theophrastus, one of Aristotle's students, and a famous alchemist. Once you begin reading, you'll find that this text involves a set of things that should interest you, including elements, the separation of body from soul, and dragons. Perhaps that's why I've given it to you..." The monk's voice trailed off, undoubtedly still unable to explain why we now had the book in our hands.

"Dragons?" I asked, prompting him for more.

"Yes, dragons." The man smiled, a wry moue. "Those who wrote this text did not entirely know what they were creating. They were pursuing a decisive goal, this one involving the transmutation of base metals to gold. And yet they chose a peculiar metaphor for the idea of chemical change: the dragon. Even stranger, Theophrastus wrote of this process of chemical change as the slaying of a dragon."

"Wow," I said eloquently.

"Wow, indeed. And you will be even more 'wowed,' as it were, when you read the contents of that article. Theophrastus may not have fully understood what he was writing, but you will. Let his ancient words speak through time, and give you the answers you seek."

"I can't believe it's that easy," I said, almost tearing up while looking at the book. "Although we will have to find someone who knows Greek..."

The man shook his head, and this time the gaze he turned on me was full of sadness. "It will not be easy, child," he said in a gentle voice. "First you must interpret the messages hidden in that text. But even more difficult will be the fact you must trust them. For what they will ask for will not be pleasant. What is the phrase used by economists? TINSTAFL?"

" 'There is no such thing as a free lunch'?" Ryu said.

"Yes, that's it. There is no such thing as a free lunch, especially in alchemy. Great sacrifice will be demanded, in return for a great act. You will be asked to do that which you do not want to do, and what you'll have to do will make no sense. But you must have faith."

I gulped. I'd never been very good at faith.

"But if you let the universe guide you, all will be well. Now, drink your tea." The old man gave me a fatherly smile, and I sipped at my cold tea obligingly, unthinkingly, my mind awhirl.

Staring down at the book on my knee, I couldn't help

marveling it would be this easy. Then I remembered how we'd thought facing Morrigan would be easy, and how it had all gone to pot.

So I adjusted my thinking as I drank tea in the presence of one of humanity's greatest spiritual leaders.

This is not going to be easy, I told myself. *This is going to be hard. Harder than anything you've ever done before. And you're going to do anything it takes.*

Because I knew I would. I'd do anything to get Anyan back. And that fact scared me a little.

"We can't begin to thank you enough," I said, my hand resting on the book on my knee, when two robed monks rushing into the hotel suite interrupted us. They were speaking frenetically in their language, and I had no idea what they were saying. But I knew it was bad when the old man paled visibly. Turning to me, he spoke urgently.

"There are dragons. On the roof."

My heart practically seized. It was bad enough facing the Red, but from the plural I knew both the Red and the White were in attendance.

Knowing I had to face Anyan, on top of everything, was infinitely worse.

CHAPTER SEVEN

Rather sensibly for ancient forces of evil, the dragons weren't actually on the roof. Instead, they were on a huge helicopter pad that was only about a quarter of the way up what turned out to be a massive skyscraper. That said, we were still very high, and between the wind whipping around and the dragons, I was pretty scared.

Scarier, however, was the fact that one of those dragons was white.

Is he in there at all? I wondered.

We were watching from a doorway as the dragons did what could only be described as play.

They pushed off one of the hotel's helicopters (yes, the hotel itself had helicopters), and then dove after it, snapping it up to throw it around like cats with a dead bird. It kept crashing against the outside glass walls of the hotel, causing me to wince every time.

Then they'd bounce off the skyscrapers themselves, the Red pouring fire forth from her jaws, the White these massive gusts of air that were as dangerous as the fire.

"What the hell are we supposed to do against that?" Ryu said, his face pale.

I shrugged, knowing my own misery showed on my face.

Behind us, I heard footsteps, and I was surprised to turn around to see a virtual army of Buddhist monks. Even more surprising was when our new friend, the old man, made a series of gestures that sent everyone to a cross-legged position on the floor. Ryu and I exchanged furtive glances, wondering what was up.

One of the monks started chanting, an oddly cadenced, hummingly eerie set of tones that made the hair rise on my arms.

To my surprise, I could also feel power rising from their ranks.

I closed my eyes, letting my senses take it in. It was, essentially, elemental power, like mine. But it was... the only words I could come up with were "harnessed" rather than "channeled." When my brethren or I used the elements, they went through us, becoming a part of us just like transfused blood became a part of our bodies even if we then bled it out.

This power was more like what happened when I lent someone like Ryu, who used essence rather than elements, a burst of my strength. He could funnel it into things like his shields, but he couldn't use it like essence. He couldn't channel it through his own body and make it his to control.

But just because it was only "harnessed" didn't make what the monks were doing weak. The power they were raising was strong, and unique, and I itched to get my hands on it.

"That's interesting," Ryu said, undoubtedly feeling what I was feeling. His voice was wary. Ryu was very used to humans, for a pureblooded supernatural, but he still wasn't really of their world. And he obviously hadn't known humans could be capable of what the monks were doing. Nor was he very happy about it, from the look on his face.

"Life is full of surprises. Now we need a plan."

"We can use this... power they've raised."

"Yes. We can. But I think they can, too." I didn't know what the monks had up their sleeves, but it was obvious from the way they were working together that they did.

Ryu grimaced. "So what do we do?"

"First we have to get them on the ground. Then..."

We looked at each other. Then?

Creature? I said in my mind.

[I am here. The monks are fascinating. Their minds are so complex...]

That's great, I interrupted. *But we have some dragons out here that need dealing with.*

[Of course. Well, we don't want to kill them yet, so that changes things.]

Right.

[But we need to get them away. Separate them. Make them have to work to find each other.]

Can we do that?

[I think I have enough power to apparate one, at least.]

My mind must have revealed my confusion over just how much power the creature actually possessed.

[My power is not unlimited, child,] the creature chided. [And much of it is with you.]

I can give some back? I offered.

[Not how the game works, I'm afraid. What's freely given is given freely.]

I didn't point out that made no sense.

But you're not, like, maxing yourself out? I asked, worried for my trapped savior.

[Oh, no, of course not,] it said. But I had the distinct impression it was lying to me.

"I think we have a plan," I said to Ryu, who'd been watching me curiously. Ryu knew everything about my link with the creature, but watching me converse mentally with my own brain had probably looked a bit odd from the outside.

"We've got to get them down on the ground. Then the creature thinks it can apparate one of them, somewhere far away. That way they'll be busy locating each other for a few days. They can't actually apparate, right?"

[No,] the creature responded to my question. [A fluke for which we must be grateful.]

"That still leaves us with one of the dragons," Ryu said.

"Yes," I said. "But hopefully it will bolt when it's on its own. I think the hard part will be to get them down, and get one of them netted in our power so the creature can apparate it."

Ryu gave me a long look. "What if the one that's left over is Anyan?"

"I'll still deal with him." My words were brave, but my heart wasn't in them.

"You have to believe he's in there, or we wouldn't be trying to save him," Ryu said.

"Of course he's in there," I said, thinking about everything I'd seen with Morrigan. When she became the Red, she was both her and not her. Her personality changed utterly, or at least it seemed on the surface, becoming much more flamboyant. But we'd never really known the "real" Morrigan, so I didn't actually know if that was true.

Certainly Morrigan had impacted the Red. The creatures had been evil, but only after Morrigan and the Red had become one did the Red care about things like racial purity. We'd witnessed the armies of the Red practicing, and they'd all been divided up by factions to train, something only Morrigan would care about.

So how much of the Red was Morrigan, and how much of Morrigan was the Red?

It seemed she was as much Morrigan as Red, but was that even how we should be thinking about their relationship? Because, after all, she'd wanted her fate—she'd wanted to host the dragon. But Anyan had been forced. He must be more like a prisoner, not a host.

Yet he had to be in there. I couldn't believe that the White had wiped out Anyan. I knew Morrigan hadn't been, so why would Anyan?

Because Anyan's not a host, like Morrigan, he's an enemy, whispered a traitorous part of my brain, a part that I ignored.

The dragons were still lazily circling in the air, but their play had gotten more destructive. Instead of focusing on each other, they were now lashing out at the buildings surrounding ours. They were trying to get our attention, and I wondered how they'd found us.

[Probably my fault,] the creature said in answer. [I didn't shield your apparation. I didn't think anyone would be paying attention.]

"How'd they get here so fast?" I wondered aloud.

[Just because they can't apparate doesn't mean they can't move quickly.]

I filed that away. Even if our plan did work, it might not give us as much of a head start on the book as I'd hoped.

The kind old monk cracked an eye open from where he sat, chanting, in front of us.

"We have reached our limit," he said dreamily. "You must act quickly, before what we've called forth fades."

I nodded, and he closed his eyes again. Turning to Ryu, I called the labrys. His eyes widened as it appeared in my hands, then squinted shut as it blazed forth light.

It knew its enemies were near.

I dialed back its power, until we could all see again.

"Sorry, it has a mind of its own."

Ryu only nodded, still looking rather befuddled. I guess it's not every day that someone you used to have to babysit reappears in your life, wielding ancient and powerful forces.

He was dealing with it quite well, really.

"Are you ready?" I asked him. He nodded again, his gaze focusing with his purpose.

"Get them on the ground," he said, repeating our plan. "Let the creature get rid of one of them, and take on the other. Somehow."

"It's a plan," I said. Not necessarily a good plan, but a plan.

And with that, Ryu and I pushed our way out of the double doors separating us from the helipad.

The first thing I noticed was that the monks' channeled power was stronger out here. They obviously could focus the magic where they wanted it, and I was shocked at their control.

I was even more shocked when another dragon appeared in the air above us. Only this one seemed to be made of golden fireworks, sparkling in the sky.

I got ready to panic as it stretched silent wings, its head rearing back as it emitted a silent roar. But then I realized what it was: an illusion, fueled by the monks' power.

You are good, I thought, thanking my lucky stars we'd wound up with such powerful allies.

Needless to say, I wasn't the only one to notice the golden dragon. The Red and the White, upon making another lazy circle around the building, paused in their knocking off bits of the surrounding skyscrapers. I'd never known what a surprised dragon looked like, but now I did. I reckon it's a bit like a gecko seconds before it's run over by a car.

With a roar that shook the foundations of the building we stood upon, the Red and the White closed in on the golden dragon. It darted upward, trailing light just like sparklers did in the hands of running children on the Fourth of July. The dragons gave chase, and our dragon, the monk's dragon, flew straight up, taking the Red and the White high into the sky before it made a sudden U-turn, plummeting downward.

Right toward us.

The golden dragon disappeared in a shimmer of power as it hit the asphalt of the helipad, the Red and the White crashing into the tarmac with far less graceful thumps that shook the whole building. It was the Red that recovered first, clambering to its relatively tiny little feet and galloping toward where Ryu and I waited.

Exactly what I didn't want to happen. But beggars can't

be choosers, and neither can people who are about to be eaten by a dragon. So with a muttered curse word, I raised my labrys and invoked the power of the creature.

[Gotcha,] the creature said, almost gleefully. And just as the Red got close enough for me to see the hungry gleam in her emerald green eyes and smell the sulfur on her breath, the Red disappeared with an audible pop.

The White roared in confusion, rushing toward where its mate had just been, but like a ghost in front of it, there arose the glittering golden form of the monks' manifested power. This time it was in the shape of a phoenix, and it glided toward the White on silent wings, an act that seemed to confuse the White even more.

The ivory, pearlescent dragon skidded to a stop, snapping its jaws at the phoenix flying toward it.

That gave me just enough time to reinvoke the labrys and run forward a few paces, where I took what I hoped was a Xena-like power stance—my feet spread about shoulder's length apart as I held the labrys with both hands, its power coiling up inside me like I was winding a jack-in-the-box. I'd come up with a plan in that instant. It was either a really good plan, or a really dumb plan, but I wasn't going to know which until I did it.

Ryu joined me a second later, adding his strength to my own. I think it was only then he realized how puny it was, in comparison with how powerful I'd become.

"Get back!" I yelled at him. "Get back and shield yourself!"

I flicked my eyes to him, to make sure he obeyed, and I saw his indecision. I'd hidden behind him for so long, no wonder he couldn't imagine a scenario in which he hid behind me.

This time, I went ahead and yelled, "Ryu, get back! You need to protect the monks! I have a plan!"

My words about the monks snapped the baobhan sith into action and he turned on his heel to dart back toward the door.

I turned back to the White just in time to see the glittering phoenix run straight into the dragon's face... and disappear.

Realizing he'd been fooled, the White galloped toward me with a roar of irritation.

Anyan, I prayed. *If you're in there, stop this now.*

But the dragon kept coming, breathing out those jets of powerful air that hit my shields like a Mack truck.

"Anyan!" I shouted, done with prayer. "Stop!"

My words did nothing. They didn't even appear to register with the creature.

With a heavy heart, I played my card.

Opening my arms wide at the very last second, when the White was nearly upon me, I let all that power I'd been coiling blast forward. It caught the White square in the chest, lifting the dragon off its feet and sending it crashing down, a dozen yards behind it, where it skidded on its back toward the end of the helipad.

It lay still for a few minutes, and I prayed I hadn't killed it.

"Anyan!" I shouted again. Maybe it would get to its feet, and the White would be knocked out, and Anyan could take control, tell us how to get rid of the White...

But when the dragon finally did rise, it was to gaze at me with green eyes full of hate.

Carefully, I invoked phase two of my plan. I held my trembling knees still with an iron engagement of will, and

I made the labrys blaze as if that hit with which I'd just leveled the White was merely what I had on for starters.

The dragon's green eyes narrowed as it assessed its chances, alone against the champion. And then it slipped backward, off the end of the building, beating a hasty retreat.

Only when it was far out of range did I let my knees unlock, sending me downward in an ungainly slide.

The truth was, I'd blasted the White with everything I had, and then bluffed more power.

"Jane!" Ryu said, catching me as I toppled the rest of the way to the ground. My ex hugged me close, telling me what a great job I'd done.

I guess that, technically, we'd won that round.

But I'd felt only loss when confronted with the White's cruel jade eyes.

CHAPTER EIGHT

For some reason, I wasn't all that surprised to find myself standing in front of a hut wearing a hat. Woven thatch made a strange cone that went low over the side walls, and the doorframe yawned in front of me.

The night was cool; I was chilly, and the warm light of a fire beckoned from inside the structure. So I went inside.

The hut's round walls were painted with bright, circular patterns in yellows and reds. They looked very Celtic. The place was also very clean, with a small sleeping area curtained off by animal skins tucked against a wall, and the rest used for living. Storage was high up, with shelves holding woven baskets and piles of stuff, so that there was more space on the floor.

I felt very at home, so I went ahead and sat down by the fire, warming my hands by holding them out in front of me.

"There you are," came a low, rough voice behind me. "I've been hoping you'd find me."

I smiled, feeling both exhilarated but oddly calm. "Of course I found you. I'll always find you."

I looked up into Anyan's smiling gray eyes.

Intense relief flooded through me, but I couldn't for the life of me think why. This was Anyan's hut; why wouldn't Anyan be waiting for me?

The barghest knelt, wrapping his arms around me from behind, cloaking me with his heavy body. We sat like that for a few minutes while he drew in long breaths, as if memorizing my scent.

"I've missed you," he whispered in my ear. "I've missed you so much..."

I appreciated the sentiment, of course, but I couldn't imagine, for the life of me, what he meant.

"Miss me?" I said. "Why? I'm always here."

He stiffened around me, and I wondered what I'd said wrong. But he didn't tell me.

"Of course you are," was all he said, and then he moved so he was sitting next to me.

I leaned against him, and we watched the flames for a long time. It felt so good to be in his arms, but I knew it should be normal, after all this time.

"How are things, Jane?" he asked eventually, his voice a low hum in the dim light.

"Oh, fine," I said. I tried to think of something to tell him about, but I couldn't. "Nothing's going on. Everything's just...fine."

The truth was, I felt like I did have something big to say; that there was something very important, to both of us, which had happened. But every time I thought I was about to remember what it was, it slipped away.

"You can't think of anything going on you want to

tell me about?" Anyan's voice was still soft and low, but I knew him well enough to detect the faintest note of desperation.

"There is something...but I can't remember. So it can't be that important, can it?" I said with a laugh he didn't return.

Anyan remained quiet for a bit, as if deep in thought, before turning to gaze into my eyes.

"What's wrong?" I said, concerned.

The smile he gave me was rueful. "I'm just wishing I had more power in this place. There are rules I cannot break."

I arched an eyebrow. "You're plenty powerful, Anyan. And what rules are you talking about?"

He shook his head sadly, as if regretting what he had to say. "It doesn't matter, Jane. I must take what I can get. I've been looking for you everywhere. I'm just happy I found you."

"Found me? Was I lost?" At this point I was totally confused.

"No, I'm the one that's lost. So I built this place for you. For us. I hoped you'd find it."

His words made no sense, but nothing could permeate my curious calm. Plus, he sounded happy, and I liked what he'd said.

"It's beautiful, Anyan. I really like it. It's ours?"

"For as long as I can hold on to it," he said, and there was grief in his voice.

"I'll help you," I said, putting my small hand into his much larger one. "We'll keep it, together." I wanted him to feel safe, like I did.

He leaned forward, pressing his lips to mine. What I felt then was anything other than calm. Our kiss was brief, but passionate, leaving me burning for more when he withdrew to speak.

"You're already helping me. Being here with you reminds me of who I am. You help me remain me, Jane."

I was confused again, but then he stood, taking me by the hand to draw me up with him. He led me to the little sleeping area.

My body kindled with its own fire as Anyan stripped me of my shirt. While he did so, I toed off my Converse. He started in on the buttons of my jeans even as I stood on the tip of one sock, and then the other, to pull them off. He pushed down my jeans, and when I was clad only in my bra and panties, he bore me down onto the soft furs that awaited us.

His lips and teeth found the soft flesh of my neck even as I ripped at the bottom of his T-shirt, trying to pull it up his body and off him. I wanted—no, I needed to feel his skin pressed against mine.

My hunger was so desperate it surprised me. Surely we'd made good use of this warm, soft nook hundreds of times before? But it was like I hadn't touched the barghest in months. As if he felt the same way, Anyan's mouth and hands roved over my body like he was relearning me, or grasping on to me so no one could take me from him.

"Gods, I've missed this, Jane," he said, his voice raspy with lust and maybe something else. Sadness? I wondered, unable to understand and yet feeling the same mixture of lust and mourning, as if I'd have to say good-bye to Anyan again after this was over.

But why good-bye? And why again? I wondered. For a second I thought I remembered, but then the memory was gone as if it were ejected.

Nothing could be as bad as all that, not with a barghest in my arms.

I'd finally managed to wrestle his shirt over his head, and Anyan helped me by pulling it the rest of the way up his arms. Then he was hovering over me, looking over my body with hungry eyes. Boldly, I moved my hand between his legs, stroking over his hard length covered by the denim that still separated us. He moaned, a low growling sound, then found my mouth again in a long, rough kiss that left me breathless.

When he moved again, it was with purpose. Kissing down my throat, over my sternum, his hands moved behind my back to undo my bra. Rather than take it off, once it was undone, he merely pushed it up, finding my nipple with his hungry, rough mouth. I whimpered, pushing up against him, still stroking him through his jeans as he found my other breast with his lips. At the same time, he grabbed one wrist, and then the other, ripping my hand away from him as he pulled them up over my head. Then he pinned them down, moving up my body at the same time so that he could kiss me again, pressing against me.

I drew my knees up, opening myself to him. Even through his jeans and my panties I could feel him, so hard and wanting. And I very much felt like giving. Bucking my hips up, I whimpered again.

"Fuck me," I begged. "Please fuck me."

With a growl, Anyan let go of one of my wrists, reaching down to undo his pants. He didn't even bother with my panties; he just shoved the crotch of my underwear to the side. I cried out as his thick fingers slid inside my folds, testing my wetness. Two fingers slid deep, impossibly deep, before withdrawing.

Still holding my wrist down with one hand, his other then fisted his cock so he could rub the broad tip against my sex. I pushed up to meet him, causing him to slip just a fraction of an inch inside me, but it was enough to break his control. Foreplay over, Anyan couldn't resist sliding deeper, his groans mingling with mine as his mouth sucked at my cries.

He withdrew slightly, and then pushed forward again, deeper this time. I'd forgotten how big he was, how much I had to adjust to him. But as always, he was perfect—giving me only what I could take until I was ready for more.

My Anyan.

The thought made tears spring to my eyes, unbidden. Unable to fathom why, I cried as he took me, a curious sensation of grief and desperate lust shaking me to the core.

I kept talking the whole time, telling him to fuck me, to use me, to make me his. Obligingly, he plunged deeper, then set up a rhythm that was bound to send both of us over the edge too quickly.

Because as much as I wanted this frantic pace, and I was helping to set it, I also never wanted this moment to end. I wanted him here, and safe inside me, forever.

I feared what would happen when this moment ended.

And so I wrapped myself around him, arms and legs pulling him close, squeezing him with my inner muscles in an attempt to keep him right where he was.

But all my actions did was drive my own pleasure higher, taking Anyan with me. His thick fingers slipped between us, finding my clit, and it was over. I broke around him, my orgasm crashing over me. His own harsh cries followed only seconds later.

A few more thrusts and he was spent inside me.

As my pleasure receded, it was replaced with a fear so overwhelming it could only be called panic. I clung to the barghest, not wanting to let him go.

He clung just as desperately to me, refusing to withdraw, wrapping his arms tighter around me.

"Thank you for finding me. It's made all the difference," he told me. What frightened me even more than his cryptic words was the fear I saw reflected in his own gray eyes. They were wild; as if frantic to impart something I couldn't yet understand.

"You must find me again soon, Jane. It's the only thing that will keep me going. He's so strong, and he's growing stronger. You have to help me."

"I'll do anything," I said, and I meant it.

"I know you will. Whatever you're doing, you're scaring them. That makes them desperate, but it means you're on the right track."

I didn't know what he was talking about, but I nodded.

"You have to stay strong, too," I said.

Anyan's mouth pressed into a grim line. "I'm trying. This helped, more than you can imagine."

Suddenly, I knew that this wasn't our hut. This wasn't a safe place, at least not really, and we couldn't stay here.

Sobs tore through my body as I clung even more desperately to the man wrapped around me. He felt like he always had—strong, like an anchor that could keep me rooted to the spot. But I knew it wasn't the truth.

I was going to have to leave.

"Don't let me go," I said.

"I don't want to. But I have to. And you must remember

this, Jane. You must try to remember and you must come again. Will you do that?"

I nodded. "Of course. I'll remember and I'll come again. I'll always find you..."

"It's not that simple. You won't have as much control as you think. You might not—"

"I'll remember," I said sharply, interrupting him. "And I'll always find you."

Anyan nodded, looking both tense and hopeful. "Talk to the creature, if you can. Tell him..."

Suddenly, Anyan's head snapped up, as if he heard something from outside.

"He's here. You must go."

"No!" I cried, wanting to stay.

"Come back," was all Anyan said, holding me closer even as I knew he was letting me go. "Come back to me, Jane. And hurry..."

I woke with a start, tears staining my face and pillow. I sat up to find myself in an unfamiliar hotel bedroom, not a hut.

I was still in Hong Kong, and Anyan was a dragon.

A sob wailed, unbidden, from my lips and seconds later Ryu was standing in my doorway. We had booked ourselves into a suite at the monks' hotel, at the behest of the kindly old monk, who wanted us to talk to someone the next day. So we'd scanned and e-mailed the important poem about dragons to Caleb, who'd either be able to translate it himself or would know who could, and we'd called it a night.

We'd also gone ahead and sent our clothes in for cleaning after ordering everything we needed, from pajamas to toothbrushes, on the tab of Ryu's compound. Sometimes it was good traveling with someone who worked for the Man, at least when he or she also had access to the Man's expense account.

"Are you all right? What happened?" Ryu asked, coming to sit on the edge of my bed.

"A dream. It was important..." I was supposed to remember something, but I couldn't. I shook my head roughly, as if I might dislodge whatever it was I had to remember.

"Easy, Jane," Ryu said soothingly. "We had a crazy day, and you're really stressed. No wonder you had a bad dream."

I frowned. What he said made sense, but it wasn't right. The dream had been important.

"Anyan was there," I said, my memory flashing briefly. Then failing.

"I'm sure he was," Ryu said, his voice grim. "Today was the first time you saw the White since he took Anyan, right?"

"Well, yes, but..."

"That's why you dreamed about him, Jane." Ryu's voice was gentle, sympathetic. He was obviously concerned for me. I sort of wanted to strangle him.

But he was probably right.

"It was just so real," I said, leaning back against my pillows in defeat.

"Of course it was." Ryu patted my hand, where it lay in the bedclothes. "You miss him."

More tears welled up. I blinked them away furiously, refusing to speak for fear whatever I tried to say would come in a garbled sob.

"Now, try to get more sleep. You need it."

I let Ryu tuck me in, felt his cool lips on my forehead as he gave me a good-night kiss. But my mind was a hundred miles away.

When he shut out the light and closed the door behind him, I blinked in the darkness.

On the one hand, I desperately wanted to shut my eyes and see Anyan again. I knew I'd dreamed about him.

Dreams aren't real, I reminded myself. And yet they were something.

Which was why, on the other hand, I wanted to stay awake. I'd felt so utterly alone, so heartbroken, when I'd woken up just now. I didn't want to feel that way again, not if I wanted to function as a normal human being for the rest of the day.

Unfortunately, no matter what I wanted or didn't want, my body had other plans. I was exhausted, and after a few minutes I felt my heavy eyelids sliding shut of their own accord.

My dreams, this time, were empty.

CHAPTER NINE

The next morning we had a surprise visitor.

A sweet-faced, deferential young monk ushered Ryu and me into a boardroom on the same floor as our suite, where we found Daniel Rankin, the British secret agent who had helped us fight the Red. He was part of a special part of MI5 or MI6—I couldn't keep them straight—that knew about supes and liaised with the Great Island's Alfar Powers That Be.

"Daniel," I said, shaking his hand. Our friend, the older monk from yesterday, smiled and nodded his own greeting to me, which I returned.

"This is Ryu Baobhan Sith," I said, introducing the two as they shook hands.

"A pleasure to meet you," the human said, his eyes aglow with curiosity. "I've heard so much about you, and we've been watching your territory's experiment in democracy with great interest."

"Is that so?" Ryu asked, his ever-eloquent eyebrows rising.

I took a moment to explain to Ryu who Daniel was, and for whom he worked. I could tell my ex had not known about Daniel's organization, and that he was not too happy to find out about it now, under such circumstances.

"The Great Island always has done things its own way," was the baobhan sith's cryptic reply. Daniel couldn't hide his obvious pleasure in discomfiting such a well-known supe.

"So what brings you to…" For a split second, I paused, unable to remember where we were. "To Hong Kong."

"I wanted to meet with you, obviously," Daniel replied.

"Okay…" I'd figured he had come chasing dragons.

"May we talk?" Daniel's eyes flicked to Ryu, whose eyebrows rose another notch. "Alone?"

The older monk made his way to Ryu's side, taking my ex by the elbow.

"I would love the opportunity to ask you some questions," the monk said, clearly bluffing. Ryu didn't look happy about it, but he let the smaller man lead him out of the room. The monk shut the door behind him, leaving Daniel and me in peace.

"What can I help you with?" I asked, taking a seat at the conference table. Daniel took a position across from me, leaning forward on his elbows and clasping his hands in front of him.

"My government wants to be a part of this operation," Daniel replied bluntly.

I frowned, cocking my head at the man. "That's very generous, but I'm not sure if I understand. This isn't much of an operation, to be honest."

"Let me rephrase, then. My government feels it represents human interests in this operation, and it wants to help. Specifically, it wants to help you."

Daniel wasn't the only one who could be blunt. "Why?"

"It's simple. Times are changing, and the Alfar are about over. Their control over the supernatural population is crumbling, and we think this latest incursion of the Red and the White is going to break it entirely. Their numbers are too low, and there are too many of your kind, Jane, coming to power."

"My kind?"

"Half-humans," he said. Only then did I start to see where he was going.

"Do you think that because we're half-human, we're more sympathetic to human causes? Or to humanity in general?"

Daniel met my dark gaze with his own pretty blue eyes. He was a good-looking man, in a nimble upper-class way, and undoubtedly he was used to charming his way through society. Supernaturals, however, were rather immune to charm.

"You are. Working with you was a revelation. You're practically human, but you're so powerful."

I couldn't help laughing. "Daniel, I'm not a revelation, I'm a freak. I'm not the status quo for anything, even halflings. Believe me."

At that moment, images of Conleth, the crazy ifrit-halfling who hated humans with a maniacal passion, sprang to mind.

"There are just as many halflings who would happily kill off humanity as those who would help it. And this power you admire isn't really mine. It's been loaned to me by a far more powerful being. Under normal circumstances, without this borrowed power, I might be able to take on a weak Alfar, but not one of the monarchs. They're too strong."

"Be that as it may, times are still changing," Daniel insisted. "Think about your own territory. It's a democracy now, Jane. Imagine how unthinkable that would have seemed just months ago. But now it's happened."

"Again, all of that happened under extraordinary circumstances—"

"I disagree," Daniel interrupted. "Our analysts believe that humanity is encroaching on the supernatural world. Our culture is infiltrating theirs. Ideas like democracy are well known in the youngest generations, and it's only a matter of time until even those most powerful of the older generations die out. Supes are long-lived, not immortal, which means not even the Alfar can exist entirely in stasis."

I thought about what Daniel said, and it did make sense if one looked at the territory that Ryu now ruled alongside Nyx. When Morrigan had revealed her true self by killing her husband and king, Orin, she'd taken most of the powerful Alfar with her when she left. Faced with that power vacuum, the supernatural community had been left with an ugly choice of which weak, fairly pathetic Alfar to push into power.

But then they'd made a totally unforeseen decision. They'd skipped over the few Alfar still around, and had decided to vote on who would be their new leader. Ryu and Nyx were nominated, and the subsequent race was so close they agreed to share power. It had worked well. They'd managed not only to hold the territory together, but by banding together and making smart defensive choices, they'd kept any wannabe monarchs from neighboring territories at bay.

"So why exactly are you talking to me about this?" I said.

Daniel gave me a funny look then, as if we were having two different conversations.

"Of course I would come to you. You're in charge."

I graced the human with one of my unladylike snorts. "What? That's ridiculous. I'm just the champion, and once that's over, I'll be back to being me."

When I said those words, it was as if they fell onto the floor in front of me with an audible plop, like that of horseshit. I stared down at the bland, if luxurious, hotel carpet and wondered how I could have been so stupid.

When Daniel spoke again, his voice was gentle. "Jane, you have to realize this won't end with your destruction of the Red and the White. If you do pull off that feat, you'll be . . . God, how to even describe it? You'll be the savior of your people. You'll be the halfling that did what no Alfar could do. And they're not going to be able to hide, not in today's world."

An involuntary shudder wracked my spine as a mini-explosion went off in my brain. My thoughts spiraled out in a hundred directions, trying to envision what it was Daniel was saying and to place myself in the center of this drama for which I'd never auditioned.

[No one can know what your future holds,] came the creature's voice, pulling me back to reality. It'd been pretty quiet since it had apparated the Red out of Hong Kong, making me think that had taken more out of it than it wanted me to know.

I dunno, I thought. *Daniel's right. What if I can never go back to being just Jane again?*

[You probably cannot go back, no,] the creature agreed, to my dismay. [But only inside of your heart. This process has changed you, but not entirely for the worse, don't you agree?]

The creature was right, of course. I'd become so much stronger and more confident. I wouldn't want to give that up.

But that didn't mean I wanted to be forced into some political role.

[And you won't be,] the creature said, reading my thoughts. [The great part about being powerful is that you can abdicate that power.]

Like Anyan, I thought, for the barghest had stolidly refused to become part of the Alfar political machine.

[And like me,] the creature added.

But you both get pulled in, I thought. *You're not really free.*

[No. But we are pulled in because we care. And no matter what happens in life, you will have things you care about, that will force actions out of you. Either that, or life isn't worth living.]

Filing away the creature's wisdom to pick apart later, I raised my eyes to Daniel's.

"So what, exactly, are you offering?"

A flash of relief and triumph crossed over Daniel's face until he schooled his expression.

"Our material resources: manpower, firepower, etc. Also our archives and our specialists. I've gathered you have a lead on a possible way to extricate your friend from the White?"

Either the kind old monk had a loose tongue, which I doubted, or Daniel and his people were good.

"Perhaps. We've scanned and e-mailed something that needs to be translated to our friend. He's working on it now. Our plan is to kill the Red and the White, for real this time. Not just contain them."

Daniel nodded. "We're behind that plan one hundred percent."

How nice of you, I thought cynically as I pondered Daniel's offer.

Considering the resources we already had at our disposal, did I really need the help of this human agency?

Then I remembered the monks' chanting, and their power, and I revised my assumptions. I'd fallen into the Alfar trap of taking humans for granted, but we were wrong to underestimate humanity. Then, on the heels of that thought, I imagined the face on Griffin, the Alfar leader's second in command, when he heard that I'd teamed up with the United Kingdom's human government.

"Oh, my, yes," I heard myself saying before I'd even really thought it through. Just the thought of how much Griffin would hate this alliance made it good enough for me.

"So you'll work with us?" Daniel said eagerly.

"I will accept your help, yes. But at the end of the day, my people and I are in charge. Not you. We do this our way, and if you're not happy with that, we'll have no problem extricating ourselves from this arrangement."

Daniel nodded. "Agreed. We want to be a part of the world you'll help build, Jane. Humans and supes, working together, finding harmony."

I knew I was making a skeptical face, and I didn't even try to hide it. Daniel tried to keep looking earnest, but eventually he cracked.

"We want the Alfar out of power," he said, and this time I knew he was being honest. "They're too intractable and they've had things their own way for too long."

"Then we have a deal," I said, reaching out to once again shake Daniel's hand.

Despite their problems, and the Kardashians, I'd take humanity over the Alfar any day.

* * *

Somehow Caleb managed to get his junk wedged into the camera's view when we Skyped. I hadn't mentally tried to clothe the satyr in a really long time, but something about the camera angle sent my mind searching for acceptable schlong coverage.

"How far have you gotten?" Ryu asked rather curtly. He'd been a bit out of sorts since I'd told him Daniel had offered, and I'd accepted, human help in our mission.

"I've translated the whole thing. It's pretty basic ancient Greek, so that was no problem."

Of course not, I thought. Just another ancient language, no biggie.

"Great. What does it say?" Ryu said.

Caleb made pincers of his fingers, rubbing his thumb and pointer finger over his eyes, as people do when they'd been reading far too long and far too late. "Well, that's the problem."

"What is?"

"It says a lot. But none of it makes a lot of sense."

Ryu fidgeted impatiently beside me, emitting a waft of yummy cologne.

"Just start at the beginning," I told Caleb. "What do we need to know?"

The satyr nodded agreeably. "Well, first of all, how much do you know about alchemy?"

"Very little," I said.

Caleb frowned. "The subject is obviously vast, and I don't want to get into it all here."

"No, please don't," Ryu murmured, and I shot him a look.

"But what you need to be aware of is the idea that, as you probably know, alchemists were interested in turning

base metals into gold. But that whole process was a metaphor for the transfiguration of the human soul into something pure, by separating the soul from the body."

"Wow," I said, clearly seeing the practical applications
of this process in terms of our current situation.

"Exactly," the satyr said drily. "It's perfect. Unfortunately, the alchemists weren't exactly into straightforward
instructions."

"From what we can tell from Grizzie's glowing act, as
well as a similar stunt pulled by our monk, the Universe
has its hand in all of this. And I know how crazy that
sounds, but it's true. So the humans involved, including
whoever wrote that poem, didn't exactly know what they
were doing," I said.

"That makes sense. Because, to use one of Iris's
expressions, this poem is a hot mess of nonsense."

I couldn't help smiling, seeing how my funny, carefree
friend had rubbed off on the very serious Caleb.

"Can you give us some hint as to what we're supposed
to be doing?" Ryu asked, still impatient.

"Theophrastus has one poem in here, handily book-
marked by your monk, that is all about the process that
starts with turning the base metal into silver, and then
from silver to gold. But, and here's where it gets interesting for us, this transmutation process uses the metaphor
of a white dragon to symbolize silver, and a red dragon to
symbolize gold."

"'Kay, let me make sure I'm following you," I said.
"This process of base metal to silver, then to gold, is
really a metaphor for separating body from soul, and that
whole big metaphor is represented by another metaphor,
using dragons that just happen to be red and white."

"Exactly," said Caleb. "And what your interactions with the, er, universe seem to be suggesting is that this synchronicity with our situation is no accident—these are *our* dragons, and the secret to destroying them is in this poem."

Caleb's craggy face had long since lit up with excitement, his tousled blond hair extra shaggy, as if he'd been unable to keep his hand out of it. The circles under his eyes told me he'd obviously been working on this problem since he'd received our e-mail, and I was again grateful to have such marvelous people behind me.

"So we have something that tells us how to destroy the Red and the White?" Ryu said.

"Yes, but only sort of. The text is a puzzle, a metaphor, and it's not easy to interpret."

Ryu made a frustrated sound and I touched my cool fingers to his in warning to keep calm. Caleb watched my movement curiously, and I wondered what my friends were thinking about me spending so much time with Ryu. I probably would have thought it fishy, too, although the baobhan sith seemed to be perfectly content with our current arrangement, and hadn't made any sort of a move on me.

I'd have to tell Iris that fact in a private conversation, after telling her to tell no one. That would assure everyone knew that Ryu and I were chaste, and just friends, within an hour.

"What do we do first, Caleb?" I asked.

"The first step, according to Theophrastus, seems to be that you make a stone."

I raised an eyebrow. "A stone?"

"Yes. A stone."

My mind was sifting through everything it knew about alchemy, which wasn't much. But I had read *Harry Potter*.

"Like the philosopher's stone?" I remembered Googling the title of Rowling's book when it had come out, and had gotten a bunch of hits on the real definition of a philosopher's stone, which was a term from alchemy.

"What's a philosopher's stone?" Ryu said.

"It's this thing alchemists tried to create. It was sort of their holy grail. A stone that would make you immortal, right?" I turned to Caleb for confirmation.

"Yes. But this isn't quite a philosopher's stone, although there must have been some kind of connection in Theophrastus's mind."

"Okay...?" I said, totally confused at this point.

"I actually found a journal article on this poem, from 1920," Caleb said, "that I think will help you understand. Here's the part we need right now: 'Divest lead or copper of its soul and spirit, endow the resulting body with a soul and spirit of a higher type and the result is gold. The change from the black of lead or the red of copper to the yellow of gold could not, however, be accomplished directly. The base metal must first be brought to the whiteness of silver before projection of the stone can produce gold.'"

"Huh?" I said.

"Listen again," said Caleb, and then he repeated the lines from the journal article, after which he summarized what he thought it meant. "What this professor has interpreted is that this is a two-step process, involving first tackling the white, or making the base metal into silver, before you can tackle the red, or making the silver into gold."

"'Kay," I said. "But where does the stone come in?"

"Sorry, that was just the first bit. Here's Theophrastus's actual translation:

The white, augmented thrice within a fire,
In three days' time is altogether changed
To lasting yellow and this yellow then
Will give its hue to every whitened form.
This power to tinge and shape produces gold
And thus a wondrous marvel is revealed."

"And the marvel is . . ." Ryu said.
"The stone," replied Caleb. "Here's the next bit:

Though not a stone, it yet is made a stone
From metal, having three hypostases,
For which the stone is prized and widely known;
Yet all the ignorant search everywhere
As though the prize were not close by at hand.
Deprived of honor yet the stone is found
To have within a sacred mystery,
A treasure hidden and yet free to all."

I sat back on the sofa, rubbing a hand over my eyes.

"I'm hearing nothing that makes any sense, Caleb," I said, feeling bone-weary. "I'm hearing stuff that sounds like it might have something to do with everything, and yet I don't understand any of it. Help."

The satyr smiled knowingly. I could imagine him standing in front of a blackboard in a university, except for the whole naked-with-goat-haunches thing.

"I've been poring over this, cross-referencing it to other things, looking at other translations and other alchemical

poems that seem to fit this same model. And I think I've
got it. You ready?"

I leaned forward, my turn for impatience as I made a
perfunctory gesture with my hands to hurry up the satyr.

"You've gotta get your hands on the White's old bones.
Then we have to perform a three-day ritual, the details of
which I'm working out from the next part of the poem,
with the help of this journal article. It's like the guy wrote
it with us in mind."

Before I could say that idea was ridiculous, I thought
about everything I'd seen when in thrall to the universe.
If a human poet could become its puppet, scribbling away
at a crazy metaphorical dragon-to-gold scheme, why
couldn't a scholar, working diligently to translate and
make sense out of the poem?

I had a moment's pang for all those vessels of the universe, toiling at what must have seemed to others like
mad whims.

Caleb continued. "What I do know so far is that the
ritual we'll do involves the sea, and fire. At the end of all
this stuff, the bones are going to yield a stone. Then we
have to get ahold of the White itself and use the stone on
him. The stone will transmute the White's essence, and
I'm thinking it's going to take it into itself."

"Wait," I interrupted. "Whose essence? The White's?
Or Anyan's?"

"It has to be the White's. This is about the dragon, not
about Anyan."

I had more questions, but Caleb kept talking.

"It's that stone that we use to tackle the dragons," the
satyr said. "Through that stone, we destroy first him, then
her. But first we have to figure out how to extract the stone

from the White's bones. So while I work out the details of the ritual, you need to get the bones."

I opened my mouth to ask my questions but Ryu got there first.

"And how are we supposed to separate the two dragons? We can't have the Red flying about while we try to murder her mate."

Caleb shrugged. "You've got to figure that part out while I translate and cross-reference the rest of this poem."

"Oh, we do, do we?" Ryu asked, clearly irritated with Caleb's high-handedness.

"Wait," I said, before Caleb started apologizing. "I have a question."

Both Caleb and Ryu turned to me.

"What happens to Anyan in all of this? Does he survive?"

Caleb chewed on his bottom lip—not a good sign. When he finally spoke, he used his "confident healer" voice. I imagined it was the voice he used to tell patients that they were probably dying, but still in good hands.

My lungs were suddenly too small, and I felt a sweat break out over my body.

"To be honest, I don't know, Jane. I really don't. From what I've translated so far, the poem is only about killing the White, not saving a host."

Caleb was clearly able to read the expression on my face.

"You know we'll do our best, Jane. We all want him back, too."

I nodded, but I knew the truth. Despite the fact they didn't want it to be so, everyone else understood that killing the Red and the White had to take precedence over saving Anyan.

At least everyone did but me.

CHAPTER TEN

You gonna be okay?" Ryu asked, his voice laced with concern.

To be honest, I wasn't sure about that one. We were standing in the last place I'd ever wanted to see again—the high cliff in Whitby where the ruins of the abbey had once stood. Now those ruins were really ruined, and half of the cliff had tumbled into the sea. The small cottages that had sat next to the abbey were burned-out husks.

And the soil here was soaked with the blood of the Original, Blondie, who'd died in Magog's arms just about where I was standing. It was also the last place I'd seen Anyan, as Anyan, before his body had been hijacked by the White.

Ryu came and stood next to me, putting an arm carefully around my shoulders. It wasn't an entirely unwelcome gesture, not least as it kept me from absconding to swim my cares away in the ocean behind me.

I'd swum immediately upon getting to Whitby, but

right now just about the only thing I could think to comfort me would be the sea.

Or Anyan, I thought. *Stripped of his dragonhood.*

The creature shifted in my mind, a comforting gesture reminding me that it was there, and equally sad to see the place its child had died.

"I'll be okay," I said, finding the strength to make that optimism a reality. Then I looked up at Ryu to give him a grateful smile, one that he returned with a peck on the forehead. It was an entirely friendly gesture, which made me happy we'd come so far. But I disengaged to take a few steps forward, scanning the ground for the disturbance I knew I'd find somewhere near the burned patch that had housed the pyre upon which we'd burned the bodies.

"There," I said, pointing. "It's gotta be right over there."

Daniel nodded, sending forth a few members of his team, armed with shovels. Knowing we'd want backup and help, we'd flown to the UK from Hong Kong on the dime of the British government, landing at an air base somewhere in Yorkshire. The drive to Whitby had only taken an hour, and so far we'd had smooth sailing in this trip to recover the White's bones.

But I knew we'd be discovered soon enough. For not even Daniel's careful plans, and his trying to use only human, governmental resources, would keep the Great Island's Alfar from discovering I was back on their turf. Not least because I already knew there had to be spies throughout the human government. Undoubtedly one layer of spies the humans knew about, so they had something to keep an eye on, and another layer of real spies.

In fact, knowing the Alfar of the Great Island, there were a few layers of spies in between, just to keep everyone guessing.

I took a deep breath as I turned my back on the men digging, enjoying the scent of the ocean and the heavy tingle of power that came rushing through me with each inhale.

Before long, I sensed another tingle, at the farthest range of the sensors I'd let drift outward from me. I sighed, dragging my power back into a heavy shield, motioning to Ryu to join me.

"We have company," I said, just as a quartet of black SUVs swept into view, their engines loud despite the sea calling behind us. Daniel motioned for his people to keep digging, even as he motioned for the men on guard to fan out behind him. Ryu and I joined Daniel, forming a greeting party to say hello to our guests.

"Luke. Griffin. Minions," I said amicably as the Alfar second and his leader slowly got out of the vehicle after a couple of goblins dressed in flunky suits had done a quick sweep with their sharp eyes and powers, and then opened the door for their masters.

I didn't seem to deserve a greeting, letting me know I was once again in trouble with The Powers That Be.

"What are you doing exactly?" Griffin said, ignoring both Ryu and me to get up in Daniel's face. Despite being Alfar, Griffin's emotions were palpable—and they mostly consisted of anger.

"We're retrieving the White's bones," the human said, remarkably calm considering that, as a puny mortal, the being in front of him could crush Daniel like a bug.

"We can see that. But why?"

"Because we are. That's all you need to know."

Daniel's voice was still calm, even affable, but his eyes were hard. I had to applaud him for standing up to the Alfar's second in command, not least because Griffin could look damned intimidating if he wanted.

Which he obviously did want to do, right then. Griffin's dark hair was slicked back into a very 1920s-looking style, and his eyes were narrowed to slits. His nostrils had also thinned out, and gone white, as if all the blood in the Alfar's body was needed to keep him from pummeling something, magically or otherwise.

"And since when is supernatural business human business?" Griffin demanded, taking a threatening step closer to Daniel so that the Alfar was nearly on top of the human.

Daniel's reply was immediate, and stated with precision, as if every syllable counted. "Since you stopped being able to control your own. And since we partnered up with the champion."

Ruh-roh, I thought, channeling Scooby Doo. Griffin's head swiveled so he could stare me down.

I also noticed that Luke hadn't moved a muscle. He was standing next to Griffin as if they could be anywhere at any time. There was no apparent awareness on the Alfar Leader's part that he was witnessing something of a historic event—the day that humans declared their overt involvement with a supernatural issue.

"You have partnered up with Jane, have you?" Griffin asked, venom dripping from his every word. The look he gave me was furious, and I wondered if we were going to end up in another firefight.

"Does that mean we are enemies, then?" The voice came from Luke, and even Griffin looked shocked. I wasn't entirely sure if the Alfar leader was all there, mentally, since he always seemed so out of it.

"No," Daniel said, even as I said, "It doesn't have to mean that, no." We cast each other a glance.

"What do you mean, it does not have to mean we are enemies?" Luke asked, his voice still utterly flat.

"I think we want the same thing," I told the Alfar leader. "I think we want to stop the Red and the White. So if that's what we're agreed on, I don't see why we have to have a problem with each other."

Griffin and Luke looked at each other as if communicating silently. I knew that was impossible for beings besides the creature and, apparently, the universe, but I'd seen it with other Alfar. It was like they'd known each other for so long, they had their own secret language, like twins.

Again, it was Luke who spoke first.

"I am afraid, halfling, that our mutual cooperation will depend on your definition of the word 'stop.' How exactly are you planning to stop the Red and the White?"

Luke had taken a few steps forward, enough to make him the clear "speaker" of the group. And even though his tone was as colorless and polite as any Alfar, he had subtly started pushing his power around, as if to remind us just whom exactly we were dealing with.

The Jane of just a year ago would have probably gone ahead and taken a step back and let Ryu deal with it. I could tell the baobhan sith was itching to get in there, and I could feel him coiling up his own power behind his shields. But I was no longer that Jane, and this situation called for a champion.

"Well," I said, taking my own carefully paced steps

forward. They were just enough to bring me to within about a yard of the Alfar. I also carefully began pushing against Luke's power with my own. I wasn't going to pull the labrys unless I absolutely had to, but I let the Great Island's leader feel the bite of the creature's power. "The fact is our plan is a bit up in the air."

Luke raised a brow, and I took a half step forward, pushing with my power.

"But we know about how it's going to run," I said. "We're working on a way to strip the White out of Anyan, saving his life. Then we're going to use that power to take the Red. And we're going to kill those monsters. For good this time."

Unstated in my rundown of events was an implied "neener-neener." For we were going to do what the Alfar had never quite managed—get rid of the Red and the White once and for all.

"I am afraid," Luke said, "that this is where we will have to diverge from your plan, and ask you to reconsider."

As the Alfar said the word "reconsider," he gave my shields a hard shove with his power, to let me know exactly what he meant by "reconsidering."

Instead of pushing back, I let my shields absorb the Alfar's strength, as if his shove had been no more than a light brush of fingertips. Griffin moved a few steps closer to his leader, ready to help in a pinch.

"Why would we reconsider?" I asked. I meant that question rhetorically, but Luke was kind enough to answer.

His voice was nasal as he started in on his droning monologue. "Your plan is pointless, halfling. More powerful beings than you have failed to kill the Red and the

White. They are indestructible. And whilst you pursue your selfish quest to rescue your bedmate, the consorts grow stronger. It is our people they will attack when they are ready, not yours."

"Rescuing Anyan is not selfish," I started, but Luke kept droning on.

"You were made our champion, given tremendous power, but then you abandoned us to our fate. I call that selfish. We need you here, protecting us, not gallivanting around on an impossible mission."

Despite my best intentions to no longer be surprised by the Alfar, I was surprised by the Alfar.

"First you try to intimidate me with your power, which isn't working by the way," I said, stepping even closer to Luke. "Then you tell me that you need me to *rescue* you? After you've called me a halfling *how* many times already?"

Luke blinked down at me owlishly as I tried to figure out what was going on here.

"There's no way you legitimately think that a halfling is needed to come in and save your ass. You guys would never believe that," I said, making a sweeping gesture with my arm to include Griffin in my assessment. I went ahead and kept talking as I tried to figure out the Alfar's true motivation in trying to get me back onside.

"You do know you need the champion, but I still can't believe you're so easily swallowing that the champion is me and that nothing can be done about that fact." Then I had an epiphany. "Oh, is that it? Are you hoping to lure me back so you can kill me or something, so someone else can take up the labrys?"

Griffin gave me a disgusted look, and Luke looked bored at my idea.

"Believe me, we are aware you are more than adequate for the task at hand," Luke said, his voice even drier than it was before.

"The task at hand..." I mused, feeling the giant puzzle pieces of Alfar intrigue move around my mind, looking for the place they fit, "...which you want to be not killing the Red and the White."

Then it hit me. Of course they wanted me as the champion.

"That's why you're okay with a halfling! You want me to be the champion because you think I can't be that powerful. You think I'll do what you tell me and just chop up the Red and the White again, because that's all I'll be capable of."

"We do want the Red and the White dealt with, yes," Luke said. His voice was still flat but did I see his eye tic?

"But not *really* dealt with, right?" I forged on like a hound on the scent. I knew I had something there. "You don't want me to actually destroy the Red and White, do you?"

"That's ridiculous," said Griffin, looking very flustered for an Alfar. "Of course we want them destroyed."

But it all suddenly made sense.

"No, you want them out of the way, not destroyed. Because if I do succeed in actually killing the Red and the White, that'll make you look awful, won't it? A halfling doing what none of the Alfar could do throughout the centuries. What would people think? You want the threat removed, yes. But you don't want me to remove it too much, so that people think a halfling like me could be more powerful than an Alfar."

With those last words, I took two long strides forward,

pushing Luke with my power as I did so. He moved begrudgingly, forced to bend before the enormous pressure of my enforced shields. My mind kept spinning as more implications unraveled before me.

"And maybe that's not all. Maybe you don't want them gone for other reasons. Maybe you *want* the threat of the Red and the White looming over everyone so people think they need the Alfar, just in case the Red and the White reappear. But if they were gone for good, *and* killed by a halfling no less, then you lose a great big reason to keep you Alfar around. Your subjects might realize they don't need you. Because you're by no means the fiercest tiger in this jungle now, are you?"

And with that, I pulled the ax. It was kind of a cheap shot, but I was really starting to loathe Luke. I had also seen the goblin bodyguards exchanging glances, as were the other supes the Alfar powers had brought with them in their entourage. If they could hear me, they could repeat what I said.

If I'd learned one thing from watching *Downton Abbey*, it was that the servants always gossiped.

So I went ahead and let the labrys's power lap over me, shoving at Griffin and Luke like an eager puppy that didn't know how big it was. The message was clear: Even when I wasn't trying to be aggressive, I could kick their ass.

Luke and Griffin exchanged an inscrutable look, and I cackled mentally.

"That's ridiculous," the Alfar second said eventually as Luke retreated back into himself. "Of course we want you to dispatch the Red and the White. They are our enemies, and they must be stopped."

Like any good politician, Griffin could flip-flop on an issue faster than a greyhound could break into a run.

"So does Jane have Alfar support, along with human?" Daniel asked, his voice cheerful. He had clearly enjoyed the show.

"Jane is and has always been our champion," Griffin said, casting Daniel a withering look. "Of course she has our support."

"Then let's shake on it," Daniel said, a completely unnecessary touch I think he threw in just to annoy the Alfar. But I wasn't much happier at having to grasp Luke's clammy paw, and Griffin looked like he'd rather bite off Daniel's.

"Well, then, that's settled. My lads have the bones, Jane. Shall we get you back to base?"

I nodded at Daniel, fluttering my fingers at the Alfar. "I'll call if I need anything."

Griffin looked ready to explode as we walked away. He knew a brush-off when he saw one.

Once we were safely ensconced in one of Daniel's military SUVs, I let the giggle I'd been holding back bubble up through my lips. Turning to Ryu, I hoped he'd join me in a laugh.

But my former lover was staring out the window, deep in thought, and when he turned his face toward my laughter, he looked at me as if seeing a stranger.

My laughter died, and we drove in silence back to the air base.

CHAPTER ELEVEN

When I fell asleep that night in one of the guest accommodations at the air base, I prayed fervently that I might have another Anyan dream. At some point during the day, after recovering from the shock of the first dream, I'd changed my tune about seeing Anyan when I was sleeping. Even if I couldn't remember them exactly, I'd decided that a dream was better than nothing. That said, I never expected my prayers to be answered, as though Morpheus were some radio DJ taking requests.

But upon closing my eyes in the dark, sterile environment of my borrowed room, I promptly opened them to find myself in the snug confines of the hut's little sleeping nook. I was also naked, and not alone.

"Oh, puppy," I cooed as the barghest stroked a calloused palm over my flank. The fur beneath me was soft and warm, tickling against the backs of my knees. The barghest was even warmer, although not so soft.

Stormy gray eyes met mine as his mouth descended for a kiss.

"We don't have much time," he said in my ear, his voice low, as if afraid someone was listening. "He'll find us quickly enough, and he'll spy, even if he can't touch us here."

"He?" I thought, confused. Why would someone want to listen to Anyan and me in bed? But all thoughts disappeared in a puff of pleasure as the fingers stroking down my sides moved inward, to the V in my legs. I groaned, a throaty growl of ecstasy, as Anyan's thick fingers dipped into my sex.

"So wet for me." The barghest's voice was rough in my ear, and I pushed my hips up into his hand in response.

His fingers found their rhythm, driving my pleasure forward. I cried out, so close to the brink after only minutes of his hands on me. He knew what drove me wild, what I needed. Speaking of which...

"Do that thing," I moaned. "That thing with your power..."

The first time we'd had sex, he'd used his power like extra hands, touching me all over. It had been incredible, like nothing I'd ever experienced.

Anyan chuckled, pinching my clit gently for my impertinence. An act that did nothing to decrease my arousal, believe me.

"Greedy girl," he said. "And I'd give anything to fuck you like that again. But my powers are no longer mine."

Why not? I wondered, but not for long. Anyan added a thumb and a pinkie to his routine, and pretty soon I was gasping for air and seeing stars.

"You'll just have to make do with plain old me,"

he said, nipping and sucking on my neck as I shattered around his fingers, crying out in unabashed pleasure until he wrapped his free hand behind my neck to clamp a hand over my mouth.

I kept singing his praises, even if they were muffled, as he kept my orgasm going until it became almost painful.

Only then did I push his hand away, curling in toward him in a boneless heap only to feel his hardness against my belly. When I could move again, I reached down a hand to stroke him. I looked up into those iron eyes, so full of sadness and affection that my heart broke. I knew that I was just as sad, and just as in love, and that there were so many things I should be saying to him, even if I didn't know what they were.

But Anyan always knew what to say, even if he didn't speak too often.

"Ride me, Jane," he told me, shifting so that he was on his back. His hands wrapped around my hips and pulled me up and over him, until I straddled his hips. "Ride me, and remind me who I am."

With tears in my eyes, I did just that. Taking him deep in my body, so deep I gasped, I set a gentle rhythm that didn't last long. Soon enough he was bucking up toward me, setting a driving pace. Our bodies slapped against each other in the warm silence of the hut, and it was like a Beethoven symphony to my ears.

The tears fell, unbidden, as I rained kisses on his also wet cheeks. Finally, Anyan came, and I sucked the cries from his lips even as I exulted in giving him such pleasure.

I fell forward on his chest, letting him hold me as I watched the flames dance in the fire pit in the center of the hut.

"And I am me again," he said eventually, stroking a hand over my hair, down my back. "At least for a little while."

I listened to the beating of his heart under my ear and I knew I missed him very much. So I told him so.

"I miss you, too, my love," he said. "But you mustn't stay much longer. I don't want him to have proof that we're meeting this way."

I moved so that I sat, cross-legged, next to Anyan, looking down at his strong, rough-hewn features. His dark curls were spread on the furs behind his head, making him look strangely vulnerable.

"Why can't I remember anything besides now?" I asked him, finally able to articulate what had been bothering me. "It feels like a veil's been drawn across my memories."

"It's the nature of dreams," the barghest said sadly, running the tips of his fingers up and down my thigh.

"This is a dream, then?" I asked.

"Yes. I'm sorry to say so, but yes."

I shook my head. "It feels so real. I can't be dreaming. This is our home…"

"This is not our home, Jane. This was a home of mine once. Now it's my prison. But I built it to be comfortable, hoping you'd find me. And you have."

"Important things are happening," I realized then. "Things I can't remember. Why can't I remember?" My voice had increased in volume, sounding slightly shrill even to my own ears. I realized my heart was beating rapidly. Was I panicking?

Anyan had also sat up, peering around the hut that no longer felt quite so much like home, or quite so safe.

"He's close," Anyan said. "And you're getting better at

remembering. You just have to convince yourself it's not a dream. Then we can talk. But now you must go."

With that, Anyan kissed, a lingering, delicious kiss. Capped off by a very hard pinch to my thigh.

My leg, charley horsing like crazy, woke me up. Swearing up a storm, I tried to stretch it out, my hands fisted in my sheets until the pain subsided and my muscle stopped twitching.

What the hell? I thought. *Must have pulled something. Or I need potassium. Aren't charley horses caused by a lack of potassium?*

I got out of bed, feeling oddly boneless, to go to the little bathroom attached to my room. I got a drink of water and splashed water on my face, then used the toilet.

Washing my hands, I studied myself in the mirror. I knew I'd had a dream, and I remember it being supersexy and about Anyan. It had obviously really turned me on, and except for the charley horse, I felt the same dreamy, subdued way I felt after sex.

Must have been some dream, I thought as I made my way back to bed. Curling up under the blankets, I shut my eyes. But I couldn't drop the idea that the dream was important.

I rolled over onto my back to frown up at the ceiling. What could have been both important and leaving me feeling all sated? It's not like I needed to remember my sexy dreams, although I wished I could. But it couldn't have been important, right?

Wrong, my brain said. It just wouldn't let it go.

This is stupid, I thought. *I'm dreaming about Anyan because I miss him, nothing more.*

So why did the dream feel so important? And why did I feel like I needed to remember it so badly?

Slowly, the dream started coming back to me. We'd had sex, and it had been amazing dream sex, yes. But not as amazing as it had been in real life, if I were honest.

Which says a lot about Anyan as a lover, I thought. For how many men could actually claim to be better than the fantasy?

But it wasn't his fault, I remembered a second later. *He said he can't use all his powers where he is. Someone else has taken them.*

This time I froze for real as a chill raced up my spine that left me shivering.

Are these not really dreams? I wondered. They were so real, after all, and so weird. When did a dream man tell you he couldn't do what he could in real life? And why was my dream Anyan so sad?

I mean, if I were just making this shit up, surely my mind would make everything lovely and hunky-dory, right? We'd be boning in a field of Oreos or something, cut through by a river of cold milk. The Oreos could dunk themselves first in the river, then feed themselves to me as I came. Now *that's* a fantasy. My dreams with Anyan didn't feel like that. They felt…real.

But maybe I wasn't trying to escape the pain, but work through it. Maybe that's why Anyan was so sad, and seemed so trapped…

More memories rushed in. Anyan's worry about being overheard. His talking about how "he" would hear us.

It's too weird, I thought. *I need to talk about this to someone…*

So I did what I should have done the first time I'd

dreamed of Anyan. I picked up my little Bat Phone to the creature and waited for it to respond.

[Jane?] the creature asked, itself a little dreamy. While I was resting, I knew it spent its time scanning the world through the eyes of susceptible humans.

I need your help, I thought at it. *I've been having dreams about Anyan. But I'm not sure they're really dreams.*

The creature's presence sort of buzzed in my mind, as if it were thinking. [Do you think he's communicating with you?]

I shrugged my shoulders, an unnecessary gesture as the creature could feel my confusion. *I have no idea. They feel like dreams, to be honest. But they're so strange. And there's you.*

[Me?]

Well, you're the only other person I know who has a body that is trapped, you know, but your mind is free… maybe Anyan can do what you do, and sort of surf.

[I doubt it, Jane. Anyan isn't like me, and his powers can't be like mine. But who knows what happened to him when the White took over his body?]

Can you do something to check? To find out if the dreams are real?

Again, the creature presence buzzed in thought. [I think I might have a way, but it will involve you giving me free access to your mind. Is that all right?]

I nodded immediately. If Anyan really was able to communicate with me, even imperfectly in dreams, that fact could be a total game changer.

The creature, feeling my acquiescence, took over. Suddenly, I was pushed firmly, if gently, to one corner of my own brain. It felt incredibly strange. I tried to move my arms and legs, but I knew I remained lying perfectly still. I could still feel, sort of, but not control.

It was an odd sensation, and very unpleasant. I thought about poor Anyan, totally pushed aside in his own brain, and I shuddered. I also wondered why the creature didn't just take me over, full stop, before remembering how weakened the White was by having an unwilling host.

Although there were times when I'm not sure I'd altogether mind being taken over. Being a champion was tiring.

Meanwhile, the creature was busy. Its mental buzzing kept increasing as if it were growing excited.

Are you finding something? I asked, and the creature somehow sent a vibe of both acknowledgment and a command to be patient. It was very good at communicating mentally.

So I did the equivalent of twiddling my thumbs as the creature rifled through my brain. I seriously doubted I had any secrets from it to begin with, but I certainly wouldn't after this...

[There it is,] the creature said, a note of marvel in his voice. [What a clever man is your barghest.]

I felt absurdly proud, even as I demanded an answer. *What did you find?*

[Just as I thought, he's not communicating with you. Even with the White's power, he wouldn't be capable of that.]

Disappointment flushed through my system. *But I thought you said...*

[Patience,] the creature said, chuckling. [He's not communicating with you; you've managed to find him.]

Me?

[Yes. You piggybacked on my own ability to reach out mentally. Obviously unintentionally. But while you were dreaming, you must have been searching for him, using my abilities. I'm a part of you in a lot of ways now, Jane, both through the power of the champion and through our time together, so close, over the past months.]

Wow, I thought, nonplussed. *I did that?*

[It makes sense. You miss Anyan. You love him. Your mind may know he's gone, but your heart doesn't. So it took advantage of the tools it could find when you were sleeping and your doubting mind was turned off.]

But how did I find him?

[You're right that he is a bit like me. He is trapped, and he does have a lot of power. I think he felt you. I think for him, he's probably constantly in a state that's a bit like dreaming. So once he realized you were looking for him, he made himself a beacon for you.]

So the dreams are real? I asked.

[Yes. They're real.]

I wept then, like a baby. Huge, tearing sobs that nearly choked me. I was making so much noise that I wasn't at all surprised when my door was flung open to reveal Ryu.

"Another dream?" he asked, rushing to my side.

"No," I told him. Then I shook my head. "Yes." And then I started laughing hysterically before I got out of bed, not caring that I was wearing only a long T-shirt and panties, to do a triumphant dance, whooping like a drunk at Mardi Gras.

"Um, Jane, what happened? Are you all right?" Poor Ryu probably thought I had been drinking.

Grinning at him like a maniac, I finally stopped my little dance.

"I'm more than all right, Ryu. I'm fabulous. Anyan's alive." And then with that, I started crying again.

Obviously completely confused and perhaps fearing for my sanity, Ryu took my hands, urging me to sit down next to him.

"You're not making any sense, Jane. You need to calm down and tell me what happened."

So I did.

"I've been having these dreams. I thought they were just that, dreams. But they were really weird. Basically, I'd meet up with Anyan in this hut and we'd, um... we'd do things." I flushed red with embarrassment, not least because it was awkward telling your ex-lover about dream sex with your current beau. Especially when he was a dragon.

"Anyway, we'd also talk, and that's the part that was weird. He was always really sad and cryptic, worrying about someone watching or listening to us. So I had the creature check it out."

"And?" Ryu said.

"And they weren't just dreams, they were *real*. I was using the creature's power to reach out to him, without knowing. And Anyan knew that, and helped me find him."

"Holy shit," Ryu said, as blown away by this knowledge as I was. "That's huge."

"I know," I said, a fresh barrage of tears flooding my eyes.

"This changes everything."

I nodded.

"Maybe we can use this," Ryu said, already starting to strategize like the baobhan sith I knew so well.

And he was right. Knowing Anyan and I could somehow communicate might turn out to be a vital weapon.

But for me it was way bigger than that. I now knew, beyond a doubt, that Anyan was alive inside the White. He was alive, and he wanted out.

And I was ready to move heaven and earth to make it so.

CHAPTER TWELVE

Using Daniel's resources, we were back in Rockabill at the end of the next day. The creature was still recovering from its apparition of the Red from Hong Kong. Meanwhile, the White's bones came with us, packed in a body bag. Everyone flipped out when Ryu and I walked into Anyan's with it, until we explained what the ominous black bag contained.

Also upon landing, I'd told my friends about my dreams, and how they weren't really dreams. I tried to be subtle about their erotic nature, so that my dad wouldn't be party to hearing about his daughter's mind-sex with her dragon-lover, but I don't think it was very subtle. Especially since Grizzie was hooting with laughter and making dirty gestures with her fingers. Everyone else listened with considered interest, reacting with various levels of excitement when I ended my talk by telling them what it meant—that Anyan was alive and well somewhere in the White.

Iris and Tracy cried with me, while Grizzie only just managed to hold back tears by complaining that she never got any "dream bonkin'." Caleb and Daoud also seemed pleased, as did Gog and Magog, even if they weren't as demonstrative.

My dad, after assiduously ignoring Grizzie's off-color remarks, gave me the kind of hug that dads excel at. The kind that told me all he wanted on this earth was my happiness, and that he would do all he could to help me along the way.

It was a good hug, and I told him I loved him.

Overcome by emotion, Amy the nahual waitress, who just happened to be at Anyan's after dropping off some food, offered to go home to get some weed to celebrate, but we refused her generous offer.

We were ready to get to work.

But first I needed a swim, to recharge my power. The creature might be lending me tons, but part of what it had done was allow me to hold more of my own water magic. So I took a quick swim, after which I grabbed some of the food Amy had brought over (priorities!), knowing that Caleb was already getting down to work. When I was ready, we all sat down to listen to his report.

The satyr was sitting at Anyan's long trestle table that had pride of place in his gorgeous kitchen. The rest of us took positions around the table, or sitting on counters. We were the full gang—Iris, of course, and Grizzie, Tracy, and my dad. Amy had stuck around after hearing my good news; and Gog and Magog were in attendance. Daoud had gone back to Boston to help Camille with a problem—some local baobhan sith had gone on a bit of a bender and killed a few humans. To my surprise, Hiral had gone with him. The gywllion and the djinn had struck up a friendship, and I think Hiral was bored waiting around doing nothing with us. But even without him, we had a lot of brains to puzzle over our problem, and with a tuna melt in my belly and the Atlantic charging my powers, I felt ready for anything.

"So, I've been going over the poem, after translating it myself. Then I found an article online, as I said, written in the 1920s." Caleb passed the article to Ryu, who passed it to me, and I had to smile at the title.

" 'The Poem of the Philosopher Theophrastus upon the Sacred Art: A Metrical Translation with Comments upon the History of Alchemy.' By C. A. Browne. Not exactly pithy, but it definitely does the job," I said, then felt my eyebrows rise as I read the next line of the printed-off article. "Wait, this was published in *The Scientific Monthly*?"

Caleb smiled. "Fascinating, is it not?"

I wanted to tell Caleb that it wasn't fascinating—it was the universe interfering again. I wondered what happened to the scientist, Browne. Was he laughed out of his university for caring so much about alchemy and writing about dragons? Or was he humored? I couldn't help picturing C. A. Browne as one more chess piece on a board set up by forces far beyond our control or comprehension.

"Indubitably," I said, because it seemed a more appropriate response than any of my other thoughts.

"This article has been invaluable, not least because Browne is constantly reminding his reader that alchemy was not just about the transmutation of metals but about the transmutation of the soul. I've printed off the relevant portions of Browne's text. I actually prefer his translation to mine, so I've used his." Caleb sent stacks of

paper around the room—one around the table and one he
passed to Gog, for those who weren't sitting with us. We
each took a sheet and started reading, while Caleb read
aloud.

"I've started with this idea of Theophrastus's that the
transmutation process had to take two steps, and that both
steps are helped along by this stone he talks about. I'll
read you this first section:

The white, augmented thrice within a fire,
In three day's time is altogether changed
To lasting yellow and this yellow then
Will give its hue to every whitened form.
This power to tinge and shape produces gold
And thus a wondrous marvel is revealed."

Caleb looked at us as if he were waiting for comment.
Everyone else in the kitchen just looked confused.

Gamely, Gog tried his hand. The gray-skinned coblynau
shifted his huge frame on his booted feet as he spoke,
as if he were a nervous schoolboy in class. "So, we have
to do something to the White. Is that why you brought
back them bones? And then we get a marvel? What's the
marvel?"

We all turned back to Caleb, since Gog had done a
good job asking all of our questions.

"Exactly. The marvel is the stone. That's the next quo-
tation on your handout," Caleb said, pointing to a block of
text on the handout that he'd kept. Then he read.

"The great agent of transmutation was the stone. 'It
is found,' said Avicenna, 'in the dirt of streets and is

trodden under foot by men.' The Greek alchemists
were no less explicit.

'It can not be bought with gold,' said an unknown
prose writer, 'yet God has given it freely to beg-
gars.' Zosimos, a Greek of Panopolis, described it as
'a stone yet not a stone, a thing despised yet full of
honor, of many forms yet shapeless, a thing unknown
yet familiar to all, of many names yet nameless.' "

"Huh?" Amy asked, her pretty, surfer-girl features
screwed up into a look of utter confusion. Confusion that
I, for one, shared.

"I know," Caleb said. "It's really obscure. And Theophrastus himself is no more help in the poem your monk
sent us, writing:

'Though not a stone, it yet is made a stone
From metal, having three hypostases,
For which the stone is prized and widely known;
Yet all the ignorant search everywhere
As though the prize were not close by at hand.
Deprived of honor yet the stone is found
To have within a sacred mystery,
A treasure hidden and yet free to all.' "

I considered banging my head against the table, but
knew that would be bad form. My dad covered my hand
in his, warning me to have patience. Iris went ahead and
spoke for all of us, though, when she said, "Caleb, come
on, this is ridiculous. What do we have to do?"

The satyr shifted in his chair, obviously uncomfortable.
"I'm not really sure. We have to use fire, I think. Or

magic. And do something to get the stone, and the White's bones have to be involved. Other than that, I'm stumped."

"You can't be stumped!" I said, regretting my words even as I said them. "I'm sorry. I know you're doing your best. But there has to be a clue in there somewhere."

Caleb waved his handout in the air. "There are plenty of clues. Clues aren't the problem. It's what to make of those clues..."

"Too bad we don't speak stone," Gog mused, staring up at the ceiling. "I'm a coblynau, and I speak to earth, but that's not really the same now, is it?"

Gog finished speaking, then looked down to find all the Rockabillian supernaturals staring at him like he'd just reinvented the wheel. He backed up a step.

"Gog, I could kiss you right now," I said, causing Magog to puff up like an enraged squirrel. Ignoring her, I turned to Ryu, who was already standing.

"I'll go get him," was all the baobhan sith said as he headed out the door.

Luckily, I'd saved Gus's life once before and our little stone-spirit owed me.

Gus's surfaces gleamed in the light of the kitchen. He was barely tall enough to see over the table, meaning that I, sitting on the opposite side from him, had a peculiar view consisting of just a bald pate and glasses, both reflecting like the moon, hovering over the edge of the table.

Gus's shiny head cocked one way, then the other. He reached out a tentative hand to touch the bones, then withdrew his fingers with a jerk.

"There's a stone in there," he said eventually. "I don't know how, but there is."

I sat up in my chair, and everyone else took an involuntary step forward. We'd been trying not to crowd the stone spirit, but now all bets were off.

"Can you help us get it out?" I asked. "Can you talk to it?"

"Oh, yes. It's very loud. It's very angry about being kept so long. And it didn't like that bag you put it in."

I glanced at Ryu, who gave me a curt shake of his head, warning me to keep it together. Gus's rapport with rocks totally skeeved me out. It was like finding out that all the toys you played with as a child were really alive. And judging.

Gus's rocks were snarky apparently, and they were everywhere. I hated the idea of being surrounded by judgmental pebbles, and tended to react with inappropriate fits of mockery.

"Please apologize to it for the bag," Ryu's smooth voice said, brokering our exchange since I was too immature to do so.

"Okay," Gus said, staring at the pile of bones in a way that made me shudder.

"Now how can we get the stone out?" Ryu asked. "We'd very much like to free it."

Gus giggled, a strange, high-pitched sound. "It knows you want to use it, you don't have to pretend. But that's okay; it wants to be used. It has a great purpose, you know."

"Yes," Ryu said, trying to keep the urgency out of his voice. "We know it has a great purpose. And we want to help it succeed. But first we need to get it—"

"It's easy enough," Gus interrupted. "It wants me to call, and it wants the girl's fire."

Gus jerked his chin at me as he said the last bit, refusing once again to fully acknowledge my presence. Despite saving both him and the boulder he called home, he'd never really cottoned to me. I resisted the urge to stick my tongue out at him.

"It will take a very long time. And a lot of power. Can she handle it?" By "she," I knew Gus meant me. For a second I wanted to snap something rude back at him, but then I remembered the poem. It had talked about the spell taking three days. Did I have enough power?

Do I have enough power? I asked the creature.

[We will, yes. And I will make sure you're physically comfortable during that time. Well, not uncomfortable at least. It will be an arduous task, though, for both of us.]

And you can definitely handle it? I said. I worried about the creature. I'd always assumed it had unlimited strength, so letting me know that was not the case had been quite a shock.

[Oh, yes. Do not worry about me, child.]

I would worry anyway, but I had to trust it. And myself. We could do this. We had to do this, to get Anyan back.

Heaven and earth, I reminded myself, in what had become my little promise to myself. *Heaven and earth.*

"I'll be fine," I said, answering Gus's question about whether I had it in me to do this task. "When should we start? I think now is as good a time as any."

Gus shrugged. "I'll have to call in sick for work." Gus was a bagger at our local grocery store when he wasn't gossiping with rocks.

Amy smiled. "I can take care of that for you, Gus. I'll call each morning you two are busy."

With a nod, Gus acknowledged we were ready.

The first thing I did, at the creature's behest, was put on some warm layers and go to the bathroom. I felt like I was gearing up for a family holiday, rather than taking part in some sacred ritual.

When I came out of Anyan's bathroom, my dad was waiting for me.

"Hey, Dad," I said, trying to sound normal and cheerful, neither of which was working.

"Hey, honey." He was clearly worried. "You got enough clothes?"

"Sure, Dad. Listen, I'm going to be fine."

"I know. It's just—"

"It's just that this is scary stuff," I said gently, moving in for a hug. He enveloped me in his arms, and I rested against the softness of his belly, like I had since I was a child.

"It is scary," he said eventually. "Do you even know what you're doing?"

I looked up at him. "Nope. We never do really."

"Oh. How does that work out?"

"Sometimes well. Sometimes…not so well. But we have to try this. And I'll be fine, the creature won't let anything happen to me."

"Yes, the great eyeball."

"It's more than just an eyeball, and it's very powerful. Plus I think it likes me."

The creature stirred in my mind, letting a gentle sense of agreement wash over me.

"Well, tell it that if you get hurt doing this thing, we're gonna have words."

I laughed, squeezing my father in one last bear hug. He was dealing with all of this spectacularly on so many levels.

"Will do. And I'll let it know you're serious."

"I am serious! Ancient creature or not, you're my baby. Now let's get you downstairs and get your Anyan back."

I shivered at his words, wondering if it could really be as easy as that.

"Oh, and Jane?" my dad said as I walked away from him toward the steps leading downstairs from Anyan's loft.

"Yes?"

"I hope he's worth all of this." My dad didn't have to clarify who "he" was. But in that moment I saw how much he did worry about me, and how frightened he was at how drastically his world had changed. I walked back to him, taking his hand in mine and squeezing it gently.

"He's more than worth it, Dad. He's worth almost as much as you."

My dad snorted, just like I always did, blinking back a few tears. Then he led me downstairs toward the others.

While I'd been getting ready and talking to my dad, Caleb and Iris had carted the White's bones into Anyan's huge backyard. Quite handily, the barghest had a nice big fire pit ready for bonfires, with felled tree trunks serving as seats lining the perimeter.

My friends made a pile of the bones, adding no other substances at Gus's instructions.

"This is a *true* bonfire, or bone-fire," said the stone spirit. "We want only the bones to absorb the magic."

Ryu had taken a cushion off the couch and placed it on the ground in front of one of the tree trunks for me to sit on. I nervously made use of it, thanking him as I did so.

"Are you sure you're up to this?" he said, sotto voce. I shrugged.

"The creature seems to think we are."

"Let me know if you need anything. And don't let that thing burn you out. I don't trust it knows your capacities."

I smiled at Ryu affectionately. "Don't worry, Ryu. It knows me very well indeed. And I've gotten a lot tougher."

Ryu ran a hand through his chestnut hair. "I know you have. And I'm trying to adjust to that fact. But I still worry about you."

"And I appreciate it. If I need anything, you'll know."

With that, I peered over at Gus, who was sitting on the trunk opposite me.

"Ready?"

The stone spirit nodded.

Ready? I asked the creature.

It gave my mind a nudge of acquiescence. I sat down on the cushion, facing the bonfire, using the tree trunk as a backrest.

"Let's get started then, Gus. What do I do?"

"Just direct your strength at the bones. Set them alight with magic. Make it burn hot and strong, and don't let it waver. I will call to the stone."

And that's what I did. Funneling the creature's power, I poured it at the pile of bones in front of me. At first, nothing happened, so I adjusted the magic. I envisioned it as flame rather than power. Eventually the bones began to glow.

"It needs more," said Gus.

So the creature gave me more, and with a loud snap, the bones burst into flame. Not the flickering orangy red of real fire, though—this was the blue-tinged fire of magic.

And then I sat there, for three days straight. I've never done anything like it, and never want to do anything like it again. The creature helped, of course. Immediately it started to take over my bodily functions. Slowing everything down, I became more of a conduit for its power than Jane True. I suppose it was really the exact same thing the creature had done right after Blondie died and Anyan was taken, but this time I wasn't numb with grief.

This time I knew what it was like to hang out in one's own mind, vaguely aware that one's body was exhausting itself—that it was hungry, and tired, and wanted the bathroom. But all of those sensations were just niggling little itches compared to the force of the power I was expending.

By the second day, everyone was starting to get worried. I knew there was activity around me—my various friends trying to make contact, to ask if I could get up, if I would eat, if I was all right. Surprisingly, I registered that it was my father who argued most vehemently to let me finish what I'd started. He knew how important it was for me to do this, and knew that I wouldn't thank whoever interrupted this ritual before it had run its course.

As much as their care meant for me, by the third day I ignored them all, not least because I had to. At some point I'd realized that my magical channels were starting to chafe and that it was only the strength of the creature insulating me with its own power that kept me from burning out entirely. I also knew that if I kicked up a fuss, or distracted the creature, I'd go up in a conflagration similar to that burning in front of me.

So instead of fighting, I added my concentration to the creature's. It was a horrible task, made worse by the fact those physical needs were growing stronger. My body was aching, exhausted, starving, and so very thirsty.

At the start of the third day, Caleb tried to give me an IV, but I knew that I'd become a vessel. I needed to remain sealed, or the power would spill out and cause chaos. Using my own personal energy, I created a rigid shield around myself, keeping everyone out.

That made everyone panic, of course, and they thought the creature had hijacked me. They were trying to figure out how to rescue me from its clutches for most of that day. But I managed to tune out their attempts, steadily pouring my power into my shields as the creature poured its power into the bones.

It was only when Gus spoke to me that I listened. The entire time I'd been working, so had the stone spirit. Maybe he found the task slightly easier since he was essentially a boulder, with a boulder's patience, but I still admired him for sticking with me that whole time. But he'd been utterly silent, staring into the fire and chanting something none of us could hear under his breath.

But then, right at the close of the third day, he shouted triumphantly.

Rising to his feet, the little stone spirit raised his chant to full volume so we could all hear. It was a strangely melodic grunting language I'd never heard before, but the sound filled the glade. As he chanted, Gus walked forward, the flames dancing in his Coke-bottle-thick glasses.

Whatever he was doing was now pulling the power out of me. I wasn't even pushing anymore, just letting Gus work his mojo. He used us as fuel, pulling so much strength that my physical shields wavered as all my strength was poured into his. Luckily, my friends were so distracted by Gus's suddenly snapping back to life that they didn't try to rescue me again.

The bone-fire, meanwhile, had gone almost entirely blue it was so hot. Gus kept approaching it, his hands held out in front of him in supplication. His chanting grew more excited and even louder as he neared.

When he was standing right in front of the fire pit, he raised his arms up to the stars and shouted one last series of grunts into the night air.

Then, to our horror, he walked into the fire.

My friends rushed forward, and the creature extinguished its power. The sudden absence of all that force left the glade eerily quiet, except for the strange crackling sound of the supernatural fire. But without the force of the creature's magic, the enormous conflagration quickly began to die down.

And when it did finally extinguish itself, there lay Gus, huddled in a fetal position in the center of the fire.

Ryu and Caleb were first to reach him.

"He's untouched!" shouted Caleb, causing me to sag in relief. I was slowly coming back to myself, the creature very carefully restoring my body's functions to normal. Quietly, so that no one would notice and they could focus on Gus, I gasped in pain as pins and needles sprang up all over my body. It was agonizing, and I tried to keep the writhing to a minimum as I also tried to pay attention to poor Gus.

"Gus. Gus. Can you hear me?" Caleb was saying. I heard a small groan from the stone spirit, and my heart soared with relief even as other parts of my body started to come to life, quite loudly and angrily.

"Gus, come back to us, c'mon," Ryu said, trying to shift the stone spirit, who was knotted up, clutching his stomach, like he'd turned into stone himself.

Finally, causing more gasps of relief from my friends,
Gus righted himself. He hadn't been holding his stomach,
it turned out. He'd been holding a baseball-sized, grayish-
brown stone. It was gray and looked totally innocuous,
but I could sense its power even from here.

"Here's the stone," Gus said, totally unaware of the
panic he'd caused by walking into the fire. "Isn't she
beautiful?"

That's when everyone remembered me.

"Jane!" Iris shouted, spinning on her heel and running
toward me.

She found me also clutching my stomach, my legs crossed
as tightly as they would go.

"Bathroom. Now. Please," I managed to choke out.

Grabbing me under the arm and hoisting me up, Iris
sprinted with me to the toilet. It wasn't the most heroic
of endings to an epic sacred ritual, but I'd like to see anybody sit for three days and not have to pee when it was
over.

CHAPTER THIRTEEN

After being awake for three days, falling asleep wasn't difficult. It was staying awake long enough to strategize with Ryu and the rest of my friends that was the hard part. But I'd managed it, and we'd come up with a good plan. Actually, we'd come up with three plans, depending on some of the answers I got from Anyan.

All these plans, however, hinged on the hypothesis that my dream Anyan was the real Anyan, and that he actually had an idea of what was happening outside that little mental space he inhabited, prisoner in his own body. We had to make a lot of assumptions and run with them, but I guess that was what war was all about. And at least we were only risking our own lives, although that was bad enough. I thought about the generals of wars, acting on intelligence they couldn't know was accurate, and sending hundreds, even thousands, of men into battles based on what could be lies.

I was glad I wasn't a general.

I was also very glad to be able to sleep after what had felt like eons spent drawing little flowcharts and making lists and arguing over exactly what I should say under which circumstances. It had only really taken us a few hours, but it didn't feel like that by the time I took a shower to relax, and then curled up in Anyan's big bed.

Minutes later, at least to my dreaming mind, I was standing in front of Anyan's hut

I raced a few steps forward, all thoughts tuned to my eagerness to see the barghest, when I stopped short.

For the hut wasn't as substantial as it had been. The first time I'd seen it, it had been so real. But now there was something gauzy about the earth piled up around the structure, and the wood looked less wood-like and more like a smooth plastic facsimile of wood. A bad facsimile.

Girding my loins, I strode forward. Something was weakening Anyan, I knew, and I knew what that something was…if only I could remember. I also knew I had to tell him something, that I was here to do something important. I tried to focus on my duties, but they swooped away like unladen swallows.

When I entered the hut, however, all thoughts besides relief were pushed out of my brain at the sight of the barghest, sitting quietly in front of the fire, watching it with sad eyes. Like the outside, the inside of the hut had lost some of its detail. The far side of the space loomed dark and empty, where once I knew there had been a back wall, full of shelves and sporting colorful paintings. The fire was still alive, though—bright and dancing, looking just like a real fire.

I came up behind the barghest and knelt, wrapping my arms around him.

"Jane," he said, his voice thick with relief. I kissed the shell of his ear in response, and held him like that for a long while.

Eventually, he pulled me around and down into his lap. I cuddled up to him happily, but my nervousness increased when I saw his face. He looked tired, and wan, as if he were at the end of his rope. Trying to remember what it was that I had to ask him, I questioned him.

Stroking a hand down his face, I said, "You don't look so good."

Anyan shook his head, his dark curls flopping adorably. "Let's not talk about it. Let me just look at you."

And that's what he did, the big softie. He studied me, as if memorizing every feature of my face. As he did so, I would have sworn the hut behind him grew a little more detailed, a little more solid.

But not as solid as it had been before.

"What's going on?" I asked gently after quite a few minutes had passed.

"Nothing," he said sadly. "But I'm glad you're here."

"I'm glad, too," I said, squeezing around him like an overzealous chimp. We sat like that in silence for a few moments, but something kept niggling at me.

"I'm supposed to tell you something," I said quietly into his ear. "But I can't remember what it is."

Anyan withdrew a bit, looking steadily into my eyes. When he spoke again, he did so carefully.

"Is it about the White?" he whispered. "I'm fighting him at every turn, but..."

Anyan was taking a risk saying his enemy's name, but it did the trick. My memories, my charge, came back to me in sharp focus.

"I'm dreaming," I whispered. "But you're here. Why couldn't I remember everything before?"

The barghest smiled, kissing my forehead gently. "It's the nature of dreams, Jane. We leave ourselves behind, to recover from reality. I couldn't remind you without risking him hearing, and I needed to see you, to be with you."

"You did the right thing, reminding me. Now this is important. Is he around yet?" I whispered back, urgency lacing my voice.

Anyan closed his eyes, as if trying to sense something. "No," he said eventually. "But he will be here soon. I think he knows we meet now. I've not been able to keep your presence hidden."

Leaning forward, I put my lips to Anyan's sensitive ear, and spoke in the quietest voice I could.

"Let him come," I said. "Let him come, and listen. Signal to me when he's close. Do you understand?"

Anyan looked at me, his iron gray eyes searching mine almost desperately.

"You have a plan?" he asked.

I nodded. Hope bloomed in those gray eyes then, and the hut around us throbbed with a burst of color. The fire blazed, warm and merry, and I knew what the trouble was.

Anyan had been losing faith in us. In me. He'd started to believe he'd never get out of this place.

"Silly barghest," I said in his ear, pulling him toward me in a rough hug. "You're mine now. I'm not letting you go."

"I know. I always knew. It's just..."

"It's hard. Now I need to ask you a question before he comes. Is he here?"

Again Anyan sensed and then shook his head. "No."

"Why are they always dragons?" I asked. We'd figured out battling the Red that when she was Morrigan-shaped, she was more Morrigan, and she was more Red when she was the dragon. Because both had their weaknesses, she'd fought us the last time as this scary dragon/Morrigan hybrid. Like a were-dragon. But ever since the White had been resurrected, they only ever showed up in dragon form.

And our plot hinged on the answer to that question.

"It's because of me," Anyan said, talking fast. "I weaken the White. Morrigan's a willing host, so they can swap between her true form and the dragon's. I'm a prisoner, trying to get free. It means the White can't change. Presumably, if he went back into my shape, I might be able to turn the tables on him. As it is, I keep him distracted. Or at least I try. I'm not very effective," he admitted, and I thought of the times the White had tried to kill me and I nodded.

"So your presence in his mind handicaps the White? Making Morrigan the more powerful one?"

Anyan nodded. "Yes."

Plan B it was, then. That was the plan that depended on the White being the lame pony in this circus. We thought that was the case, but we had planned for every contingency.

Our voices had never risen to full volume, and we'd withdrawn enough to talk to each other's faces, rather than in each other's ears. But I cuddled forward again, loving that intimacy.

"Well then," I whispered before giving Anyan's earlobe a little nibble. "We need to distract ourselves until we have an audience. Whatever can we do to pass the time?"

With a growl, Anyan manhandled me onto my back,

his lovely heavy body draping mine. We'd managed to entertain ourselves for a quite a while when Anyan stiffened. Stiffened more, I should say, and with his whole body. Not just his special parts.

"He's here," he murmured in my ear.

Show time, I thought, and then I started talking. Plan B was in effect.

"Are you certain he heard?" Ryu asked as my dad passed me a second bagel smothered in cream cheese. I was still making up for those three days without food.

"No," I told the baobhan sith, giving him an evil look as I started in on my second breakfast. I'd woken up on the wrong side of the bed after my dream-night with Anyan.

"Jane," Ryu admonished, casting me an equally illtempered glare. I sighed.

"Sorry, I'm just nervous as hell. But I'm serious, I don't know if the White heard. I said everything I was supposed to say, and Anyan was sure the White was lurking around, but I can't guarantee he heard, or listened, or cared."

My dad leaned over my shoulder, patting my hand that rested on the handle of my coffee mug.

"You did all you could, Jane," he said, turning back to Anyan's big farmhouse sink to wash dishes.

Caleb, sitting next to me with the remains of his own breakfast, nodded. "And I doubt the White would waste such information, or be oblivious to it."

"But what if he knows it's a trap?" I asked, my voice small.

Iris piped up from where she sat across from Caleb, her voice like honeyed ice cream.

"I don't think they can risk assuming it's a trap, any

more than we could if we thought they were moving on a new weapon."

Plan B hinged on the fact that the White was weaker than the Red. We needed to separate the two dragons, and we needed them as far away from each other as we could get them. The good thing about them being dragons, meanwhile, was they couldn't communicate. Dragons had no pockets to hold a cell phone, and massive fuck-off claws made dialing difficult. So if we could get the Red and the White really far apart, we could work on the White, using the stone.

We could get Anyan back, and have a fighting chance at taking the Red.

The hard part, however, was not necessarily separating the two. The hard part was making sure they both went where we wanted them to.

In other words, we had to create two sets of "dangers" that they'd have to split up to follow, only one had to be significantly less dangerous than the other. Presumably, they'd send the less powerful dragon, the White, after that group, and the Red would go after the more dangerous group.

As I qualified as "most dangerous," being the champion, I needed to be Red bait. But we had to invent another story, equally compelling, after which the dragons would send the White. For if they both chased after me, we were fucked.

Not least because the creature had admitted it wasn't sure it could apparate something as big as a dragon again, without serious consequences to itself. And we needed the creature for so many reasons.

"I agree with Iris," Ryu said, interrupting my reverie.

"They've got to check this threat out. And if I were them, I'd send someone after both of our groups to be safe."

What I'd told Anyan, so that the White could overhear, was a mixture of fact and lies. The facts were that we'd learned of a stone that was an important ingredient in a process that could separate the White from Anyan. I lied, however, about the fact we already had it. Instead, I said that we'd only heard of it, and that it was located very far away, in China. We'd concocted a whole story about it being in the collection of the Communist regime, blah blah blah. We were sending a team to investigate.

The kicker was that the ritual involved a bunch of other stuff, which we had to prepare in Rockabill. That was the other lure—the one that would hopefully bring in the White, and that was baited with the power of the creature.

"The second we get our hands on that stone," I'd told Anyan, my voice radiating excitement, "the creature will apparate me right back to Rockabill. And then we can start the ritual. We can take you back in seconds, just like they did."

And that was my little personal pot sweetener. I'd gone over those last minutes in Whitby, when the Red had stolen Anyan from me, a thousand times. And they weren't even *minutes*. It had taken only seconds for the Red to lash out that damnable tail of hers and send Anyan flying onto those bones. Another few seconds for her little chant to power up their mojo...and Anyan had been lost.

And it had been all an accident of fate. Everything had been going according to plan, or so it seemed, when Jarl had showed up, and everything was suddenly back in the Red's hands. Er, claws. But then Jarl was dead and we were going to win...

Only we lost. Big time.

So that was why I said what I had to Anyan. I knew, after seeing what had happened in Whitby, that huge things could happen in seconds. And because of our connection with the creature and its power, it appeared like we had time on our side. The Red and the White didn't know the creature actually had limits on its strength—all the dragons knew was that the creature could apparate either one of them at will.

And the Red and the White obviously knew the power of time, since they'd used it against us so well in Whitby.

If the White had heard me, which I had to have faith it did, it would know that all I had to do was lay a hand on that stone, and it and I could be back in Rockabill in seconds, starting this mysterious ritual I'd told Anyan about.

Which meant they had to send someone here, to make sure that ritual never got off the ground, at the same time they tried to keep me from reaching the stone.

Only, in reality, we already had the stone, and I wasn't leaving Rockabill.

At that moment, we were distracted by the lady of the day coming down the stairs.

Magog walked down slowly, looking distinctly uncomfortable. She'd washed all the gel out of her jet-black hair, and combed it flat and straight. Iris had taken some scissors to round it off at the ends, and to give her some bangs. Her massive amounts of eye makeup were toned down, and she'd taken out her facial piercings. To cap off the "Jane" look, she'd borrowed a pair of my jeans and my Converse.

If it weren't for the wings, we could have been sisters.

Are you sure it'll hide the wings? I asked the creature, who sent a warm wave of assent through me.

[So completely no one will be able to sense the glamour. You just have to explain to it what you need it to do.]

I stood up from the trestle table, and walked toward Magog.

"You look great," I told the raven before realizing how arrogant that sounded. "I mean, you look just like me. That's good. We'll only need to cover those wings and we'll fool 'em."

Magog nodded nervously. I wondered why she was so antsy till she asked her next question.

"And you're sure I can give it back?" she said, her singsong Welsh accent prominent.

"Of course. I'm just asking it to let you carry it, and to lend you some power. That's all. It knows to come back to me when I call. Are you ready?"

The raven nodded, and I pulled the labrys.

It answered my summons, blazing forth in my hands as if it knew it was about to go on a mission. It probably did, actually, as it had become such a part of me.

Do I just talk to it? I asked the creature. Again, it seemed to nod in my mind. So I stared at the labrys, and I mentally explained what we wanted it to do, feeling like a bit of a tit.

I felt less like a tit, though, when it shimmered in my hands, reappearing in one of Magog's to our mutual surprise. It was eager to get this show on the road. A second later, while Magog was still looking down in shock at her new burden, the air shimmered around the raven.

When it cleared, I was standing there. A perfect simulacrum of me, down to the unique power signature I recognized as mine, now that it stood in front of me.

"Wow," I said as I blinked at myself for a few seconds.

"Weird," Gog said, walking up to his bedmate and love and peering down at her with an expression of curiosity mixed with a mild distaste I tried not to take personally.

"All right," Daniel said. "Let's move out. We've got a chopper ready to take us to the air base. From there we go to a British carrier, where we will meet with an Alfar contingent from the Great Island, to fill out our numbers. When we're close, we'll switch again to choppers. They'll take us to our goal. The Chinese government is expecting us, and is allied with us in this mission."

I grimaced, despite the fact that this should be good news. The truth was that the Chinese were with us only because they were so against supernaturals. Their government was very aware of the existence of the supes, and was determined to wipe them out. So they were more than happy to join with us in the destruction of the Red and the White, but for reasons I found more than distasteful.

"Are we ready?" Daniel asked. Magog nodded and Gog took her hand.

We all headed out to Anyan's massive backyard, which was now dwarfed by the presence of a massive military helicopter. Gog, Magog, and Daniel, all bent low to the ground, raced over to the open doors of the helicopter and climbed inside.

It had all happened so fast, I hadn't gotten to say good-bye to myself, or my labrys, before they were both high in the air and flying away.

CHAPTER FOURTEEN

I'd sort of hoped I'd be able to lean and loaf and invite my ease for the next twenty-four hours, but no such luck. While Magog traversed the globe, we kept a tight shield on Anyan's cabin. I also kept a lid on the labrys's power. For although it was so many miles away, I still had control, and we didn't want the Red or the White to know our exact whereabouts until we were ready to engage. That said, I knew at least one of them was close—it felt like a prickle at the back of my neck. I prayed it was the White, and that the Red had gone after the bigger (seeming) fish.

My dad, Grizzie, and Tracy had gone out with Amy and Daoud to run errands. We'd given them *lots* of errands, so that we could make battle plans without them around. They were actually turning out to be really helpful, but I knew they also worried. They'd had enough stress, especially with Tracy pregnant.

Nell and Trill were patrolling Nell's borders, to ensure the White didn't sneak up on us or send in any minions.

That left Ryu, Iris, Caleb, and me to figure out what to do with the White once we had him. So we sat down once again with Caleb's journal.

"You have to be kidding me," I said as I started to read the section he'd highlighted.

Caleb shook his head, his expression grim. I read it again, growing more horrified with every line. Finally, I resorted to reading it out loud, thinking maybe it wouldn't sound so bad. Trying to keep my voice measured, I read:

"This dragon seize and slay with skillful art
Within the sea, and wield with speed thy knife
With double edges hot and moist, and then,
His carcass having cleft in twain, lift out
The gall and bear away its blackened form
All heavy with the weight of earthy bile."

I tried to keep control of my temper as I looked up at Caleb. "What the hell is this? Are you kidding me?"

The satyr only shrugged. "It's what it says."

"We can't cleave Anyan in two! That's absurd."

"But he's not 'just' Anyan anymore, Jane. He's also the White. So it makes sense that he would need to be divided..."

"But not *physically*, Caleb. I can't hack Anyan into pieces, like the Sunday roast." My voice was more than a little hysterical.

"It's not all that bad," he said. "Keep reading."

So I did:

"Great clouds of steaming mist ascend therefrom
And these become on rising dense enough

To bear away the dragon from the sea
And lift him upward to a station warm,
The moisture of the air his lightened shape
And form sustaining; be most careful then
All burning of his substance to avoid
And change its nature to a stream divine."

Caleb visibly flinched when I glared at him again.
"How is this better? It still says we have to chop him in
half."

"Well, we don't have to burn anything this time, like
we did the bones," Iris said, trying to be helpful. I shot
her a look that made her eyes widen. I turned back to the
poem.

"With quenching draughts; then pour the mercury
Into a gaping urn and when its stream
Of sacred fluid stops to flow, then wash
Away with care the blackened dross of earth."

I groaned. "Great, so we need mercury, too? Isn't mercury poison?"

Caleb shook his head. "It's a metaphor. Our good man,
C.A. Browne, writes of these passages, 'The union of
copper and silver is referred to by Theophrastus as taking
place within the sea, the latter being a common term for
the liquid metal mercury.'"

"Oh. So more water, then," I said, only slightly molli-
fied. I was nowhere near "over" the idea we'd have to hack
up Anyan.

Although now it was starting to make sense why the
champion's weapon was a labrys, of all things...

I refused to entertain such thoughts, at least not yet, and instead kept reading:

> *"Thus having brightened what the darkness hid*
> *Within the dragon's entrails thou wilt bring*
> *A mystery unspeakable to light;*
> *For it will shine exceeding bright and clear,*
> *And, being tinged a perfect white throughout,*
> *Will be revealed with wondrous brilliancy,*
> *Its blackness having all been changed to white;*
> *For when the cloud-sent water flows thereon*
> *It cleanses every dark and earthy stain."*

I stopped reading and looked up at Caleb for help.

"That sounds positive?" Iris said. "Except for the entrails. But the rest sounds good. We want cleansing, right?"

Ryu had been suspiciously quiet throughout this whole exchange, but at Iris's words, he cracked a smile. I didn't think it was very amusing, especially the use of the word "entrails."

Seeing the stormy look on my face, Ryu suppressed his amusement before speaking. "I think this is where the stone is going to come in. There's something revealed here that is white, and cleansed of the stain. I think that's what the stone is going to do . . ."

"Clean the stain?" I asked, trying to keep my voice from sounding snarky. It wasn't Caleb's fault that ancient prophecies sucked in terms of clarity but excelled in being exceptionally scary.

"Read the last bit," Caleb said, his sonorous voice

almost soothing but not, considering the circumstances. But I did as he said.

> *"Thus he doth easily release himself*
> *By drinking nectar, though completely dead;*
> *He poureth out to mortals all his wealth*
> *And by his help the Earth-born are sustained*
> *Abundantly in life, when they have found*
> *The wondrous mystery, which, being fixed*
> *Will turn to silver, dazzling bright in kind,*
> *A metal having naught of earthy taint,*
> *So brilliant, clear and wonderfully white."*

We all sat, contemplating the last lines, before I spoke. My voice was crackling with emotion when I did—strained and high-pitched one minute, husky and low the next. I didn't know whether to laugh, scream, or cry at this point.

"Caleb, no offense, but this makes no sense. This has to be wrong, or something. It tells us nothing."

Finally, Ryu spoke. Looking at me with compassion in his eyes, but a hard expression on his face, he laid it all out.

"No, Jane. It's quite clear. We've got to capture the White, surround him with water to weaken him, and then you need to cut him in half. Then we have to sluice him with more water, and hope for the best. That's what the poem says, in quite clear English. Well, ancient Greek, translated into English."

Ryu stopped talking, and I continued to stare at him, looking like a fish gasping for air.

"You're crazy," I insisted, not wanting to acknowledge he was right. "I can't cut him in half."

"You're going to have to. To kill the White, you're going to have to cut the dragon in half."

"But what about Anyan? I can't..." My voice trailed off. I couldn't kill Anyan. I couldn't.

"Will you give us a minute?" Ryu asked. The others obeyed, Iris shooting a concerned glance at me as she filed out of the cabin with Caleb. When we were alone, Ryu leaned over the table, placing his hands palms down to rest his weight on them.

"Jane, you have to do this," he said.

"We don't even know if the poem is real!" I shouted, belatedly turning down the volume of my voice. "We don't even know if we can trust it."

"No, we don't. But you saw that monk glow, and Grizzie. You heard the universe speak through them. We have nothing else to go on. And time is running out."

"What do you mean, 'time is running out'?" I babbled. "That's ridiculous. How is time running out? We have plenty of—"

"No, Jane. Pretty soon the Red and the White are going to start coming after people. Our people. The only reason they haven't already is probably because the White's not at full strength and we've been a worry to them with our activities. But that won't be an issue for long," Ryu said grimly.

"Anyan will keep the White busy. While we find another—"

"Jane," Ryu interrupted. "You said yourself that Anyan's fading."

"But he's not fad*ed*," I said, almost whimpering.

"Do you think he wants to live like this? And what happens when the White does take control? When they start killing innocents, with Anyan trapped inside that thing?"

I looked down at my own hands, which clenched into fists in my lap.

"Think it through, Jane. I know you love Anyan. He knows you love him. The gods know none of us wants to lose him. Even *I* don't want to lose him. But this isn't just about us anymore."

I looked up at Ryu, and felt hot, wet tears coursing down my cheeks.

"You would say that, wouldn't you? You've always hated Anyan, and now you hate him even more because we're together. Don't tell me you're being all 'save the world.' You just want Anyan gone . . ."

It was a low blow, and unfair, and I regretted it even as I said it. But I regretted it even more at the look Ryu gave me. It was cold, but also full of pity. Like he kinda wanted to smack me, but knew just what a wretch I was at that moment. I didn't like being either person—the girl who said such hateful things or the one who deserved pity.

So I took it back, or at least tried to, since we can never really take back what's already been said.

"I'm sorry, Ryu. That was uncalled for."

"Forget it. I know you're stressed. But you need to know I'm right. This is the only hope we've got, and we have no reason to think the universe is steering us wrong."

Tears blurred my eyes again, and I looked back down at my lap. But Ryu kept talking, although his voice was gentler.

"We have to stop the White, and this is how we do it. The first part of the poem worked—we made the stone. And look at Gus. He walked into that fire, and there he was, good as new when it was all over.

"Plus, Anyan *is* running out of time. We all know it. And he'd rather be dead than be that thing. Anyan and I may have been rivals in the past, yes. But I also respect him, and I know him well enough to know he wouldn't want any of this. None of us would."

The tears kept falling, but I knew Ryu was right. Anyan was losing his battle, and he'd rather be dead than a shadow in the mind of the White for all eternity.

"But why do I have to do it?" I said, my voice breaking on an ugly sob.

"Because life sucks," Ryu said, moving to my side of the table and squatting down to take both my hands in his. "But we'll all be right there with you, if it helps."

I looked at Ryu through the tears and nodded. "It does. Not much. But it does."

"Good. And I do think this will work. I didn't want to believe that was really the universe, speaking through Grizzie or the monk. The whole thing seemed ridiculous. I was convinced you'd do some weird chant for three days, and at the end of that time we'd have a tired Jane and a pile of burned bones. Instead we got that stone. And whatever it is, it's powerful. We can all sense it."

We looked at the object in question, which was sitting on top of the refrigerator. It had seemed like a safe enough spot, considering it couldn't really be hidden since it beamed out so much power.

I hadn't really thought much about the stone, to be honest. And I hadn't thought about it the way Ryu had—as proof the monk's poem worked. But that's exactly what it was, and what Gus had done walking into that conflagration had seemed just as crazy and dangerous at the time as carving someone up.

I picked up my copy of the poem and read it over again as Ryu went to get Iris and Caleb. They filed in and sat down.

Then, with the creature's help, we came up with a bunch of strategies to get the White on the ground, and surrounded by water, so that I could carve him up like a turkey. We worked for hours, only taking a break when the others returned from their grocery-shopping trip. So as not to be recognized, they went to a supermarket an hour away, with a few coolers in the truck to pack up the frozen and perishable goods. Amy wasn't strong enough to glamour all three of them, but they needed to get out of the house. My shenanigans had made them all virtual prisoners, another thing I had to keep in mind.

This has to end, I admitted to myself finally. One way or another.

The next few hours were torture as we waited for the word to come that Magog and her team were in Chinese air space and near the target we'd chosen— an abandoned factory that the government claimed wasn't inhabited. Daniel had done quite a bit of negotiating to get the Chinese to agree to our use of their air space and their territory, and he'd been relieved when they'd acquiesced without too much of a fuss. We were, after all, bringing a dragon into their air space, but he claimed they understood the global threat the creature represented.

And speaking of global threats, there had also been

reports of the Red in that area, and we'd had a few sightings of our own—a glimpse of something large and white on the horizon, which disappeared as quickly as it appeared.

So we knew we wouldn't have long to wait once we threw off shields and made a fuss. That came the next day.

When we were given word that our troops in China were on the ground, Amy took my dad, Grizzie, and Tracy over to her house. They wouldn't return until we'd given them the all clear. When the civilians were gone, we made our way to my cove. That's where we'd decided to do battle with the White. It had years of protections on it to keep out wandering humans, and it didn't matter it wasn't that big. Because we were going out to the ocean.

We waited for Daniel's signal—a text message to Ryu. It was such an easy, everyday way to begin what could end up being the loss of my world, that I hardly noticed it when Ryu's phone sounded.

But then he nodded to me, and I knew it was time.

I commanded the labrys to light up, feeling it like a distant flame in my breast. At the exact same moment, the creature literally moved heaven and earth. A mirror cove to match mine sprang up across from where Iris, Ryu, Caleb, Nell, Trill, and I spread out across the beach.

We all had a role to play, but Nell and I were the real powers, so we stayed in front, while the others took their places behind a powerful shield.

The mirror cove rose slowly in front of us, the actual seabed rising at the creature's command. Water streamed off, leaving mud and all sorts of gasping fish and other sea creatures. Ryu, meanwhile, kept a careful eye on his phone, waiting for a report from our people in China.

I felt like time stood still when it finally rang. He listened for a few seconds, and then he nodded again at me.

"They're in position. The enemy is advancing...and it's the Red."

I sagged as relief flooded through me, but I had no time to gloat.

It was show time.

First, I called to the labrys. From across the ocean it answered and suddenly it was with me again. It blazed up first in welcome, but then it blazed up again, as if recognizing something else out there in the dusky evening sky.

If all went according to plan, at that same moment back in China, the Alfar who had met our team on the aircraft carrier would invoke a special charm they'd brought—a hugely powerful nullifier that would make them, and quite a bit of the surrounding area, "go dark." The Red would know she'd been had, but it wouldn't matter. She'd have to get all the way back here to find the White, and by then it should be too late.

It *would* be too late, dammit.

That's what I focused on as I looked at Nell. "You ready?"

The gnome nodded. I turned to my friends behind me. "Are you ready?"

They also nodded, although Iris's lips were white with fear. But she'd insisted on being part of this, and I wasn't about to tell her no. Not after what Morrigan's cronies had done to her. For as much as I was doing this to get Anyan back, at some point I'd also realized just how much this was going to hurt Morrigan and the other monster she had living inside her.

And that was going to feel good, not just to Iris.

"We're ready!" I called to the creature, although I could have just thought it. Fact is, it was fun to shout.

We were all so very, very ready.

CHAPTER FIFTEEN

It didn't take the White long to make his appearance.

I'd been pretty specific in Anyan's dream-hut, telling the barghest all about our plans—about going with an Alfar contingent to retrieve an important sacred object while my friends in Rockabill set up everything we'd need to complete a ritual that we were pretty sure would take care of the Red and the White for good.

Because they'd already seen the creature's powers of apparation, we wanted them to believe they couldn't take any chances. Just like the Red had changed my life with the flick of her tail, I made it sound like the second we managed to lay a hand on the object, the creature could have my crew back and completing the ritual before either of the dragons could blink.

Basically, we wanted them to believe they had to be in both places at once, to ensure the threat was mitigated. As I was supposed to be the "lure" for the Red, the more powerful dragon, we couldn't let the White know they'd been tricked till he'd landed in our trap.

So I stayed where I was, safe under one of Nell's powerful glamours. Her territory extended to the waterline, and I was well inside it, standing as I was in the real cove. The creature was also pouring power into Nell's defenses, so that the White would see nothing more than a few dinky supernaturals standing on a beach.

Easy picking for an ancient force of evil like him, right?

When he did glide in, he did so quite lazily. He wasn't expecting us to put up much of a fight, after all, what with the champion thousands of miles away.

The White landed on the sand of the new cove, as we'd wanted him to. The creature had used its power to make it look like a strange rocky bluff extending out into the sea.

But once its claws hit land, we were in motion.

I raced forward, plowing through Nell's glamour the second my feet hit the fake bluff, where the safety and shielding of the gnome's territory ended. In that instant, I raised the labrys, which ignited with an explosion of light that hit its target with staggering force. The White, not expecting an attack, tumbled onto its side even as we sprang the second part of the trap.

With an audible whooping sound, the fake cove retreated back into the sea, drenching the White and me both.

Step one, drown the dragon, was complete.

Step two took a massive amount of power both from me and the creature. First, I held down the White, gone powerless in its enemy element of water, as I voided that very element out of the area around it. Then the creature held the water at bay, but surrounding us.

Basically, we'd created a watery Thunderdome, in which I could battle the White, once and for all.

The dragon rose gamely to its feet, shaking off the water like a dog. In those few seconds, I swear I saw a hint of iron gray take over the emerald eyes of the White.

I'm getting you out, Anyan, I swore on everything I held sacred. *I am getting you out…*

In seconds, however, the beast's eyes were once again pure green, and full of murderous rage. It dried itself with a puff of its air magic, sparking with power.

"Now you die," it hissed, sounding much more like I would expect a dragon to sound than Morrigan had, as the Red. She'd sounded more like herself, but bigger and more dragony. This was pure dragon.

I reminded myself that was the point—what I was about to kill was the dragon, not Anyan. We had to kill the dragon part to get at Anyan, trapped inside. The fact was that seeing that glimpse of my lover had rekindled my fear as much as it had my hope. Yes, Anyan was in there. But was carving up that big body in front of me really the way to get him out? Or was I just going to kill both of them?

"I don't think so," I said, responding to the dragon threats even as I took a fighting stance.

And that's when it really hit me that I was about to fight a motherfucking dragon.

Before I could dwell on that fact, however, the beast was in motion. It blew a gust of that crazily strong wind from its belly, the air elementals version of the Red's blast of fire, even as it charged physically. I met the gust of wind with a blast of my own that streamed from the labrys and caught the White in mid-gallop. It hit it like it would a wall, roaring at me and trying to strain forward physically, before giving up and retreating a few steps.

We circled each other warily, undoubtedly a ridiculous picture. My tiny shape against that of a dragon the size of at least two elephants, maybe three.

[But you have me,] the creature reminded me, even as it took charge of my body.

Suddenly, I was flying through the air, Crouching Tiger style. The labrys blazed in front of me, and as I flew, I grew. No, I realized, I wasn't growing. My shadow was. And that's what engaged with the dragon.

On the ground, I swung, deflected, and snarled, while above me, my shadow self—but one made of pure power—beat the snot out of the dragon.

At least at first.

When I initially attacked, my first swing took the White by surprise, not least because it was watching the real me. It never saw the giant shadow fist until it was too late, and I'd blindsided it against one watery wall of our cage.

It recovered quickly, charging back at me. It stumbled before we could clash, however, one of its feet tangling with the others. My shadow self was on it a moment later, a fist of power coming at the dragon's vulnerable under-belly, then another, and another. The dragon wrenched itself free eventually, retreating to the far side of the cage.

Then it started fighting with itself.

That's the only way I can describe the odd little dance it was doing. The White's beautiful head—for it was beautiful, even if it was pure evil—whipped around in the air as its jaws snapped at nothing. Its feet scrabbled around as if some were trying to scratch itself, while others were trying to defend from the scratching.

Both the creature and I watched, dumbfounded, till the creature realized what was happening.

[Your Anyan. He fights.]

Of course he does, I thought, pride coloring my thoughts.

Then we were in action again, coming at the dragon with shadow fists and feet. It was taking quite a beating from us, but it seemed oblivious, trapped as it was in its own private battle.

Meanwhile, I was fighting with the creature. Unlike the first time it had used my body to fight, when I was a passive witness, this was more like team fighting. It took care of powering the shadow, and gave me tips, nudging my body here and there. But I was in charge—I was the one doing the hitting, weaving out of the way of the White's random tail lashings.

I was also paying close attention to the White's internal battle. Maybe Anyan could win, and we wouldn't have to perform this ghastly ritual? Maybe he could trap the White, and it would die when he did, of old age?

But that didn't happen. Instead, I saw the moment Anyan lost to the White with vivid clarity. One second those eyes flashed almost entirely gray, causing my heart to swell in my chest, and the next they were a pure emerald green. And then the dragon dove away from my attack, rising to its feet and visibly regrouping.

This time, when it charged, there was no Anyan present to stay its course.

He lost, I thought; that kernel of hope that had grown with the spread of gray through those eyes died then, and I knew. Not knew because everyone told me, but *knew*.

Anyan would rather die than live like this, and the White had to be destroyed. Either the ritual worked the way we wanted, and Anyan lived, or it only worked because it killed the White *and* Anyan. But either way, it had to be performed.

This time, I didn't pull my blows. I hadn't realized I was pulling blows until that moment, but I had been. I wondered why the creature had let me, but it probably wanted me to come to this realization on my own. I probably had to be in this one hundred percent for the ritual to work.

The first punch of my shadow fists that connected knocked the dragon to the ground. A second destroyed its jaw, and a third smashed down on the dragon's back, a horrendous crunching sound ripping through our watery cage.

It was easy, to be honest. Not least because we'd already beaten the White half-senseless while Anyan was doing battle with it internally. And it wasn't the Red, fully charged with two beings' power and will. It was divided, just as the creature and I had been, when I didn't want to hurt the White's hostage.

Undivided, I was not only powerful, but incredibly pissed at being forced to make the kinds of decisions that would have me carving up the man I loved like I was Jack the Ripper.

[You must use the ax, child. The shadow can't deal the final blow,] the creature said. And then it left me. Its power was still there, but I think it couldn't take part in these final actions.

It had to be me. Probably because it would hurt more. We like to think the universe cares, and it had told me itself that it does seek balance. But balance runs both ways, and the other side of caring is watching us squirm.

At that moment, the universe definitely wanted me to squirm.

I found myself racing forward, screaming like Mel

Gibson in *Braveheart*, holding the labrys aloft. Never letting myself think, the bane of action, I attacked. With a massive, two-handed, overhead swing, I went for the White's head.

And I fucking missed by a good foot.

Swearing like a sailor, I tried again, but I'd taken too long. The White had recovered enough from its wounds to lash out at me with those deadly claws, which no magic could heal.

I backpedaled furiously, actually pulled by the ax, which seemed to have come into its own. It pulled me left, right, weaving through the White's lashing front claws. Its spine must not have been healed yet, as its back claws stayed put, but I knew I had only minutes to finish this before it was back up and we were at it for round two.

"Fuck round two," I said with a snarl, as I used what I remembered of the creature's power to make a mini-shadow, just an extension of my hand that I used to bop it once again on the same place we'd whacked the White before. Its green eyes rolled back in its skull and its head hit the dirt.

Channeling Little Bunny Foo Foo, I struck again, only instead of a bop, I gave a lop. Totally running on pure adrenaline, I struck again and again and again, until the creature spoke in my mind.

[Er, Jane . . .]

I came to, panting like an overrun horse, and still in midswing. The ax landed with a sickening sound in the mass of blood and bone at my feet that had once been the White's head.

"Oh," I said out loud. Then, in my mind to the creature, *I guess I overdid it.*

Not bothering to reply, the creature's words urged me on. [Now you must work fast. I know that looks final, but its head will seek to reattach itself. We must complete the ritual.]

I couldn't help being skeptical that the head pudding I'd made could ever be repaired, until I actually saw one of the severed tendons wriggle under the white skin, seeking to attach itself to its other half. I shuddered, and turned to the body of the White.

"Um, where do I start?" I asked.

There was a mental shrug from the creature. [Wherever you like.]

I didn't bother to remind it that I didn't "like" any of this. Instead, I started hacking.

Needless to say, the process was gruesome. Within minutes, I was covered in blood. The White wouldn't actually die, of course, so its blood was pumping away until I cut out its heart, giving it a few whacks for good measure and throwing it to the side so it wouldn't repair itself and start geysering blood about again.

Meanwhile, I was scared shitless.

"I thought he'd be in here. Like an egg," I said to no one in particular as I kept hacking. I was commenting on the fact that no matter how much I hacked, Anyan didn't pop out like a stripper from a really inappropriate birthday cake. And that's sort of exactly what I'd hoped would happen.

[The ritual isn't complete,] the creature reminded me grimly. [The poem said the spirit would rise out of the entrails. We're not there yet.]

With an equally grim expression, I kept hacking. The bowels were the worst part, as you can imagine, and I went ahead and leaned over and puked at the smell.

I may have been the champion, but I'd missed picking up my champion's stomach.

"He's not in here," I whimpered when I was done with puking, and once again hacking away, my feelings of desperation growing. Maybe Anyan was hiding in the liver? It was a big liver, after all...

But no. Anyan wasn't anywhere. I hacked and hacked and hacked, till all that was left was a quivering mass of body parts, trying to reconnect themselves to each other. I'd discovered early on that I could heat the labrys to sort of cauterize the wounds as I made them, but it wasn't a perfect solution and the White was desperate to fix itself.

[Easy, Jane,] the creature interrupted, physically stopping me from cutting any more. I had gone a bit bonkers, hacking away as I was.

I made mincemeat, I thought, more than a little hysterical. Later, I'd realize I'd been in a state of shock from about the time the White landed. Since I wasn't a natural warrior, the creature had helped me repress my trauma, but it was coming out big time now. Not least because the results were not as I'd expected.

"I killed Anyan," I said, sounding perfectly calm but feeling like I was about to keel over and die. "I just hacked up my lover with an ax... How very serial killer of me."

[Jane, stop. The ritual isn't complete. Call the water.]

I blinked. I'd totally forgotten that last step, no small feat since our plan had just three—make the White land, hack it up, and then drench it again.

Feeling a spark of hope that I begrudged, so convinced was I that I'd just hacked up my lover for good, I called to the water. Just a single column that poured down, like a waterfall, to sluice over the bloody red ruin of the White.

"By drinking nectar, though completely dead," I said aloud, suddenly remembering the line from the poem. Completely dead, it had stated, not a little bit dead, or dead but for the living guy trapped in its belly. Completely dead.

Well, I've definitely made the White as completely dead as it's going to get, so here goes nothing...

The water hit the body with an audible hiss of energy. I straightened my spine, peering forward eagerly.

But nothing happened. So I called more water, drenching the remains. I remembered the poem calling water "liquid mercury," and that's what it looked like in the dim light of the moon shining through the ceiling of water above us.

Still, however, nothing happened. I kept pouring, and pouring, my heart growing heavier and heavier in my breast.

And then, finally, it happened. The pile of remains began to twitch. So hopeless was I, at that point, that I figured the White was just re-forming again. I contemplated letting it do so, so it could eat me and put me out of my misery, when something broke free from what had been the White.

It was a beautiful globe of silver-white light, gliding straight upward till it spun in the air like the purest of stars. It was so riveting that I almost missed seeing the pile begin heaving again.

Another blotch of color broke free from the pile of viscera, only this one was black, and more of a glob than a sphere. In fact, it was like a stain, rising eerily black against the already dark wall of water behind it.

It oozed up toward the sphere of white as if in thrall to it and then spread out beneath it, tendrils of it creeping away as if trying to escape before they were pulled back.

"What the hell?" I asked, even as the creature spoke in my mind.

[The stone, Jane. Now we need the stone.]

So I pulled the stone out of where I'd stashed it in my hoodie's zipped front pocket. Unsure of what to do, I held it aloft.

Power bloomed from the grayish-brown rock, and it seemed to focus on the dark stain. It responded sluggishly, unwillingly, trying to dart right or left. But it was like the stain was trapped between the white sphere and the stone, with the stone pulling and the sphere pushing. The stain crawled toward me, causing me to shiver as I watched its slow creep.

The stone kept pulling, my arm tingling with power as I held it, until with a last burst of energy it sucked the black stain into itself.

Then, so fast that I jumped, the white sphere came whizzing toward me. I nearly dropped the stone, catching it at the last second and clutching it to my chest, so that when the white sphere hit the stone, it also hit me with the strength of a truck.

I was knocked backward, my head smacking hard against my own watery walls. I blacked out for a split second, and when I came to, I dropped the stone with a yelp. It was molten hot, and my hand was badly burned. But I was too busy blearily staring down at the stone to notice either the pain, or the cool, tingling sensation of the creature healing my wounds.

For the baseball-sized stone had gone from a normal, grayish-brown rock to a brilliant silver sphere, winking in the moonlight.

[Jane, look up,] the creature said suddenly. [The White!]

I did as the creature said, and I looked at the pile of goop that had once been a dragon. From the evidence of the stone, it should have been completely dead—its stain contained, ironically, by its own power.

But the pile was still moving, and it took my recently concussed brain a second to figure out why that might be. Then I did.

"Anyan!" I shrieked like a banshee, scrabbling forward on bloody hands and knees to reach the corpse of my enemy.

CHAPTER SIXTEEN

The only thing grosser than creating a giant pile of eviscerated dragon parts is digging through said pile.

If I hadn't been covered in dragon innards, blood, and shit before, I certainly was then. But I didn't care. The pile was moving. The pile should not be moving. Ergo, I was gonna get to the bottom of that pile no matter how many intestines I had to fondle.

My heart was still located in my throat, where it had rocketed after first seeing the pile move. That said, it was slowly starting to creep downward, weighed down by not finding anything. Throwing chunks of dragon bits behind me like a mole rat in a digging frenzy, I wasn't seeing anything remotely barghestian.

Beginning to give up hope, I feared the quivering had been some magical death throes as the White's power exhausted itself fully. It was only at the urging of the creature that I kept digging...

But then I saw a hand—a fully formed, definitely human, hand. And a very familiar one at that.

The hand, however, wasn't moving.

With an undignified squawk I grabbed at the hand, a nightmare scenario of it coming away from the pile, severed neatly at the wrist, flashing through my brain. But when I grasped the fingers, they were warm, although that could have been from the hot dragon meat in which they'd been encased.

"I'm coming!" I shouted at the fingers. "Hold on!"

Even though it slowed me down considerably, I never let go of that hand, digging with only my one free arm. There was no way I was letting Anyan go. Not ever again.

So I kept digging, and pretty soon there was his arm. The creature reminded me I had magic at that point, and I nearly brained myself with the labrys. I was still human enough that, in a panic, I forgot I had mojo. But powered by my magic, I dug considerably faster.

Meanwhile, I felt the earth around me shifting. The creature was raising the mirror cove back to its original position. The water retreated above us until only the sweet shine of moonlight fell on my activities.

By that point, I had Anyan mostly dug out. I'd know that big body anywhere, but to anyone else he'd be well nigh unrecognizable, covered as he was with dragon effluvia.

But my friends never questioned as they ran forward, even little Nell crossing her own territory lines, something gnomes were absolutely loath to do, to help me dig out my lover.

If I hadn't appreciated them all before, I certainly did then. Covered in ichor, they never looked better to me.

Even fastidious Ryu helped, his white button-up quickly soaked with blood and worse.

Soon enough, with all hands on deck, we'd dug out Anyan. I tried to feel for a pulse as I held his hand, my fingers tracing up to his wrist.

Caleb knelt down beside us, and I felt that warm healing glow tingle up through my fingers as it spread through Anyan's body into my own.

I knew how mothers of newborns felt just then, when Anyan took his first strangled gasp of the night air, his naked body arching up in a strong spasm, then crashing to the earth. He took in another long breath, then another, until finally, after what felt like a century, his eyes blinked open once, twice, and then they stayed wide.

His beautiful, iron gray eyes, without a hint of that dreaded emerald green.

I was crying by that point, great blubbering sobs that sent both tears and snot running down my face. Considering what else my face was covered in, the snot was actually an improvement. My body, meanwhile, was literally paralyzed with a combination of joy, relief, and…I don't know. I can't explain what I felt at that moment. After a lifetime of huge things going wrong; after being in this same position so many years ago with Jason, whose eyes never opened…seeing Anyan alive just about broke me.

In a good way.

When he sat up and wrapped his filthy, sticky, shit-smelling arms around me, I sobbed again and held him right back. We must have been quite a sight, me sobbing and crying and him still half-conscious but trying to comfort me, despite looking like we'd all just murdered a family and bathed in their blood.

We kissed then, and despite the fact I probably got a mouth full of dragon poo, I had never experienced anything so wonderful.

Although I definitely planned on brushing my teeth when I got home.

Eventually, Caleb and I got Anyan to his feet. The barghest's long legs were flimsy as a colt's after his long stay wherever the hell he'd been stored by the White. I couldn't imagine how the dragon could be Anyan, but obviously not Anyan, but I guess that was the joy of magic. It defied logic.

When he was up, and supporting his own weight with only a little help from Caleb and me, he looked around at all of us.

"Thank you," was all he said. But his voice held enough emotion to power Hallmark for a good year and a half.

Everyone hemmed and hawed, glowing with their own happiness to see him. I let them bask in his thanks, while I basked in his stinky, dragon-goop-smelling warmth. Anything was better than him actually *being* a dragon.

Then we took a couple of stumbling steps forward, to help Anyan get his sea legs. I also pointed with my chin at the beautiful silver stone that I'd dropped a few feet away. The labrys had long since disappeared to wherever it got to when it wasn't needed, but I'd almost entirely forgotten the stone, natural champion that I was.

Ryu went to where it lay and grabbed it, eyeing it as he did so. He marveled at it before raising an eyebrow at me. I grinned at him. We'd done all right.

I felt a touch at my chin, and I turned my face over and up, to meet Anyan's eyes. He'd let go of Caleb, letting me support him fully. He gazed down into my eyes, a thousand emotions playing over his features.

His next words moved me more than anything I could ever have heard. They told me that everything was going to be okay—that he was still Anyan and that nothing had changed about what the two of us shared.

"Take me home," he said, his growling voice deliciously commanding. "Help me clean this shit off of me. It's like a goddamned episode of *True Blood*."

Iris rushed ahead of us, darting upstairs. I heard the water turn on in Anyan's big shower, and I blessed my friend's considerate succubus heart.

She ran down to help me get him up to his loft bedroom, no mean feat, and then she darted off without a word. But she did pause to take my hand and squeeze it, tears filling her lovely blue eyes. She was happy for us.

Hell, I was happy for us.

"Call my dad?" I said.

She nodded. "Of course."

Then Iris made her way downstairs and out the front door. I had no idea where everyone was going, since Anyan's was our base camp, but I didn't give a hoot at that point. Certainly not enough to risk this almost sacred privacy I finally had with Anyan. The real Anyan, and not a dream.

I gave him some alone time in the bathroom as I peeled out of my blood-soaked clothes. It took a ridiculously long time to do so, as it was like shedding a second skin. Then I had to figure out what to do with the sodden bundle of nastiness. Anywhere I set them would stain, so I finally just chucked my filthy clothes out of the back window and onto the lawn below.

I could burn them tomorrow.

When I tapped on the bathroom door, I heard a muffled "Come in" from the shower. Anyan was already under the showerhead, leaning against the wall as he let the water sluice off the first layer of gunk.

Dragon shit and all, I'd never seen a more beautiful sight.

Feeling ridiculously energized for someone who'd just fought a Titan, I paced forward toward the shower, practically purring. When I climbed in, the first thing I did was wrap myself around the barghest, just because I could.

I'd never take a hug from him for granted ever again.

He held me back, lowering his cheek to rest it on the top of my head. We stayed like that for a long time, the water running red beneath us as it slowly made us clean.

"I missed you so much," I finally managed to choke out around the knot in my throat.

"I missed you, too. And I'm so proud of you."

I raised misty black eyes to his iron gray. "I've never been so scared as when I hacked you up."

He chuckled. "It wasn't me. It was the White. You freed me."

I shuddered with relief. I'd been so afraid that he'd been aware of the whole thing, from the first ax blow to the last.

"Where were you?" I asked.

He shrugged. "Who knows? I was in there, but as you saw me. Trapped somewhere, in that space I built the hut. I figured it was just my mind, but I guess it was all of me somehow."

"Was it horrible?"

"Not too bad. Not after you found me, at least." His voice was scratchy. I think it had been that bad, although he'd not admit it yet while I was still so shaken up.

I made an inarticulate noise, then reached up my right
hand to try to rub some of the blood off his face. He
caught my hand, kissing my knuckles.

"I love you," he said. My heart swelled and broke, then
swelled and broke again. The barghest was going to be
the death of me at this rate.

"I love you, too," I said. "Now let's get you clean..."

The first round of shampooing and soaping was not at
all sexy, believe you me. Anyan had bits of dragon stuck
in the unlikeliest places, and it took both of us to clean
him off. I wasn't much better, although the fact I'd been
clothed helped. We had to clean out the drain twice, since
it looked like someone had tried to make stew in it, and I
had to be careful to help Anyan keep his feet underneath
him. He was still weak, and would probably be so for
another day or two, even with some supernatural healing
help.

The second round of soaping was a lot nicer, however.
The major cleaning was done...this round was just about
being thorough. And perhaps also about being able to
touch each other for real after so very long.

I did spend an awfully long time gliding the soap over
Anyan's long arms, loving the feel of his biceps under my
hands, and the soft hair on his forearms. His chest needed
quite a bit of attention, obviously, especially those ten-
der nipples. That I kept licking them just meant I had to
soap him up again, and then they were so clean they just
begged to be licked when he'd washed off the soap...

And it wouldn't have been fair just to clean his top half.
Those lovely long legs needed attending to. Moving up
from Anyan's calves to his muscular thighs, I soaped him
to a fine polish. And that brought my face so perilously

close to the other part of Anyan that begged to be tasted. Of course, I couldn't resist, even if taking him in my mouth was risky since he was already a bit unsteady on his feet. Even with the help of the wall propping him up, his hands were soon in my hair, pulling me roughly away. Another gentle tug let me know he wanted me on my feet, so I obliged.

"I can't stay upright. At least not on my legs anyway," Anyan said with a chuckle, kissing my mouth hungrily even as he wobbled.

I rubbed my belly against that part of him that was having no problem keeping erect, sucking on the moan he emitted, then his bottom lip for good measure.

"Let's get you to bed, then," I said, pulling away and turning off the shower. "Although I fully intend to take advantage of your current weakness."

He chuckled, using my shoulder for support as he followed me out of the shower. "Finally get your chance at dominance, eh?"

"I'm a dragon slayer, and don't you forget it," I reminded him as I swept my long black hair up into a towel then began vigorously drying him off with another. By the time I was done with the barghest, I'd shaken most of the water off myself and only needed a few passes with another of the clean, dry towels that Iris had set out for us.

Then I led him back into his own bedroom, as if he were the visitor, and laid him on the bed. He watched as I pulled the towel off my hair, scrubbing at it vigorously for a few minutes, then pulling my fingers through it so it was only slightly crazy looking, rather than full-on Mad Shrubbery style.

But there was no way in hell I was spending another

second of my time on my toilette, not with Anyan lying naked in front of me.

I threw the towel on the ground and crawled onto the end of the bed, starting with Anyan's toes. Each little piglet got a kiss, then my hands swept up his calves, carrying me with them. I scissored his legs apart so I could kneel between his thighs, my mouth returning to that heavy, hard cock.

"Gods, Jane," Anyan moaned, his hands knotting in my already snarled hair. Within seconds of my lips on him, he was chanting my name, and other deliciously filthy expletives, until he came. I swallowed him down, keeping my mouth on him until he pulled me up by the hair so he could kiss me. He never lost his erection, though, and after a short, hard kiss, he sat up just enough to manhandle me into position.

Then he pulled my hips down hard, and I saw stars as he shoved into me. I moaned, hugging him to me, his face buried in my breasts as I pushed myself down on him, forcing myself down, down, stretching around his thick length.

He groaned the whole time, and then I pushed him back, hard, onto the pillows, and rode him like a cowgirl.

I wish I could say we held each other and whispered sweet nothings while making gentle, decorous love. But it wasn't like that at all. It was hard and rough, and it was exactly what I needed. I needed to know that he was there inside me, under me, all around me, and that he wasn't going anywhere. He was mine, goddamnit, and no ancient force of evil could change that.

So I fucked him, surprising both of us with my vehemence. Not that Anyan was complaining—not at the bite marks I left on his neck, or the scratches down his arms and chest, or the filthy things I whispered into his ear. He was mine, and I told him so, and I think he liked it.

At least he seemed to like it as he writhed beneath me, trying to touch me, to bring me off, but allowing me to pin his wrists to the bed despite the fact he could have taken control at any time he wished.

It was only when I knew he was nearly at the brink that I let him touch me. His fingers found my nipples, pinching with delicious cruelty that made me gasp. Then he pulled me down so he could suckle the sting away as his thumb found my clit to swirl gently, shatteringly, around the center of my pleasure.

I gasped, thinking how much better this was than a dream, even if the dreams had been pretty good. Nothing could be like this, with my real Anyan underneath me, with his powerful body at my command.

And his power. I'd forgotten about his power.

But I remembered then, when I felt a cool brush like two heavy hands roaming down my back. As one of Anyan's real hands held my hip so he could ram up into me, his other real hand was busy frigging me into oblivion. But those hands of power that he could conjure up, those were busy stroking my back, pulling my hair just the way I liked, kneading my backside.

I knew I was a goner when those hands parted my cheeks, stroking that most intimate place. When I felt an invisible finger of power push inside me, then another, stroking in and out in a dizzying rhythm that matched the thrusts of Anyan's cock, I was done.

I came, screaming his name, and maybe offering to have ten million of Anyan's babies and/or gift him with a kidney, should he ever need one.

Anyan's own orgasm broke seconds after mine, and the part of me that could still think over the buzzing of my brain thought yes, yes, yes, yes, yes...a universal affirmation of the fact I loved this man, more than I'd ever loved anything, and that he was here with me now, and he was safe and whole, and we were fucking.

If that wasn't a moment of triumph after the shit show that had been my life for the past few weeks, I don't know what was.

We didn't move for quite a while after we'd finished. I just lay there on top of him, his heavy arms wrapped around me, my hands twined in his hair.

It was only when Anyan started snoring that I realized he was dead asleep. I clambered ungracefully off him.

I covered him up and went to the bathroom to clean myself up a bit. And when I returned, I sat in the darkness, holding Anyan's hand and watching his chest rise and fall, till exhaustion swept me away, too.

That night I dreamed of Anyan, but it was only a dream. And the real man was there, still with me in bed, upon waking.

CHAPTER SEVENTEEN

It took me a while to drag myself from Anyan's side. I'd awoken about an hour earlier, and crept over to use the bathroom and freshen up. But despite every intention of heading downstairs for some much-needed coffee and breakfast, I ended up back in bed, staring at the barghest with what were probably enormous seal eyes.

Who needed breakfast when the man in front of you was good enough to eat?

Part of me just couldn't get over the fact that my lover was here, and safe, and no longer trapped inside a homicidal dragon. I also couldn't believe I'd rid the world of said dragon. There had once been a scourge on humans and supernaturals alike, free to roam the world, and I— Jane True!—had killed it.

Granted, I would probably have nightmares about the killing part for the next few decades, but I knew it was all for a worthy cause. All that life lost over the centuries, and I was the one to take away that threat.

In other words, for the first time in, well, ever, I felt like what I was supposed to be—a champion.

And here's my prize, I thought smugly, leaning over to kiss Anyan gently on the cheek. He didn't even twitch, his heavy breathing continuing unchanged. The barghest was exhausted.

Eventually, my grumbling tummy wrestled control from my puppy love, and I got up from the bed again. I put on clothes—yoga pants and one of Anyan's T-shirts— then headed downstairs.

My steps were light as air as I descended, and for a second I imagined myself tripping lightly downward like Cinderella, my steps buoyed by the help of singing birds. I giggled at the thought.

But all giggling ceased when I saw what awaited me.

I'd thought Anyan and I were alone in his cabin, as there wasn't a peep from downstairs. I was wrong, however. Ryu sat with his chin in his hands on Anyan's big, overstuffed chair and a half. Iris was cuddled against Caleb on the sofa, both looking utterly dejected. I noticed the gwyllion had returned, although Daoud didn't appear to have come with him. Even Hiral, whose skin was blue already, looked decidedly bluer. Tracy and Grizzie were sitting at the kitchen table, Tracy with her hands on her stomach as if holding on for dear life, Grizzie watching her worriedly.

No one had made any coffee.

"Um, what's up, guys? Y'all look like someone died."

I immediately regretted my choice of words when Ryu informed me that, yes, someone had died. A lot of someones.

I sat down on the bottom stair, where I'd stopped upon

seeing everyone looking so depressed. Luckily I hadn't gotten any farther into the room, as my legs weren't up for carrying me anywhere.

"All of them?" I said, my voice strangely calm.

"All of them." Ryu's reply was patient, if distant.

It still took me a second for my brain to catch up. "Gog, Magog, and Daniel? All dead?"

"Yes. Their helicopters were destroyed."

"But I thought the Red—"

"Not by the Red. By the Chinese."

"What?"

Ryu got up and strode into Anyan's kitchen, where he started making coffee. I think he just needed something to keep his hands busy so he wouldn't choke anyone.

"We already told you how the Chinese feel about supernaturals. They took the opportunity to rid the world of what they consider a scourge—a few supes and the humans who supported them."

I watched Ryu dump in water and coffee grounds, trying to figure out which question to ask first.

"But I thought they had that glamour..."

"It blocked magical probes and regular eyesight. Not heat-seeking missiles working on human technologies." Ryu's answer was blunt. So was the way he slammed down the mugs he pulled from the dishwasher.

"So why did we work with the Chinese at all? If they were going to—"

"Because they weren't 'going to,'" Ryu said, his voice gone sharp with anger. "They had reached out to Daniel's government in the beginning, telling them that they knew the dangers of the dragons and would help in any way they could. They promised to lend their support, to fight a greater evil. Asking them for help seemed obvious. Faraway location, lots of military support if we needed it, no explanations necessary as to why we needed the airspace. Daniel and his people thought it was the perfect answer. So did I."

Ryu gazed out the kitchen window as the coffeemaker burbled and dripped, its brew scenting the air with far too homey and peaceable a smell for the conversation we were currently having.

I finally felt my legs could hold me enough to make it into the kitchen. I flopped down into one of the available kitchen chairs, and both Grizzie and Tracy reached out a hand. I took theirs, squeezing them lightly, before getting back to Ryu.

"But how could they blow Daniel up, too? He worked for the British government. And did they blow up all the helicopters?"

"Yes. There were only three. And we know Daniel worked for the British, but there'll be no trace of him anywhere. He's probably on the books as some sort of tax collector or claims adjuster or something. Maybe a meter maid. The unit he worked for didn't technically exist, so how could he exist within it?"

"So they can just blow up three helicopters, killing how many people?"

Caleb answered that question, his rumbling voice deep with grief. I think he'd spent a fair amount of time with Gog and Magog, picking their brains about life overseas.

"Sixteen, total," he said. "Nine supernaturals, including the three Alfar in each of the other choppers, and then the one with Gog and Magog. And seven humans, including the pilots and copilots, and Daniel."

"Fuck," was my only response, but my grief ran a lot deeper than that. Losing Blondie had felt—still felt—like a knife in my heart. But she'd been killed by her greatest foe. I would never be okay with her death, but it made sense.

But to get randomly blown up by a supposed ally when the danger was over?

I couldn't wrap my brain around the fact I'd never see Gog and Magog again, or Daniel. They hadn't been in my life long, but we'd been through some heavy shit together.

If my reaction to the news of our friends' death was to slide downward, inside myself, Ryu's response was to slam down more coffee mugs on Anyan's granite counters. I didn't tell him to take it easy, for fear one of those mugs would find itself winged at my head. I don't think I've ever seen the baobhan sith so angry, ever.

Numbly, I watched as he poured coffee, and then I helped him pass the mugs about. I even brought Tracy a glass of orange juice, since she couldn't have coffee, and brought everyone else sugar and milk, letting things cool down before I began another barrage of questions. I also knew I had about twenty minutes, tops, till it sank in that the people I'd called friends for such a short time were dead, and I had a meltdown.

"Seriously, how can they get away with this?" I asked once everyone had had a few sips.

Ryu's voice was back to normal when he spoke again, although his hazel eyes were still blazing. "Any number of ways, Jane. They'll blame the attack on us. They'll say that the helicopters were full not of supernaturals, who aren't supposed to exist, but of Western spies. The British government will say that's ridiculous, but won't do anything about it. Somewhere there'll be a few closed-coffin funerals, and end of story."

"But why won't Britain do something? They were citizens—"

"Who were in Chinese airspace, with no formal clearance since everything was done under the table. If Britain really pushes this, all the Chinese have to say was that they never had permission, the helicopters were obviously full of spies, and they deserved to be shot down as they were in armed military helicopters in Chinese territory, unannounced."

Under normal circumstances, I would have said something like "tuckerdoodles." But these weren't normal circumstances. These circumstances sucked. So I stayed quiet. We all did. Except Ryu, whose calm had only been temporary.

"Damn them!" he shouted suddenly, throwing his mug at the sink. Coffee went everywhere as it broke, spectacularly and loudly. He got up and strode to the sink, leaning over it, his breathing heavy with suppressed emotion. I listened for any movement from upstairs, but Ryu's temper tantrum didn't seem to have awakened the barghest.

"What's going on, Ryu?" I asked, trying to make my voice soothing. But I stayed where I was in case he wanted to throw anything else.

"Damn the Red and the White. This is exactly what they wanted. The fucking humans will start killing us, and there will be nothing we can do."

I blinked, surprised at the outburst. I'd always known Ryu held a modicum of contempt for humans—they were his dinner, after all. But I'd never heard him express anything so bitter. Then again, under the circumstances... and Ryu hadn't even been that close to Gog and Magog.

He'd barely known them. He hadn't known how in love they were…

I choked down a wave of grief, and concentrated on Ryu.

It was the idea of what had happened that rankled him.

So instead of asking what he meant by "the fucking humans," I tried to put myself in his shoes. Out loud.

"Let me get this straight," I said. "You're mad at the Red and the White for exposing us, correct?"

Ryu straightened up, giving me his patented "No shit, Sherlock" look.

"And you think that this attack by the Chinese is only the beginning?"

Tracy and Grizzie had begun looking distinctly uncomfortable the minute Ryu started throwing things and blaming humans, and I didn't blame them. After all, Ryu could annihilate any trace of them with the snap of his magic-riddled fingers.

And that was the problem.

"They fear us, Jane," was Ryu's response, as if echoing my own thoughts. "And they have every right."

"The baobhan sith is right," Hiral said, his long nose twitching. "The humans'll be after us if we're not careful."

"But you guys *are* humans. Or were. Whichever." We'd learned the truth about the supernatural origins from the creature right before I'd become the champion. I'd been fighting Phaedra in the creature's underground lair, and it had beamed out the truth into our minds, and most of the minds in the surrounding area. The supernaturals were really a type of mutated human, who—unlike "normal" humans—could do things with the elemental power that was all around them.

"Do you really think that matters?" Hiral asked, his beady eyes staring into mine.

I wished I could respond that it wouldn't matter. That humans would be better than they were, and see that we were really all the same, but I couldn't. I knew my people—on both sides—too well. And the humans were no better than the supernaturals, and vice versa.

The truth was that supernaturals were scary. They were the things that went bump in the night, and could easily bump you off in the night. They were terrifying—some even looked terrifying, and even the ones that looked totally human, like Ryu, had powers that any individual human could only dream of, probably in a nightmare.

That wasn't the whole story, however. Yes, one-on-one humans were no match for their supernatural counterparts. But humans and supernaturals wouldn't have to be one-on-one if it ever came down to a real race war. Humans outnumbered the supes at least thousands to one, maybe even more than that. And they had big guns, and missiles, and tanks. Yeah, a powerful Alfar could probably last awhile, maybe days, against a thousand humans, all armed to the teeth. But what if they caught someone like Trill, my sweet kelpie friend, on land? She'd be a goner, unless she was in the water, where she was strong. Iris wouldn't last seconds against ten humans, let alone thousands. Even someone really strong, like Ryu, wouldn't survive an all-out, sustained attack.

In a race war, the supes would lose. But they'd do a lot of damage before they died.

Then the other shoe dropped.

"And she has nothing to lose. A war is what she wants."

My voice was a low breath that barely carried. But everyone heard it. "Does she know yet?" Everyone knew what I meant.

"We think she does," Caleb said from where he sat on the couch. With some clomps and shuffling of fabric, he and Iris extricated themselves and came toward the table. They both took seats at the free end of the trestle benches.

"Before they were shot down," the satyr continued, "Daniel was reporting. The Red was furious they'd disappeared, and was trying to find some way to get them to show themselves; figure out where they'd got to. But then he reported she just stopped. Went dead in the air, even started to collapse toward the earth. Then she screamed. We could hear it, even over the sound of the chopper. It sounded...heartbroken."

"So she knows," I clarified. The Red must have felt the White's death.

The others all silently nodded in agreement.

"And now she's got nothing to lose. She's lost her White, and she's not going to stop at anything to get revenge," Hiral said.

"More than that," Tracy said, before casting an apprehensive glance at Ryu as if she were worried he'd throw his mug at the human for talking. When he didn't budge, she continued. "Even more than that, she knows you've got the power to destroy them. So she's lost her partner, yes, but she's also lost her immortality."

"Oh, snap," Grizzie said lightly and inappropriately. We all stared at her for a second, and she shrugged an apology before pointing at her wife's bulging stomach. "Sympathy hormones."

"If I were the Red," I said, thinking about how I'd

felt when I'd lost Anyan, "I'd want the biggest, baddest revenge possible, as soon as possible. And what better way to do that than to have us kill each other?"

"She's going to show herself again, and soon." Ryu's voice was grim, and he avoided looking at Tracy and Grizzie.

Sitting in the grim atmosphere of the kitchen, I was glad Anyan was still upstairs sleeping. He deserved a tiny amount of time away from all of this worry before it slapped him right upside the head.

And we had some friends to grieve.

Having hashed out our situation with the Red as much as we could at that point, we spent the next hour reminiscing about Gog, Magog, and Daniel. I told the others about our time in Britain, and we talked about how they'd helped us here in Rockabill. The sad thing was none of us really knew much about them, except Hiral, but he had some funny stories to tell about them.

It was only after a good hour that I'd realized we were missing someone. I'd been so wrapped up in our mutual doom and gloom, I hadn't noticed we were short one person.

"Hey, where's my dad?"

"Out in the workshop," Iris answered. He'd made Anyan's workshop into his personal Man Cave, to get away from all the bustle in the house.

"Does he know?" I asked.

The succubus shook her fair head. To be honest, I was glad he hadn't heard all of what we'd just said. He was rolling with everything really well, but there was no point in scaring the crap out of him.

"I'm going to take him some coffee," I said. "Clear

my head." Then I remembered my dad's coffee addiction. "Wait, can he have some?" I asked my human friends.

Grizzie laughed and Tracy smiled. "Yes, he can have some," the latter said. "But only one cup a day, that's his maximum. Or he turns into a crackhead."

I sighed, filling my dad his one mug of coffee and adding a splash of milk, the way he liked it. I took it out to the barn, smiling at the sight of him napping in his old recliner. They must have smuggled it out of our house somehow, and bought him a smart new flat screen. Good thing, too, because if he didn't see his soaps, he got quite cranky.

I crept in, not wanting to wake him, and set his mug down on the work stool he'd pulled up next to his recliner. Then I reached for the remote that was sitting on his knee, swiveling around to turn the television off.

My finger froze on the button. Those weren't soaps.

My dad had fallen asleep watching the news. Greeting me that morning was live coverage of London, under attack by a monster out of a horror film: a great red dragon.

Swiftly, I ran back to the house to get the others.

It had begun.

CHAPTER EIGHTEEN

"Guys!" I called, flinging open Anyan's front door. "Guys!"

The panic in my voice was obvious, and everyone reacted accordingly.

"What's up?" Ryu asked as I ran past him to turn on Anyan's big flat-screen television.

I didn't reply, instead hitting a few buttons to turn on one of our local networks. As I'd assumed, all of the world was watching the Red's attack on London, including Maine's news networks.

"...there doesn't seem to be any rhyme or reason behind these attacks," droned an anchorwoman's voice, commenting on what appeared to be footage from someone's cell phone. "As stated earlier, they began around dawn, with the creature attacking Westminster, and then St. Paul's Cathedral." The fuzzy footage cut to a few pictures of Big Ben, lying across the split roof of the British Parliament building.

Ryu sat down next to me, and then Iris and Caleb joined us on Anyan's massive sofa. Hiral was standing, clearly shocked, in front of the television. The Great Island was his home, after all.

"Since this morning, the creature has been sighted all over London, attacking sites indiscriminately. Emergency crews are active throughout the city, and the military has been called in. The death toll has been reported at anywhere between twenty-eight and a few hundred, with reports of injuries coming in from all over..."

The anchor kept talking as more photos were shown: wounded people being attended to by paramedics; buildings flattened or burning; other bystanders, unhurt, reacting to the sight of the Red.

Sounds came from behind me, a soft, choked grunt. I turned to find Anyan, wearing sweatpants and his favorite Eukanuba T-shirt, watching the television. Hate and fear burned in his eyes, and I remembered that he'd been a prisoner for all that time, not a guest.

He also looked too thin and too weak, so I stood up and gestured for him to take my place. Then I forced on him a coffee after I'd popped a bagel in the toaster for his breakfast. He needed to regain his strength, and fast.

For this war was far from over.

The others kept watching the reports of carnage as I waited for the bagel to pop up, then smeared it liberally with full-fat cream cheese and took it to the barghest.

"Eat it, don't argue," I said, right before I picked up the remote and turned off the television.

"We've gotta move out," I said. "Ryu, resources?"

Without blinking an eyelash, Ryu told us we had access to his private jet. He'd already called to have it flown into Eastport, our neighboring town, from where it lived at the compound outside Montreal.

"Good," I said. "Daoud can stay with the girls and my dad. Iris? Caleb?"

"We're with you," the succubus said automatically. The satyr nodded his agreement.

"Ryu?"

"With you, of course."

"Hiral?"

The look the gwyllion flashed me was of pure rage. Obviously he was going with. That was his island the Red was attacking.

I then almost looked around for Gog and Magog, to ask them if they wanted to come, before I remembered. They'd never go on any more missions again. I choked down a wave of grief, adding my dead friends to the list of things I'd have to mourn later, when all of this was over.

I turned to the barghest, who was wolfing down his bagel after his first few tentative nibbles. He finished it off in about three bites as I contemplated him.

"Anyan..." I began, planning on telling him he might want to stay home, considering what he'd just been through.

"I'm going with you if I have to follow on foot," was all the barghest had to say after choking down his mouthful of food.

"Are you sure?"

"Yes. Can someone make me another bagel?"

I didn't point out that if he couldn't toast himself breakfast, he probably shouldn't be entering battle, because I'm a considerate girlfriend. I had to trust that between his own healing powers and those of good food and some rest, he'd be back to normal soon.

"All right. So that's our team. When we get to London,

we'll have to coordinate with the supes, and figure out how to reach out to the human government with Daniel gone. But Luke and Jack will know..."

My voice died as another sound overwhelmed the cabin. Choppers. And lots of them.

"What the fuck?" Anyan said as those sitting sprang to their feet.

We all moved to the big back doors of the cabin, watching in alarm as three enormous helicopters landed in Anyan's large backyard. They were sleek, black, and heavily armed. Not exactly a comforting sight.

"Grizzie, Tracy, you stay here. Amy, take them upstairs. As soon as you get a chance, I want you to get out of the house. Go to your house and wait there. Take my dad."

Once the girls were safely hidden upstairs, we walked out onto Anyan's deck, throwing up some powerful shields—both magical and physical—just in case the choppers opened fire. I noticed Hiral didn't appear to be with us, but I knew better. He'd used his powerful glamour to disappear—not out of cowardice, but on the off chance he could spy.

The whirling helicopter blades began to slow as men in black SWAT gear poured out of the choppers. They made a large circle around Anyan's big deck, keeping us securely in front of them.

But they never attacked; they just stood, watching. I saw my dad peeping at them through the windows of Anyan's workshop and I prayed he'd keep down until they left.

Finally, when the helicopter blades had all but stopped, three men emerged from the middle chopper. They were dressed like Men in Black: all black suits, black wrap-around shades, and shiny black shoes. They even sported earpieces. Two were fit and strong, both well over six feet. But the man between them was short, probably only about five-seven, and pudgy, with a bald pate ringed by a thickly curled hedge of human clown-hair.

He looked a bit like the clown on the Simpsons, only not at all funny.

"Jane True?" he called from where he stood. I nodded my head warily, amping up my shields just in case he was waiting for me to clarify who I was before he began shooting.

But he only smiled, showing off teeth far too small for his gums.

"It's a pleasure. May I come forward?"

"No." He blinked at my curt response. "Not until you tell us who you are."

"That's simple. My name is Trevor Martinez, and I work for your government,"

I couldn't help sighing. Just what we needed. Another superspy. I looked at Ryu, then looked at Anyan. They both shrugged their shoulders at me, equally confused. So I waved the little man forward.

The SWAT-looking guys stayed where they were; only Trevor and his goons came toward us. When he was closer, he pulled a badge out of his pocket, showing it to me. It said CIA.

"What do you want?" I asked, cutting to the chase.

He stopped smiling then. "We want you to come with us, ma'am."

A throb of power went through our combined shields, nudging Trevor and his goons back with an invisible shove. If they were surprised, they didn't let it show.

"And why would we do that?" My voice was calm, but my mind was reeling. Was I being arrested? Could champions be arrested? What would that mean for my dad? Was I going to have to turn fugitive?

"We just want to talk to you, ma'am. We've been keeping tabs on your people through our unit's shared operative, Daniel. But now that he's no longer part of this operation..."

"Because he's dead," I pointed out. I hated tiptoeing around things.

Trevor ignored me. "We needed to reinstate contact, what with Daniel out of the picture."

"I thought Daniel worked for the UK government," Anyan said from behind me. We all looked at Trevor accusingly.

"He was on the British payroll, yes. But he was part of a unit made up of operatives from across North America and Europe. We're a bit like Interpol, except we don't police humanity."

"You police supernaturals," I said. "So you want to replace Daniel?"

"As the closest member of our organization geographically, it makes sense that I would pick up Daniel's baton. But I also represent American interests in this matter, and you are an American. We wish to offer you our support if we can."

Everything about Trevor screamed honesty, sincerity. His eyes met mine in an unwavering gaze, and he oozed kindly, paternal authority.

I didn't trust him any farther than I could throw him.

"So why exactly do I need to go with you?" I asked. "Can't we make plans here?"

Trevor smiled. "We wish to offer you the full range of our services, Ms. True. We want you to see what we have available. We can also get you into Britain a lot faster than the jet you have coming in from Canada."

Ryu's eyes narrowed. He was undoubtedly displeased at seeing how much Trevor's people knew about what went on in our compound.

"We also want to be able to talk," Trevor added when the silence had stretched thin as dental floss. "We want to make you an offer…"

So that was it, I thought bitterly. They want a piece of the champion.

"Okay," I said curtly. "I'll go with you. But with all my people. And we leave now. I don't want any of you lingering."

I could text my dad as soon as I had the chance, make sure he and the girls had gotten out of there. They'd be safe and out of the way at Amy's, while we could always fight our way out of wherever Trevor and his people took us.

Trevor nodded, giving me that reassuring smile I wanted to wipe off his face. Then he gestured us forward. First I made sure that every single one of those soldiers got back on the choppers. Then we boarded, with his goons, on the middle chopper. After we'd climbed aboard, I texted my dad to stay put till we were gone, and then go with Amy and the girls. We'd be fine, I assured him. We were safe with our government.

The base Trevor took us to was sparse on the outside— just a cluster of low buildings, mostly hangars, around a central helipad, with an airstrip next door. But inside…

Ryu, Anyan, and Caleb were suitably impressed by

all the machines that go ping taking up the wall space, and the center areas had more machines doing all sorts of noisy, apparently complicated things. I was very happy to know that Hiral was our unseen companion. He was completely invisible, but I knew he was around because of occasional whispered commands from somewhere around my knees, such as "I'm coming with. Hold the door open," or "Scoot over, fat arse." I kept his presence a secret, as he obviously wanted. Meanwhile, I tried to look cool, like secret military bases were a dime a dozen in my experience. I'm pretty sure I failed at that.

At the base, Trevor walked in front of us, pointing out the functions of various people and things. It was all very technical and very important. And all perfectly useless when I thought about the fact the Red was actively attacking London even now. Part of me wanted the creature to apparate me straight there, to confront her. But I knew that was a bad idea on a number of levels. I couldn't waste the creature's power apparating me and my team, and it was stupid to face her alone. Even more stupid without a plan, and having ignored the promise of resources that Trevor offered.

Eventually, we were led into a good old-fashioned conference room and asked to take a seat. Trevor took the chair next to me, leaning forward as if we were the only ones in the room.

"I would have asked you to meet with me privately, Ms. True," he said. "But I know you would have refused."

Damn Skippy, I thought, but I didn't say anything. My silence was answer enough.

"I know these are some of your most trusted friends and advisors, so if you're comfortable, we can proceed as if alone."

I arched an eyebrow at him. What was he playing at?

"We've been aware of the legends of the Red and the White for a long time. And through them we were, of course, aware of the legend of the champion. But we were thrilled to discover that you'd been made that champion, Ms. True. May I call you Jane?"

I nodded, but I knew my eyes were squinting at Trevor. I didn't trust him, and it showed.

"Good. We had a lot of reasons to be thankful that you were chosen. Can you guess why?"

It didn't take a rocket scientist. "Because I'm American? And half-human?"

"Clever girl," Trevor said patronizingly. Anyan was watching our exchange with avid interest, partially because he could probably guess how close I was to beating the snot out of the CIA agent.

"You're one of us, Jane, and you've been given this wonderful gift." Trevor's voice was hushed now, as if revealing the secrets of Capone's tomb. His eyes were limpid with emotion. I could hear an imaginary orchestra playing "The Star-Spangled Banner" in the background.

I considered puking on Trevor's shoes.

"Maybe," I said instead. "But that would probably depend on how you defined 'us.' "

"I mean your interests are our interests, Jane. You want to stop the Red, as you did the White," he said, nodding at Anyan.

"Yes, which reminds me, the Red is sort of destroying an entire city . . ."

"And we'll get you there shortly. I promise. But I want to make sure you're aware just how important you are. How much we value you."

My already narrowed eyes narrowed further. "You mean because I can fight the Red."

"Of course!" Trevor beamed, laughing heartily as if we were all in on some great joke. "You must destroy the Red. That's our first priority—"

"That's *the* priority," I interrupted.

"Er, yes. The priority. But after that's over…"

Trevor made a gesture in which he first narrowed his hands, palms together, then widened them out, lifting his palms to the heavens as he did so. He was indicating, I think, that the sky was the limit.

"After that's over, we can…pray?" I asked, feigning confusion. I knew what Trevor wanted from me, but he had to say it to get a reaction.

"No, Jane. After the Red's defeated, we can think together how best to use your powers to serve yourself, your race, and your nation."

"My race?"

"The human race. You were raised human, despite any, er, outside influences."

Internally, I was reeling in horror, but Trevor probably thought I was thinking over his generous offer. In fact, he was staring at me like I was an unwrapped cookie.

But I didn't want to be a cookie, unwrapped or not.

"Look, Trevor," I said, leaning forward to mimic his body language. "That's a super-generous offer, but you're barking up the wrong tree. I don't want to be the champion, I don't want to fight the Red. I have to, however, and I'm going to do it because it's the right thing. But as soon as that's done, I'm done. If I survive, that is. I'm not joining your little team, or joining some big fight. I'm not going to battle terrorism, or fight your wars for you, or collect taxes from little old ladies scared I'll laser beam them with my magical death-eyes."

Trevor listened to me talk, his smile patient. When I was finished, he sort of half nodded, half shrugged.

"You're under a lot of stress, Jane. I can understand that. These have been very trying times for you, and circumstances are constantly changing.

"But the fact is that you have power. And you have to use that power somehow. You can use it for good, to help your country and your people, or you can refuse our offer."

"Is that a threat?" I asked rhetorically. It was definitely a threat.

"With us or against us," Trevor said, smiling inappropriately as if he could make his words less poisonous with his facial expression. Ryu, meanwhile, visibly twitched. I'd thrown those words at him when we'd broken up.

"That was the shittiest offer anyone has ever made me," I said, leaning back in my chair and giving Trevor my shaming stare. It didn't faze him.

"It's actually a very generous offer, which I think you'll realize after some thought. Now, shall we get you to London?"

With that, Trevor stood, offering me his hand. I refused it, getting to my feet by myself. I also wasn't finished talking.

"Trevor, I'm serious. I know you have to do what you're doing, that this is your job. But as soon as this hell is over, I'm done. I'm not a warrior. I never was, and I never will be. I'm just someone who was in the wrong place at the wrong time, and ended up having to save the world. That doesn't make me a hero."

Trevor looked at me, and he dropped the mask of genial politeness with which we'd talked until then. "Who said anything about being a hero?" he asked. "This is about power. You've got power that people want, Jane. You'll never be able to walk away from that fact."

And with that he left the room, taking my hopes for the future with him.

CHAPTER NINETEEN

Turns out our new military friends had what was basically a Concord at their base, so we made it to London in amazing time. Surrounded by Trevor's own men and women, I couldn't spill my guts to Anyan about my feelings over Trevor's speech. But the barghest slept the whole way anyway, after eating an enormous meal. Considering I wanted him at top strength for a number of reasons, I didn't begrudge him the recuperation time.

When we arrived at Heathrow, we were met by official-looking vehicles that whisked us through a set of security lines for which we didn't even have to get out of the car. I felt like a scary Beyoncé from all the special treatment, coupled with the way the guards looked at our vehicles. Trevor might look a bit like Dilbert, but he was obviously a major player in his world.

I tried to tell myself his help at this time was a good thing, but I wasn't convinced.

"So where's the Red now?" I asked as we started the drive into the city.

Trevor checked his iPhone again before speaking. "No reports. She's gone quiet after a long night."

"Damn. What's the plan?"

"If you're up for it, we'll tour the damage?"

I nodded. Maybe we could glean something about the Red's mental state from the attacks, although I doubted it. I was pretty sure she wasn't working on a plan at this point. She was venting her rage and loss.

The fucked-up thing was that I understood why she'd do that. I mean, not why she would hurt others as part of her grieving process, but I could understand being so full of rage and hurt. We'd killed the love of her life, her brother and mate. That might have been creepy, but it was also quite a powerful set of relationships, all rolled into one incestuous dragon package. Considering she was evil to begin with, no wonder she was randomly striking out.

The scary part was that I also understood this striking-out stage would pass. Then she'd go for her real revenge. If her tantrums could kill a few hundred people, it was horrifying to think about what she could do given time to plan.

My thoughts continued along such dark paths as we drove through London's deserted streets, seeing only emergency crews and soldiers directing everyone to stay indoors or take to the Underground to use as shelters, just like they did in World War II. London looked and felt like I would imagine a war zone would, something I never thought I'd experience in my lifetime.

"Here we are," Trevor said as our vehicle approached a smoking ruin. "Westminster. Or what's left of it."

Our vehicle stopped, and the others in our cavalcade pulled up beside us. Anyan and I got out of the car we'd been riding in, and I unconsciously reached for both the labrys and the silver stone in my pocket. My mind brushed against the place the labrys hid, waiting for me, as did my fingers on the stone. It was less of a comforting gesture, although it was that, and more of a subtle reminder that if we were at war, I was the warrior. It was a necessary reminder. Seeing the destruction of a building that was part of my cultural imagination of Britain made me want to run home to my childhood bed.

Iris, Caleb, and Ryu had gotten out of the car they'd ridden in, and were looking with similar expressions of horrified awe at the crumbling ruin in front of us. None of us asked about definitive death tolls, probably because we didn't want to hear them. I felt a small, invisible hand press my knee, a bizarrely comforting gesture from our secret gwyllion ally.

"So this is where she attacked first?" Anyan asked from beside me. He was looking almost his own self, and now that we were back on the ground, I could feel a steady pull of his earth magics. He was healing himself with every step, building back up his physical and magical strength. As for his emotional and mental... only time would heal those wounds. Time and lovin', and I planned on helping him have both.

"Yes. Westminster first. She struck Big Ben and then attacked the Parliament, then St. Paul's. Then it was just... random."

I pursed my lips, considering, before I spoke. "I wouldn't say it was random. She got the attention of the world first, and then she showed off what she could do."

"Well, we definitely saw that. The military didn't stand a chance against her."

"You need water," I said, moving forward a bit to get a clearer view of the wreckage.

"Water?" Trevor asked, already reaching for his phone.

"Yes. Fire trucks are good. Daniel knows all this," I said, but then remembered Daniel was dead. And who knew how the chain of command for reporting things worked when you were dealing with government organizations that weren't supposed to exist? Someone should have known, through Daniel, that water was a weakness for the Red and the White, but obviously they didn't. Considering Trevor's words to me, I was pretty sure there were all sorts of territorial disputes within this secret unit, and Daniel had been as involved as Trevor.

"Fire trucks," I repeated, "and those crop duster planes might work, although the Red would probably just swat them out of the sky. Maybe drones could be rigged with water?"

I was talking out of my ass by this point, having no idea what a drone could do other than what I'd learned on the nightly news.

"We'll look into it," Trevor said, his chubby fingers texting furiously. "Maybe we can hold her back until we figure out what she wants."

"Wants?" Anyan asked, rounding on Trevor. He'd been quiet for our walk, taking everything in his usual way. But I could see some of that old barghest spirit rising in him. "She doesn't *want* anything. She just wants to destroy everything she can. That's what she wanted before we killed her lover and brother. Now, there's nothing she wants that we can give her, as we took the only thing she loved. All she's got left is revenge."

Trevor stopped texting, raising his eyes to Anyan's. A flash of fear went through them at the idea of an enemy who genuinely wanted nothing. We may not understand the mind-set of a terrorist, for example, but we could learn about them and make guesses about what they wanted. Hell, they usually made videos telling us in great detail what they wanted. And even if their demands seemed illogical or impossible, their desires were there for us to mull over.

It was rare to have an enemy who genuinely wanted nothing except to kill. Rare and horrifying, as there was suddenly no room for negotiation.

Hiral started feeling up my leg again, but this time he was tugging on my jeans like he wanted me to walk forward. I cleared my throat, meeting my crew's eyes carefully before again addressing Trevor.

"We want a few minutes to look around. Alone."

Trevor looked uncomfortable. "I'd prefer you had some of my men with you. For safety."

I arched an eyebrow. There was nothing his men could save us from, quite frankly, no matter how big their guns. I forced my brow back to normal before speaking, keeping my tone carefully modulated.

"Trevor, let's not kid ourselves. You and your people are here as a favor. We'll let you play with the big dogs, but don't think for a minute we couldn't be out of here the second we wanted to. You know what we're capable of."

I saw Trevor's Adam's apple bob as he absorbed my not-quite-entire truths. The fact was the creature could poof only one or two of us out of there, especially after all the mojo it had expended helping create the stone; and then getting Anyan back had necessitated an enormous output of energy. It couldn't keep up this pace forever, any more than we could.

But Trevor didn't need to know that. I'm sure he already knew we had the ability to appear out of nowhere before, and of the Red's sudden disappearance in Hong Kong. If he thought such occurrences were normal, we'd be a lot better off...

"Yes, well, if you're certain you'll be safe..." the little man said, his voice trailing off when his words were met by my contemptuous little smile.

"We'll call you if we need you," I said drily, moving forward and motioning to my friends to follow.

We walked forward in a tight knot, following the cordon placed around Westminster, along streets that normally would have been full of tourists but were now eerily empty.

"Hiral?" I asked when we were out of earshot of any of Trevor's cronies. We kept walking as we talked.

"Here," the gwyllion said, letting his rotten-toothed smile appear, floating in front of us, just for a second, like that of the Cheshire cat.

"What's up?"

"I'm off, just wanted to let you know that. Figure we need a set of eyes in the enemy camp."

I felt relief wash over me. "Good. Because this can't last, the random attacks."

"She'll want more than random revenge soon," Anyan said. "She'll calm down enough to make a plan."

"Then we're really fucked," said Ryu.

The gwyllion's voice spoke from the empty air. "I'll find her people; see what they're working on. The Red and the White were never the most practical buggers, so I imagine she's got advisors working on something horrifyingly modern in terms of destruction."

We all cast each other looks as we continued walking, thinking through all the doomsday scenarios possible when dealing with a supernatural creature willing to use the human world to exact vengeance.

"Don't miss me too much," was Hiral's parting shot.

"Good luck," I whispered. The gwyllion had become a more important, courageous ally than I'd ever imagined he would be, and I deeply regretted my first assessments of him. Even if he was smelly and unpleasant, he was loyal and fierce and incredibly skilled.

We continued walking as I addressed Caleb.

"How'd your work on the plane go?"

Caleb's face was pensive, as it had been since we'd disembarked at Heathrow. Considering the circumstances, a little gloom and doom was probably called for, but I was worried there was something more. The satyr had, after all, been translating the rest of Theophrastus's poem, comparing it to the journal article he'd found and trying to figure out what the last stage of killing the Red would entail. For we couldn't just repeat what we'd done with the White. The whole process of alchemy was about building on stages of development, so the White got one ritual (the stone's transmutation into silver) and the Red got her own (the stone's changing from silver to gold).

"It's . . . going," he said eventually. "I need a little more time . . ."

"Is it something bad?" I asked sharply. "Because if it is—"

"I don't know yet," the satyr interrupted. "But bad or good, I'll let you know whatever I discover."

There was something about Caleb's tone that worried me, like he knew something more than he was saying, and it wasn't going to make us happy. But I had to trust him—if he wasn't sure what he was talking about yet, there was no point in getting worked up.

Not that I had a tendency to get worked up or anything.

So we kept walking, stretching our legs and getting a good view of the carnage. Anyan swirled a powerful glamour around us, so that the occasional teams of workers or soldiers we passed wouldn't notice our presence and try to stop us. In general, the streets were almost entirely empty of anyone resembling a civilian, and that fact combined with the smell of smoldering ash lent the whole scene a very post-apocalyptic feel.

When we turned back to rejoin Trevor and his team, Ryu spoke up.

"So what do we do now?"

Anyan and I both shrugged as if on cue. I gestured to him to answer.

"Nothing we can do except wait out the Red. Try to stop her if she attacks again. Hope that Hiral discovers something we can use."

"What if she doesn't make another appearance?" Ryu asked. "What if she's done venting?"

"She won't be," Iris said. "Not until she's about to do something bigger. Right now she'll wreck havoc until either we stop her or she forms a plan for some ultimate revenge."

I gave the succubus a questioning look, and she shrugged. "I know anger," was all Iris said. It was enough.

"Well, if she does lay low for a while, we can always try to find where she holes up. Take the fight to her," Ryu said, but he was wasting his breath.

Running toward us, as fast as his little legs could carry him, was Trevor.

"It's her. She's at the London Eye."

Anyan snapped to attention. "Get as many fire trucks as you can on deck and ready to roll. We need water. Jane can use the Thames, but if there's any way you can help pump some water…"

"There are fireboats out already. But it's probably too far to reach the Red…"

"All she needs is water in the air. She can handle getting it to the Red."

I nodded at Anyan's words, letting Trevor know the barghest was right.

Trevor nodded, calling up contacts on his cell even as we ran back to the waiting vehicles.

It was show time.

CHAPTER TWENTY

When we arrived on the scene, we found the Red had invented a new game: throwing the London Eye around like it was a Frisbee.

"Extreme Destruction?" I muttered to myself, giving the new game a name.

"What was that?" Anyan asked, turning to me.

"Nothing. We need a plan."

The barghest frowned, watching the Red fly. She hadn't seen us yet, as we'd parked in an unobtrusive place behind some low-lying buildings. I watched with curiosity as Anyan took a power stance, then moved his head right, then left, stretching his neck muscles. At the same time, he pulled power from the earth, sending it out in a tight but very strong shield in front of us.

He's warming up, I realized. *Making sure he's ready.*

When he was finished, he turned back to me. "Okay. I'm good."

"Ryu? Caleb?" I asked. They both nodded. Iris was

staying back with the car. She had her own strengths, but kick-assery was not one of them. I turned to Trevor.

"Fire crews are in place, as are the fireboats."

"Tell the fire crews to stay put till we need them. Tell the fireboats to start getting that water in the air."

Trevor spoke into his phone and immediately I felt the effect. I could feel the Thames a short distance away, but now the water was arcing up. There I caught it, holding it high in a net of my own making. I kept collecting it, keeping the swaths of water low so the Red wouldn't see them from where she was flying. While I worked on the water, Anyan spoke to the others.

"Somewhere around here have to be the Alfar and the supernatural rebels. We lost our main contact with them when we lost Gog and Magog, but I've no doubt they'll be following the Red's movements and planning their own counterattack. When they show, try to work with them."

Ryu and Caleb nodded, but Ryu was looking skeptical.

"So, do we have a plan?" he asked.

I looked at Anyan, who shrugged. So I went ahead and made a plan.

"The plan is to keep her busy and feel out her strength. The Red and the White were always a unit; now half of that unit is gone. We have no idea what we're dealing with out there."

"Will you use the stone?" Ryu asked.

I shook my head. "I think it's best we keep it out of sight for now. Unless Caleb's had a breakthrough with the poem?"

The satyr wouldn't meet my eyes. "I think I'm close, but not quite there. It's...complicated. I'm not sure exactly what you need to do yet."

It was obvious that there was something up with the poem, something that Caleb didn't want to tell us.

"Right, then. As I said, it's best we leave the stone out of it till we know how to use it. For now, I think our main focus is figuring out what the Red is capable of on her own. Better yet, we need to get her out of London and make her think twice about showing her ugly mug here again."

I sort of felt like the star of a noir crime thriller when I said the last bit, but I'd found that pretending to be a real champion was a great way to end up actually being a champion. As Kevin Costner taught us, if you build it, he will come. If I acted like a hero, maybe I could be one.

"So the plan is to just…go fight?" Ryu didn't look pleased.

"It's become an old favorite," Anyan replied drily.

Ryu, the planner, looked at Anyan, the seat-of-his-pants man, and they both frowned.

"As fun as this is," I said, pulling the labrys from where it dwelt, "I have things to do. Dragons to see." And with that, I let the labrys unleash its mojo as I strode purposefully along the narrow street that led out to the square that had formerly housed the London Eye.

The nice thing about having a giant flaming ax with a consciousness of its own was that getting attention was pretty easy.

"Easy, killer," I groaned at the labrys as it started winging random shots of power at the Red. It took the dragon a second to figure out where the shots were coming from, but it quickly caught sight of me.

A roar of such fury and pain rent the air that, for a split second, I almost felt sorry for the Red. The agony in that furious shriek struck deep in my bones. But then the dragon threw the Eye, for maximum damage, at a nearby building, taking out at least two floors and whoever might have been hiding inside them.

Pain or no, something so destructive had no place on this earth.

The labrys was still spitting at the Red as she made a lumbering circle in midair, breathing fire down at us. I turned the ax's spitting missiles into a shield that arced out over me and my friends, and I felt them add their power to my own.

The fire continued unabated as I pushed up with my shield, creating more space between us and the heat of the flames. The whole time, my little water nets were continuing to collect.

I looked at Ryu, who'd earlier said he would keep in contact with Trevor. "Tell him to bring in the trucks," I shouted even as I pulled my nets forward.

The baobhan sith got on the horn at the same moment I went on the offense. I pushed hard with my shields, causing the Red's own fire to boomerang back on her. It didn't hurt her, since she was fire to start with, but it distracted her, letting me lob a few strong volleys of the labrys's power at her. She shifted in midair, her heavy body avoiding the missiles. The potshots did keep her attention on me, however, just as I wanted.

But the Red also knew my tricks at that point; knew that I knew her weaknesses. Sensing the water in the air, she was ready for my net. Just as I went to dump it on her, she pirouetted in midair, plunging down to the earth to duck most of the water as she did so. But a considerable amount was still coming at her head, and she concentrated on steaming that away with a huge burst of fire from her belly.

"Go go go!" I shouted, waving at the waiting trucks that had rolled up at Ryu's signal as the Red dealt with my water net. Distracted by the water above her, she wasn't able to avoid the water below. The fire trucks' massive hoses drenched the dragon. Covered in her enemy element, the dragon shrieked in pain and frustration, plummeting toward the earth as her magic failed her.

I rushed forward, letting the labrys's magic boom out around me. When she hit the ground, I'd be ready for her in her weakened state...

But she was ready for me instead. I watched the huge shape of the dragon hit, roll, and...change. The form shrank, compacting into itself like a dragon-shaped black hole. When it came to a standing position, it was neither Morrigan nor the Red, but that lizard-like human hybrid I knew was far more dangerous, to me at least, than the awesome power of the dragon.

For what it gave up in strength by letting Morrigan play, it more than made up for in smarts and evil. The Red might be an ancient force of chaos unleashed upon our lands, but Morrigan was a right bitch, capable of just about anything and cunning enough to make that anything happen. Out of pure dragon form, it also lost its vulnerability to my element, water.

Our shields butted up against one another as we sized each other up.

"Jane," Morrigan hissed through her distended lizard's muzzle, her dragon's forked tongue flicking out at me. But the eyes above that muzzle were the sapphire blue of Morrigan's, not the Red's green.

"Morrigan slash Red," I intoned seriously, pushing at her shields with my own, to get a sense of their strength.

"You have been a naughty halfling," Morrigan said, pushing right back. "The Red isn't happy with you at all, and neither am I."

"Think of it this way, Mo. Now you don't have to share with the White. And who cares about the Red's feelings anyway? Aren't you the one in control?"

That comment didn't go over well. Morrigan's blue eyes flashed green as she shouted, "I care, you stupid cunt. I am the Red, and she is me, and we loved him... We loved both of them."

For a second, I thought Morrigan was talking about her husband, Orin, but that was daft.

"Oh, you mean Jarl," I said, probing for weak points in her shields with sharp bursts of the labrys's power.

"Do not say his name!" shrieked Morrigan, returning my magic jabs in kind. She also started to move in a slow circle. We must have looked ridiculous—just two people (well, a person and a giant red-scaled lizard-woman) circling one another and chatting away. Only a supernatural would have felt the power sparking in our otherwise invisible shields and know that, if either of our defenses fell, we'd crush the other, quite literally, under the weight of our power.

Which was why I wasn't happy to see Anyan creeping around as if he were trying to sneak up on the Red.

He's not up to full strength, I thought. I had to keep our enemy distracted...

So I pulled out my Shotgun of Annoyance, firing with both barrels. "I can say his name if I want to, and you can't stop me," I chanted. "Jarl Jarl Jarl Jarl ..."

Morrigan didn't appreciate my chanting, but I found the name rolled off my tongue so easily I kept it up.

"Jarl Jarl Jarl . . ."

"Shut up, you bitch!" Morrigan snarled, lunging toward me both physically and magically. I pushed back hard, stopping her. But it took a lot of power. Which begged the question . . .

Creature?

[Yes?]

How you doing?

[Recovering. You fight the Red.]

Yes. Can you get a bead on her power? I'm trying to figure out if we've weakened her . . .

I increased the wallops of my power against the Red's shields, and she answered with renewed volleys of her own. We circled and circled, hammering at one another. Every once in a while I would chant "Jarl . . ." She didn't like that.

[She's as strong as she was before. There has been no increase or diminution in her strength,] said the creature eventually.

That was good news actually, if not the best. I'd been worried that, despite what I'd seen with the stone, the White's power would somehow revert to the Red when he was killed. That did mean the Red was still incredibly powerful, but no more than she had been before.

Thanks, I told the creature. *You rest. We'll need you soon.*

[Let me know if I can help,] came that gentle voice in my mind, and I realized that somehow our roles had changed. The creature no longer automatically took control of me in a dangerous situation—I was in charge of myself.

And right now, we'd accomplished the first part of our plan, to figure out how powerful the Red was, after the death of the White. Now was time for plan B. Get rid of her and put the fear of God into her.

And it looked like Anyan planned on helping me with that one. The barghest was crouched low, on the other side of Morrigan, and I could feel him drawing up his earth powers.

I stopped circling with Morrigan, keeping Anyan behind her, and I let the labrys have its head. It pulled at me, wanting to engage with its enemy hand, er, claw.

"Look, Morrigan, this has been fun. But now it's time for you to crawl back into your hole, at least until we can figure out how to get rid of you for good."

The red-scaled beast in front of me hissed, lunging forward again. She bounced harmlessly off my shields, although I had to pull some power forward to keep her away.

"You arrogant little shit," she said, her blue/green eyes blazing as she and the dragon fought for control inside her. "You only took the White because we were foolish, thinking an inferior creature could house his greatness. You won't be so lucky with me."

I couldn't help laughing at that. "So you think we got the White because you used Anyan?"

"Of course. Your pathetic halfling-loving barghest will be the first creature I kill when all this is over..."

She probably would have continued threatening my loved ones if I hadn't run out of patience. "Oh, Morrigan," I said as I pulled my shield in tight to my body as if it were a suit of armor. "The problem with you is that you're so blinkered by hate. I mean, obviously you're blinkered by hate, because you let yourself become a great big fucking gecko in order to get power. What do you eat anyway? Shitloads of insects?"

Morrigan watched me, her own shields still crackling with energy now that I'd pulled mine away. But she didn't advance on me, confused by my actions.

"The reason your precious White fell is because Anyan fought. He wasn't an inferior vessel, he was a superior vessel—he fought your mate with everything he had in him. And you know why he did that? Because he loves me. Unlike Jarl, who fought you every step of the way so you wouldn't pull him into your crazy scheme."

I knew I'd hit a nerve. When Jarl had died, he'd been running away from Morrigan's attempt at turning him into the White, and toward me to save him. I'd even been willing to do just that, but one of Blondie's last acts on this earth was to kill my Alfar nemesis, forcing Morrigan to take Anyan in a fit of panic.

"He loved me, you bitch. He was confused by you; you forced him away from me . . ."

I could feel Anyan's powers growing from behind her, and I tapped into the water I kept in reserve . . .

"You know that's not true," I said. "You were keeping him prisoner. He had to be drugged . . ."

"Liar!" she screamed, forgetting her earlier caution as she lunged toward me.

I was ready, for this was what I wanted. It was my turn to affect a power stance, my labrys pointing forward with all my power and the creature's borrowed strength poured into sharpening its blade to cut through Morrigan's shields . . .

But then she stopped, smiled, and turned neatly on her heel. To sprint directly toward my friends.

"Fuck," I said, and then I did call for the creature.

"Speed!" I yelled, letting it know what I needed even as my little legs started churning. Sprinting far faster than I ever could have on my own, I felt Anyan's coiled power strike, sending up a wall of earth to protect Ryu and Caleb from the Red's onslaught. I felt them brace the earth barrier with their shields even as I threw power at them. Anyan caught it, weaving it into the earth he controlled. It wouldn't hold the Red long, but it was enough.

She was running hell for metal, probably expecting the earth barrier to shatter before her. But it held, and she bounced off it with an enraged roar. She then raised her claws to start slashing her way forward, but I was there.

The labrys carved through her shields like they were butter I was so amped up, and I caught her a glancing blow on her red-scaled shoulder. Blue blood spurted and she wheeled around, lunging toward me as she did so. Her claws glanced off the blade of the labrys, only inches from where my fingers gripped the haft. I shuddered, and then I began fighting.

We closed in against each other, her a whirl of claws and distended muzzle, me using every trick in my arsenal, and more than a few of the creature's, to match her blow for blow. I blocked a clawed fist, then a clawed foot, and somehow managed to pivot fast enough to stop that damned tail from slashing across my back. Unsure how long I could keep this up, I turned to my friends for help.

Anyan was already in action, hauling the fire hose of

a nearby firefighter out of his hands and training it on the Red and me. The water blasted with excessive force at both of us, but I met the blast with a laugh.

For while the water wouldn't hurt the Red as much in this hybrid shape that was as much Morrigan as dragon, it was just the weapon I needed.

The water danced around me as I began flailing at the Red, striking her blow after blow with clubs of water. I imagined it felt like being forced to belly flop, over and over. The water also charged me as I used it, washing away that dangerous moment of doubt that had preceded Anyan's help.

I may not have put the fear of God into the Red that day, but I did make her retreat. With a growl, she sprang back, shaking herself like a dog as she did so. Then she was running in the opposite direction to the Thames, letting the speed of her sprint dry her of her enemy element. I considered chasing after her, but knew we'd accomplished what we'd wanted to. We'd stopped her initial, grief-fueled attack on London and we knew her strength after the fall of the White.

Behind me I heard cheers, and I turned my neck just enough to catch the crowds behind me in my peripheral vision. Only the humans were cheering; my friends were waiting to make sure the Red didn't return like the killer in a horror movie.

One human wasn't cheering, however. Trevor was watching me, his chubby cheeks raised by a smile that made me shiver. He was pleased with my performance. I turned back to the Red's retreating form.

I watched her shapeshift into the dragon and fly away, and then even Iris whooped with pleasure. But the rest of us remained silent, knowing that our plan had one major flaw.

Now that she was no longer able to take her anger out on this city and its people, she'd move on to her next phase.

Taking her anger out on the world.

CHAPTER TWENTY-ONE

The barghest's hairy chest made an exceptionally good pillow. As did his whole body, really. So who could blame me for staying sprawled across him after we'd made love that night?

His hands busied themselves with long, slow strokes over my hair and down my back. The steady thrumming of his heart beating against my ear sounded as epic as the opening of Verdi's *Otello*. It would be a very long time before I took Anyan's presence for granted again.

We were in our own apartment in a grand house owned by the U.S. State Department, courtesy of Trevor. Once again, our friendly government representative had spared no expense to make me feel at home. Our quarters were as big as some of Rockabill's houses, including my own, and were decked out in a lavish style more befitting a prince than rubes like us. Not that we hadn't happily indulged in the bottle of Veuve waiting in ice in a silver wine chiller, and we'd been more than willing to clean up nearly all the gourmet open-faced sandwiches and chocolate-dipped strawberries waiting on a silver platter. The only thing that had kept us from cleaning them up entirely was that Anyan feeding me strawberries had pretty quickly led to him feeding me other things, and next thing we knew, we were naked.

Blondie had been right, bless her—post-battle sex was pretty amazing.

"Are there any sandwiches left?" Anyan's chest rumbled against my ear as he spoke.

"Yes. Quite a few."

Anyan was silent for a few seconds while I happily listened to his heart beating. "That was actually a hint for you to go get them," he said eventually.

I pinched his love handle gently, causing him to squeak, before I sat up.

"Look at you, ordering me around like a pasha. I'm the champion, I'll have you know." But I went and got the sandwiches anyway. And the strawberries. And the champagne. When I got back to the bed, Anyan had sat up. I laid the tray of food across his lap, filling up our empty champagne flutes before setting them down on the nightstand.

"Fancy," I commented, giving the flute a little flick with my nail, causing it to ping in the way only crystal does.

"They're sparing no expense for you," Anyan replied, watching me with inscrutable gray eyes as he crammed a few of the little round sandwiches in his mouth. He was still eating for two, him and the dragon, despite his change in circumstances.

"I've noticed that." I nibbled on my own sandwich, no longer quite so hungry.

"Well, you are the champion." Another few sandwiches disappeared off the tray and into the barghest's craw.

"Yeah, but if all goes well, I'll have killed the only remaining thing I'm supposed to be, er, championing against. So not the champion for long."

"You sure about that?"

"Yes. Um, yes."

"That doesn't sound sure." Anyan's voice was gentle, but his words grated against my ears.

"Sorry that I don't know exactly what I'm doing here, dude. I mean, it's not like there's a long line of champions to talk to, get their stories. There was one, but she died."

"I love it when you call me dude."

I glared at Anyan, defiantly finishing my own little sandwich. I would not be held back from eating by this conversation, goddamnit. That would mean I was taking it seriously.

Anyan used my full mouth as an opportunity to keep bothering me. "That's true. It would have been nice to ask Blondie more about your condition."

"My condition?" I said after swallowing. "You make it sound like I'm pregnant."

"It's not a totally ridiculous metaphor. The question becomes, then, will you ever give birth?"

"That doesn't even make sense."

"What I mean is that we don't know whether you'll ever really lose this power of yours. I take it you're assuming it'll go away when you finish the Red?"

"Of course it will. Blondie's went away. I have it, after all—"

Anyan interrupted me again.

"Did it? Go away, I mean. Blondie was so strong—"

"Blondie was an Original, hence strong," I said, butting in myself. I didn't want to be having this conversation.

"Blondie was also the only Original we ever knew. So we can't really compare her to another one, to know if she was stronger or weaker than other Originals. We also don't know if she ever really did give up that power. We know she gave up the labrys, but couldn't you have just gotten new power when you were made the new champion? I don't think we can assume the power really transferred—"

"Well, so what if I'm powerful forever? I don't have to use it. Once the Red is dead, I can go about my business..."

My voice trailed off as I realized how ridiculous that statement was. Anyan didn't speak, watching me look around the gorgeous room we were staying in, part of the luxurious apartment we'd been given all to ourselves.

Trevor wasn't doing that out of the kindness of his heart. He wasn't being generous or thanking me for my efforts so far.

He was recruiting me.

And he wouldn't be the only one. The Alfar monarchs—all of them—would want a piece of me if I kept this power. It would be like an arms race, only I was the arms. I was peripheral to all of this, of course—I was just the vessel. My voice wouldn't matter.

Then there were the halflings. My people—subordinated and abused to varying degrees throughout the world. They'd want something. Some, like Jack and his lot, would expect a lot. They'd want me to fight for them, too. They'd also want a piece of that power.

Humans, halflings, and purebreds, all fighting over me.

The girl who couldn't get a date to the senior prom to save her little life, not least because she'd been drugged to the gills in the loony bin after inadvertently bringing about the death of her first great love.

She was suddenly the belle of the ball.

"What do I do?" My voice was bleak when I finally spoke. Anyan took my hand.

"I shouldn't have been so negative. Maybe the power will go away. Or maybe the creature will take it back."

I remember Blondie telling me, right after she'd duped me into taking the labrys, that it was all mine now. She'd seemed sad when she said it, and I now wondered if her words weren't loaded with other meanings.

Automatically, I reached for the place the creature inhabited in my mind. It could probably answer my questions. But since taking on the White, it had been mostly absent in my mind, showing up only when I was in danger.

I knocked and got no answer, so I replied to Anyan.

"No, you were right to bring it up. Especially now. We've got to keep an eye on Trevor. It's not like he can disappear me to Guantánamo, not with the creature able to apparate me out, but he knows more than enough about me to make my life miserable if he wanted to. Hell, everyone knows enough about me—Jack, Luke, all of them. I don't want to spend the rest of my life rescuing friends and relations abducted to get me to cooperate."

"We can keep people safe," Anyan said, but his voice was doubtful. He knew better; he was just trying to ease my mind.

I snorted. "Yeah, we can, by kidnapping them ourselves. My dad doesn't want to live out his life in hiding. And Grizzie and Tracy are having their babies. They won't want to raise them in the supernatural world. Can you imagine living out your life as a human at Ryu's compound? Trapped there with people like Nyx?" Ryu's delightful cousin had once brought a human "snack lunch" to a compound dinner party that had ended with a giant melee. The human had been killed, and I doubt Nyx had even noticed. She certainly hadn't cared.

"They don't have to go to the compound; they could be with us..."

"While we hide out, too. That'd be a fun life. All of us on the lam together."

"I shouldn't have brought this up now. You were amazing today..."

"No, you were right to bring it up. I can't take this treatment for granted and I can't let my guard down, even for a second, around people like Trevor."

Anyan handed me one of the little sandwiches, the last one spread with cream cheese, smoked salmon, and a little cucumber. A peace offering. I smiled at him and took a bite, chewing thoughtfully and swallowing before talking again.

"The irony of all this is that if one of them does 'get' me, they're going to be sorely disappointed."

Anyan cocked his head. "Why?"

"Because I'm a terrible champion." Anyan was obviously about to protest, so I raised my hand to still him. "Seriously, I am. Yes, I've got all this power, but I'm not doing all this stuff alone. We're a team. We brought you back as a team, and you're like the most valuable player on this team. Alone, I'd be nothing."

Anyan moved the tray over to the nightstand, then reached forward to draw me into his arms. He pulled me across him, so we were cuddled close. I let the warmth of his body seep into mine, gone cold.

"You'll never be nothing, Jane. And I'll always be on your team; nothing could ever change that. But I understand what you're really saying."

Of course he did. Anyan listened.

"I couldn't ask it of them," I said, and Anyan stroked a hand down my back, letting me know he'd heard me. He didn't have to say anything, for it was the truth.

I'd changed my life when I unwittingly stepped into the champion's shoes; there was no question about that. But someone had to battle the Red and the White, because as long as they were around, they were a threat to everybody. Fighting them wasn't only my battle; it was really everyone's. So Team Jane wasn't really fighting for Jane... Team Jane was fighting for everyone, and I was just the (ax-wielding) figurehead.

But if I managed to kill the Red, then what? Trying to keep Team Jane around me would be pure selfishness. The threat would be gone, and the gods only knew what all the various factions competing for my favor would want me to fight for. And meanwhile I was useless without my cohorts. I also couldn't imagine living my life without my friends, my family, my routine...

I may have become a champion, but I was no soldier. I hated this life, even if I enjoyed moments within it. I loved getting Anyan back, but I'd trade that feeling of triumph in a heartbeat for never having to feel his loss. I loved kicking the Red's ass, but in the moment I was always scared shitless, working on pure adrenaline edged with terror.

If I kept this power, I would be viewed as a soldier for

the rest of my life. No, not even a soldier—I'd be viewed as a weapon. At least a soldier has his or her humanity acknowledged. I'd just be something everyone was trying to use. And I couldn't ask anyone, even Anyan, to follow me into that life.

And without Team Jane, I was pretty sure this weapon would break fairly quickly, like a cheap toy used inappropriately.

I knew I needed to talk to the creature about this issue, but right then there was another knock at the door. Only this was frantic pounding, and it also had no power signature.

The two of us glanced at each other as we stood up from the bed. I reached for the robes we'd discarded next to the bed, throwing Anyan one and donning my own. Then we went out into the sitting room, Anyan moving to open the door as I took point, standing about six feet behind the barghest. I called the labrys, which came to me lazily, not bothering to light up. I took that as a good sign, but still kept up my guard as Anyan swung open the apartment's front door.

Instead of an enemy, it was Hiral, the gwyllion. I'd never known the little creature to knock, but he was obviously not in his right mind. The normally blue-skinned creature looked green, his large eyes skipping over our faces as we moved toward him.

"Not good, not good, not good," he mumbled, stumbling into the apartment.

"Hiral, are you hurt?" I said, squatting down to give him a once-over.

The little man waved his hand at me absently, as if he were swatting away a fly.

"Not hurt. But we need to talk. This is not good."

We all made our way back into the kitchen, me leading the blabbering gwyllion.

"They're planning something big," Hiral said as I set a glass of water in front of him. He drank thirstily, using both of his long-fingered hands to hold the cup. When he finally spoke, his voice was strained.

"It involves human weapons. I think nuclear. They're being more careful as they know I'm a factor. Using the same shields you are," he said, making a circular motion around his head to indicate our own protections. "But a lot of people know, and not all of them are intelligent. Or circumspect. There have been hints."

"We need more than hints," Anyan said.

"And we can get them. There's one of 'em, really high up in Morrigan's council, who has a problem with whores. Can't get enough of 'em. He's got a favorite brothel he visits in secret, as they're all supposed to be on lockdown until the big event. But I've followed him more than a few times, and he's as routine as they come. He'll be easy to nab, and we can get the information we want then."

"Good. How powerful is he? How big a team will we need?" Anyan was, as always, practical.

"Not big at all," Hiral said. "The creature we're after is—no offense, Jane—a halfling, but not a powerful one. Half goblin. Barely any power at all, though he's a mean, clever son of a bitch."

We all stared at Hiral. Anyan's eye twitched visibly.

The gwyllion never noticed, his eyes still scanning the handout as the bomb he dropped exploded.

"Calls himself the 'Healer,' he does."

CHAPTER TWENTY-TWO

V.I.P Jacuzzi Shower Facilities was only one of the amenities listed on the Ladybugs Sensual Massage website. Oddly, they also pointed out they had customer toilets, something I'd think any good brothel would have as a matter of course.

But what did I know.

I'd taken the time to Google the place before we went, using Blondie's iPhone. She didn't need it anymore, obviously, and I'd somehow ended up with it. Not that I didn't feel a little pang every time I used it, remembering sitting across from her on trains, Googling away at our problems.

Research made me feel better about things, and confronting the Healer was definitely knocking my equilibrium out of place.

There was no reason for me to be that jittery, of course. Yeah, the Healer had kidnapped me, and yeah, I'd seen that hellhole torture chamber of a mansion he'd set up for himself. In his sadistic tastes, the goblin-halfling Healer was a combination of Dr. Mengele and Pinhead from *Hellraiser*, although he affected a polite and educated Scottish brogue while he tortured his victims mercilessly.

Although I hadn't really suffered at his hands except to be knocked about a bit, I had seen what he'd done to others. I'd talked to his victims, and seen the scars they carried both emotionally and physically.

And one of those victims was my friend Iris.

That the succubus had suffered so horrendously so recently was actually hard to imagine. She'd been kidnapped and abused by the Healer and his followers for almost a month before we could rescue her, all to get back at me and my friends. When we'd first rescued her, she'd been a shell of her former self. But she'd proven her strength and her resilience by building herself right back up again. She'd also found a partner out of the whole mess. Caleb, Ryu's deputy at the time, had been with us when we rescued her. They'd immediately fallen for each other, and it was a relationship that might not have happened otherwise.

Despite, or maybe because of, her history with the Healer, Iris had insisted on coming with us. I hadn't thought it was a very good idea, but Caleb had supported her decision, and he was a healer.

Maybe she needed to confront her captor for reasons I couldn't understand but he did.

"You okay?" Iris said to me, her voice concerned. She was wedged up against me, sitting bitch between Ryu and me.

"Yes. Are you?"

"Yes," she said, although she didn't look at all okay. She looked pale and drawn. I took her hand in mine and gave it a squeeze.

"You don't have to do this, you know. You don't have to confront him."

"I know. But I want to try."

I put my arm around her shoulders and gave her a squeeze. She'd be safe with us, even though Iris wasn't the most powerful of supes when it came to offensive magics. Her natural succubus talents were amazing; she could make the sun dip down and say "Hey, how you doin'?" on a good day. Lobbing mage balls was another thing, however. But the Healer wasn't powerful, either. He was just supersick in a way that made him perfect for plotting strategies for someone like Morrigan, so he had the strength of her patronage. On his own he was nothing.

"He'll be coming along anytime now," Hiral said. The little gwyllion was standing on Anyan's knee on the front seat, peering over the dashboard at the massage parlor that did the kind of massages that involved a lot more vagina than normal.

"He's as regular as Big Ben. At least before it got knocked over." Hiral's joke fell flat, as it was undoubtedly intended to.

"I'm surprised they let him in," I said. "I can't see someone like that going in for vanilla sex."

"He never touched us," Iris said from beside me. Her voice was light, despite the subject matter. "He watched, and he liked to tell his men what to do with us, but he never actually touched us."

"Oh," I said, simultaneously nauseous and curious at the same time.

"Well, aggression isn't his thing, apparently," Hiral said. "He likes to be dominated."

"What?" I squeaked. It was both TMI and so incredibly weird I couldn't help wanting to know more.

"That's what the girl told me. Yvonne is his favorite. She's a domme, as well as a prostitute. Nice girl, very polite, and has a good sense of humor."

"Um, Hiral? How did you get to know Yvonne?" I asked, totally confused.

"I went up and introduced meself, what do you think?" The gwyllion was clearly not impressed with me at that moment.

"Glamoured?" I asked, just to be sure.

"Hell no, I wasn't glamoured. When I glamour meself, I can't be seen."

"Um, is that sarcasm?" I was so confused at this point.

"No, I really did go up and introduce meself. Why wouldn't I?"

"Because you're two feet tall. And blue," Anyan said. The gwyllion gave the barghest a dirty look.

"She's a dominatrix and a whore, fercrissakes. You think she's not seen weirder shite than a two-foot-tall blue man? She barely batted an eyelash."

I shook my head, amazed at Hiral's tactics. "And she talked to you?"

"Oh, yes. She not only talked, she was good enough to make a deal, once I explained why we wanted our boy. Girls in her circumstances understand the importance of the sisterhood, even if they're the first to be booted out of it."

I'm not sure what I found more mind-boggling, Hiral's sensitive appraisal of intergender politics and how women often shun their most vulnerable sisters, or the fact that any human being would calmly hear out a gwyllion. Contemplating this, Iris beat me to my next question.

"What's your deal?"

"Our boy likes to be tied up, flogged, the whole nine yards. I just asked her if she would be kind enough to tie him up a little more firmly this time. And maybe leave the room so we would have our own chance to play with her naughty boy."

I shuddered at the imagery, but couldn't help applauding Hiral's methods. The Healer was kidnapping himself, effectively.

"She only asks we don't leave any, er, remains. They run a clean establishment."

They certainly do, what with those V.I.P Jacuzzis, I thought.

"No remains, period. We need him for questioning," Anyan said.

Ryu agreed. "Although I doubt it, Morrigan might be willing to barter to get him back. Or we can use him for bait. Or keep pumping him for more information, once we get what we need now out of him."

Iris was quiet, as was Caleb from where he sat in the driver's seat. I didn't like the sound of all that silence, and I worried that bringing Iris wasn't a good idea. She was a grown woman, decades older than me, but I don't know if she'd made the right choice. I could understand her desire to confront her tormenter, but maybe it was too soon?

"And bingo," Hiral said, pointing forward with one of his spectacularly long fingers. "There's your boy."

Iris's body beside mine went rigid, vibrating with contained energy. I again squeezed her hand, a gesture she returned with painful force.

"So what now?" Ryu asked.

"We let him get upstairs. Yvonne'll take care of him. Then she'll give us the signal."

Ten minutes passed, then twenty. We were getting fidgety, watching the dumpy old former warehouse that housed the massage parlor, when suddenly a stream of people came out the front door. Men and women in various states of undress, the women looking bored and unapologetic, the men's expressions running the gamut from embarrassed to exasperated. The johns ran to their cars, some hopping into their trousers as they did so, while the girls dispersed leisurely into the night.

One figure, dressed in a leather bustier and short shorts, paired with some seriously pointy dominatrix boots, detached herself from the group and came toward our van, lighting up a cigarette as she walked. The flare of her lighter revealed a sharp-featured, thin face, capped off by a mop of curly brown hair. Large brown eyes inspected our vehicle with cool calculation.

Anyan rolled down his window as Hiral moved around on the barghest's lap so he was facing the girl.

"Hey, Hiral," she said, her voice rich with boredom. "You're all set, love."

"He's incapacitated?" the gwyllion asked.

"Oh, yes. Bound tight as a roast goose. He's not going anywhere."

"Which room?"

"The rubber room. The hose is in the little cupboard by the sink, by the way."

"You *are* a good girl," said Hiral gleefully as I wondered what Yvonne thought we'd need the hose for.

Yvonne smiled, but it wasn't a humorous expression.

"From what you've told me, he has it coming. I figure he's getting off lightly. Whatever you do to him won't be as bad as he made others suffer."

A shudder ran through Iris's body, but otherwise she didn't react to Yvonne's words.

"We'll not be back till morning. I've warned everyone away. Text me when you're all done, and I'll come back to lock up. Just don't leave a mess."

"No, ma'am," said Hiral.

Yvonne made a vague gesture of farewell, and Hiral sighed as he watched her strut away. "What a woman."

I couldn't help agreeing. Opening our doors, we all hopped out and walked toward our destination. Anyan and Ryu took the lead, Caleb and Iris took the middle, and I took our backs. Partially, that was so I could keep an eye on Iris. I didn't want her getting into anything she couldn't handle, or fainting at the sight of her captor or something. She was tough as nails underneath all that soft flesh and blond hair, but there were some things too tough for any of us.

The brothel, when we walked into its low front door, was as sad and dingy as I'd expected it to be. It wasn't dirty, just drab and definitely depressing. It had been some kind of industrial building before, and it had been carved up into rooms using the same sort of thin walls companies make cubicles from. Which meant there would be no privacy whatsoever, and any goings-on would be heard by everyone else in the place. But maybe that was part of the appeal?

Our little group walked on silent feet down the thin gray carpet lining the concrete floor till we neared what had to be the end of the establishment. Hiral gestured to a door at the end of the corridor on the left-hand side of the hall. The walls here were proper walls, but we still crept forward as quietly as we could.

Until, that is, I felt a tug at my hand. Iris had stopped, her face pale as death.

"I can't do it. This was a mistake. I shouldn't have come."

I placed both of my hands on her shoulders, gazing deep into her eyes. "You do whatever you're comfortable with, you hear me? If you want to wait for us here, none of us will think less of you. You were brave just coming."

She dropped her head, a small sob racking her body. "Thank you, Jane. I'll just stay here. Don't worry about me, though. I'll be fine."

"Are you sure? Do you want me to stay with you?"

"No. Please. I'll be fine. And they may need you."

I was torn between staying with my friend and going to help take care of the Healer.

"Seriously, go," Iris told me, obviously seeing my hesitation and interpreting it correctly.

After another second of deliberation, I nodded. "All right. If you need anything, just shout."

"I will." She took a seat on one of the little chairs in the waiting area, wringing her hands nervously. I turned and ran down the hallway, catching up with the others quickly. They'd been waiting for me.

"Iris all right?" Anyan asked.

"Yes, but she doesn't want to go in."

"I don't blame her. You ready?"

"Yes."

Hiral did his little disappearing act to scout ahead, and we didn't see him again till he popped back into visibility, standing right in front of the room Yvonne must have stashed the Healer in. He cocked his head to the side, shaking it slowly, gesturing for us to move forward.

We ended up all crowded inside the doorframe, peering inward with various expressions on our faces. Mine, at first, reflected confusion. In front of us lay what had to be the Healer, although his back was to us. Green goblin scales covered the back of his head and neck, trailing down his spine, broken only by some sort of strap across the back of his head. I wasn't sure what that was about, because his face was turned to the other wall. The rest of his body was a hodgepodge of goblin scales and human skin, and there was definitely a lot of skin to see.

For the Healer was naked, except for a giant adult diaper and a crisscrossing of ropes binding him up like a hog for the slaughter.

There was nothing so off-putting as seeing the bane of your nightmares wearing some giant Pampers.

He must know something's up, I thought. In my naïveté I thought the goblin halfling was struggling, for who wouldn't know something was wrong after at least ten minutes of being hog-tied in a diaper?

That's not struggling, my libido pointed out delicately. A second later, I realized it was right. The Healer was humping the floor. Or his diaper. I'm not sure how that fetish worked, really.

Gritting my teeth, I pulled the labrys. I wasn't fucking around.

At my unspoken but very bright signal (the ax didn't seem to like the Healer one bit), we all strode into the room. Squirming to turn his tied body, the Healer eventually made his way over to the new source of light in the room. The labrys flared brighter, then brighter, and he squinted at us, unable to see our shadowed forms in the glare. It wasn't till I spoke that he realized he was in more of a bind than he'd paid for.

"Hello, Healer. We meet again."

This time he squirmed for real, and not in a fun way. His cries of alarm were muted, however, by the ball gag explaining the thin strap at the back of his head.

Yvonne is a clever thing, I thought admiringly. I'd have to ask her where she learned to tie knots.

"Why don't we make our guest comfortable," I told Anyan and Ryu. I was channeling every Bond villain I'd ever seen, trying to mimic the creepy combination of polite threat at which they all excelled. Acting as my evil minions, the barghest and baobhan sith moved into the room. Caleb stayed behind me.

There wasn't much in the room, which was, indeed, made of rubber. Black rubber, to be exact, and the floor had been left concrete but painted black. A drain was set in the middle of the floor, and I remembered Yvonne's comments about the hose. Perfect for a quick cleanup, I realized, trying not to think of all the things one might do with a diaper fetishist.

Ryu and Anyan picked up the Healer roughly by the armpits, swinging him in a way that made his bound body jerk painfully. The goblin halfling batted at them ineffectually with his magic, but he was no match for either supe, physically or magically. I would have thought it wasn't a fair fight, except that the Healer himself specialized in unfair fighting. His victims had ranged the gamut from weak supes to human children, so I didn't feel too badly about dropping the auspices of chivalry.

"Oh, that is perfect," I said, channeling my inner villain, as Ryu and Anyan untied the Healer's bindings long enough to bind him back in place, tied to the only furniture in the room.

Ironically, that piece of furniture was the same type of medical gurney that the Healer had used to torture so many of his own victims. It was the sort that could fold up, or down, from almost a chair to more of a bed.

"Aren't you a hot mess of issues," I marveled, walking toward our bound captive. Anyan and Ryu had raised the back of the gurney up so it was more like a chair than a bed, and they'd left the ball gag in for now.

"You torture people in the way that you want to be tortured? Is that it? Orchestrating the pain you want to feel yourself?"

The Healer's eyes, radiating a combination of fury and fear, blinked wetly at me.

"Maybe you think they enjoy it, too?" I mused. I was genuinely curious. It wasn't often one got to question a true sadist.

"No," I said after I'd thought through the issue. I took a step forward, studying the pink human flesh of the Healer's face and the eyes that bulged at me over the ball gag. "You know they don't want it. And that's part of why you love it so much. At the end of the day, you're an imperfect victim. Not only do you want the pain, you can only let it go so far before your self-preservation kicks in. But when you hurt another person...they can take whatever you give them, because you don't care if they die."

Our eyes, locked on each other's, shared something then. And that something was...nothing. I would never understand the Healer any more than he would ever understand me. I don't know what made one person so eager to hurt others, and another willing to help, and I could study a hundred Healers and never be any closer to the answer.

I moved out of spitting range first, then nodded to Anyan. "Take the gag out."

The barghest did so, using his power to keep the Healer's head back against the gurney's headrest. It was a reminder to the Healer that it wasn't the ropes binding him that really kept him there; it was the fact that every single one of us in that room was far more powerful than he was.

I reveled in watching him squirm, and I know I wasn't the only one. We all loved Iris like a sister, except for Caleb, who loved her in another way entirely, and we all wanted revenge for her kidnapping and abuse. Our motivations were far from pure, although I didn't feel too sullied by wanting the Healer to feel just an ounce of the fear he'd made others feel.

"Listen, you," I began, ready to put the fear of God into the Healer. I raised the labrys to emphasize my point, assuming we were going to have a tough time getting anything out of one of Morrigan's closest acolytes. "If you don't tell us what we want to know..."

"I'll tell you everything! Anything you want. Absolutely everything, just let me live..."

For a second, I thought I'd misunderstood the Healer's strong Scottish accent.

"You'll what?"

"I'll tell you everything. Anything. Just ask. What do you want to know? My secrets for my life."

I couldn't help feeling a bit disappointed. I'd had a

whole Evil Spiel ready about how we would cut off his appendages, and I mean all of them, and I'd been working on some "descaling like a fish" ideas, but instead he just folded.

"What is Morrigan planning next?" Anyan asked, since I was sulking like a disappointed child.

"Nukes," the Healer said promptly. "She's sending her people in to commandeer a nuclear submarine. She'll fire on whatever target they're set for."

The news hit all of us differently. Caleb gasped, clearly understanding the full implications of such a threat. I just shook my head, wondering if we really were in a Bond film. Everyone else looked suitably serious.

"Which sub? When? How?"

For the next twenty minutes, the Healer told us everything. Ryu took notes on his phone. We also got some good info on just how many troops Morrigan had, what their general feelings were about what they wanted from their affiliation with the Red (which ranged from wanting Armageddon to wanting a place in the New World Order), and where Morrigan/the Red was mentally.

"You've killed her soul," the goblin halfling said, his eyes flicking at me. "The Red is broken without the White, although just as powerful. And Morrigan's more Red every day, and vice versa. I think Morrigan helps keep the Red going at this point, and the Red's wrapping Morrigan up in her grief over the White. They're not wholly separate, but not wholly together, either."

The others looked confused at this information, but I remembered my own symbiotic relationship with the creature right after Anyan had been taken, and I understood.

"Well," I said, looking at Anyan. He nodded. "That's

enough for tonight. We have what we need, but you're coming with us, buddy. Only sans diaper. Where are your clothes?"

"There are lockers by the door," the Healer said, not meeting my eyes. "I'm number 69."

"Of course you are. Sit tight while we get your clothes."

We filed out of the room, Caleb leading us back down the hallway. We left the Healer where he was so we could talk, Ryu slapping a binding of power on him on top of the ropes already holding him in place. None of us were reading any power signatures from anywhere nearby, as none of the Healer's cronies knew he was in danger. So we took advantage of the opportunity to discuss in peace what to do with him.

"Did he tell us everything he knows?" I looked at Anyan, who shrugged.

"Probably not," the barghest said. "But maybe. I don't think their organization is all that organized in terms of a master strategy. The Red doesn't work that way, and Morrigan's goals can only go so far, especially now that we know they're so blended in her body."

We sat down in the entryway chairs as we hashed over our initial findings, figuring out who (in terms of Alfar, humans, et cetera) needed to know what now and what we should leave for later. When that was done, we had only one more issue to confront.

"So what do we do with the Healer?" asked Anyan.

"First of all, we put him back into his pants," said Ryu. "His locker's right over there. I'll get his stuff."

"And then what?" I said.

Anyan shrugged. "Hand him over to the Alfar?"

"'Cuz they do an awesome job keeping prisoners," I

said bitterly, remembering the moments before Anyan had been turned into the White, after both the Alfar and rebel security had failed spectacularly.

"What if we had the creature apparate him to his cave?"

"He'd probably hump its eye. And I don't want the creature wasting that much power."

"Well, let's get him back to base and we can think of something. Maybe just leave him with the humans?"

"They'd be sitting ducks if Morrigan tried to rescue him."

"Will she even notice he's gone? She seems a bit preoccupied at the moment—"

"Here's his clothes," Ryu interrupted, coming down the hallway holding up a bundle. "No more diaper for him..."

"Where's Iris?" I asked, suddenly realizing we were missing somebody.

We all did a weird little shuffle as we flung ourselves around to look.

"Where the fuck did she go?" I repeated, my voice cracking with anxiety.

My heart was in my throat, thinking she'd been kidnapped again, until I saw Caleb. He didn't look at all panicked. He looked guilty as hell.

"Caleb," I said through gritted teeth. "Where's Iris?"

The satyr's eyes betrayed him, shifting to where the Healer waited, tied up like a sheep for slaughter, in his room.

"Shit," Anyan said, running down the hallway with a fluid motion that had him halfway to the room before I could blink. We took off after him as we watched him gain the doorway.

"Shit," he repeated, sliding to a halt. I gurgled when I saw why.

"Sorry, I had to do it," Iris said from where she was calmly washing her hands at the sink. She didn't sound sorry at all. In fact, her voice was back to its original pure sexy sweetness.

When she was done cleaning her hands, she washed the knife she'd used to cut the Healer's throat. Iris must have been standing well behind the goblin halfling when she'd done it, as her clothes were pristine but the room was literally covered in blood. I learned that day that arterial spray is called "spray" for a reason. The knife now cleaned, Iris replaced it in her large handbag.

She must have hidden in another of the closed rooms while we questioned the Healer, and then waited till we were back in reception to sneak past us.

The Healer was already very dead, his human face ashen white and his goblin scales gone dull. After a long minute of stunned silence spent alternately gazing at the dead body and Iris's cleanup efforts, Caleb went to go to the succubus, but he slipped on some of the blood sprayed throughout the room. His hooves scrambled to regain purchase, a weirdly slapstick moment that made the whole scene all the more surreal.

The satyr finally regained purchase and then led Iris out of the room, although he was the only one who looked upset. Either he hadn't known she was actually going to kill him, which I doubted, or seeing the aftermath was different than he'd expected. Because Iris looked as serene and angelic as she used to, before her stint at the Healer's mansion.

A year ago I might have seen such an event as proof

that the supes were anything but human. Now I saw it as proof we were all one and the same. An eye for an eye, and all of that.

Anyan and I exchanged glances. Eventually, he spoke. "At least they have a hose."

CHAPTER TWENTY-THREE

"Are you sure you're ready for this?" Anyan asked me, adjusting the straps across my wet suit. I didn't need it for the cold water, but unlike the ancient Picts that peopled this island, I wasn't about to go into battle naked.

"As ready as I'll ever be. And I have Trill," I said, nodding at the kelpie, who stood, happy to be naked in her human form, watching the sea. The creature had apparated her in at my request. I thought the use of its power was worth it as I needed some watery backup.

"I still don't like this," Ryu grumbled, his face pinched with nerves.

"Neither do I," Anyan said. It was rare those two agreed.

"Why would the Red do something in your element?" Caleb asked for the umpteenth time. "You're already the champion, and this just panders to your strengths."

I sighed. "I know. It doesn't make any sense. Plus she has to know something's up since the Healer never returned home. So it's probably a trap. We've established this."

"So why are we sending you in again?" Anyan said, still unnecessarily adjusting my wet suit.

"Because we have no other choice, as we discussed already," I said gently, gathering his hands in mine. "We can't risk the Red getting a nuclear submarine. And what can the trap be that's so bad? She's got no power in the water. It's not her element. She'll have to rely on her followers."

Anyan frowned. "We already know she had a kappa on her side. She probably has others. For all we know, she has an army of water elementals waiting to attack…"

"She doesn't have an army of water elementals," I said to the barghest soothingly. "Trill would have gotten wind of that if she did. Or the creature would have. It's hard to hide an extra army, and we've already seen the army she has, which didn't include any water elementals."

"But you're going in alone…"

"Anyan, I'm the champion. And I have Trill. I'm not going in alone."

"But I'm not with you…"

I sighed. So that was it. I led the barghest a little ways off, so I could speak to him privately.

"Anyan, honey, you can't swim. You've had one lesson." The barghest turned a bit red, probably more out of frustration than embarrassment, but what I said was the truth. "If you came with me, I'd spend more energy and concentration keeping you afloat than I would doing my job. And you can't connect with your elements underwater. You'll be totally cut off from earth and air."

Anyan's eyes wandered over to where Ryu waited, also in a wet suit. I resisted the urge to roll my eyes.

"Ryu can swim and he's used to functioning with only

his reserves of magic." As a baobhan sith, Ryu got his power from essence—which was basically a form of concentrated magic that humans passed off in their blood and bodily fluids. Humans were surrounded by the same elements we used for magic, but couldn't use them like we could. That said, the elements still permeated them, and like anything foreign in our bodies, they had to get rid of them somehow. Essence was potent stuff, making baobhan siths usually very strong. But it was also finite, in that you had to go out and find someone to harvest essence from every time you needed a top-up. Elementals like me or Anyan, or the majority of supes, just had to be in contact with our element. For Anyan, being cut off from his elements of earth and air was a near impossibility, so he wasn't used to rationing his power. He just charged in, blasted away, and topped up as he went. If he did that in the water, with no way to recharge, he'd be weakened and vulnerable in minutes.

"But I hate not being there with you." Anyan actually pouted on that one. It was sweet, and adorable, and frustrating. Everything I liked about him really. But he had to get over this.

"Anyan, I wanted nothing more than to get you back fighting at my side. You're everything to me, you know that, right?" The barghest nodded glumly. "But you were also a dragon for quite a while, and I learned to do things for myself. And this is something I have to do by myself. Also with the whole huge team of people over there wearing wet suits that are going to help. Many of whom helped me get you back, remember?"

Anyan sighed. "I know. I just hate the thought of you going it alone."

"We all gotta do what we gotta do," I said, but I leaned in to kiss him to mitigate the harshness of my words.

When I pulled back enough to meet his gaze, I saw that his left eye was twitching. He really hated me going in alone.

"Hey, I've got a good team," I said, nodding to the group of assembled, wet-suited figures. It was quite an assortment, as we were working closely with the Alfar and the rebels of the Great Island on this one.

The Alfar leadership had volunteered a few of their more adventurous soldiers, and for once they were all fellow Alfar. Normally the Alfar had a tendency to stay well behind the lines, offering up scads of lesser elementals as cannon fodder before joining in the fray. But because the Alfar had access to all elements, and pureblooded water elementals tended to stick to themselves in the sea, they had to step up themselves for this one. So we had their small, elite team of what were sort of supernatural Navy SEALs, used for the rare situations in which a water elemental had to be brought in for some reason or, more commonly, because there was an out-of-control supe on a boat or an island or something. That said, the Alfar would only have access to water, since that's what they'd be surrounded by, so they wouldn't be anywhere near as powerful as they were normally. I knew this to be the case as I'd captured Phaedra by cutting her off from the majority of her elements.

Because the Alfar were so weakened by being submerged, it was really the rebels who had come through for us in terms of this mission. Standing next to the Alfar in their underwater SWAT gear were a mixed bag of halflings—all children of underwater folk who had spent enough time on land to reproduce, and then abandoned their progeny when they turned out to be too human to be true water folk.

In other words, they were all like me. In fact, three were selkie halflings. There were also quite a few siren halflings, another breed of water creature that looked mostly human except for a fish tail they could shift into human legs if they wanted. Because supes had to leave off all magic to be most fertile, that meant creatures who could "naturally" appear human, like selkies or sirens, had a better chance of successfully living on land long enough to purge the magic from their systems and meet someone.

One woman, however, had an enterprising kelpie father who'd chosen a blind hermit human for his mate, and there was a kappa halfling whose mother swore she'd been seduced by a man dressed as a Teenage Mutant Nina Turtle. She'd apparently had a crush on Donatello as a child, and she'd been drunk when she'd wandered away from a bonfire on the beach.

These water-halflings had volunteered as they were all strong in the water, if mostly human in physiognomy. They also all apparently had combat experience, something that wasn't dwelt upon since the only people they would have been fighting were the Alfar, as the Sea Code would have prevented anything else.

Basically, the Sea Code was a nice of way saying that the water folk stuck to themselves, and would happily let the rest of the world fuck itself. Water elementals were pretty rare, not least as they had to constantly use their magic to support their watery existence. Breeding didn't occur often anymore, and when it did, it was usually with humans. Sometimes the progeny would favor the supernatural parent and could live in the sea like a pureblood...other times they didn't, and they ended up left on land, like me and the other halflings surrounding me that day.

All of which left the few supernaturals in the water with a lot of space in which to play, and no reason to interest themselves in Alfar politics. They kept to themselves, and wouldn't interfere unless bothered. If the Alfar ever did try to take back the seas, as had happened a few times with particularly megalomaniacal monarchs, then all bets were off. The sea folk would come together and push back the invaders, usually quite easily as they were surrounded by their power source, and then go about their business again when everything was over.

"We've got a good force," I said, reiterating my thoughts to Anyan. "I don't see how Morrigan can have any real purebloods. That kappa was definitely a fluke, according to Trill." I was referring to the kappa that had kidnapped my own mother. He'd turned against the Sea Code and sided with the Alfar. He was dead now, shot by our own forces on a raid that had saved the other water elementals he'd captured.

"We've got a good batch of halflings, another thing Morrigan isn't going to have. And we've got me, and Trill. She's weak on land, but believe me, she kicks ass in the water."

Anyan nodded. "I know. It's just—"

"I like fighting with you, too," I said. And I meant it, much to my surprise. I never really liked fighting, but knowing Anyan was there took an edge off somehow. He always had my back, and that was comforting.

"You just like watching me handle my mage balls," Anyan said, waggling his eyebrows at me. I giggled. I do that when people say "balls" around me, because I'm supermature.

"Are you gonna be okay, then?" I said. "I don't have to worry about you getting a snorkel or anything?"

Anyan shook his head. "No, ma'am."

I stood on tiptoe to kiss him just as one of the SWAT-looking Alfar made a gesture over his head. After saying "see you soon" to Anyan, I trotted over to join the others.

Trevor was there, as was our new Daniel, the guy who was our new liaison with the British government. This guy, Rory, was clearly cowed by Trevor, however, and had barely said two words to me. He just nodded at everything that came out of Trevor's mouth. Rory had been useful in providing our Alfar soldiers with all the info they needed on the sub's location, and the like. Hiral, meanwhile, had been sent back to Morrigan's estate to make sure that they went ahead with the attack. Despite the Healer disappearing, he'd reported that they were still gearing up for something big, and that it still looked like the scenario the Healer had described.

Once all of us who were part of the mission were surrounding the Alfar underwater team's leader, he started barking out orders.

"We're dealing with a sub, so never forget that. It's got humans on board and quite a payload. If that sub explodes, we go with it. And whilst we care about our own lives, and the people around us, we can assume the Red's forces don't.

"We can also assume this is some kind of trap. Which means assume aggression, but keep your eyes open.

"In other words, this mission is kill over capture or immobilize. They want a doomsday device, but they're going to get their doom instead. Understood?"

All heads bobbed. Trill looked positively gleeful at the thought of a little ultraviolence. She had a bloodthirsty side and didn't often get to show off her water mojo. Personally, I felt a little nauseous. Despite everything, I'd never fancied myself much of a killer.

The SWAT leader spoke again. "We've got an update from Hiral. He managed to get on a shuttle that left yesterday from Morrigan's compound. It arrived in Scotland today, and hit the coast a few hours ago. Hiral counted nine Alfar on the team, and there were at least two water folk that met them on the beach, a kelpie and a rusalka.

"So this should be straightforward, even if they do have something up their sleeve. Our mission is to take out the team attacking the sub, make sure the sub stays untouched, and get out. Understood?"

The Alfar's own troops, six men in total besides him, all gave a professional shout. The rebel halflings nodded, giving the Alfar's show of soldierism rolled-eye disdain. I nodded to myself, making my own plans.

I would cover the sub, I'd decided. Push anything back that came near it, and let the others do the killing. It might have been cowardly, but it also seemed smart. I was much better at being repulsive than I was at doling out death.

"We ready?" the Alfar shouted rhetorically. His own troops gave an answering shout, which caused the rebels to sigh. We all moved as one down to the beach. Ryu joined me on my other side, looking admittedly rather hot in his tight wet suit.

Anyan glowered.

"Jane," the barghest said, catching me to him when we'd reached the edge of the water and the waves were lapping at my feet. He lifted me, kissing me thoroughly before setting me down.

Ryu made a point of looking unimpressed.

"I love you," I whispered in the barghest's ear. "Now stop showing off. There's no competition."

Anyan rested his forehead against mine. He was still holding me aloft, and it was all very sweet.

"I love you, too. Don't worry about killing anyone. Just keep them away from the sub."

I smiled. "That was my plan already, big guy."

"Good." He turned to Ryu. "Take care of her."

Ryu nodded. I could tell he was enjoying this immensely. It wasn't often he got a chance to do something the barghest couldn't. "Of course. I'd never let anything happen to her."

Anyan reverted to glowering, and I turned away from both of them to Trill. My friend had joined us, her large swamp-colored eyes looking eagerly out at the sea. The sun reflected wetly off her pearlescent gray skin, and her seaweed hair flowed down her back in a neat queue. She turned to me and gave me a fierce smile.

"It will be good to fight with you in the water, Jane, where you belong."

I wasn't quite as excited at the prospect as Trill was, but I didn't tell the kelpie that. Instead I held my hand up for a high-five. Her webbed fingers smacked mine and we both grinned, reminding me for the umpteenth time that month how lucky I was to have my friends.

"Move out!" the Alfar shouted, and move out we did. The halflings surged forward, meeting their element with eagerness, while the Alfar and his soldiers moved with more deliberation, but no less enthusiasm. I gave the barghest one last squeeze, then trotted forward with Ryu and Trill.

Power swirled around me as we entered the ocean—that of the sea herself but also that of the elementals around me, drawing forth and expending energy as we powered through the water. We'd decided to eschew boats for this mission, shooting for maximum surprise. That meant we had about a two-hour swim till we reached our destination.

Once we hit real ocean, the Alfar leader made the gesture we'd all been waiting for, and the halflings, Trill, and I moved forward. We made a sort of V-formation, with two rows. Our first row of real water elementals went first, Trill and I in the lead. Ryu and the Alfar made up the row behind us. Our row cocooned the back row in a bubble and began to tow them forward.

After much arguing and grandstanding earlier that morning, the Alfar had finally agreed that this was the best way to get where we needed to go. I could swim for days without really tiring, I was so symbiotic with the water. The Alfar had limited access to their water channels—they had access to all four elements, but only so much access to each. When they could use multiple elements simultaneously, they were superpowerful. But limited to one, they were pretty average.

Once we had the Alfar in our tow, we could really move. Jetting through the water, after about an hour of swimming, we spotted our goal. A submarine, floating in the deep. We stopped then, watching from a distance for the enemy to show.

Eventually, there was movement on our watery horizon. I could feel their power from here: Alfar, as Hiral had warned, and two much stronger water signatures—the kelpie and the rusalka.

I looked around. We had superior numbers, we had laid our own trap, and we had the champion. This should be a piece of cake.

So why did I still feel like we were the ones who had been set up?

CHAPTER TWENTY-FOUR

Putting on a burst of speed, we catapulted ourselves and our Alfar backup through the water. We had to meet the enemy at a distance from the sub, not least because it and the men in it were so very vulnerable to attack.

Our swimming shapes streaked over our target, and I was the only one who slowed. I took a defensive position floating above the submarine, pushing the rest of my team forward with a strong shove that lent them much-needed distance from the vessel we guarded.

We didn't want to take down the thing we were trying to protect with ricocheting power.

I watched as our own forces met Morrigan's in a flurry of magical weaponry and physical muscle. Our halfling water elementals moved with ease through the water, and I could feel them using the tricks Trill had taught me when we'd fought the kappa that had kidnapped my mother. They would try to catch and hold one of the Alfar, keeping the power of the sea away from them until they drowned. It worked on a few; lifeless corpses floated away on the current without a scratch on them. But not all of Morrigan's troops were so easily killed, and a few of our own forces were similarly weak. We lost at least one of our Alfar to the power-sapping trick before a halfling could save him.

Once the weakest had been weeded out, the real fighting began. Nets and tridents were our halflings' weapons of choice, created out of magic but just as dangerous as a physical counterpart. Underwater mage balls also began flying, and I carefully spread out shields, catching those that streaked toward the sub. Some were definitely accidental ricochets, but at least a few of Morrigan's troops kept their eyes on the prize and were trying to target the sub.

As for Trill, she went right for the big prey, moving in on the kappa and the rusalka. The kappa seemed happy to engage with her. The rusalka, however, darted away. He was male, and looked like a Disney version of a merman, but I knew from past experience with his race that he'd have a hollowed-out back. I knew because one of the Healer's victims had been a rusalka, and this bastard was working for the same forces that had raped and mutilated one of his kin.

If that didn't make my blood boil.

Unfortunately, the turncoat was also a very good fighter. He pivoted away from the kappa and kelpie, only to be met by one of our half-selkies and a half-siren. All three closed in on each other, power flying. I saw the selkie nearly net the rusalka as the siren made a fierce jab with his glowing trident, but somehow the rusalka managed to dart under the net, grabbing the selkie so that it was her body that met the siren's thrusting trident. I gasped as the trident cut deep, but the siren was clever. Jerking her whole body forward, and I can only imagine painfully, on her fellow halfling's trident, she jerked herself away from the enemy. Then the selkie halfling used the trident to dart with her away from the enemy. At a safe distance he stopped to pull out the trident, and I could feel his healing powers as he concentrated on her.

Which left the rusalka free to move.

An Alfar of ours got in his way, but was no match for the rusalka in his element. A quick slash with a weapon that appeared and disappeared in the rusalka's hands and suddenly the Alfar was minus a head. That meant the rusalka was free to make his way toward his real target...the sub.

I swam forward, putting a burst of power into my sprint to create a nice distance between me and the submarine. Unfortunately, the rusalka did the same. We careened off each other's shields like a couple of kids playing bumper cars, spinning through the water in arbitrary directions— me back toward the sub and him upward toward the surface of the water.

When I got my sea legs back, giving my head a firm shake to clear it, I darted back toward my enemy. This time I didn't get very far, however, and I was very aware of the vulnerable hull of the submarine scant yards behind me.

The rusalka wasn't fucking around, either. A weapon flashed in his hand, and as it came slashing at my face, I solidified my shields just in time to match it, even as I pulled the labrys. It floated in my hand with no weight whatsoever, like a good magical weapon, lighting up under our attack. I slashed back at the rusalka, only my weapon carved through his shields like they were butter. His eyes went wide as he swam hurriedly backward. Then, undoubtedly realizing I wasn't such easy pickings, he focused behind me and took off toward the sub.

I swore, albeit soundlessly, and tore off after him. The labrys gave me speed, and I closed in on the rusalka with no problem. Throwing up a barrier in front of him to protect the sub, he only managed to stop just short of my shield's power signature, turning to face me again. I swung the labrys in front of me cockily, motioning to him to come on over.

It was time to finish this.

His face mashed up into a snarl of rage, the rusalka came at me, throwing mage ball after mage ball. I met his volleys with my own, my shields easily absorbing the impact. When he was close enough, I slashed forward with the labrys. It was still way too far away to make contact with him, but it did what I wanted it to do.

Cutting through his shields, which he kept pretty far out from himself as most water folk did in a fight, I had a convenient hole through which to aim my next volley. One mage ball caught him in the face, one in the stomach, and one in the crotch. I had meant that last one as a follow-up to my gut shot, but I like to think that karma intervened.

I was pretty sure the rusalka died immediately, but just to make sure, I paused, letting my selkie senses probe for any sign the merman was alive and quietly healing himself. When I felt nothing, I let the ruined corpse drift away.

I guess when the stakes were high enough, I could kill and not feel that bad about it.

Returning to the sub, I watched our forces mop up the

enemy. Trill had dispatched the kappa and was helping to capture the last of the Red's forces. We wanted to take a few of them alive if we could, for questioning.

I floated above the submarine, just in case, until Trill and Ryu came toward me.

"That was easy," she mouthed. I nodded. It had been. Maybe my spidey senses had been wrong and this wasn't a trap, just a cockeyed plan that must have been plucked whole from the brain of the mad dragon queen.

But I found that hard to believe.

The Alfar leader of our troops made a gesture with his arm to circle up. I ignored it, as did Trill and Ryu, and we watched as he dispatched a few of his men to go ahead with our prisoners. He then turned to where we floated a few feet away. He gestured again that we were leaving, but I shook my head.

He gestured again. I shook my head again, making my own gesture for him to get going with our prisoners. Obviously frustrated, he made the same gesture of retreat.

We might have kept at that game forever—him trying to order me around, me refusing, mostly out of spite at being commanded by an Alfar but also because everything felt too easy. I wanted to stick around and make sure the sub was safe.

We never had a chance to continue with our little duel, however. For one minute the Alfar was gesticulating angrily at me, and the next he was swallowed up.

And I mean swallowed. A huge beast had risen from the depths underneath the Alfar and had gulped him up in one negligent opening of its massive jaws. It happened so fast that I only caught a glimpse of huge white eyes and a massive underbite armed with razor-sharp teeth.

"What. The. Fuck," I mouthed to no one in particular. Trill took my hand first, then Ryu took my other hand. We raised shields around ourselves and the sub.

We watched, unable to help, as the titan swooshed right, and then left, its way lit by a light dangling like a nightmarish streetlamp off its forehead. I realized then what it was, having seen that Disney movie about a fish a few years back.

It was an anglerfish, grown to the size of a suburban condo.

Its apparently random swimming was anything but: Trill and I watched in horror as it swiftly gulped up our Alfar allies and their prisoners easily. The halflings proved more difficult prey, their control over their element giving them speed and reflexes the others didn't.

It all happened so fast that we'd only managed to squeeze off a few mage balls at the thing, testing its shields. Meanwhile, I was battering on the mental doors that separated me from the creature. It responded swiftly to my calls.

[What is that?]

You're supposed to tell me!

[Open your senses...]

I responded promptly to its terse command, opening all my senses up to the creature.

[It's not an elemental,] it mused. That had been my first thought as well, that it had been like the creature itself—one of the offspring of the elements that created our planet. But it presumably would have been a water element, then, and therefore directly related to the creature. Why would it work for Morrigan?

[It's not even magical,] the creature said eventually. We

kept hitting it with mage balls, and I nodded to myself. The mage balls were all striking, indicating the creature had no shields. But it was so big that each strike was like the shots of a BB gun against an elephant. It also didn't react at all to the damage, like it was impervious to pain.

It's gotta be something, dude. Anglerfish don't grow to the size of houses on their own! I watched as the beast caught up with one of the selkie halflings, chomping it down in one horrendous bite.

[You're going to have to get closer. I think I know what it is, but I can't feel from here . . .]

"I've gotta go in," I mouthed to Ryu and Trill, whose eyes followed my lips as she read what I was saying. "You stay here. Guard the sub."

Trill shook her head no, as did Ryu a second later. "I'm coming with you," mouthed the kelpie. Ryu nodded, pointing between me and Trill.

I pointed with both hands down at the sub. "You have to keep it safe."

Trill rolled her eyes then pointed at the massive fuck-off anglerfish, then used one of her own fingers to mime slitting her own throat. I sighed. We were stronger together, it was true, and Ryu had volunteered to stay behind if we got chomped. Not that he'd be able to do much besides get eaten himself.

I nodded, motioning toward the fish. Trill and I swam toward it, bulking up our shields as we went. I also pulled the labrys, and to my surprise, it lit up as if Morrigan herself were right next to us. Could the Red also turn into an anglerfish?

But that didn't seem like the right answer, as the anglerfish was acting just like a fish. It darted around, trying to scoop up our halfling team, but didn't do anything particularly intelligent or magical.

I think it's really just a giant fish, I told the creature.

[I think you're right,] it said.

But it's connected to Morrigan. The labrys pulsed frantically as if agreeing with my thoughts.

We were close now, and the fish was intent on eating one of our kelpie halflings. The kelpie was doing a good job defending itself, but was clearly tiring. Trill and I exchanged glances, then we went in.

We used our shields first, like a battering ram, swimming them into the anglerfish to get its attention. Its freaky white eyes swiveled toward us as its body followed. Its long, needlelike teeth looked like carefully sharpened elephant tusks, and they were so large. I tried to stop the knot of panic in my belly from unraveling as its luminous headlamp thingie swung around to cast an eerie glow over the two of us.

This was some primordial shit we were dealing with, and I knew how my human ancestors must have felt when cornered by an irate mastodon.

It lunged at us, and it took all of us and the labrys to keep our shields both big enough and strong enough to keep the thing from swallowing us both whole. I really didn't fancy playing Jonah and the whale, after all.

We managed to shove it back, but it came at us again like a dog lunging at a bone. To our horror, it grabbed on to our shields with its teeth—something I'd never seen before.

How the hell can it do that! I screamed at the creature as the thing began gnawing its way through our shields.

I heard the creature mumble something about minichampions, even as I felt it take control over the part of my magic that worked like a probe or a radar. It reached out toward the fish, and I could feel what it was feeling.

While the word "mini" was inappropriate, I suddenly got what the creature was saying. However our ally had imbued me with its strength to make me its champion, the Red had done the same with the anglerfish. The Red had never bothered to make its own champion before, because it didn't need one. It was free to wreak its own havoc while the creature was underneath Rockabill, underneath a large chunk of the Eastern Seaboard. It was trapped, and had been for a very long time. It had voluntarily given its power to another to help stop the Red and the White because otherwise it would have to release itself, taking a big chunk of the continent with it. The Red could fight her own battles, so why waste power on a champion when she could use that power herself?

But she couldn't face me in my own element—water. So she'd gambled with catching me unawares using her own champion. It was a brilliant strategy, really. After all, while water was my element, it wasn't any of the rest of my team's.

And I'd already figured out long ago that my real strength came from the people who surrounded me. The Red must have figured that out, too, and gambled that without all of them, maybe I'd be vulnerable, even in my own element.

But I wasn't alone, not even then. Trill was with me, and Ryu was ready to back us up. He'd moved forward to throw more power into our shields as I let the creature use mine to probe the fish.

At first, all we felt was fish—dull brain waves intent on its next meal, a sort of mindless hunger that was a bit like I imagined a zombie's would be.

What are we looking for? I asked the creature. If it was using my senses, the least I could do was help.

[There has to be a tie connecting it to Morrigan,] it said. [I was able to give you the labrys; that's your tie. As long as you have the labrys, you have my power. But she couldn't do that with a fish.]

No hands, I thought, having figured out the problem with a fishy champion a few seconds after the creature spoke.

[Exactly. So look for the tie...]

We scanned all over that stupid fish, our magic stroking around it like a masseuse with a big tipper. Meanwhile, it was busy literally eating at our shields. Just like the labrys could cut through magical barriers, the fish's massive teeth had the same effect. Luckily, it was a fish, and therefore wasn't smart enough to use its teeth to slash in a more effective way. Instead, it was trying to chew its way through with teeth not really meant for chewing.

Wait, there! I thought, suddenly feeling something. We'd been so busy with the body of the fish, but the power surge I was sensing came from the light on the end of its angler.

The creature pounced, confirming my suspicions with a feel of relief. The tether, for that's what it felt like, extended from the light, up toward the surface of the ocean, where undoubtedly the Red hovered.

[You have to cut it!] the creature told me, just as I was afraid it would. The fish's body had, after all, evolved to eat anything that was attracted to that very angle. That massive underbite was made to swoop forward, snatching up anything that came at it from the front.

Fuck, I thought, turning to Trill. Ryu had since abandoned his post above the sub and joined us, never being one to abstain from action. But he'd have to follow Trill's lead, as he wasn't as good at reading lips.

I took their hands and put them together, indicating they were now a team. Then I gestured at the fish.

"I can stop it. You distract it."

Trill pursed her lips. I nodded my head vehemently, as if to counteract her doubt. "You distract it," I mouthed "Only way."

The kelpie nodded, tugging Ryu back when he tried to follow me as I swam toward the anglerfish. Its eerie eyes watched me hungrily, and it attacked our shields with renewed vigor.

Just then two massive mage balls hit it from the side. Trill and Ryu came at it from the left, pummeling it with the biggest mage balls they could muster. The fish emitted a watery stream of bubbles, I guess the equivalent of a fish roar, and turned to its attackers. Its angler wobbled through the water a second behind it, like a recalcitrant puppy on a leash.

Its peripheral vision was good, however, for just as I went in to use the labrys to cut the tie connecting it to Morrigan, it lashed back around, nearly catching me with one of those sharp teeth. It cut through my shields, and I frantically backpedaled, building back up my protections as I slashed forward with the ax. It hit tooth, slicing off one of those massive needles and causing the fish to retreat a pace.

Trill and Ryu went in again, this time separately. Trill, as the more powerful fighter in the water, took the lead, using her body to lure the fish. It lunged toward her, but Ryu was there, pushing it back with a mighty shove of his shields even as he aimed a mage ball at one of its eyes. The blast hit with horrifying effect and one of those milky orbs became a blackened, viscous ruin. Enraged and in pain, the fish lashed forward blindly, and I darted in toward its angler. Using my magic to sense my target's random movements through the water, I held still waiting for the perfect shot...

It came a few seconds later. The fish's frantic movements stilled for just a second, and that's when I struck. The labrys severed the cord binding the angler to the Red. With a weird underwater sonic boom, the power eclipsed from the fish. I looked down to see a fish no larger than my forearm darting down into the depths. Now that it couldn't eat me or my friends, I was glad it survived. It hadn't wanted to be a pawn of the Red's any more than the rest of us.

I started when someone grabbed my arm, turning to find Ryu, his face white. I looked down to see why, and mentally screamed for the creature.

Grabbing for the baobhan sith and his bloody bundle, I felt the creature apparate us as my eyes tried to take in the full extent of Trill's terrible injuries.

CHAPTER TWENTY-FIVE

With an agonized mental groan, the creature landed us straight back in the Scottish military base from which we'd first set out. I'd ask it later about how its power was holding up, but for right now all my thoughts were on Trill.

"Medic! We need a medic!" Ryu was shouting, and I felt his power wrapped around the kelpie in a blanket of healing. I knew Ryu wasn't the best healer, but I nonetheless added my power to his. We could hopefully keep her stable.

Various forms hurtled around us, many of them making an aggressive push toward us as others took a defensive line. We had appeared magically in the midst of a bunch of soldiers, after all. So those who recognized us tried to keep us from being attacked by those who didn't. I only half registered what was happening, however, as my attention was mostly focused on Trill.

Her pearl gray skin had paled to a ghastly white, her

black fingernails looking even more eerie against her pallor. Her eyes flickered back in her head as she lost and regained consciousness. I clutched her cold hand, my mouth moving in a silent prayer as I took in the horrible belly wound. I think she'd been speared straight through.

It was only when I heard the familiar sound of clip-clops behind me that I dared breathe.

"Move," Caleb said curtly, and I shuffled like a crab to the side. The satyr did what I'd seen him do only once before, with me, when I'd been hurt after an attack by the ifrit-halfling, Conleth. He took Trill into his arms and literally wrapped her up in his healing magic. Hope rushed through me as the satyr's strong healing power lapped at my shields. But it was quickly dashed when he opened his eyes, a pained look on his face.

"We need to get her to the infirmary. Now." Caleb looked around at the watchful human soldiers around us, and one quick-witted individual made a motion to follow. She led us swiftly out of the doors opposite us, across a tarmac over which a gray sky threatened storms, and into another building. We turned right, trotting down the hall to a set of double doors that led us into the welcome sterility of a hospital ward.

"She's been impaled," Caleb said to the doctor on duty, a frazzled-looking woman with wiry red hair held back in a tight ponytail. "I'm healing her as much as I can, but something's blocking me."

"The fucking Red," I hissed as the woman motioned to a bed. Caleb laid the kelpie down gently. Trill was totally unconscious now.

Caleb frowned. "The dragon was seen over the waters. How did she—"

"She made herself a champion," Ryu said curtly. "An anglerfish."

"She must also have given some of her ability to wound without recourse to healing magic to the fish. Not all of it, though. I can make a dent. But Trill's wounds..."

While Caleb talked, the doctors were at work. The satyr never stopped sending power pulsing through that lifeline of healing magic he'd created between him and the kelpie. Ryu and I fed him power, through which I could feel a little of what he was able to do.

It wasn't much. Basically, he was keeping Trill alive, but he couldn't do a lot to actually heal her. It was more than he was able to do with someone wounded by the actual Red, but not a lot.

The doctor was shouting commands for blood, various medicines, and other specialists. Needles were inserted all over the place while Trill's wound was cleaned and prepped for surgery. Not a single doctor or nurse balked over the fact that their patient had gray skin, a foreshortened muzzle, or seaweed hair, and my heart swelled at their professionalism. I knew I was clinging to straws by that point, but it seemed right that one of our little band would be taken care of by human and supernatural alike.

When they whisked the little kelpie off to surgery, we followed. Caleb kept sustaining her, and we kept feeding him power. The surgeons quickly got down to business, and I admit I turned away. My forehead found the cool tile wall in front of me as I leaned toward it, exhausted. I knew it wasn't so much physical or magical as mental tiredness, but it felt like I'd been hit by a truck.

Hands on my waist pulled me around, then one hand moved up to cradle the back of my head, pulling my forehead away from the tile and toward my favorite man-wall. Anyan lifted me, and my legs moved around his waist as he walked me over a few paces. Then he sat on something. I don't know what, as I kept my eyes closed the whole time, greedily lapping up that sudden feeling of security that came over me.

"Go feed, I'll take over for you," Anyan said, his strong arms keeping me in a comforting squeeze. I pulled back to look at him, and saw a pale, worried expression. His arms around me tightened spasmodically, and for a second it looked as if he would cry.

Ryu didn't respond verbally, but I felt his power slip away as Anyan took over for the baobhan sith. Before he left, the Ryu's hand found my shoulder.

"You were great out there," he said wearily.

I craned my neck to look at Ryu. "So were you. And Trill probably wouldn't have made it if you weren't so quick."

He shook his head. "Not quick enough."

"Nonsense. You saved her. Now, go rest up. Restore your power."

Ryu nodded, giving Anyan a curious look. The bar-ghest did look really pale, but of course we would all be upset about Trill.

"Thanks," Ryu said, turning on his heel to stride away. His wet suit clung to his strong back and thighs.

Some soldier girl's about to get lucky, I thought, but without jealousy. I already felt pretty damned lucky, at least when it came to Anyan.

Now we just needed Trill to pull through...

It was a long few hours as the surgeons worked. I think I dozed, lulled by the steady beat of Anyan's heart, which

I concentrated on to tune out the muffled sounds of surgery. Various machines made pings and beeps, while the
doctors murmured commands the nurses echoed. Every
once in a while, something would squelch or suck wetly,
causing me to shiver.

Throughout it all, Anyan held me, the both of us feeding Caleb our power while the satyr patiently did his own
work, shoring up the efforts of the surgeons with a layer
of magic and keeping Trill's body functioning.

After what felt like a day, Anyan tapped me gently on
the back. I raised my head from his chest and then stood,
my legs feeling a bit wobbly. I turned to face the doctor,
who by that point looked almost as pale and fatigued as
her patient.

"She's not out of the woods. But we've done what we
can. The next few hours will be critical."

I nodded, tears blurring my vision. I didn't want Trill
to be critical, or in any woods, let alone bad woods.

"Your people have another healer on hand to take
over for yours," she said, nodding at Caleb. If the doctor looked tired, Caleb looked worse. His craggy face had
gone crevasse-like, his blue eyes reddened like he had
pink eye, blinking blearily out of dark pits.

"I'd go rest. Come back in a few hours. If anything
happens, we'll wake you."

I mumbled a protest that Anyan ignored, steering me
toward the doors. Iris was waiting for Caleb, and she
whisked the satyr off without comment, although she
did give me a fierce hug. Caleb and Anyan exchanged an
inscrutable glance, but it could have been about a thousand things.

I might have wondered about that glance more if an

Alfar I didn't recognize hadn't walked into the room, his healing powers already extended toward Trill. A halfling came trotting up a second later, also extending a powerful healing feeler. I couldn't help smiling at that. The rebels and Alfar were still trying to outdo each other, but for once I didn't mind.

The rebel healer did pause, giving me an update on the rest of our forces. Many of the halflings had made it back safely, although quite a few had died. The Alfar forces had been wiped out.

I was so emotionally numb by that point that I could barely process what the healer was saying. But I was grateful some had survived and saddened others hadn't. With every death, I had more and more motivation to go after Morrigan.

Anyan took me to a little room with a cot, where he reached for the zipper on my wet suit.

"You need rest," he said roughly, peeling the suit the rest of the way off me.

"So do you," I said, peering at him. He looked exhausted.

He shook his head. "I'm fine. Now, in bed."

After the barghest tucked me in, I cadged a few hours of much-needed sleep. After which Anyan insisted I take a quick swim. Luckily we were right on the coast, if a bit high up. But Anyan used the earth to make me a set of stairs leading to a rocky beach. I swam fast and hard, soaking up as much of the ocean's power as I could to fill my own reserves. Then we were back at the base, being shown to the recovery room, where Trill slept.

We weren't allowed to go in this time, not least because I was covered in seawater and a general coating of grime. But we could see the little kelpie through the doors.

Trill looked so small, covered in bandages and surrounded by machines.

"We've got to end this." My voice was husky, my throat clenched with a combination of grief, relief, and fear.

The barghest gave one of his trademarks grunts, but this one seemed even more full of emotion than usual.

"Part of me thought that, after we rescued you and got rid of the White, maybe we could just keep a handle on the Red. Maybe we wouldn't have to go after her. And then, after today . . ." I didn't finish my thought. I didn't want to say that we'd nearly seen our friend die, so I moved on. "She'll just keep doing things like this until we stop her."

Anyan put a hand on the nape of my neck, not to stop me from talking but to comfort me as I clarified for myself what I must have known all along. "I'll lose all of you, one by one, just like we almost lost Trill. Next time we might not be so lucky. The creature might not be able to apparate us —I think it just about knocked itself out doing us three this time. Or the wound will be a few inches to the right or left, somewhere that kills instantly. Or we won't have healers around to keep someone alive till we can get help.

"She'll just keep coming, and coming, and coming, until there's no one left."

We watched the shallow rise and fall of Trill's chest for a moment. Then I turned to Anyan and buried my face in his body, wrapping my arms around him.

He held me for a long while, and when he did speak, his voice was rough with grief.

"You're right, Jane. We do need to end this. But there's something you need to know . . . Come with me to the café?"

Confused, I followed obediently as he led me to the

little room that served as a café for the soldiers. He bought us coffee from the machine and sat down across from me.

"I didn't want to have to show you this yet, but there's no better time. While you were saving the sub, Caleb and I had a chat. It was about this. Caleb made it."

With that, Anyan gave me a handout. That's when I knew I was in trouble. The only reason one needed a handout was if (a) the information was so complicated it needed to be seen (which this clearly wasn't), or (b) the person giving the information didn't want to have to give it.

"What's it about?" I asked, not really wanting to read it.

"It's about the second part of the poem. About how to get rid of the Red. The whole second part of the text is actually quite short. The bulk of the work was done by you and Gus, creating the stone, and then doing that first transmutation of the stone into silver. Now, in alchemical parlance, we have to get that silver to gold, or what Theophrastus calls 'the second slaying of the dragon.'"

Anyan motioned toward the handout, his expression grim. I read aloud what was written, the knot in my stomach tightening evermore:

"Then seize again this dragon changed to white
(A change divinely wrought, as I have said,
By means of albifaction twice performed)
And slaying him again with knife of fire
Draw all his blood which gushes blazing hot
And red as shining flame when it ignites.
Then dip the dragon's skin into the blood
Which issued from his belly's gory wound
(As thou wouldst dip a whitened robe in dye

Of murex purple); so wilt thou obtain
A brilliant glory, shining as the sun,
Of goodly form and gladdening the heart
Of mortals who behold its excellence."

We all sat in silence, staring at our sheets of paper.

"Does this say what I think it says?" I said eventually. My voice was remarkably calm.

Anyan shook his head, his shaggy hair swinging vigorously.

"I don't know what it says yet, Jane. We're still trying to work out all the possible meanings—"

"It reads pretty clear to me," I said, interrupting the barghest. My hands clenched into fists around my handout of doom.

"And I won't do it," I added for good measure.

"Jane, if that's what we have to do, it's what we have to do. The Red can't be allowed to live. And if this is the only way…"

"I just won't do it," I insisted. "This whole thing is ridiculous…"

Anyan raised his voice. "We don't know yet—"

"Anyan! Stop it. It's clear as day, just like the other texts. It's telling me I have to gut you and bathe the stone in your blood. That's not going to happen. We'll find another way. Or we'll just chop the Red up again and keep her in some sort of giant blender. Whiz her up every time she starts to recongeal. I'm not killing you."

Clearly taken aback by my blender imagery, it took Anyan a moment to respond. When he did, his voice was gentle, but firm.

"Jane, you said it yourself. We have to end this."

I blinked at him through a haze of sudden tears, seeing the determination written all over his face.

For I knew then that he was ready to die. Because he loved me so much, and everyone else in his life, he would die for us. If sticking the labrys in him and bathing the stone in his blood was the only way we could take down the Red, he'd do it.

My first reaction at that thought was to scream at fate and stomp my feet and go ape shit. But I managed to suppress that urge. Instead, I forced myself to think through the problem.

My voice this time was muffled.

"I want to see the poem. The real one."

"Okay," he said, his hand stroking over my hair. "We can go over it."

I looked up into his beloved gray eyes. "No. I want to read it alone. I need time to think."

I wondered what he thought then. That I needed time to adjust myself to the idea of killing him?

He bent to kiss me. The touch of his lips was full of promises that we could not keep.

"Let's find Caleb," was all he said. We did just that, and the satyr handed over the book he was using without comment, but his expression was full of pity.

Later, alone with the poem, I applied my not inconsiderable English major skills. Unfortunately, it was exactly the same as Caleb's handout. I focused on the section that was freaking me out:

> *Then seize again this dragon changed to white*
> *(A change divinely wrought, as I have said,*
> *By means of albifaction twice performed)*

And slaying him again with knife of fire
Draw all his blood which gushes blazing hot
And red as shining flame when it ignites.
Then dip the dragon's skin into the blood
Which issued from his belly's gory wound...

It was that "again" that sent me into fits, me and my inner English major. It seemed so specific. That and the male pronoun.

But no amount of pronoun specificity or "agains" would change my mind. I wasn't killing Anyan. I didn't care if the world would go up in a ball of flame and everyone I knew died. I wasn't killing Anyan. I didn't think I *could* kill Anyan. I had enough trouble killing someone coming at me in full attack mode, although I had gotten better at it, as my taking out the rusalka confirmed.

But it was one thing to blast away an aggressive attacker, and another thing to slit open the belly of my lover and stick a stone in him. It also seemed so ridiculous. Why have a ritual that saves someone only to have the next ritual kill them?

Of course, my English major brain pointed out how deliciously sadistic that idea was, and therefore what a perfect sacrifice. But it was too perfect.

And at the end of the day, none of the syntax mattered. The fact was I wasn't killing Anyan.

Creature? I asked. It mumbled sleepily in my mind. We'd done a number on it, asking it to apparate all three of us. In hindsight, only Ryu and Trill really needed the emergency evacuation; I should have stayed behind.

[Yes, child?] it said eventually, after it had fully roused itself.

I need your help.

[Of course.]

I told it everything. We went over the poem for an hour, our silent communion racing as our brains merged the way they had right after Anyan was taken. When I emerged from our link, I blinked in the darkness of my room.

The creature had an idea, but it wasn't convinced so it was hiding its theory from me. I'd felt it realize something, then pull back, leaving me to wake on my own. My attempts at contacting it after that were futile, although it was still a part of me.

But for some reason I felt buoyed, as if a silent, secret part of me understood that all would work itself out. I didn't know if the creature had just planted that feeling there, inside me, but I didn't care. I'd take it.

I got up, showered in the little communal shower down the hall using the toiletries that had been left in my little room, and then got dressed. Trill's room was my first stop, and I watched the kelpie breathe for a while. She looked horrible, of course, but she was still with us.

Then I went and found my friends. They were sitting by themselves in a corner of the cafeteria, empty now as it was about an hour before dinner. Sounds of food prep clattered from the kitchen, but otherwise silence reigned.

Iris and Caleb were there, Caleb looking much better after a rest. Ryu looked well fed and as handsome as ever. Anyan looked disheveled and adorable, and happy to see me when I went and sat down next to him. It was only then that I saw Hiral had rejoined us.

"Hey," I said, giving the gwyllion a smile. "What's going on?"

"I thought I'd come back and check in," he mumbled. "The Red's in a state after you knocked out her champion. She'll be recovering for a few days, at least."

"That's perfect," I said, feeling like we'd finally been dealt an ace. "We need to figure out a plan. A trap. We need to end this."

Ryu and Iris nodded, but Caleb looked sad. I ignored the satyr and the implication of his expression.

"But first, we need to do something important. Something I've been thinking about for a while now, but haven't felt it was right to bring up until now."

Everyone looked at me expectantly, waiting for my big plan.

"What we need . . . is to go dancing."

They all stared at me like I'd been drinking, until Iris laughed and clapped her hands.

Dancing it was.

CHAPTER TWENTY-SIX

We borrowed a car from one of the halfling rebels to drive the few short hours to the Scottish city of Edinburgh. Once there, we checked into a hotel on the Royal Mile.

Anyan and I had a tiny, perfect little room in the turret of the hotel. There was room only for a queen-sized bed and a bathroom that could barely fit a shower cubicle, sink, and toilet. But the view was magnificent, as was the company.

Anyan immediately pulled me into his arms, then sank both of us onto the bed.

"We're supposed to be getting ready," I giggled as his lips found my neck.

"You're always ready," his voice rumbled in my ear as his hands slipped down my pants. I hissed when his fingers found my wet heat. I gasped as he spoke again, his voice smug. "See?"

We were definitely going to be late meeting the others, but I didn't care. Luckily, quickies are called quickies for a reason, so it wasn't too long before we were doing a tango trying to clean ourselves up in the little bathroom.

"I've been thinking about what you said about ending this," Anyan's voice rumbled from the bedroom behind me, where he was getting dressed.

I poked my head out of the bathroom long enough to glare at him. "We are dancing. We are not planning anything," I reminded the barghest. He ignored me, as usual.

"I've got an idea. A way to lure the Red here, to Edinburgh. I figure we're all here already, after that bit with the submarine. And Edinburgh has the perfect bait..."

I sighed, hoping it wasn't too late to cut him off now that he was officially strategizing.

"That's great, Anyan. I can't wait to hear it. But for right now..."

"For right now, we're dancing," he said agreeably, coming to stand in the doorway while I washed up in the sink. He watched me sponging off, his eyes filled with an expression I couldn't place.

"Exactly. I'm excited, I've never ceilidhed before. Can I say that? Ceilidhed? I don't know if it's a verb or not..."

"Jane. You've got to be prepared. If we're really ending this, you've got to be ready..." Anyan's voice broke through my ruminations, and we were back at square one.

"Please," I said, and I was really begging at that point. "Please don't bring that up again."

"I have to. It's the only way. Everything the poem said has been right so far..."

"Yeah, but that doesn't mean it's right this time."

"We can't let her keep attacking people. Attacking our people."

He was throwing my words back at me, and it worked. "You know I know that, Anyan, but..."

"But nothing. Come here for a second."

I followed the barghest the short few steps back to our bed, where we sat.

"I thought I was dead inside the White," he said, taking my hands in his. "It's not that I ever doubted you would do everything you could. I knew you would. I knew you would turn over heaven and hell to bring me back. But I didn't think anything *could* help me. When I woke up inside that thing, I thought I wouldn't even have a body to come back to."

"But you did. We got you back. And..."

"Just listen, please."

I clammed up, looking down at our joined hands.

"But despite everything, you brought me back. And we've had this extra time together." Anyan let go of my hand to brush back the hair from my face. Then he lifted my chin, forcing me to meet his eyes.

"This time has meant more to me than you can ever know. I know we were busy, running around and fighting and chasing the Red. But for me it was time I thought I'd never have again. Every second has been a luxury."

"And we'll have many more seconds," I said, trying to keep my voice steady.

"I don't know if we can, Jane. Because as much as I love you, I don't know if we can live like this. If we know we can kill the Red, and we choose not to do this last ritual, every death that occurs from now on is on our heads. Can you live with that?"

I glared at him, refusing to answer.

"I don't think I can," he said gently. "Not if it's Trill. Or

Iris. Or Caleb. God, what if it's you? Your dad? Everyone you care for? You're not going to love me then, Jane. Not even you are good enough for that."

I blinked back tears. His words had hit home. Watching Trill lie in that hospital bed, I hadn't been able to resist thinking of all the other battered bodies that bed could have contained.

"I don't want to talk about this now," I said, my voice angry, broken with tears. "We're supposed to be dancing."

"And we will, honey. But this isn't something we can walk away from, I want you to think…"

"All I can do is think about this shit, Anyan. And I hate it. Can I just have fifteen minutes to not think? Is that too much to ask?"

Anyan looked at my reddened face. I could feel the heat from where I knew my blood was pounding under my cheeks. I'd never been so angry in my life, but I wasn't angry with him. I was angry at everything—at the world, at fate, at my life that had gotten so good and then so fucked up, all at the same time.

At the universe, with its balances that never seemed fair.

"No," he said, leaning forward to kiss my forehead. "It's not too much to ask. You finish getting dressed, and I'll go tell the others you're coming."

"Thank you," I said quietly. I waited till the door closed at his back to get up and dig out the dress I'd borrowed from Iris.

I put it on with purpose, determined to have my dance. Even if I couldn't forget everything Anyan had just said, at least I could pretend I had.

*   *   *

Ceilidh dancing isn't hard, but it's definitely vigorous. It's traditional dancing, kept very much alive in Scottish culture, and the venue we'd found was a regular nightclub the nights it wasn't hosting a ceilidh.

When we arrived, there were already quite a few sweaty dancers twirling each other around in complicated reels, accompanied by a full ceilidh band of fiddle, flute, drums, and accordion. There was also a caller for us newbies, and they'd slow down before each song just long enough to teach the dance, but then it went to full speed and you either caught up or got whirled out of the reel.

Luckily, I was a fast learner, and all of my other friends seemed to know what they were doing. Caleb, heavily glamoured, worried me with those heavy hooves around all the daintily shod human feet, but he danced like a naked, goat-haunched Astaire. Iris looked like an angel in his arms, all that darkness she'd carried around so long totally lifted with her dispatching of the Healer. Ryu, of course, looked magnificent in his metrosexual duds, and the ladies were all doing their best to get reeled in his general direction.

Anyan was the real surprise. I'd never pictured him dancing, but he was as confident and quick on the wooden floor of the club as he was in bed. Our bodies moved together in perfect sync, and our eyes rarely left each other's as I was passed from partner to partner then back to him during the more complicated dances.

We'd dance a few dances till we needed to wet our whistles, then we'd hit the bar. The beer was cold at the nightclub, no warm ale, thank God, and we may have also sampled the whiskey. Once we'd filled our tanks, it was back to the floor for a few more songs. We did this again and again, dancing Strip the Willow, The Dashing White Sergeant, The Eightsome Reel, the Highland Barn Dance, and the rather Yankee-sounding Virginia Reel.

I was laughing nonstop when I wasn't panting or spinning about like a top toward Anyan, whose strong arms were always waiting to catch me.

It wasn't until the third Strip the Willow that I officially needed a break. It was the least challenging of the dances, but it had a lot of spinning, and there were some dancers on the floor who seemed to fancy themselves preparing for the Olympics in discus. I decided my thirst was greater than my willingness to have my arms ripped off again, so I motioned to Anyan to head toward the bar. He joined me, and together we made our way past the downstairs bar to the one upstairs, placed on a loft with a perfect view of the dancers below.

We ordered a pint and a water each, taking a stool at the railing to watch our friends. Iris's white teeth flashed in laughter as Caleb practically hurtled her through the air. Ryu had found himself a vivacious-looking blonde, and I had no doubt he'd be stripping her willow later that evening. I remembered how very well he stripped willows, and I wished them both all the pleasure in the world.

It felt a bit like being God at that moment, sitting above my friends. I let my mind toy with that idea. I pictured Iris and Caleb's golden, goaty babies, and all the women Ryu would pleasure in his long, handsome life. I thought of Trill, back in her hospital room, and pictured her here. She would love to dance like this, and I would have glamoured her so that she could. Her bare, black-nailed feet would have pounded out the rhythms of these dances, and for a second the beating of the drums became the pounding of my friend's pearl gray legs and of her heart, which beat ever stronger from that hospital bed.

Maybe it was the whiskey, or the pint still in my hand, but that feeling of omniscience grew until I felt that I was floating, suspended as if on a cloud above the roiling dancers below me.

Watching that seething mass of humanity with my friends dotted among them, all sweating and laughing and living, I saw my choices laid out in front of me like stars. The lines of attraction and repulsion created by the dancers Stripping the Willow made a spiderweb of cause and effect that brought clarity. From my great height I understood the poem finally, and that it was right. Watching my fate swirl like a dervish, driven faster and faster by the wild piping, I knew what was really important.

These people were important. This life was important. Yes, my own relationships meant the world to me. Anyan was *my* life, but every person in this room also had a life.

My life was just one more glowing star, and my love was worth no more and no less than anyone else's.

I took Anyan's hand in mine. He was watching me, his iron gray eyes inscrutable, but I could imagine he was also wondering about our fate, and whether I could do what he thought I had to.

And of course I could. I was the champion, and my life and my love had been fated to follow a special path, long before I was born. I'd railed against that idea of destiny for so long that to accept it felt like a strange relief, and as the spinning web before us wove faster and faster, the music wailing, the dancers panting and shining, I reveled in the motion and the joy. The universe had won and at that fact I laughed, standing to pull Anyan to his feet, just as the pounding beat ceased, everyone suddenly stock-still.

The threads binding the web were cut with the music's cessation, just as all webs must inevitably be met by Fate's scissors. It all made sense.

Anyan seemed to know I'd decided something as we left the club and made our way home. The others would spend the night dancing, drinking, living. But we had so much we needed to say.

"Jane," Anyan said as I pushed him inside our little room back at the hotel. "You've made your decision..."

But I didn't want to talk with words. I pulled him down roughly to me. My hands fisted in his T-shirt, and my mouth found his in a fierce kiss. His lips answered mine with equal vigor, saying everything that needed to be said.

I pushed him toward the bed, stripping him as we went. His shirt, his jeans, those damned motorcycle boots he loved but that took forever to remove. He peeled off his own socks as I made short work of my clothes and my easily removable Converse.

He pulled me on top of him. Neither of us needed, or wanted, any foreplay then. This was about being alive, about being with each other, about our joy at living and loving. He moved inside me with a force that left me gasping, but I met him stroke for stroke until we both broke, biting each other's shoulders to keep from screaming and waking the crowded hotel.

Afterward, we lay panting until our hearts slowed enough to start all over again. But this time our lovemaking was slow, gentle. We tasted, and smelled, and touched, memorizing each other's every movement, savoring each other's bodies. If the first round had been about life and love, this round was very different.

This round was about saying good-bye.

CHAPTER TWENTY-SEVEN

Morrigan's troops are massing in Dalkeith," Griffin said, pointing to the map in front of us. Hiral had already brought us footage of her troops, where they were bivouacked at a local estate. She seemed to know all the rich folks, our Morrigan did.

"I hate the word 'troops,'" I said to no one in particular. Anyan grunted a soft laugh.

In the grand scale of things, our "armies" weren't that big. We weren't invading Afghanistan or Iraq. But still, there were nearly a thousand people on each side waiting to kill the other.

That seemed like more than enough to me.

"We've done a good job putting together a force large enough to combat hers," the rebel leader Jack said, slightly defensively. He had been, of course, responsible for the majority of the troops making up our regiment. But we'd pulled in people from other territories, as well, including a contingent of soldiers from my own territory.

One of them was Nyx, who was currently standing across from us at the conference table we were using in the military base.

"The troops won't be a problem," said the baobhan sith babe who I'd once thought the scariest thing in the world. Her chestnut hair was still boy short, and she was wearing a latex catsuit à la *Underworld*. I couldn't keep my eyes off her. Not because she was admittedly gorgeous, but because she used to scare the piss out of me, and now I was all "whatever." If I hadn't known I'd changed since first learning about my mother, I certainly did now.

Her eyes met mine briefly as she continued talking, and I didn't even flinch. I deserved a cookie.

"Our forces are equal to theirs and we're more integrated, better fighters. Morrigan's splitting everyone up by faction is not only crazy, but suicidal. They can't cover for each other's weaknesses."

Nyx was right, and we all nodded.

"The problem is Morrigan herself," Ryu added. Over the course of our various planning sessions, I had seen why they worked well together, now that Nyx wasn't determined to be an evil cunt. They both had the same cool, assessing style of thinking that could see both the big picture and the minute details.

"We've got to get her out of the way as quickly as possible. Our communities won't stand for much more from her." Trevor, our U.S. government liaison, was blunt, but I knew he was right. One of our debriefings had been an overview of current human sentiment about what was happening, as depicted in the media and in the blogosphere. It wasn't good. Obviously, everyone knew something was up and no amount of "it's all fine" would cover the fact a massive fuck-off dragon kept popping up, and then being battled with what looked like magic.

I knew the Alfar Powers That Be all over the world were confabbing about how to handle this dilemma. Hiral had taken some time off from spying on Morrigan to spy on one of Griffin's conference calls with the other seconds in command (who almost inevitably had more political acumen then their powerful but dazed leaders). Their suggestions for how to handle the humans had ranged from complete eradication of the species, which was immediately dismissed, thank God, to trying to act like it was a *War of the Worlds*–type publicity stunt for a movie.

I wondered if I'd be made to star in said movie.

No final plans were made, but it was pretty clear something would have to give in the complete secrecy that ruled our world. The thought was both terrifying and exhilarating to halflings like me, who straddled both spheres anyway. On the one hand, it would be so nice not to hide. On the other hand, I knew full well how badly my fellow humans dealt with change, let alone with difference.

"Leave her to me," I said, my voice quiet but steady. "Just get her where we want her and I'll take care of her."

My hand found the silver stone I kept in my hoodie's zip-up pocket. I'd decided to start carrying it. On the one hand, it reminded me of what was coming. On the other, I also wanted to keep it safe in case Morrigan had her own Hirals in our court.

Nyx gave me an appraising look, but she didn't openly sneer like I was expecting. She'd obviously changed, as well.

"You sure you can end her?" Nyx said, although her voice was only mildly skeptical. To be fair, claiming to an ability to end the Red was big.

"We got the White, didn't we?" My words shut her up, not least at my reminder that there was no "I" in this team.

"All right. Let's go over this one more time. Tonight is going to be tight; we don't want anything going off the rails."

I watched Griffin go through our plans once more by pushing little troops around on the map in front of us, but I couldn't help letting my mind wander. My task was relatively straightforward, after all: Let everyone else do his or her job, then kill the Red.

But if I thought too much about what killing the Red really entailed, I'd go crazy.

So instead I watched the odd combination of humans, Alfar, rebel purebloods, and halflings that I'd come to depend upon. They were working well together now, something none of us commented on; but I knew we were all aware of that fact.

Watching Jack, Griffin, Trevor, my friends, and all the other soldiers in that room bent over those maps, I realized then that, no matter what, Morrigan had failed. Even if she killed all of us, the Alfar queen's real goal had been to divide. She'd wanted a pure Alfar society ruling the world, and her purist agenda had been so powerful that it had even infected the Red. But all she'd done was bring us together. We were fighting side by side, and although I didn't know what would happen when all this was over, I knew things couldn't go back to the way they were before.

Ironically, by attempting to "out" the supernaturals, no doubt hoping that would cause humans to attack and the Alfar to mount an offensive that would make them supreme, she'd only made the supernatural community work with the human community. And paradoxically, that engagement with both humans and the Red had meant an increased reliance by the Alfar on the halflings they'd tried so hard to ignore for so long. Halflings were part human, after all—they were a bridge between the humans and the Alfar that both sides sorely needed.

If we did kill the Red, and the world went on, it wouldn't be as it was. I couldn't imagine the changes that were coming, but change would be inevitable.

And if we didn't kill the Red, we'd probably all die together. But even that was spit in Morrigan's eye, not that I wouldn't prefer a slightly less dramatic spitball.

Yet it comforted me, looking around that room, that Morrigan had lost even if she won.

And at that moment I needed all the comfort I could get.

Once again, we were in costume. I'm not sure why supernatural wars had to involve costuming—maybe we'd all seen too many movies. Or maybe the mad Alfar with the *War of the Worlds* plan had won, and we were all going to pretend it was Joaquin Phoenix inside the dragon.

I was wearing something I'd never have been caught dead in otherwise. The Alfar had spared no expense outfitting us, and Griffin had actually put a few of his most fabulous minions on the job of making us look like fire dancers.

Low on my hips rested a pair of dark burgundy belly dancing pants. They were basically stretchy yoga pants that flared out into cool, split bell-bottoms. They also had a little scarf-skirt combo built in, which could be ruched up or down with little strings dangling from my hips. For a top, I was wearing basically a furry bra, decorated with shells and coins that jingled as I walked. My stomach and arms were bare except for some fake tribal tattoos painted on by Anyan, who'd done a beautiful job.

Of course, we'd gotten incredibly distracted in the painting process, smudging Anyan's first attempt and having to redo it all. But that was half the fun, to be honest.

Over my face I wore a great horned mask, which made me look like an owl with antlers. I'd been transformed into a wild, half-human creature from Celtic mythology.

Anyan was resplendent, meanwhile, in black leather pants that clung to him like a second skin. His chest was bare and also painted, as was his broad, muscular back. His face was shadowed by a mask of black feathers, with a raven's beak. He was menacing and beautiful, and I couldn't keep my eyes off him, despite the circumstances.

The rest of our troops were similarly attired, and we watched as similarly dressed humans eyed us while they crossed the Meadows. For we were dressed perfectly for a social event that was on the other side of town—the Beltane Fire Festival. That was on Calton Hill, but we were planning on going up Arthur's Seat, a very different hill altogether.

It had been my idea, actually. Something I remember Anyan telling me when we first got to England and he'd been trying to explain the supernatural politics of the Great Island. While all other Alfar monarchs were called king or queen, Luke called himself the leader of the Great Island. It was a game of semantics, for there existed an ancient legend that whosoever ruled the Island ruled the race.

That idea had stuck with me, mostly because it was so ridiculous. But there had also been a frisson of romance to the whole thing, and I'd always loved a legend.

So when we were trying to come up with lures for a

creature who loved nothing now that we'd killed the White, and who seemed to have figured out that the best way to avenge herself on me for his loss was to terrorize everyone around but me, I'd turned to the legend. If Morrigan was so obsessed with race, I couldn't imagine anything worse in her mind than having the race run by a halfling.

Hiral and I had holed up in a corner, letting our imaginations run wild. We'd come up with something brilliant, and if I hadn't already started to feel affection for the little gwyllion, his place in my heart would have been sealed then. He smelled bad and had atrocious manners, but he was brilliant—crafty, cunning, and bold.

"Let's give her the kind of conniption you can only give a real purist," he'd said, grinning evilly. "The thought of everything in your hands will make her shit bricks."

To get our forces into the city, close enough to our target to mobilize quickly, we'd used the cover of the Fire Festival. It was a huge event, drawing people from all over the world. A few hundred more congregating in costumes wouldn't alarm human authorities, so we wouldn't have to skulk in or waste energy on glamours.

We could also parade around a bit, to drive Morrigan even battier.

Once we had the plan, we had to make her aware of what we were doing. We figured the best way to do that was to take Hiral off the case—at least on the surface. It turned out that Morrigan did have her own spies in our camp, but that Hiral knew who all of them were. He hadn't told The Powers That Be who they were, because he had his own ways of doing things that he considered more effective. And I had to agree with him that he was right. After all, it had been easy for the gwyllion to engineer little accidents at key moments, to keep the spies from learning anything crucial. So the spy carefully placed in Luke's ranks got terrible food poisoning at the meeting where he was supposed to be updated on our important plans regarding the submarine attack. Or the human spy whose role was to go through our things when they cleaned our barracks rooms slipped on the way down the hall, needing medical attention. Hiral's way of doing things was totally effective. No new spies were brought in, as the current spies' failures were seen as simple accidents. All of which meant Hiral knew his enemies and could continue to keep one step ahead of them.

So to get any information we wanted back to the Red, all Hiral had to do was stop working. When Anyan and I went to train with the labrys one morning, we left out a few interesting tidbits alluding to notes of a secret stash of power somewhere in Edinburgh. Other, similar hints that a revelation was on the horizon were left out for Morrigan's various spies. Hiral jumped back and forth between our camp and Morrigan's, reporting that the Red's people were abuzz with news that we were up to something big.

All we needed to do was let the buzz grow to a roar, then have a final meeting, one in which Luke's advisors—including Morrigan's top Alfar spy—were included.

We'd been masterful that day, Ryu and me. Anyan had let us handle it, since Ryu was the showman. The baobhan sith had brought in a huge pile of scrolls, books, and other old-looking sources. He'd shown us all the "evidence"—most of it cobbled together from existing legends with added embellishment. Then he'd let us know the crucial info: that the legend about ruling the Island wasn't a legend. It was fact. For Arthur's Seat wasn't called that by accident—it was an

ancient seat of power, containing a hidden force so raw and
untamed anyone who wielded it would be like a god.

We'd made the whole thing up, of course. Arthur's Seat
was just a dramatic-looking plateau. But it was the perfect
dramatic-looking plateau for our operation.

All I had to do then was pull the labrys and make some
crazed declarations of my intentions to find this source
and take it for myself, so that I could defeat the Red and
all she represented and rule all the supernaturals under
my benevolent grace.

Cut to startled looks from all involved, then a combination of cheers from the halflings, startled shouts from the
humans, and anger from the Alfar, then everyone hustling
to start the preparations we needed to make. The only one
who'd left looking calm was Morrigan's spy, but that's
because he thought he was the cat who got the cream.

And that had brought us here, dressed in sexytimes
costumes. It was growing dark finally, and that's when
we'd start. Already some of our folks had lit torches or
poi, both of which they swung around in elaborate fire
dances. Confused humans gathered, thinking they were
off to the wrong place, so we prodded them along to their
real destination with gentle magical nudges.

Slowly, Ryu, Caleb, and Iris made their way around the
crowd, getting everyone into formation. Across the other
side of the city, Beltane rites were beginning that would
see the crowning of the May Queen and the sacrifice of
her consort, the Green Man.

Meanwhile, we started our own procession, going in
the other direction. Anyan and I led the way, our joined
hands held up high so that all could follow as we marched
toward our destinies.

CHAPTER TWENTY-EIGHT

The climb up Arthur's Seat was bracing. Despite the chill air, sweat ran down my back, soaking the hair at the nape of my neck. My calves sang with tension, but nothing could top the anxiety whisking around my stomach.

When we got to the top, we moved forward, our troops amassing behind us. We formed a circle, Anyan and I at the center. Our fire dancers moved around the edges, front and back, whirling their poi or their torches, while others with flaming banners waved them around. We were being as noisome and frolicsome as we could, as if in the beginning stages of some massive ritual.

Anyan and I watched the proceedings, my hand clutching his. I knew mine was slick with sweat, my heart pounding in my throat as he surveyed the scene with sad eyes.

I raised my free hand to finger the stone, strung in a mesh net that dangled from my neck like a heavy necklace. It bumped against my own belly, as if to remind me of what I must do.

"They're coming," said a voice next to me from out of nothing. Hiral popped into view a second later, the gwyllion having served as one of our scouts.

"When?" was all Anyan asked.

"They're coming from the Dalkeith side. They'll be here in minutes. She's brought more troops than we have."

Anyan and I exchanged looks.

"We have to get her down immediately," I said. "Put an end to this as quickly as possible."

Hiral nodded. "Leave it to me."

Suddenly, the dancing around our circle ceased and our numbers fanned out, as ordered. That left Anyan and me facing our enemy.

Morrigan came first, in her half-dragon, half-human form. Her long limbs rippled with muscle, covered in scales that caught our fire and reflected it in a bloodred glow. When her troops appeared, they revealed that she, too, had done some costuming. They were wearing red tabards with a white embroidered dragon. She wanted everyone to know for whom she fought; for whom she sought revenge.

We eyed each other over the expanse of the grassy top of Arthur's Seat. Then she raised her hands, creating a mage ball that glowed as red as her scales. Her troops created their own missiles, and we raised powerful shields. To combat the glow her side was creating, I pulled the labrys, which lit up like a strobe, knowing its enemy was near.

I don't know who launched the first mage ball, but it wasn't Morrigan. She stood the whole time, staring at me with hate etched on her features as her troops attacked. Our own forces surged past us, in front of us, guarding us as they met the brunt of her forces. Our goblins and goblin halflings, armed with enormous broadswords and axes, charged first, their long legs carrying them out of the crowd. Harpies swooped overhead, as did ravens and nahuals who'd grown wings, clashing in the night sky, armed with mage balls, talons, bows, and swords.

Ryu and Nyx fought together. They were a formidable team, both in tight leather armor and armed with swords lit up with power. They fought as one being, smoothly defending the other's back as one of them went on the offensive, fluidly switching roles as the battle demanded.

Caleb, and other healers like him, roved about alternately fighting and doctoring our troops. I'd feel a surge of earth magic from the satyr as he exploded an enemy's upraised arm, only to feel a similar surge as he healed the fallen dryad at his feet.

Our fighters were outnumbered, but they were also skilled. And Morrigan's prejudices meant her troops had trained only with others of their own factions—something that was eminently stupid on a number of levels. In the melee of battle, those groups were quickly broken up, and fighters who had no idea what the other's skills were had to suddenly defend each other's backs. Our people were used to capitalizing on each faction's strengths and weaknesses, so we had defensively powerful creatures, like dryads, paired up with offensively powerful ones, like ifrits. The one shielded them both, the other attacked with no mercy. Morrigan's scattered troops quickly tried to emulate our strategies, but they didn't know how. A few who had obviously fought before signing up with Morrigan barked orders trying to help, but their voices were swallowed up by the din of the fight.

Eventually, a knot of hard-fighting Alfar came at Anyan and me. We met them with a wall of power so fierce we pushed two backward all the way off the cliff. The others stood their ground, braced behind their own shields.

When we realized we could do this all day, we stopped, and let them come. I took a defensive stance with the labrys; I would try to carve through their shields, allowing Anyan to attack.

It was Griffin and Luke who stepped in then. Surprisingly, Luke had insisted on fighting. Griffin hadn't been able to stop his leader, although it was obvious he wanted to. But I was glad he hadn't. I knew we'd have been able to take Morrigan's Alfar eventually, but it would have taken a lot of time and energy better spent combatting the White.

And Luke proved why, despite his being completely unaware of reality, he was the Great Island's leader. I felt a huge swell of power from behind me as the first two Alfar charging us were literally obliterated by a mage ball winging over our heads. Griffin and Luke stepped around Anyan and me, Griffin throwing his own mage ball a second after Luke's. It wasn't as strong, but Luke's had decimated the Alfar's shields, along with their first two soldiers, so Griffin's missile took out the next in line, a fierce-looking Alfar female.

The pair closed in on the remaining Alfar, and were sucked into the melee. I knew they'd won when what looked like a bomb exploded from behind a wall of fighters. Bodies flew everywhere—living and dead—until finally Luke and Griffin emerged, looking grim but triumphant.

Caleb and his team rushed about healing the flying

bodies from our side, while Anyan and I braced ourselves for Morrigan's next trick. That's when Hiral popped back up. He'd somehow managed to acquire a red tabard that fit him, and I threw up a hasty shield around the gwyllion as a mage ball from one of our fighters nearly caught him as soon as he appeared.

"Ready?" he asked.

I looked at Anyan, who nodded. "Yes."

The gwyllion popped away without comment. The creature, a silent presence in my mind the whole time, let me see Hiral's progress through his own eyes. The gwyllion was way behind Morrigan's lines, where her advisors milled around her, protecting the queen as well as keeping an eye on the battle.

The gwyllion approached a nahual sitting shyly by the sidelines, clutching a briefcase. "Gofer" was written all over the girl.

Dispersing his powerful shield and glamour, Hiral burst into motion, coming up on the girl and grabbing at her hands.

"They've started! They've started the ritual! Only I could see what they were doing. The Alfar she sent are dead and they've started!"

The girl stared at the gwyllion, comprehension dawning in her eyes. Then her face took on a crafty, greedy look. She obviously saw a promotion coming her way.

The gofer girl approached one of the less senior Alfar on the sidelines, and I watched as the process repeated itself a number of times, the rumor running up the chain of command. One or two Alfar in, the gwyllion disappeared as his lies became fact. He stayed on, though, to see the fruition of his actions.

Morrigan threw back her head and roared. Her body shimmered with magic as her skin stretched and pulsated. The Red obviously wanted out, and the Alfar queen who hosted her was obviously doing everything she could to keep the dragon from taking charge. Morrigan knew they were smarter and tougher in this hybrid skin, even if the Red didn't accept that.

When the fit of magic ended, and Morrigan had regained control, the eyes she raised to the melee were filled with fire. That fire spread over her body till she'd lit up like an ifrit. I couldn't help shuddering. Reminders of Con would always have that effect on me.

"She's coming," I said to Anyan, and seconds later we saw her flaming presence making itself felt across the field. Combatants parted like the Red Sea, and those who weren't fast enough were blasted out of her way regardless of whether they were our soldiers or hers.

Ryu, Nyx, and Caleb hastily cleared our soldiers out of the way, pushing everyone back into a semicircle behind us.

When Morrigan appeared, she was obviously irate.

"What is this ritual, you stupid bitch!" she roared. The long muzzle distorting her face was full of sharp teeth and a snake's tongue, all of which contributed to a definite lisp. What came out was more like, "Whas iss diss widual, you dupis biss!"

Any humor created by her speech impediment, however, was mitigated by her throwing the head of one of our goblin fighters at us. I felt bad batting it out of the air but I also didn't want to get dinged by it.

The Red followed up the head with herself, lunging her own neck forward using her Go-Go-Gadget-neck trick that never ceased to horrify me. The Red blazed in her eyes as she again fought for control over her own body. I followed after her retreating jaws, the labrys blazing before me like a comet.

Slashing, I could feel myself melding with the creature as we fought the Red together. Preternaturally swift and sure on my feet, my arms moved through the air like a ballerina's, if ballerinas were armed with flaming axes of death.

Her neck still extended unnaturally, the Red pranced in front of me, slashing with wicked teeth and claws. I kept my shields beefed up as much as they could, because any wounds made by the Red were immune to magical intervention. But the same kind of primordial power that animated my labrys animated the Red, and my shields were not immune to her slashing attacks.

So it was up to me to be quicker than she, and the creature helped with that. But I felt the first burning score across my hip like a tracing of fire, and bright blood swelled to the surface when I looked down.

"Son of a bitch," I growled, slashing forward. My labrys found the Red's shoulder as if in punishment for the hip slash, and she growled back at me with equal ferocity. Dancing around each other, we fought with wicked ferocity until we finally fell apart, panting.

Only then did Anyan nod at me quietly from the sidelines.

Launching myself forward, I again attacked the Red. She snarled her rage, coming to meet me after the briefest pause. But this time, I didn't close with her. Instead, I began a weird slashing dance that sent me prancing around her like a deranged dervish. All of my power

went into the labrys, leaving me vulnerable. So despite
the speed lent to me by the creature, I felt a fiery slash
across my left arm, then my right, and another dug deep
across my calf. That one made me stumble, but buoyed
by adrenaline and egged on by the labrys, I erupted back
onto my feet, only to continue my weird twirling circuit
around the Red.

Obviously confused, she didn't realize what I'd done
till her shields crumbled around her, slashed in a thousand different places. Before she could erect new ones, I
shouted for my backup even as I struck.

The ax wasn't meant to be thrown, but Anyan and I
had practiced all day. Good aim and a nudge from the
creature's power meant the strike was perfect, the labrys
burying itself in Morrigan's chest. From inside her, the
double-headed ax struck again—a pulse of power that
actually knocked me back on my ass and tore through
Morrigan like a grenade.

Without losing a beat, Iris ran forward from where
she'd been hiding, waiting for her moment. She carried a
single, precious bucket of water that she threw with perfect aim over the Red.

As the water arced over Morrigan, I raised my hand
and commanded it to slow and spread till it resembled
a net of water that fell over the Red, pinning her to the
ground for the next, awful stage of this ritual.

Anyan came racing up from behind me, grabbing my
hand and hauling me to my feet and to the Red. Writhing
in agony, the labrys pumping a series of tiny explosions of
power through her mutilated chest, Morrigan still looked
at me with hate in her eyes as we stood above her prone
figure.

The barghest took the stone from where it hung at my belly and pressed it into my hands.

"You must do this!" he shouted over the Red's angry shouts and the commotion of the battle still raging around us.

I met his eyes, and it was like time stopped. Wanting to memorize every plane of his beautiful, rough-hewn face, I raised a trembling hand and brushed it down over his cheek.

"I will always love you," I told him. "Never forget that."

"And I you. I'm doing this for you. You must live without me; live for both of us."

I nodded, pulling him down to me in a kiss. He tasted of love, and regret, and so much life.

Before we had even pulled away, my hand found the haft of the labrys. I'd have to do this quickly, as once the labrys was out, the Red would heal herself in seconds and we wouldn't be able to keep her on the ground.

Anyan's hand fisted itself in my hair as his forehead met mine.

"God, I love you. I love you, I love you," he chanted, his eyes frightened but determined.

And that's when I pulled the ax from Morrigan's chest with a great sucking sound. It took me a second to adjust the grip on the haft, and then I struck.

Anyan's eyes widened as he screamed, a single, piercing "No!" His power rent the air around him.

The pain, of course was excruciating. There was a reason shamed samurai ended their lives by self-evisceration. It was a horrible way to die.

My knees buckled as my blood bubbled from my gut. The labrys still pulsing in my hand, I used the dregs of my physical strength to push the silver stone into the wound I'd made.

When bright red splashed against silver, the stone and the labrys began to pulse the same shade of coppery gold. I could feel Anyan's magic trying to close the wounds I'd made, but they'd been made to serve a magic far older than his, and would not answer the throaty pleas he shouted into the air above me.

With bloody hands, I raised the stone above the Red, where it glowed down on her, raising her body up an inch in the air. Her green eyes, slit like a cat's, met mine. After the first shock of fear had passed from them, they seemed pleased.

"Now you die," I told Morrigan, plunging the stone back into the wash of my fresh blood. Her dragon's face smiled at me, her expression almost serene. Her hand reached up to the stone, as if accepting her fate. Then she spoke.

"And so do you, little halfling. My life for yours."

CHAPTER TWENTY-NINE

Dying hurt, and dying the way I'd chosen to, hurt a lot. But I'd known it had to be me, for a lot of reasons.

After all, it had never made any sense that Anyan would have to die to complete the ritual. He wasn't the White, after all—not anymore. The White was the stone I was bleeding all over. There had been that pesky "again" in the poem, as well as the male pronoun. But everything was a male pronoun back in those days, and as for dying twice—well, I had that covered after dying once over Jason.

And that's what I'd realized the night at the club. All of the niggling hints and things that had never made sense came together for me as I watched over the crowd like a god. Things like why the creature didn't just tell us what we needed to do; why it was important I figure things out for myself.

It also answered that bigger question: Why make me the champion? I'd joked a number of times that I was a lover, not a fighter. It had never made any sense that I'd be chosen over someone like Blondie, who'd already made such a good warrior-champion.

But that was the whole point. This job, killing the Red and the White for real, didn't require a fighter. It required a lover.

What I'd seen that night, arcing above the crowded nightclub, hadn't *really* been destiny, although that had been a good enough word. More accurately, I'd seen a really good choice. I'd figured out the motivation behind the universe's actions, and realized what I had to do. I was the *sacrifice*—the Green Man—not the May Queen who would bring renewal to the land. I had to die before that could happen.

In other words, it wasn't destiny at all, even if the universe itself was involved. The creature, Blondie, Anyan, me: We'd all been the pawns of ancient forces beyond our comprehension since the first stirrings of the Red in Morrigan's consciousness. I'd been cast as a sacrifice, and having realized that, I knew what a smart choice the universe had made. After all, a sacrifice had to be a *real* sacrifice. I was loved, and loving. I didn't want to lose this life and these people I cared so much about and who cared about me. So yeah, I wasn't that great at fighting, but because my friends loved me, they would keep me safe until the time came. And then I would do the same for them, in the only way I knew how.

I would die for them, and do it gladly.

Don't get me wrong, I didn't feel all that glad right then. My life's blood was pouring out of me over a silver stone that, except for a bit of a glow, wasn't doing much. And Anyan was shouting, staring into my pain-widened eyes with a gray gaze full of despair.

"It was supposed to be me. It was supposed to be

me!" he was shouting, trying to heal me, trying to pull me away from the magic in which I was caught. But the labrys wound wouldn't heal any more than one made by the Red's claws, and the otherwise innocuous glow of the stone wouldn't let me go.

The Red's wounds, meanwhile, were healing, and she was fighting her bonds. Staring up at me with a hideous form of hope, she reached up to where I bled. Grasping the stone, she pulled, meaning to get it away from me, away from herself, so that she could attack again...

But as soon as her red-scaled, black-clawed hands made contact with the stone, it boomed with a sonic wave of power that flattened everyone but Anyan and me. We stood in its glow, the May King and his sacrificial bride, as the stone levitated upward on its own.

The glow it cast turned brighter and brighter, casting heat on my so-cold skin. As my blood continued to seep over the stone, slowing now, I felt something else pouring into that damned rock.

My life began to leave me, giving the stone what it needed to complete the ritual. Born of fire, made to contain evil, it would take nothing less. As my consciousness faded, as Anyan's shouts turned to panicked screams and my friends fought to get through the barrier created by the stone's power, I felt the magic grab hold.

Morrigan felt it, too. Her green eyes narrowed, then went wide with fear. I'd not yet seen her look afraid, and even as I died, I felt satisfaction.

With the last dregs of my consciousness, I felt the stone's power hook deep within the Red, and pull. The same black ooze that had crept out of Anyan came out of Morrigan, as well as a bright sphere of power. But this sphere was gold.

Like before, the stone pulled at the black ooze, only this ooze fought twice as hard as that which had been the White. As I bled out over the stone, I could feel the direct link between my blood and the stone's power—as if knowing its terrible effect, my draining blood seemed to empower it, and it pulled with even greater urgency.

Finally, after stretching itself as thin as it could get in an attempt to survive, the black ooze was sucked up into the stone. A split second later, the gold glow clapped on to it. Between the rivulets of blood still flowing over the once-silver stone, I saw bright yellow metal.

Then I saw nothing as I fell to my knees. Having performed its ancient birthright, the stone was suddenly just that—a stone. Made of precious metal, yes, but without agency. Without its power keeping them at bay, my friends all rushed to my side, Anyan lunging over Morrigan's body. But I was already toppling over, and no one was quick enough to catch me.

The last thing I saw as I died were the dead eyes of Morrigan, returned to their former shade of brilliant, sapphirine blue.

I'd died before, of course, but I hadn't remembered it. Still, when I woke up in a bright white space that wasn't a room, that had no horizon to speak of, I wasn't panicked. I knew I'd been there before.

I was still lying on the ground. I picked myself up carefully, afraid I'd lose my intestines. But there was no pain, and when I looked, my belly was unscathed.

The only surprise was that the rock was still there, although it no longer hung in a net around my neck. It was clutched in my hand, everything now clean of my blood.

"Jane," came a voice from behind me—one carved into my memory. I turned immediately to one of the only people I'd obey without hesitation.

My mother looked exactly as I remembered her—long black hair swirling down over her curvy body, encased in a white robe. The robe was a nice touch.

"Is it really you?" I asked, strangely calm, considering. Ever since I'd woken up in the white light, I'd felt... not a lot, to be honest. My thoughts would occasionally coalesce enough for me to remember I should be panicked or upset, but then such thoughts would scatter like dandelion seeds in a strong wind.

"Yes, and no," my mother said, smiling kindly. "I am a part now of everything."

I knew we were getting into some serious eschatological issues.

"Um, are you the universe?"

"I am everything," she repeated.

I took that as a "yes."

"What you did was brave," she continued. "You took a great evil into yourself. We thank you."

I looked down at the golden stone, so beautiful now. It was hard to believe something so glistening could hide such evil, but I'm sure I wasn't the first person to have thought something similar.

"Is that it, then? The Red and the White are dead?"

"Yes. They are contained, and permanently, because of your sacrifice."

I blinked at the mention of "sacrifice." A vision of

Anyan swam before me, and I felt grief for the first time since waking.

"You mourn," said the figure that looked like my mother. "You must cross over, and forget."

I looked up, suddenly blinking back tears. I didn't want to forget.

But I'm dead, I realized. That's what I'd done. I'd killed myself, which meant I was dead. And there was no going back this time.

Mutely, I held out my hand. I couldn't do *this* alone, too. My mother's hand met mine, just as it used to. Only mine was bigger now—an almost mirror image of the one it clutched.

"Come, Jane," she said, her shining black eyes so content, so at peace. We took a step forward, then another, and the air began to shimmer in front of us, coalescing into...

A giant yellow eye, slit like a goat's.

"Stop!" boomed the creature's voice in the white space. It wasn't in my mind this time, but everywhere.

The form of my mother cocked her head to one side, as curious as me. Before either of us could ask what was happening, the creature spoke again.

"You will go no further, Jane. Your task is done."

"Um," I said, "I'm dead. As you knew I would be from the moment you chose me." My voice crackled with bitterness as fury swept up inside me. Suddenly, I could feel, and all I felt was anger.

"We knew you'd be brave enough to make this choice, yes," the creature said calmly. "And someone had to."

A thousand furious rejoinders flashed through my mind, but before I could say any of them, my anger faltered

and died. What it said was true. Someone had to destroy
the Red and the White—why not me?

"But I didn't want to die," I said weakly. My mother's
hand squeezed mine and the eye blinked.

"And that's why you were perfect," the creature said
sadly. "You were a true sacrifice, the oldest magic there is.
Your ancients knew this to be true, as did those you wor-
ship as gods."

"And Aslan," I mumbled, a bit awed by this conversation.

"Your death was powerful," my mother said, confirming the creature's words, "and its power was great because
you were full of so much life, so much love."

"That's fucked up," I pointed out. Then I asked the
questions that had been lurking in the back of my mind
since I'd realized what I had to do. "Was any of it yours?
The power? The scheme?"

The creature paused. "My power was mine, yes. But
the champion's power...that was the universe's."

"So it was the one that chose me?"

"With my aid, yes."

"So were you really running out of power?"

"No. You had to experience certain things for yourself,
and have the time to process them. I would use my power
to speed things along when it was appropriate, but there
were times you had to work at a human pace. You needed
to make the connections for yourself."

I rubbed a hand over my stomach. "So I'd know what
to do when the time came?"

The creature paused, choosing its next words carefully.
"More so that you could accept what you had to do. It was
important that you *accept*, that you act willingly. And I
needed to keep my strength."

"For what?"

"For this," said the creature. "Give me the stone."

I looked at the eyeball, which—rather obviously—looked back.

"What?"

"Give me the stone. You have done your part. Now let me do mine."

"But…"

"Trust me. Give me the stone."

I looked at my mother, who shrugged eloquently. The decision was mine.

"What are you going to do with it?" I asked as I held up my precious golden cargo to the giant eye. The snarky part of my brain wondered how I could give anything to an eyeball with no hands.

"I don't need hands," the creature said, causing me to blush. We were apparently still connected mentally. "And as for what I'm going to do with it, I'm going to make sure it never comes back."

Suddenly, the white nonroom started to rock. Enormous power was building, greater than anything I'd ever known. It was the kind of power that had created our world, and that could be harnessed by only one being.

"It loves you very much," my mother said musingly as she drew me closer to her side. It was a protective gesture that made my heart lurch, even as I felt that power swell ever greater.

Till it broke in a flood of force so strong I felt myself unraveling. Looking down, my eyes glimpsed insubstantial legs, arms, and an unscathed belly beginning to grow transparent. My mother held me comfortingly throughout.

"I loved you very much, too," she murmured into what had been my ear as her arm tightened around nothing.

I was only a presence then as the creature's giant eye grew larger, blazing with power, until it whispered in a harsh, unfamiliar voice.

"Finally," it said. Its eye met mine, full of love and triumph and hope and a thousand other emotions I couldn't begin to name. It spoke one last time.

"I told you, child. There are always options."

And then it died.

The moment of its death hit like another big bang. Everything exploded around me in a flood of white light that shattered eternity.

I was flung too far to comprehend with a force beyond flying.

To be honest, I wish the creature had been able to give us some sort of warning of its intentions.

Because Anyan just about had a heart attack when the corpse he'd been sobbing all over sat up in his arms, gasping for breath.

EPILOGUE

R eader, I married him," I said to Iris as I watched Anyan dandle Layla on his knee after passing Grace over to my father.

"No, you didn't," my succubus friend reminded me absentmindedly before chasing after Grizzie and Tracy's just-toddling boys, Tom and Dennis. Their mothers had come in long enough to pass their kids over to Iris and then they'd sacked out next to my dad on our couch. They still had their coats on and the girls' birthday presents in their hands, and they looked about as tired as I felt.

"I was being literary," I called out after Iris in my defense. It was true that Anyan and I never married, simply because supes don't go in for that type of thing. But I had given him a promise to love him as fiercely as I could, and then I'd given him babies.

Twin girls to be exact, currently resplendent in Pampers and matching blanket rompers. I watched as my father and Anyan cooed over them, thankful for their adoration. The truth was, I think Anyan and my dad only really forgave me for eviscerating myself once I'd given them babies. Before that, there had been a substratum of our relationships made up of a steely wall of anger that never quite gave way.

I couldn't blame them, of course. If either of them had done what I'd done, I'd have killed their dead bodies. Twice.

"Oops, I think Layla needs changing," Anyan said, standing up with a groan. He looked as tired as I did. Twins did that to a body. But standing there with his hair sticking out at every angle, his gray eyes shadowed by dark circles, and baby sick staining his Eukenuba shirt, I'd never thought him handsomer. My love caressed my dark head with his strong hand as he went to change our girl.

My dad rocked Grace gently as she promptly fell asleep. Layla was Anyan's child—big gray eyes and enough energy to keep both of us on our toes. Grace was mine.

In case there was any doubt, the air around Grace shimmered, and lying on my dad's chest was a tiny, perfect seal dressed in a blanket romper.

"I'll never get over that," Grizzie said, her voice awed.

"Me neither," I said drily. After seeing Grizzie and Tracy go through it themselves, I thought I'd been ready when Caleb told me I was having twins. Until I gave birth to one girl and one seal. A true selkie, Grace had gone ahead and reverted to her watery form in utero.

"Thank the gods I never let you talk me into a human doctor," I reminded my father.

"I know," he replied with a chuckle. "Although I do sometimes like to imagine the conversation when the ultrasound found flippers."

"Something tells me the doctor would not have found the situation as funny as we would."

"Probably not," my dad replied, still chuckling. He stroked a gentle hand down my daughter's fur. To be honest, I still wasn't entirely comfortable with having a seal pup for a baby, although Anyan dealt with it much better than I. He was the one to coax her back into human shape, after all, when I'd been squeamish about nursing a baby seal.

"They're a miracle on so many levels," my dad said, touching upon the elephant that, although it had shrunk in size, still stood in a corner of every room.

Grizzie and Tracy both looked away uncomfortably.

"Dad, I had to do it," I said for about the millionth time. Of course, Anyan chose that moment to return with Layla, who was squirming around in his arms trying to see everything there was to see.

Hearing what I said, Anyan growled. Layla hiccoughed and looked up at her daddy.

"Are we really going to have this conversation again?" I thought it had died with the babies' birth.

"I know you did what you had to," my dad said, to my astonishment. "I've thought about it a lot, obviously, since I was told what happened. And I'm starting to understand. I just wish…"

His words trailed off. He didn't have to say what he wished; it was what we all wished—that I hadn't had to make that choice, that I'd known and could have warned everyone, that I hadn't had to actually go through with it.

"That's not how sacrifice works," I reminded my dad and Anyan. "It had to be real. It was real. And I'd do it again to save you and save everyone we love."

"No, you won't," Anyan said flatly. But his eyes were on our twins. He'd been willing to die for me, and it was particularly unreasonable that he'd taken so long to accept I'd be willing to do the same for him. But he'd been that unreasonable. Anyan had been furious with me after I'd woken, an anger fueled by all that fear he'd felt seeing me die.

We'd had to start almost from scratch when I came to. He'd felt betrayed in a way I couldn't figure out until Iris made me stop and put myself in his shoes. Even if I'd done it for the right reasons and it had worked out, that moment of losing me had hurt Anyan as deeply as a person could be hurt. It didn't matter why I'd done it or that it had ended all right, my actions had wounded him in as final a way as possible.

Once I understood that, I'd been able to approach him differently. Instead of being upset that he didn't get that what I'd done had been for him, I acknowledged the fact that what I'd done had eviscerated him as messily and as painfully as it had me. I'd asked for forgiveness for real, and he'd been able to give it to me.

He'd also given me twins less than a year later. I couldn't help wondering if my fertility was a parting gift of the universe or the creature, or if there was simply something in Rockabill's water. But our babies had certainly been the magical fix to our relationship that babies usually aren't.

I think they reminded the barghest that we can *all* love others more than ourselves, and that he didn't have the monopoly on martyrdom. That's when he'd apologized to me for being so hurt, and everything had gone back to pretty much perfect.

We watched as Layla shimmered again, turning back into a human baby. I shook my head, wondering what she was dreaming about, and wondering how long she'd stay with us. Instead of looking forward to a kid going to college, I had to look forward to a kid moving into the sea.

Parenthood was going to be as interesting as anything else in the supernatural world.

"So, tell us about your date last night," Anyan said to my father. "You like this lady, don't you?"

"Patti's real nice," my dad said, blushing almost as red as the sofa he sat on. "She cooked dinner over at her place, and it was nice."

Anyan chuckled. "Nice, huh?"

"Yeah," my dad said. "Real nice."

My eyes darted between the two men, who seemed to be communicating on some level of testosterone I couldn't quite comprehend, but I was pretty sure I didn't want to translate.

Grizzie butted in, coaxing a few more details about Patti from my dad, and then we continued to chitchat. The gossip from Rockabill was blessedly normal, something I still appreciated, as I was still grateful I'd been able to go back home.

And that was when the rest of the guests showed up.

"Sorry I'm late," Caleb said, clip-clopping inside still wearing his medical scrubs. Well, at least his shirt. He'd gotten a job at the local clinic, under a glamour obviously, and was making a good living in Eastport as Dr. Caprone. Iris walked back in from the porch, where she'd chased the toddlers, one squirming bundle of Grizzie-spawn under each arm. She kissed her mate, passing him Tom at the same time. She kept the other toddler, Dennis, for herself.

"Ryu's just coming now," Caleb said. "He and Daoud are unpacking gifts."

"Hopefully not out of Daoud's pants," I muttered, going outside to help.

"Hey, boys!" I called, wandering down to where Daoud and Ryu were trying to extricate an enormous package out of the tiny trunk of Ryu's latest sports car. I couldn't help laughing.

"She who laughs gets no presents," the baobhan sith said, glaring at me over the top of his dark designer sunglasses, before continuing to mutter swear words at his car.

"I'm sorry. Can I help?"

"Nah," said Ryu as Daoud pushed down in a way that must have released whatever was stuck. The big, wrapped package came out, looking only slightly the worse for wear.

Daoud had dressed comfortably in jeans and a T-shirt, knowing he'd be covered in spit-up within minutes. He carried the gift toward the house, pausing to give me a peck on the cheek.

"Way to give birth a year ago," he said, winking cheekily.

"Thanks," I said drily. "Get in there and grab a baby. I swear they're multiplying like Tribbles."

The djinn chuckled, and did as I bade him, leaving me with my ex. Ryu gave me a big hug, then withdrew to look at my critically.

"You look tired," he said.

"Twins," I said with a shrug. "You look as gorgeous as ever."

He chuckled, striking a pose before taking off his sunglasses and tossing them in his car. "I can't help but be beautiful."

"So what's going on? How's the compound?" I asked as we moved toward the house.

"Everything's good. Busy, but good."

His charming smile never wavered, nor did his confident voice. But I knew Ryu well enough to know he was being evasive.

"So how's the Initiative going?" I asked, referring to the North American human-supernatural governmental alliance that Trevor, Ryu, and a counterpart in the Canadian government had set up.

"It's going great," Ryu said, but his smile was forced. "Negotiations are good, and we're working toward an accord based on mutual understanding. The humans sent to help us are very…helpful. Especially the American." That last bit was forced out, as if Ryu was trying to convince himself of what he was saying.

I narrowed my eyes at the baobhan sith. I'd met the woman Trevor had sent to work with Ryu at the compound. A tall, leggy, no-nonsense redhead, she'd intimidated the crap out of me. Not that she was supposed to be an antagonist. The Initiative was really more of an exchange program—we'll show you our world if you show us yours—than anything else. Once both sides understood each other better, formal talks could begin, and supes and humans might start to work together more.

So I couldn't understand why this woman was causing Ryu to grit his teeth like she was a pain in his molar. Unless…

"What's the American's name again?" I asked.

"Maeve."

"Pretty name," I said, watching him closely.

"I'm sure it is."

"She's pretty, too."

"I guess. But she's just so...full of herself." Ryu was actually grinding his teeth as he shuffled restlessly on his feet.

"She's gotten under your skin."

"What?" Ryu looked shocked.

"Nothing," I said, smiling at him innocently. Whatever was going on, I'd not seen Ryu this discombobulated over a woman, ever. And I'd once been the woman who was supposed to discombobulate him.

"Trevor here yet?" Ryu asked, obviously wanting to change the subject from Maeve. I couldn't wait to question Daoud about what was going on between those two, but it would have to wait till later. Not least because of Trevor. I looked at my watch.

"He should be arriving in three...two...one..."

Just as I said "one," a black car pulled into Anyan's long driveway, smoothly rolling up.

"How'd you know?" Ryu asked, clearly impressed.

"Trevor is always exactly on time," I said. "Although I doubt Trevor is in that car."

Indeed, when the sedan rolled up, it was a minion that got out. In fact, it might have been an intern. The young man was barely old enough to be called "man," and he was visibly nervous as he passed me a small present.

"Our government wishes you and yours a happy birthday. For your twins. Um, so we wish them a happy birthday. And you a happy birthday because they're yours. Thank you, ma'am." The nervous young man retreated back into the car without letting me respond, and the sedan backed sedately down the driveway.

"What the fuck was that?" Ryu asked, his head cocked at the awkwardness of the preceding exchange.

I sighed happily. "That, Ryu, is the stilted dialogue of freedom. Trevor has officially given up. After nearly two years of stalking me, convinced I still had power after the creature died, he's finally lost hope. I only rate a minion now. Thank God for minions."

Ryu turned to me, looking over me critically. "And you're sure all that power's really gone?"

I blinked at him. "Are you kidding me? Of course! I died that night, Ryu. And then the creature took my death into itself, and used the last of its power to give me life. I'm just like I was before."

Ryu's lips twitched. "Good speech. That's very convincing."

I was about to protest but he walked past me. "Did you make that taco dip of yours?" he asked as he walked toward our front door. I wanted to follow him to insist on how powerless I was, but more guests were arriving.

They were a mix of glamoured supernaturals and friends from Rockabill and Eastport. For despite my trepidation, I'd gone back home. First I'd made it up to Anyan, and that had been my focus. Then I'd started appearing around town, and then I'd started working again at the bookstore.

After a long discussion, we decided not to try to glamour the locals. Instead, we told them nothing. We let the rumors fly, neither denying nor confirming anything. Half of the town was convinced I was part of some government hoax; the other thought I was part of some government conspiracy. Both were wrong, but both sets of rumors granted me an iota of respect I hadn't had before.

Either that, or it simply shifted my identity in the town's consciousness from the girl who'd been responsible for Jason's death to a girl who occasionally fought dragons. I was still the object of scrutiny and gossip, but I liked this type of gossip better.

And I enjoyed every moment I could of being "normal," something I never thought I'd get to be again. So greeting guests and watching them gossip in my living room about people I could still interact with felt like a huge blessing.

Eventually, after food was eaten, cake was distributed, "Happy Birthday" was sung, and presents unwrapped, the guests left one by one. Iris, Caleb, and my dad helped to clean up, and to wear the babies out so they'd sleep. After seeing Tracy and Grizzie's struggles, I'd been very happy to learn that supe babies are easier than human babies. It's something to do with their already beginning to process their elemental power, which wears them out no matter what they're doing. But I didn't ask too many questions, letting myself enjoy the fact that they were already sleeping almost entirely through the night.

After Anyan and I sought out our own bed, the barghest's warm hand found my stomach. He'd started holding me like that when I was first pregnant, but considering our recent history, it had more meaning than the usual gesture.

"I meant it, you know," he said. "Never again."

I placed my small hand over his, snuggling closer against his side.

"Anyan, I think the chances of me twice becoming

the champion of the universe, chosen to battle an ancient force of evil, are pretty slim."

"I know. But still. Never again." His voice was steely, adamant.

I sighed. "I had to—"

"I know you did," he interrupted. "I get that. And I was willing to do the same for you. I get that, too, now. But things are different. We have the girls—"

"And we would both do anything for them," I said, my turn to interrupt.

"Yes. But my point is that sometimes the ultimate sacrifice is to live. It's to survive, despite what else we have to give up. That's what I'm saying."

I turned over on my side, pressing my body against his as I nuzzled his long, gorgeous nose with mine. "You're a wise man, Anyan. Er, dog. Dog-man . . ."

"Barghest," he murmured as his mouth found mine in a gentle kiss.

That gentle kiss quickly turned hungry, his tongue filling my mouth as his hands slipped under my nightie. He'd divested me of my clothing in seconds, and as he'd come to bed naked, we were now even. His hands roamed over my body as I did the same to him, loving the feel of us warm and solid against each other.

"I love you, puppy," I told him, just because I could.

"You just love my doggie style," he said, taking my wrists firmly in his. And then, suddenly, he flipped me, so I was lying on my stomach. He kept my wrists in his big hand, pinning them to my back, and me to the bed. His knees nudged my thighs apart and I gasped as his free hand knotted in my hair. He pulled my head back to whisper in my ear. I was expecting something delightfully dirty, but his voice was rough with more than just passion when he spoke.

"I love you, too."

That's what I adore about my barghest. He's like a box of chocolates: sometimes filled with something sweet, other times filled with pure filth.

Together, we may have saved the world—but we also knew how to save each other.

And have a damned good time doing it.

Acknowledgments

Writing acknowledgments is harrowing. I always worry I've forgotten somebody, and I usually do. But writing the acknowledgments for the last book in a series is especially daunting. After all, this series made me an author, something I'd never thought I'd become. And I have so many people to thank for that honor.

First of all, to my family. I've said it before, and I'll say it again: You let me become who I am. No matter how distant or daunting was my next adventure, you always supported me. All of my experiences have gone into my books, and I would definitely not have gotten where I am so early if it weren't for your support.

Next up is my dedicatee, Rebecca Strauss, and everyone else at McIntosh and Otis. You have all been incredibly patient with an author who knew absolutely nothing about the business. You have guided me with patience and wisdom, and you have been not only a source of professional support, but a friend. I can't begin to thank you, and I really do feel we're a team.

I also owe a huge debt of gratitude to Orbit Books. To my editor, Devi Pillai, for buying my books and for telling me when they rocked and when they didn't. To Jenn Flax and Susan Barnes for helping make my writing better. To Alex Lencicki, Jack Womack, and Ellen Wright for making sure my books reached as many people as possible. To Sharon Tancredi and Lauren Panepinto, who made Jane beautiful. To Tim Holman for leading the pack. And thanks also to the UK Orbit team, especially Anna Gregson, Rose Tremlett, and Joanna Kramer, for getting Jane overseas, where she belongs.

I must also thank all of my friends who supported me. James Clawson, Christie Ko, and Mary Lois White get special mention for all their readings of Jane. But there are so many of you who supported me, gave me inspiration, and answered questions on various bizarre subjects. To all of my author friends and the League of Reluctant Adults and the Pens Fatales, especially: Thank you for all of your support, advice, and talkings down. To my critique partner, Diana Rowland, who has been Jane's partner throughout. And thank you to my employers, LSUS and Seton Hill, and to all of my wonderful colleagues.

Finally, to the fans. I can't believe how much you love Jane. It humbles me and thrills me, and I am so lucky for your support.

I know that's a lot of people, but one woman does not a series make. I'm also sure there are people whom I've forgotten, and there are a ton of people I wish I could list by name. But please know I'm well aware of how lucky I am to have you. I've loved writing Jane, and I couldn't have done it without you.

extras

orbit

meet the author

Nicole D. Peeler received an undergraduate degree in English literature from Boston University, and a PhD in English literature from the University of Edinburgh, in Scotland. She's lived abroad in both Spain and the United Kingdom, and has lived all over the United States. Currently, she resides outside Pittsburgh, and teaches in Seton Hill's MFA in Popular Fiction. When she's not in the classroom infecting young minds with her madness, she's writing urban fantasy for Orbit Books and taking pleasure in what means most to her: family, friends, food, and travel. To learn more about the author, visit www.nicolepeeler.com.

introducing

If you enjoyed
TEMPEST REBORN,
look out for

BLOOD RIGHTS

House of Comarré: Book One

by Kristen Painter

Born into a life of secrets and service, Chrysabelle's body bears the telltale marks of a comarré—a special race of humans bred to feed vampire nobility. When her patron is murdered, she becomes the prime suspect, which sends her running into the mortal world... and into the arms of Malkolm, an outcast vampire cursed to kill every being from whom he drinks.

Paradise City, New Florida, 2067

The cheap lace and single-sewn seams pressed into Chrysabelle's flesh, weighed down by the uncomfortable tapestry jacket that finished her disguise. Her training kept her from fidgeting with the shirt's tag even as it bit into her skin. She studied those around her. How curious that the kine perceived her world this way. No, *this* was her world, not the one she'd left behind. And she had to stop thinking of humans as kine. She was one of them now. Free. Independent. Owned by no one.

She forced a weak smile as the club's heavy electronic beat ricocheted through her bones. Lights flickered and strobed, casting shadows and angles that paid no compliments to the faces around her. She cringed as a few bodies collided with her in the surrounding crush. Nothing in her years of training had prepared her for immersion in a crowd of mortals. She recognized the warm, earthy smell of them from the human servants her patron and the other nobles had kept, but acclimating to their noise and their boisterous behavior was going to take time. Perhaps humans lived so hard because they had so little of that very thing.

Something she was coming to understand.

The names on the slip of paper in her pocket were memorized, but she pulled it out and read them again. *Jonas Sweets*, and beneath it, *Nyssa*, both written in her aunt's flowery script. Just the sight of the handwriting calmed her a little. She folded the note and tucked it away. If Aunt Maris said Jonas could connect her with help, Chrysabelle would trust that he could, even though the idea of trusting a kine—no, a human—seemed untenable.

She pushed through to the bar, failing in her attempt to avoid more contact but happy at how little attention she attracted. The foundation Maris had applied to her hands, face, and neck, the only skin left visible by her clothing, covered her signum perfectly. No longer did the multitude of gold markings she bore identify her as an object to be possessed. She was her own person now, passing easily as human.

The feat split her in two. While part of her thrilled to be free of the stifling propriety that governed her every move and rejoiced that she was no longer property, another part of her felt wholly unprepared for this existence. There was no denying life in Algernon's manor had been one of shelter and privilege.

Enough wallowing. She hadn't the time and there was no going back, even if she could. Which she wouldn't. And it wasn't as if Aunt Maris hadn't provided for her and wouldn't continue to do so, if Chrysabelle could just take care of this one small problem. Finding a space between two bodies, she squeezed in and waited for the bartender's attention.

He nodded at her. "What can I get you?"

She slid the first plastic fifty across the bar as Maris had instructed. "I need to find Jonas Sweets."

He took the bill, smiling enough to display canines capped into points. Ridiculous. "Haven't seen him in a few days, but he'll show up eventually."

Eventually was too late. She added a second bill. "What time does he usually come in?"

The bartender removed the empty glasses in front of her, snatched up the money, and leaned in. "Midnight. Sometimes sooner. Sometimes later."

It was nearly 1 a.m. now. "How about his assistant, Nyssa? The mute girl?"

"She won't show without him." He tapped the bar with damp fingers. "I can give Jonas a message for you, if he turns up. What's your name?"

She shook her head. No names. No clues. No trail. The bartender shrugged and hustled away. She slumped against the bar and rested her hand over her eyes. At least she could get out of here now. Or maybe she should stay. The Nothos wouldn't attempt anything in so public a place, would they?

A bitter laugh stalled in her throat. She knew better. The hellhounds could kill her in a single pass, without a noise or a struggle or her even knowing what had happened until the pain lit every nerve in her body or her heart shuddered to a stop. She'd never seen one of the horrible creatures, but she didn't need to in order to understand what one was capable of.

They could walk among this crowd without detection, hidden by the covenant that protected humans from the othernaturals, the vampires, varcolai, fae, and such that coexisted with them. She would be the only one to see them coming.

The certainty of her death echoed in her marrow. She shoved the thought away and lifted her head, scanning the crowd, inhaling the earthy human aroma in search of the signature reek of brimstone. Were they already here? Had they tracked her this far, this fast? She wouldn't go back to her aunt's if they had. Couldn't risk bringing that danger to her only family. Maris was not the strong young woman she'd once been.

Her gaze skipped from face to face. So many powdered cheeks and bloodred lips. Mouths full of false fangs. Cultivated widow's peaks. All in an attempt to what? Replicate the very beings who would drain the lifeblood from their mortal bodies before they could utter a single word of sycophantic praise? Poor, misguided fools. She felt sorry for them, really. They worshipped their own deaths, lulled into thinking beauty and perfection were just a bite away. She would never think that. Never fall under the spell of those manufactured lies. No matter how long or how short her new life was.

She knew too much.

Malkolm hated Puncture with every undead fiber of his being. If it weren't for the bloodlust crazing his brain—which kicked the ever-present voices into a frenzy—he'd be home, sipping the single malt he could no longer afford, maybe listening to Fauré or Tchaikovsky while searching his books for a way to empty his head of all thoughts but his own.

Damn Jonas for disappearing without setting up another reliable source. Mal cracked his knuckles, thinking about the beating that idiot was in for when he showed up again. It wasn't like the local Quik-E-Mart carried pints of fresh, clean, human blood. Unfortunately.

The warm, delicious scent of the very thing he craved hit full force as he pushed through the heavy velvet drapes curtaining the VIP section. In here, his real face, the face of the monster he'd been turned into, made him the very best of their pretenders and got him access to any area of the nightclub he wanted. Ironic, considering how showing his real face anywhere else would probably get him locked up as a mental patient. He shuddered and inhaled without thinking. His body tensed with the seductive aroma of thriving, vibrating life. The voices went mad, pounding against his skull. A multitude of heartbeats filled his ears, pulses around him calling out like siren songs. *Bite me, drink me, swallow me whole.*

Damn Sweets.

A petite redhead with a jeweled cross dangling between her breasts stopped dead in front of him. Like an actual vampire could ever tolerate the touch of that sacred symbol. Dumb git. But then how was she to know the origins of creatures she only hoped were real? She appraised him from head to toe, running her tongue over a set of resin fangs. "You're new here, huh? I love your look. Are those contacts? I haven't seen any metallic ones like that. Kinda different, but totally hot."

She reached out to touch the hard ridge of his cheekbone and he snapped back, baring his teeth and growling softly. *Eat her.* She scowled. "Chill, dude." Pouting, she skulked away, muttering "freak" under her breath.

Fine. Let her think what she wanted. A human's touch might push him over the edge. No, he reassured himself, it wouldn't. *Yes.* He wouldn't let it. *Do.* He wouldn't get that far gone. *Go.* But in truth, he balanced on the edge. *Fall.* He needed to feed. *To kill.* To shut the voices up.

With that thought he shoved his way to the bar, disgusted things had gotten this dire. He got the bartender's attention, then pushed some persuasion into his voice. "Hey." It was one of the few powers that hadn't blinked out on him yet. Good old family genes.

His head turned in Mal's direction, eyes slightly glazed. Mal eased off. Humans were so suggestible. "What'll it be?"

"Give me a Vlad." Inwardly, he died a little. Metaphorically speaking. The whole idea of doing this here, in full view of a human audience, made him sick. But not as sick as going without. How fortunate that humans wanted to mimic his kind to the full extent.

"A shot?"

"A pint."

The bartender's brows lifted. "Looking to get laid, huh? A pint should keep you busy all night. These chicks get seriously damp over that action. Not that anyone's managed to drink the pint and keep it down." He hesitated. "You gotta puke, you head for the john, you got me?"

"Not going to happen."

"Yeah, right." The bartender opened a small black fridge and took out a plastic bag fat with red liquid.

Mal swallowed the saliva coating his tongue, unable to focus his gaze elsewhere, despite the fact he preferred his sustenance body temperature and not chilled. A few of the voices wept softly. "That's human, right? And fresh?"

The bartender laughed. "Chickening out?"

"No. Just making sure."

"Yeah, it's fresh and it's human. That's why it's two hundred and fifty dollars a pop." He squirted the liquid into a pilsner. It oozed down the glass thick and viscous, sending a bittersweet aroma into the air. Even here in the VIP lounge, heads turned. Several women and at least one man radiated hard lust in his direction. The scent of human desire was like dying roses, and right now, Puncture's VIP lounge smelled like a funeral parlor. He hadn't anticipated such a rapt audience, but the ache in his gut stuck up a big middle finger to caring what the humans around him thought. At least there weren't any fringe vamps here tonight. Despite his status as an outcast anathema, the lesser-class vampires only saw him as nobility. He wasn't in the mood to be sucked up to. Ever.

The bartender slid the glass his way. "There you go. Will that be cash?"

"Start a tab."

"I don't think so, buddy."

Mal refocused his power. "I've already paid you."

The man's jaw loosened and the tension lines in his forehead disappeared. "You've already paid."

"That's a good little human," Mal muttered. He grabbed the pilsner and walked toward an empty stretch of railing for a little privacy. The air behind him heated up. He glanced over his shoulder. A set of twins with blue-black hair, jet lips, and matching leather corsets stood waiting.

"Hi," they said in unison.

Eat them. Drain them.

"No." He filled his voice with power, hoping that would be enough.

They stepped forward. Behind them, the bartender watched with obvious interest.

Damn Sweets.

The blood warmed in his grasp, its tang filling his nose, but feeding would have to wait a moment longer. Using charm this time, he spoke. "I am not the one you seek. Pleasure awaits you elsewhere. Leave me now."

They nodded sleepily and moved away.

The effort exhausted him. He was too weak to use so much power in such a short span of time. He gripped the railing, waiting for the dizziness in his head to abate. He stared into the crowd below. Scanned for Nyssa, but he knew better. She only left Sweets's side when she had a delivery. The moving bodies blurred until they were an undulating mass, each one undistinguishable from the next until a muted flash of gold stopped his gaze. His entire being froze. Not here. Couldn't be.

He blinked, then stared harder. The flickering glow

remained. It reminded him of a dying firefly. Instinct kicked in. Sparks of need exploded in his gut. His gums ached, causing him to pop his jaw. The small hairs on the back of his neck lifted and the voices went oddly quiet, save an occasional whimper. His world converged down to the soft light emanating from the crowd near the downstairs bar.

He had to find the source, see if it really was what he thought. If it was, he had to get to it before anyone else did. The urge drove him inexplicably forward.

All traces of exhaustion disappeared. The glass in his hand fell to the floor, splattering blood that no longer called to him. He vaulted over the railing and dropped effortlessly to the dance floor below. The crush parted to let him through as he strode toward the gentle beacon.

She stood at the bar, her back to him. The generous fall of sunlight blond hair stopped him, but the fabled luminescence brought him back to reality. So beautiful this close. He rubbed at his aching jaw. *You'll scare her like this, you fool. You're all fang and hunger. Show some respect.*

He assumed his human face, then approached. "Looking for someone?"

She tensed, going statue still. Even with the heavy bass, he felt her heartbeat shoot up a notch. He moved closer and leaned forward to speak without human ears hearing. Bad move. Her scent plunged into him dagger sharp, its honeyed perfume nearly doubling him with hunger pains. The whimpering in his head increased. Catching himself, he staggered for the bar behind her and reached out for support.

His hand closed over her wrist. Her pulse thrummed

beneath his fingertips. Welcoming heat blazed up his arm. A chorus of fearful voices sang out in his head. *Get away, get away, get away…*

She spun, eyes fear-wide, heart thudding. "You're…" She hesitated then mouthed the words "not human."

Beneath his grip, she trembled. He pulled his hand away and stared. Had he been wrong? No marks adorned her face or hands. Maybe… but no. She had the blond hair, the glow, the carmine lips. She hid the marks somehow. He wasn't wrong. He knew enough of the history, the lore, the traditions. Besides, he'd seen her kind before. Just the once, but it wasn't something you ever forgot no matter how long you lived. Only one thing caused that glow.

She bent her head. "Master," she whispered.

"Don't. Don't call me that. It's not necessary." She thought him nobility? Why not assume he was fringe? Or worse, anathema? But she'd addressed him with the respect due her better. A noble with all rights and privileges. Which he wasn't. And she'd surely guessed he was here to feed. Which he was.

She nodded. "As you wish, mast—" Visibly flustered, she cut herself off. "As you wish."

He gestured toward the exit. "Outside. You don't belong here." Anyone could get to her here. Like Preacher. It wasn't safe. How she'd ended up here, he couldn't fathom. Finding a live rabbit in a den of lions would have been less surprising.

"I'm sure my patron will be back in just a—"

"We both know I'm the only real vampire here." For now. "Let's go."

Her gaze wandered to the surrounding crowd, then past him. She sucked her lower lip between her teeth and twisted her hands together. Hesitantly, she brushed past, painting a line of hunger across his chest with the curve of her shoulder. *Get away, get away, get away…*

She was not for him. He knew that, and not just because of the voices, but getting his body to agree was a different matter. Her scent numbed him like good whiskey. Made him feel needy. Reckless. Finding some shred of control, he shadowed her out of the club, away from the mob awaiting entrance, and herded her deep into the alley. He scanned in both directions. Nothing. They hadn't been followed. He could get her somewhere safe. Not that he knew where that might be.

"No one saw us leave."

She backed away, hugging herself beneath her coat. Her chest rose and fell as though she'd run a marathon. Fear soured her sweet perfume. She had to be in some kind of trouble. Why else would she be here without an escort? Without her patron?

"Trust me, we're completely alone." He reached awkwardly to put his arm around her, the first attempt at comfort he'd made in years.

Quicker than a human eye could track, her arm snapped from under the coat, something dark and slim clutched in her hand. The side of her fist slammed into his chest. Whatever she held pierced him, missing his heart by inches. The voices shrieked, deafening him. Corrosive pain erupted where she made contact.

He froze, immobilized by hellfire scorching his insides. He fell to his knees and collapsed against the damp pavement. Foul water soaked his clothing as he lay there, her fading footfalls drowned out by the howling in his head.